MW01138885

AFTERMATH

Invasion of the Dead
Book 1

OWEN BAILLIE

Copyright © 2013 Owen Baillie

All rights reserved.

ISBN: 1494344548
ISBN-13: 978-1494344542

This is a work of fiction. Any similarities to real persons, events, or places are purely coincidental; any references to actual places, people, or brands are fictitious. All rights reserved.

Edited by Monique Happy Editorial Services
Copyeditors Monique Happy & Tracey Fitzgerald Rose
www.moniquehappy.com

Cover design by Clarissa Yeo
www.yocladesigns.com

ACKNOWLEDGMENTS

Thanks to Brent Henry for owning guns and answering my silly questions, Vinnie Orlando for his brisk reading and ideas, and Michiko Malcolm, for her clever observations, and getting through the story. A big thank you to my amazing editors at MHES, Monique Lewis Happy and Tracey Fitzgerald Rose, whose support, enthusiasm, and of course expertise, has helped beyond words.

Thank you to my wife Donna for her support, encouragement and logic, and our three girls for putting up with my writing time.

And finally, a big thank you to the readers who let me know how much they liked the first part, or left a positive review. Never underestimate your generous words and encouragement.

WARNING: Adults only. This book contains high-level violence and coarse language.

PREFACE

January 10, 2014.

Headquarters Joint Operations Command, ACT, Australia.

Major General Frank Harris tossed the yellow folder onto the desk and rocked back in the chair, clasping both hands behind a ring of short grey hair. The wall clock said it was a little after six in the morning. He closed his eyes and felt the sweet pull of exhaustion. He hadn't slept yet, probably hadn't totaled four hours over the last few days, and he couldn't see a bed in his immediate future. A knot of the deepest concern he had ever experienced twisted his gut, and he couldn't remember the last time it was absent. He knew nothing short of a miracle from a God in whom he had never believed would relieve the sensation. Life as he had known it, as the entire world had known it, was over.

He rubbed a coarse layer of stubble and stood, his back cracking and his behind aching. He pushed the chair back and walked to a mahogany buffet at the rear of the office. How long since he'd left the bunker? Eight days? Ten? He'd lost track. He was in the "deep"—far below the ground-level base; commanding officers were transferred here during high-level security situations. Some of the officers had refused, preferring to be with their families. Harris understood that. He wanted to be with his own family more than anything in the world, but … they were no more. He gritted his teeth as an image of Maggie formed in his mind—sweet, beautiful Maggie, forever his adoring wife, suffering through his long and distinguished military career. And the boys. John and Dale. Harris took his own nose between thumb and forefinger, then twisted. Pain flared and the images fled. He had managed to avoid thinking about it too much; now wasn't the time to start. He reminded himself that millions above ground were suffering the same fate.

Twenty-one days since they had classified the virus, and it had dragged them to their knees like sick children. The decay of society, of governments, banks and defense systems, had been rapid. As much as the world relied on computer systems, it still required humans to monitor and manage them. Without keystrokes and mouse clicks, nothing subsisted. The government had abandoned its post. Somewhere, probably within twenty miles of where Harris sat, ministers and senior officials were bunkered down, planning a recovery. Their handling of the crisis in Australia had been woeful, barely acknowledging the existence of an infection, let alone the subsequent collapse. They had peddled the line about a variation of H1N1 when, in truth, it was a new strain that displayed an aggression well beyond the former's capabilities. The British and Americans had also suffered. Communications had ceased with both countries. The last report Harris had received indicated similar levels of chaos and destruction. There was no help beyond their own crumbling shores.

Sliding back a wooden panel, Harris retrieved a bottle of Scotch and a short glass etched with the Australian Defence Force symbol. He cracked the seal, poured an inch, paused, and then topped it off. He sipped the smooth amber liquid, running it over his tongue and around his mouth. *This might be the last bottle I ever open,* he thought.

Perhaps Harris was only alive because he had followed protocol and stayed underground. Reports from the surface stopped three days ago; he could have ordered one of the lower ranked officers to investigate, but to what end? Confirmation of the inevitable? It was over. There was no more *surface*. The predictions proved true. The only hope now was that Weinstrem and his team could formulate a vaccine.

He glanced at the folder on the desk. He had memorized the contents, having read it four times. The information was days old, and he wouldn't be receiving any more figures. It didn't matter, though. A collapse was a collapse. What more could one say beyond the projections? In Australia alone, from a population of twenty-three million, less than one hundred thousand, or 0.5 percent, would survive. If such a survival rate translated worldwide, it meant the number of humans left alive on the planet would fall to 350,000. The death toll wasn't the *major* issue, though. What *happened* to the dead was what terrified him. If the remaining 350,000 had only themselves and the collapse of society to contend with, maybe they stood a chance. But there was more than that. Six and a half billion bodies, some of which *would* reanimate in varying states of aggression and madness, pursing the blood of those who remained alive. It was the worst of horrid nightmares.

Harris sat in the chair and pulled himself to the desk. The computer screen displayed an old e-mail from Lieutenant General Matheson, his ranking officer, outlining the go-forward plan: *create a vaccine, then re-establish.* Their last briefing had been five days ago, and Harris had not since seen or heard from any of the officers present in that meeting. He supposed they all became sick, or they'd died. He took another mouthful of Scotch and welcomed the burn in his throat.

They had captured several of the infected and kept them in one of the containment cells up top, examining their behavior and analyzing their blood. Most remained passive, in a vegetative state of wandering, but in some, the virus reacted differently, the level of aggression *and* intelligence far greater than average. It was similar to a terrible form of rabies. Harris had first seen it a week ago, watching the cells through a reinforced glass screen. The thing had attacked the window; he and the other observers had *all* leapt back like frightened schoolchildren. It had scared Harris more than anything he had seen on the ground in Iraq or Afghanistan. Probably more than anything *anyone* had seen *anywhere.* The group of officers had stayed for a demonstration. The scientists put a different class of the infected in with it. With a frightening calmness, the more aggressive subject had bitten the other. Nothing had happened immediately, but hours later, Harris had received word that the passive subject had become more aggressive.

A frightening thought.

Harris touched the screen on his desk phone and waited as it dialed the laboratory. The name "Klaus Weinstrem" displayed on the screen. The world, he supposed, was now relying on the likes of Klaus to find a vaccine. But there was nothing on the horizon yet, and if Dr Weinstrem was correct, it might take months to make progress. Harris would be stuck underground for the near future—if his sanity lasted that long.

A pleasant-looking man with long blonde hair and smart glasses appeared. Klaus was in his early forties, and stumped people with his boyish looks.

"How goes it, Klaus?" Harris asked in a flat, tired tone. "Anything to report?" He had asked the same thing every day and suspected he would get the same response. *Nothing new.*

"Good morning, Major General. I have some news for you."

Harris leaned forward. "What is it?" The sudden warmth of hope flushed him, the first hope he'd felt since the final discussion with Matheson, who had *insisted* they would prevail.

"Not good, I'm afraid, in terms of a vaccine. Nothing here yet."

Harris slumped back.

"But I seem to have found evidence that the virus has been manipulated to cause the second phase of the reaction."

Harris cocked his head. Did he hear right? Manipulation? The second phase referred to the subject's reanimation coupled with a compulsion for blood and human flesh. "What do you mean by manipulated?"

"The virus is not naturally occurring. Well, correction. It is to a point, that point being the first phase, which is a particularly nasty strain of influenza that can easily be fatal."

"Are you suggesting *somebody* has tinkered with this virus deliberately to cause the second phase to occur?"

"I believe so. Yes, that is my conclusion, with the evidence I have on hand. There is definitely a synthetic component."

"Who would do that? And why?"

"Bio-terrorism. Introduced into controlled populations, it would be a way of self-eradication. The general subjects will feed on themselves if no immediate source of sustenance is located, until there is only one subject remaining."

Harris shook his head. "Unbelievable."

"However, I don't believe whoever modified the virus counted on the mutation."

"The aggressive types?"

"Yes. They don't eradicate, they populate."

"Jesus." *They populate.* "So, potentially, there could be a growing population of the aggressive types?"

"That is my thinking at this point. However, the analytical timeframe has been quite short. I'll need longer to confirm these theories."

"We need a vaccine, Klaus. When are we going to have it?"

"Not soon. It won't happen for six months, assuming the people and resources required to formulate it will survive."

"How many people does it take?"

"The more we have, the quicker it would happen. But for now, it's just the three of us."

"Would a vaccine prevent the spread of the virus from, say, a direct bite?"

"I can't yet say. But we would aim for that."

He had many more questions but knew there were no answers. Waiting was the difficult part. The more he spoke, the longer he kept Klaus from finding those answers. "Good work, Klaus. Keep working on it. Let me know if anything changes."

"Yes sir."

Harris cut the phone call, gulped down the rest of his Scotch, and settled back in the chair. It was time to see Admiral Gallagher.

Part I

1

Callan would later think that coming off the mountain was the last time their lives had been normal. Until that moment, they still had football and cold beer, another Star Wars movie, celebrity magazines, and Chinese takeout. People were still walking around pissing and moaning about taxes and the failures of the government, about how so-and-so was driving a new BMW, or that the couple everyone thought would stay together forever had separated. That moment had been another time, lost forever, and he would always reminisce about it with a sad, aching soul.

* * *

Kristy turned the dusty green Jeep off the dirt track onto the thin strip of scarred bitumen baking under the mid-summer sun. It was the first real road they had seen in over a month, but Callan hadn't missed the sign of civilization. The lake and its isolation had been perfect, satisfying and relaxing in its own charming way, although he and Sherry hadn't been able to rediscover the magic that had initially drawn them together. He was desperate to find that again.

"There," Kristy said, shifting the gears into second. "*That* was some kick ass driving."

It was, Callan thought. The boat had jumped and jiggled, almost jack-knifing twice on two particularly sharp bends where rainwater had worn ruts into the track, but she had managed the heavy load. She had wanted to drive; Callan didn't think she would have done such a thing five weeks ago. He hoped the change was permanent.

"Not bad," he said from the backseat. "Thought you were gonna lose it once or twice."

Kristy adjusted her Dolce & Gabbana sunglasses. "I'm surprised you haven't had some kind of fit, sitting back there."

"There are finger marks in the door handle."

She was a first year resident in the emergency room of the Monash Medical Centre in Melbourne. For her, the trip had been an escape during three months of personal leave. Kristy had never quite adjusted to the realities of ER life. The strain of long hours and relentless death had worn away her emotional resolve. It was no surprise to Callan, though. While her academic achievements had won a university scholarship, she had cried like a child when they found dead animals on the farm. Callan didn't think she could cope with seeing the lives of patients end, often so abruptly. The camping trip had been Callan's idea, to isolate her from the routine and give her a clear head to decide if she still wanted to be an ER doctor.

On their left, a gas station appeared between a gap in the thick scrub. "We need fuel," Callan said, recalling the cute old couple who had served them at the store on their way out to the lake. He remembered wishing he and Sherry would turn out like that one day, married for fifty years, enjoying their golden years together.

"Let's hope they've got cold beer," Greg said from the front seat, where his tall, bulky frame had room to stretch. He rubbed at four weeks of ginger growth on his cheeks.

Kristy said, "Let's hope they *don't*. We'll be stopping for you to use the little boys' room every five minutes."

It was a little before one and Callan felt sweat on his forehead. The weather had been perfect, low to high nineties every day, no need for a shirt until after dusk. So far, they had knocked off an hour of the four it would take to get the car and boat back to Albury, their hometown on the border of Victoria and New South Wales.

He had seen the resentment in their faces as they drove away from the clearing they had called home for most of the summer. Just one day earlier, they would have been

8

skiing or paddling in the shallows. Callan's father had cleared the area years ago with a chainsaw and mattock, creating the perfect tent site among the gumtrees. It was their own private camping ground on a remote tip of Lake Eucumbene, a vast waterway known for its outstanding trout fishing, unsullied wilderness, and clear, sunny waters. Nobody bothered travelling that far up the lake, settling for the more popular areas near old Adaminaby or Frying Pan Creek Road. Low, flat banks made swimming in the shallows pleasant, and the wider areas further out provided ample space for skiing. The bushland surrounding the lake disguised deer, wallaby, possums, wombats, and the occasional wild pig.

The Jeep pulled into the gas station and rolled up to the pumps under the cool shadow of a crooked awning, its white paint flaking from rusty patches. Weeds sprouted around the roof posts, and the concrete floor had cracked and broken loose in places. The garage was no more than a small dwelling in the middle of the bush where falling leaves regularly clogged the rain gutters. Customers could purchase items and pay for fuel from the quaint shop, built in sections using a combination of wood and tin, now faded and peeling under the intense, seasonal weather of the region. It seemed quieter now than it had been on the way up.

"I am thirsty though," Greg said. "Drier than a mother—" He glanced at Kristy. "I could use a drink. You know I don't take the sun as well as you guys do." The girls had insisted on driving with the Jeep's plastic top off, but sometimes it was nice to have a little respite from the heat.

"That's better. See, you can do it. It's only taken five weeks."

"Who knows what dizzying heights I might achieve with your help?"

Greg loved the banter with Kristy, but he had worked to curb his swearing, asking Callan for tips to impress her.

"Start by cleaning up your potty mouth," Callan had said, splitting redwood kindling for a growing ripple of flames and drinking a cold beer after returning from a day of skiing on the lake. It didn't feel strange that his best mate liked his sister. In fact, it was perfect. He loved them both and knew Greg was a decent man. Aside from his mother, they were the two closest people in his life; if they ended up together, he considered it a win for all.

Greg swung out of the passenger seat and stretched. He sat up front most of the time because his legs were long and he always ended up touching somebody's ass in the backseat while fumbling for the seatbelt buckle. He worked part time in security at one of the pubs in Albury to supplement his job as an electrician in local building developments. In the lead-up to the trip, he had worked long, demanding hours on a huge project at the Army base about seventy miles away in Wagga Wagga. The five weeks at the lake had been reward for all the laborious work. He and Callan had been best friends since the third grade, playing sports at every level, even making the Regional team together. In later years, however, Greg had swapped the bat and ball for a beer and the remote control. He loved a laugh and a joke and didn't take life too seriously. "My treat," he said. "Who needs a drink?"

"Pepsi," Kristy said, pulling the hand brake.

"Make it two," Sherry said.

She and Callan had been a couple for almost two years. Her rich red hair and sharp blue eyes had a magnetic charm on most men. She was opinionated and could be a real bitch, but he loved her passion and the fact that she knew what she wanted. In the early days, they had laughed often, but of late, there were fewer fun times. Callan tried to ignore his concern, but she seemed distant, withdrawn. He had tried everything from flowers and gifts to dinner and romantic drives to reignite their spark. He'd begged her to come on the trip, promising it would change things, but she'd spent much of the time complaining, and nothing had improved.

As the girls walked from the Jeep, he noticed Dylan, the last of their group, watching Kristy with his flashy green eyes narrowed in thought. Callan frowned. Dylan's interest in Kristy had grown as the trip progressed. Had something happened between them? Callan didn't think so, but they had a connection that was starting to concern him.

"Get me a pie or a sausage roll," Callan called. "I'm starving."

Their supply of most food items had run out going into the final week. Bread, potatoes, fish, and rabbit had become staples. The boys had spent dawn and dusk nearly every day hunting to ensure they had fresh meat. Callan had done some basic outdoor survival training as a Boy Scout and had supplemented their diet with various natural berries and greens, but the limited options soon became tasteless. They had a Stevens 350 shotgun for rabbits and a Remington .30-06 pump action for the big stuff. They had killed two pigs and spotted a deer, but scared it away. They were all comfortable with guns, having shot them since adolescence in country paddocks under the supervision of their parents.

Callan took the battered nozzle out of the bowser and unscrewed the gasoline cap. He caught his own reflection in the side mirror and laughed. His dark cropped hair had grown spiky, while his bronze skin and lean, muscled body presented a sharp contrast to the pale, fleshy man that had guided the boat up the mountain five weeks ago. His physical conditioning had been poor, sabotaged by too many beers and limited exercise. But from day one, he had embraced the physical exertion required to set up a long-term camping site. Hunting, fishing, wood-chopping, even the cooking and general cleaning had kept them active. Add in the swimming races, water skiing, and their daily game of cricket, and no one would wonder at the fact that they had all lost weight. Callan particularly, had carved away the fat and defined his muscles under an incessant, golden sun.

Callan noticed Dylan hadn't moved from the back seat. He wore an odd expression, as though listening for a distant sound. "What's wrong?" Callan said.

He had thought the two of them wouldn't survive a month together. When Kristy told him she had invited Dylan to replace Johnny, who had pulled out at the last minute, Callan had torn into her. Johnny and Dylan had fought in high school and despised each other. Johnny would be angry knowing Dylan had taken his place. "He can't replace Johnny," Callan had yelled. "His old man sacked Dad from his job." Dylan's father ran the most successful business in town and employed half the locals. Callan thought the man considered himself better than everyone else. "Mr. Top Shit," Callan's father, Keith, had called him. The company had dismissed Keith in controversy after a safety breach on an industrial packing machine. Management claimed he had neglected his occupational health and safety obligation, and that as a result, a fellow worker lost a finger.

"That's between them, not us."

Bullshit," Callan had argued. "He should never have sacked Dad. It wasn't even his fault."

Kristy had laughed. "You know Dad's a pisshead, Cal. He might have fed you a story about what happened, but I promise you there was more to it than that."

"I don't care. Dylan's different. He doesn't fit in and I don't trust him."

Kristy suspected the real reason for Callan's deep resentment. "You're not still holding a grudge about Emma Sandhurst, are you?"

Fuck yeah. In the tenth grade, Callan's girlfriend had left him because of her feelings for another boy. He hadn't learned who the *other* boy was until the eleventh grade.

Dylan turned and stood up in the backseat. "There's nobody here."

"What do you mean?"

He nodded toward the window. "The paper headline is weeks old. It's faded and crinkled, and there's mail on the ground at the door." Dylan leapt out of the car, landing on two feet, and walked toward the shop.

The door chime sounded and Greg came out holding a six-pack. "Beer?"

Dylan stopped at the package of mail. "I wouldn't go in there," Greg said. "It doesn't smell too good."

Callan said, "Shit man, maybe you better stay off that stuff until later?"

Greg's endless consumption of alcohol worried Callan. They all knew he had a drinking problem. He tried to ignore his addiction by making a joke every time someone commented on it. As teenagers, Greg had been the first to start drinking. Now, at twenty-eight, he downed four or five beers a night and at least a case on the weekend. They'd brought a dozen cases of beer for the trip and Greg had drunk more than half. "It's in my genes," he told Callan. "Why fight it?" He was only a baby when his father had died. They didn't know all the details, other than it being alcohol-related. His mother had a nervous breakdown when Greg was ten, and he had lived with his grandparents until he turned eighteen. He should have been emotionally ruined; instead, he was the most reliable person Callan knew. On the football field, in a barroom brawl, or whenever Callan had gotten himself into trouble, Greg was the one to whom he turned.

"Fuck you." Greg opened the top and swallowed a mouthful. "Ahhh." He burped. "Warm as piss."

"You'd drink that too if it had alcohol in it."

"Fuck yeah."

"You've tasted piss?" Dylan said, picking up the stack of mail. Greg spat a stream at Dylan's feet and they both chuckled.

"Postmarked two weeks ago," Dylan said.

Kristy appeared in the doorway, holding a newspaper. She was about five and a half feet tall, and although the activity and rationed food had helped her drop a few pounds, she still complained about her weight. Callan figured dissatisfaction with their weight was part of the female's DNA. He didn't think it was a problem, and neither did Greg or Dylan. She wore a yellow shirt that contrasted nicely with her blonde hair, golden tan, and sparkling blue eyes.

"The place is dead. I found this newspaper. Look at the headlines."

VIRUS REIGNS OUT OF CONTROL. MILLIONS DEAD ALONG THE EAST COAST OF AUSTRALIA.

"What the fuck?" Callan exclaimed, jamming the gas trigger into the bowser with a rattle and clunk. A cold shiver touched his skin. He recalled hearing about a virus on the news before their trip, an influenza pandemic in Hong Kong. There had been a few cases in Sydney, one in Melbourne, but it was minor news. He walked toward Kristy as Sherry came out, holding two bottles of Pepsi.

Dylan took the paper from her and read silently, his face twisted with disbelief. Overhead, a flock of cockatoos squawked loudly.

"What does it say?" Callan said. "Read it aloud, man."

"It's that virus. It's killing people everywhere. They've shut the doors at the Royal Melbourne and Monash hospitals." He read further along. "The Army's been called in. They're telling everyone to stay inside and limit contact."

"What's the date on the newspaper?" Sherry asked.

Dylan turned it over. "The fourteenth."

"Twelve days ago?" Kristy said. "If the Monash is over capacity, there must be a *lot* of sick people."

"It's reached Adelaide. They're saying…" He scanned the text. "…that flu shots and antibiotics are not effective.

It's viral. They don't know what's causing it, where it's come from, or how to stop it."

Greg said, "Maybe they've got it under control by now. I read that after the bird flu, the government put in all sorts of measures to cope with this sort of thing."

"What's the government saying?" Kristy asked.

Dylan skimmed the pages. "Not fucking much."

Callan said, "Sounds bad though."

Dylan said, "Yeah. Let's check our phones. Anyone got reception?"

Callan retrieved a slim device from his hip pocket, glancing down at it. "Fucking phone networks. We're still too far out."

"No Internet or e-mail either," Greg said.

Kristy said, "There might be a landline."

"Good thinking, Doc," Callan said.

They followed her inside, and the smell hit Callan immediately. He wrinkled his nose in disgust. Greg separated another can from the pack and popped the seal.

It was a typical country gas station—dark and dingy, a fifty-foot square room with a dirty window out to the pumps that probably hadn't been opened in twenty years. The counter consumed too much space and any more than four customers meant queuing out the door. Perforated hardboard lined the walls so the proprietors could hang every product a person might need for a camping expedition. Convenient food items like potato chips, lollies, chocolates, even a couple of bread loaves filled the remaining shelves. This was the last place to stop before the hour-long drive up the winding dirt road to the upper reaches of the lake.

Callan stood in the center of the room as the others poked about. Mingled with a strange, musty smell was the aged scent of rot. He didn't like the look of the place or his intuitive feeling of concern. It might have been the newspaper article. The fridge was dark, and the light switch didn't work, but the front door hadn't been locked and the gas pumps still worked. Why would someone do that and then disappear?

"Shit, no power means we can't buy ice," he said. "The cubes I made in the car freezer might not last the rest of the trip. I don't want that meat stinking up my boat." They had shot a dozen rabbits the previous night and stored the meat in the big boat fridge with a little ice to last the trip home. In this heat, though, it had probably melted. The fridge would smell horrible by the end of the day.

Dylan disappeared into the back room.

"This bread is moldy," Sherry said.

Kristy said, "There's no cash in the register." She reached the landline and lifted the phone to her ear, pressed the reset button a few times, then placed it back on the holder.

"Guys! Get in here," Dylan yelled.

Callan felt his nerves tingle. He pushed past Greg and Sherry and stepped through a small doorway into a storeroom, where inventory was haphazardly scattered. Empty boxes lay strewn about, along with canisters of salt, pepper, tomato ketchup, cans of baked beans, and sachets of powdered mashed potatoes. Another door along the back wall led to a second room. Callan strode over the supplies and went through.

The room was neat and orderly. Books filled long shelves, blankets sat piled on a chair. A pink and green floral rug covered floorboards on which a sofa couch had been folded out into a bed. An elderly couple lay with their arms curled around each other, eyes closed. Their pale skin had dried like parchment, and flies buzzed around the room. The smell was horrendous, biting into his nostrils with putrid teeth. On a wooden bedside table sat a bottle of medication.

Pills, Callan thought, ramming the crook of his elbow over his mouth. *They committed suicide.* He wondered what might drive them to do that.

"Shit," Dylan said. He took a deep breath with his nose pinched shut. "I don't think we need a doctor to call it."

Sherry pressed her lips in a thin line, which, for her, meant severe concern.

Kristy stood at the bed, peering at the bodies. "Why?"

In a low voice, Dylan said, "Let's see if we can find any more newspapers." He walked out, followed by Greg and Kristy.

Sherry stepped to Callan's side.

"I don't like it," he said. What if the old couple had committed suicide because of the virus that swept through Sydney and Melbourne? If it was bad enough to make killing yourself a better option, they were in big trouble.

He signaled for Sherry to leave and followed her, closing the flimsy wooden door after them. He pulled her to him. She initially resisted, but he squeezed her hand and she let him put his arms around her. It was their first hug in a week.

"I've got a bad feeling," he said, sighing into her hair. "Taking pills to die isn't the way I imagine myself going out."

"You think they killed themselves because of the virus?"

"Maybe. The only other thing I can think of is that one of them had a terminal illness and the healthy one didn't want to go on alone."

"That's stupid."

He wouldn't call it stupid. The thought of living without Sherry dropped a hot coal into his stomach. He could understand why a person might do that.

Callan led her toward the exit, feeling the softness of her fingers. He missed the contact. "Let's just get home and see what we can find out, okay?" He took her face in his hands and pulled her to him.

She turned away. "Not now, Cal. I feel strange."

"Sure, I understand. There are two dead people in the other room." He watched her walk through the doorway, feeling a familiar defeat. Originally, he had courted her for six months, enduring several knockbacks. Sherry came from a wealthy family in Albury; that had made his task challenging.

"Do you know how fucking hard it is to be the daughter of my parents?" she had asked him one day. "*Nothing* is good enough. They try to tell me who I can see, what I can do, when I can do it."

"You do what you want," Callan had said. Her independence was one of the things that had impressed him.

"I'm always conscious of what they'll say. I fucking hate it." She had smoked back then, and had pulled out a cigarette, lighting it with a stiff hand. He still didn't know why she'd quit. "Expect to get a call or visit from my father, too. He'll read you the *family laws*—what they will and won't accept as far as your behavior. Tell him to fuck off."

"I won't give you up easily," Callan had said. "You're everything to me. I love you, Sherry, and I haven't said that too many times before."

He recalled how her lips had curled at the edges, showing perfect teeth and a hint of the love she would one day possess. What had happened to them? Somewhere, it had started to unravel, and he had no idea how to fix it.

In the shop, Dylan filled a cardboard box with items from the shelves: matches, batteries, mosquito repellent, wicks for the gas lantern, and a packet of firelighters.

"What's that for?" Callan asked.

Dylan shook his head. "You never know."

"The milk has curdled," Kristy said, peering into a carton.

Greg leaned against the brown laminated counter, drinking his third beer. "This isn't looking too good. I dunno about you guys, but that voice inside my head is telling me some heavy shit has gone down."

"Any older newspapers?" Callan asked.

18

Kristy said, "Nothing. This is it. We've got twenty copies, though."

Sherry asked, "How long do you think they've been dead?"

"A few days, maybe more."

"Maybe this virus is the reason we didn't see anybody up at the lake," Dylan said.

Callan said, "It's always dead up at that end of the lake. Even at the height of summer you don't see many people."

"But *nobody*? No water skiers or fishing boats? I don't buy it. I wish I could talk to my father," Dylan said. "Virus outbreaks are like a hobby of his. He follows them pretty closely. He'll know what's going on."

Callan prickled. "He's an expert on viruses now?"

"I didn't say—"

"I'd like to talk to my father, too. I'm sure he'd have a good handle on things."

"I'm sure, but I know my father will have been tracking this thing. He kept a detailed record of the bird flu outbreak. Kristy read it. You were impressed, right? We'll see what he's got when we reach my place."

Callan had promised to stop arguing with Dylan, but Sherry's rebuff stung, and any talk of Dylan's father just pissed him off. Mention of Kristy reminded him of her growing friendship with Dylan. He didn't want that to go any further, at least for Greg's sake.

"I'm not sure this is the time for arguing," Kristy said. "I saw Dylan's father's work and it was impressive. Hopefully he's done the same again and we can learn from it, *if* it's needed. We're getting ahead of ourselves though, aren't we?"

"Doesn't mean Dylan's house is the first stop," Callan said.

"It makes sense though," Greg said. "It is the closest."

"Shut up, man. Whose fucking side are you on?" He couldn't believe Greg would agree with Dylan. "There's a quick way to my place. If we take the back roads, it won't take any longer than getting to Dylan's or to anyone else's house. We'll be there in five minutes and then we can go wherever you guys want."

"Don't be a shithead, Cal," Kristy said. "I thought you'd stopped taking those asshole pills."

"Okay," Sherry said, stepping in. "That's enough. We all want to get home, right? That's our goal? To get back to Albury safely?" She waited. "Anybody disagree?" Sherry had a Business Management degree from Deakin University, and was classified as "highly influential" in the DISC personality profiling system. It was really like impatient bossiness, but Sherry preferred the term "leadership." She was well organized, too, and Callan had seen her form a coherent, successful team among a previously dysfunctional group of people. She had Callan tied around her little finger, but he didn't mind. When she walked into the room, his heart stopped. He would walk through a burning house for her.

"It's time to get organized. Imagine there's no power or water for a few days. What do we need?" Sherry continued.

"Beer," Greg said, crushing his third can. He tossed it into a full bin and it rolled off onto the floor with a clunk.

"Matches, water, fuel," Callan said.

"I've already got some of those," Dylan said.

"You can never have too many."

"Okay," Sherry said. "We're getting somewhere. How quickly can we pull this together?"

"Quickly," Callan said. "You're right, we should do this." He felt hope, seeing her enthused again. It proved to him that managing people was her thing.

"You fill the rest of the fuel tanks and the gas bottles. Kristy and I will get drinks. Maybe a beer or two for Greg," she said, feigning a smile. Greg burped. "You belong in a sty. Dylan can gather another box of emergency supplies. Greg, you get the food, and not just

20

the stuff you normally eat. Try to find something that has a milligram of nutritional value."

"Sure," Greg said. "Hang around while I duck out to the fruit and vegetable shop and load up. Any vegans here? I could always get some lentils or legumes."

She shook her head. "I wonder what would need to happen for you to take life seriously. We all know your idea of a salad is pizza with a lettuce leaf on top. Just don't fill us with chips and chocolate, okay?"

Greg made a face and opened his forth beer. So far, Greg's drinking hadn't caused an issue, but Callan thought it wasn't the time to get wasted. He would shut his mouth for now, but if Greg kept drinking, he'd pull his buddy aside and say something.

Sherry clapped her hands. "Let's do it. I don't want to hang around here any longer than I have to."

The sun was a yellow blazing eye and Callan wished they were back at the lake. Sweat dripped down his forehead as he unloaded gear and lined the empty Jerry cans up at the pump. There was an urgency in their movement, as if the five had an important appointment. Even Greg had stopped sucking down beers, grunting as he carried box-loads of food from the shop. They worked in comfortable silence as the birds chirped and tweeted from the woods around them.

Callan would miss the peace of the countryside. The last five weeks had been more enjoyable than the entire four years he'd spent in his office job, cooped up in a shitty little cubicle with a picture of Sherry stuck to one wall. He didn't have Kristy's brains and would never reach the mercurial heights of the academic or career achievement for which she was destined. He dreamed of working as a fishing or hunting guide, taking rich clients up into the mountains every weekend, teaching them how to catch trout and shoot game. He loved the smell of the trees and the leaves, the snarling vegetation, even the algae on the rocks at the river's edge. It was his dream job. He recalled a conversation with Sherry about the possibility of one day moving away from town.

"You're not serious?"

"Have you ever been up to the Snowy Mountains? It's peaceful and beautiful, and smells amazing."

"It's boring, Callan. There's nobody there."

"That's part of it. Don't you get sick of having all these dickheads around you at work?"

"No. Those *dickheads* give me things to do. They're my job."

He thought the camping trip might change her mind, but that had failed. Even now, in the short time since she had taken control and allocated tasks, she was happier. She needed people. His dreams would have to wait. Sherry was the most important thing to Callan. He would follow her wherever she went and hope that, someday, she might see things differently.

The girls stacked separate piles of bottled soft drinks and cases of water wrapped in clear plastic beside the Jeep. Greg had done his best to vary the food, but it was limited to powdered mashed potatoes, tinned beans, and canned fruit. Dylan added three more boxes of camping supplies and a pack of 3M breathing masks.

"I found these," he said, holding up the box of ten. "You never know."

"Good idea," Callan said. "Was that it? Just the one box?"

"That's all I could find. They probably didn't have time to prepare for an outbreak."

Twenty-five minutes later, Callan had cleared the pile, stacking all of the items into the boat around the large portable ice chest, which contained the skinned rabbits and a couple of pan-sized trout.

"We *can* get our asses into gear when required," Sherry said. "Let's hope we don't need any of it."

"I don't think we have enough to pay for it all," Callan said. "I've only got a fifty and the card machine won't work."

Sherry said, "Does it matter?"

"Probably not, but it's the right thing to do. I'm not about to start stealing just because we can."

"Good point," Kristy said, sticking a hand into her pocket.

They scraped together one hundred and sixteen dollars, and left it in the squeaky till. It wouldn't pay for everything, but Callan felt satisfied that, under the circumstances, they wouldn't be branded as looters.

"We could always drive down to Cabramurra," Callan said as they waited for him to pack the last few things. "See if they've been affected."

"I just wanna get home," Kristy said.

Sherry said, "Me too. I've had enough of the country."

Callan felt another stab of disappointment. He secured the last few straps on the boat trailer, closed his eyes, and sucked in several deep breaths of pure country air. It would be the last time for a while, if Sherry had anything to do with it. You couldn't beat the smell of the gum and eucalyptus trees. In town, or worse, a big city, there were so many different odors that you couldn't distinguish one from the other. Out here, smells were unique, as if separated so you could appreciate each one. Some of his clothes still smelled of smoke from the campfire too, and although they had complained about it, two days from now he would miss that. Albury was delightful compared to the city, but out in the real country, when you closed your eyes, your senses marveled. When Callan opened his eyes, Kristy approached.

"I'll keep driving, if you don't mind," she said.

"Sure."

"You okay?"

The more thought he gave Sherry, the more he realized she had been acting strange before the trip. "Has Sherry said anything about being unhappy?"

Kristy looked confused. "No. Why?"

"She's been different."

"Today?"

"No, longer. Before the trip. Don't let her know I'm worried."

"Are you?"

Callan ached when he considered life without her. His mother once told him that in any relationship, there is always one person who loves the other more. Callan was that person. He felt her slipping away. Lack of physical affection was one thing, but she seemed less interested in him, too. Any time he mentioned moving to the country, or what he wanted for his future, she became disengaged, as though she didn't consider a future with him. And they hadn't had sex since before the trip. There was just no interest there, despite his attempt to romanticize their time together. "Yeah."

Kristy put a hand on his arm and gave a conciliatory smile. "Let me talk to her."

As they rolled away from the gas station, Callan looked back at the ramshackle building and felt a pang of concern. Were they driving into trouble? If he didn't need to check on his parents, he'd be glad to head back up to the lake and wait it out until they got word that the virus had passed. They had fuel and enough food to last several weeks. He couldn't sit up there wondering whether his loved ones were safe, and he doubted the others could either. They would discover what had happened soon enough; the idea filled him with a cold apprehension. Surely the government had control of the situation now.

2

Kristy gripped the wheel tighter as they cruised along the winding highway, fighting tight corners and steep hills. She pressed the accelerator to the floor, trying to coax the Jeep over the rise and onto the downward side. The sun cast warm rays through towering gums; out here, only brown earth and hardy, sun-loving bush existed. They had seen the odd dead kangaroo on the dusty gravel edge and, once, an echidna preparing to make its suicidal trek across the black stretch. As much as Kristy loved town life, like her brother, she had a soft spot for the real country too.

A nervous tension swept over her again. Its absence had been blissful for the last three weeks, and she thought she might have won after a year of fighting the stresses of thirty-six hour shifts and people dying under her care. As they crept toward home, though, it was back, familiar yet unwelcome.

She hadn't thought about working in the ER for weeks, but now the memories crept back with a sharper edge. She always thought of her first loss, the old man who had come into the ER complaining of breathing difficulties after suffering symptoms of the common cold.

"What were his initial signs?" the attending physician had asked after Kristy requested a consult.

"Cough, sore throat, mild breathing difficulty, painful right ear, headache."

"Diagnosis?"

"Upper respiratory tract infection."

"Treatment?"

"Analgesic. Come back in two or three days if it doesn't improve."

It didn't improve, and by the time the man returned, the infection had moved to the lower respiratory tract. She chased the original attending around the ER as he sought to save the life of a car crash victim.

Her tone was higher, panicky. "His breathing is very short, he's complained of chest pain, and is coughing sputum. I'd like to perform a chest x-ray."

He had agreed, and she had the x-ray taken, confirming pneumonia. She had administered antibiotics immediately, notifying his son and his elderly wife of the diagnosis. They suspected afterward that a virus *and* bacteria had caused the infection, but combined with the man's age, it proved too strong; he had not recovered. The attending had found her sitting alone in one of the doctors' quarters in tears, more than three hours after her twenty-six hour shift had ended.

"It's not your fault," the attending said. Kristy had blown her nose and tried to speak but emotion had impaired her.

"He waited too long to come back in."

"I should have known," she managed. "What sort of doctor am I, losing a patient to pneumonia?"

He had put a hand on her shoulder. "A good one. I consulted on this too, remember."

Kristy had never forgotten what she saw as her negligence, though, and that had been the beginning of the erosion of her confidence. Now the newspaper headline and the dead couple at the gas station, along with the prospect of returning to work, unsettled her. She supposed she was nervous by nature, but this had touched a sensitive place. The unknown consequences of the virus had disturbed the group, and a contemplative silence had fallen.

She wondered from where the pathogen had come. Was it global? Did they have a pandemic, or was it limited to Australia? The papers said a virus had caused the deaths. She suspected a high virulence based on the death toll and the rapidity with which it had moved. What if it was airborne?

Stop it. Don't think about this until you have to.

Kristy forced herself to concentrate on the road ahead; in the distance, thin white clouds gathered in the west. It had only rained twice in the last month. Most days had seen vivid blue skies and only the occasional clouds. One of those times, she and Dylan had stayed behind to clean the camp while the others had gone skiing. They had ended up having a fight with the dirty dishwater until relentless laughter had hurt their bellies.

Dylan had made her time at the lake more enjoyable. While they hadn't been intimate, she felt a connection, and was certain he did too. They had known each other since high school, and had always been good friends. Why had the romantic spark failed to turn into a flame earlier? She thought that was probably her fault. Her list of failed relationships was impressive: angry, brooding, aggressive types, much like her father, she supposed, all the opposite of Dylan. His quiet, passive nature, his ability to listen and give sensible responses to her comments, provided a pleasant change. He was cute, too, and she found herself sneaking more glimpses of those sharp green eyes and waves of dark hair as the trip lengthened. Her favorite moments had been their quiet, late night talks by the orange embers of the campfire, smoke lazily circling them as they sat together, discussing the world in general. The romance of it all made her tingle. How she had wanted to snuggle up in his arms and fall asleep! He wasn't big and manly like Callan or Greg, but he possessed an intelligence that she thought made him stronger than any man she had known before.

Kristy saw him talking to Sherry in the rearview mirror and her stomach flipped. Admittedly, she hadn't been forthright the way Sherry would be if she liked a man. Sherry was blunt, to the point. Perhaps Kristy should seek her advice. She promised herself that once the virus business was resolved, she would make a move.

"Kristy! Watch out!"

An old man in a tattered grey suit staggered along the side of the road.

The tires screeched and the steering wheel shuddered as Kristy jammed the brakes and tightened her dreamy grip, fighting to keep the car straight. She managed it, but they might have whiplash or bruising from the seatbelts.

"I didn't see him," she said in a high voice, her chest heaving. "Is everyone all right?"

Callan said, "Yeah, but I don't know about this guy. He stepped out of nowhere."

Ahead, on the right shoulder, the man stood looking at them. They had stopped on a gentle downward slope; the road onward crossed a short wooden bridge, then began another long, slow incline. Loose, rusty wire strung through rotted posts served as fencing on either side. Beyond, tussock grass rolled into a hill dotted with the occasional tree. The breeze tickled their noses and on it came the scent of cow dung and farm animals.

"What's wrong with him?" Kristy asked. Her heart raced and her hands shook. Callan jumped over the side and landed on the bitumen. "Be careful, Cal."

"Wait!" Dylan said.

Callan stopped. "What?"

"Put a mask on."

Callan considered this, and then walked to the back of the Jeep where he took a mask from the box and slipped it on. "Just to be extra safe."

That's what makes Dylan different, Kristy thought. He was always thinking two steps ahead and cognizant of everyone's safety, not just his own. Callan would never have thought of such a thing. There were so many parts to Dylan she didn't yet know.

Callan approached the man with a cautious hand out. "Hey, buddy. You okay?"

The man looked up; he had dark rings around bloodshot eyes. His red nose and pasty complexion suggested a condition Kristy had seen before. He wore a faded, oversized grey suit jacket. His pants were torn and his boot seams had split. He began to cough. "No."

"Maybe you should leave it, Callan," Sherry said. "It's not our problem."

"He's got the flu," Kristy said. "At the very least."

"What about the virus?" Callan said.

"The flu is a virus."

Callan stopped six feet away. "What's wrong, mate?"

The man blinked twice and rubbed his eyes, then shook his head, as if to clear it. "I've caught it," he said. "It must have been that bastard who tried to grab me back at the farm."

"Caught what?"

The man sneezed and snot sprayed forth. He coughed, choking on phlegm, and for a long moment Kristy didn't think he would stop. Finally, red-faced and spewing spittle in a long string, he ceased. From the Jeep she could hear his wheezy chest.

"He's coughed up blood," Callan said.

Kristy opened the driver's door and got out.

"Don't be stupid, Kristy," Sherry said.

She went to the rear of the Jeep and rummaged until she found a towel and a breathing mask. *You can do this.* While she had stitched a wound and fixed minor problems for Callan and the others on the trip, this was the first outsider she had treated in six weeks. *He's not going to die on you.* She faced the question with every patient. If they died under her care, did it make her less of a doctor? She thought so. The attending who had consulted for her on the pneumonia patient told her the guilt of loss would pass, that she would realize she couldn't save them all. He had told her to focus on the ones who lived, and that her business was to do her best to keep them alive.

"Kristy," Dylan said from the back seat. "Don't get too close. We don't know if this guy has the virus or not."

The man abruptly sat down on the road as though he had just finished a marathon. "I don't feel too good," he said, cupping a hand over his mouth.

Kristy squatted beside him and offered the towel. "How long have you been sick, sir?"

He took the cloth and wiped his face. "Thank you." He coughed again, short and sharp. "Since yesterday. Comes on fast. I'll be dead by nightfall."

A chill touched her. *You're treating him.* "What makes you say that?"

"Seen it already. The missus died yesterday. Bastards got her the day before, and they came back for me. Do us a favor and kill me right now, would you?" He looked to Callan. "You got guns?"

Kristy felt cold dread penetrate her. The red skin around the end of his nose had begun to chap; when he inhaled, the mucus sounded thick and viscous.

"It's… the virus," Callan whispered.

It might well be the virus. What could she do for him? She had her medical bag with everything required for an emergency. She had even used a surgical needle and thread to close a cut on Callan's foot. There were pain relievers and sedatives that might ease his suffering, but it appeared he did have a virus, and they would offer little assistance against that. Respiratory problems were common with influenza. Did he have a fever? She reached out with the back of her hand.

"No," Callan said, and she jerked it back. He stood in front of the Jeep with the Remington pump action.

"What are you doing, Cal? He's sick, not trying to kill us."

"You have got guns," the man said.

"Just being careful, mister. Don't be alarmed. No touching, Kristy. He's got something and I don't want you getting it."

"What's your name, sir? Where do you live?"

"I need to take a look at that gun." He convulsed with another deep, hoarse cough.

Kristy felt compelled to do *something*. She decided to get her medical kit from the car and administer pain relief to improve his comfort.

The man pushed onto one leg, then made a face and sneezed three times, his head snapping forward. Kristy shuffled back, despite the facemask.

"Let's just go," Sherry said. "We can't help him. We'll call an ambulance and send them out here, or something."

"Let me get some paracetamol," Kristy said.

The man was on his feet, dragging his battered boots toward her. In a sudden, swift movement, he snapped at her the way a dog might try to catch a fly buzzing too close to its mouth.

"Kristy!" Callan screamed. "Get back!" He stepped forward with the gun aimed at the old man and pumped a cartridge into the chamber. "Back, mister, get back."

"Don't shoot him, Callan. He's done nothing wrong."

"He makes one more move toward you and I won't hesitate." The gun wavered. "I'm sorry, but I won't risk my sister's life for anyone. You come any closer to her and I *will* shoot you."

The Jeep's engine kicked into life. Dylan sat in the driver's seat. "Just in case," he said in a quiet voice.

Callan adjusted his aim. "No objections from me."

"All right," Kristy said. "Maybe it's time for us to go."

The man opened his mouth to speak, but another coughing fit seized him, saliva and blood spraying over the blacktop.

"What's he saying?" Kristy said.

"Who gives a fuck? He's walking death. Get back." Callan directed the gun to within a foot of the man's head. "If you don't want me to shoot him, Kristy, get in the car now."

She was missing something. He was trying to communicate, and she needed another moment.

"Kristy!" Callan screamed. Veins bulged in his neck.

With astonishing speed, the old man snatched the nose of the shotgun, turning it away. The pump action exploded with a heavy, metallic bang, echoing across the paddocks.

Kristy screamed and fell backward onto the road.

The man pulled on the barrel, twisting left and right, tossing Callan off balance. The pump clicked and the gun thundered again. Part of the man's right arm exploded like a grapefruit, showering the bitumen and dirt with red, lumpy muck.

Sherry screamed. Kristy ran to the car, smelling the familiarity of ER trauma. Greg stood at the rear, reaching underneath their luggage.

The old man finally twisted the gun free with his remaining hand.

Greg sprinted to Callan's side with the Stevens 350 shotgun, then aimed it at the old man's head. "Put it down."

The old man turned the Remington around until he was staring into it. He staggered, found his balance, and engaged the pump action. When he placed his thumb on the trigger, Callan and Greg stepped away.

Kristy stood at the driver's door. She knew what was going to happen. She had seen the look of hopelessness in patients before, people begging for death to take them.

"Thank you," the man said.

He put the shorter barrel into his mouth.

Callan and Greg shuffled back. Kristy turned away.

The gun boomed, followed by a wet, squishy sound. The weapon clattered on the road. Kristy turned back to see the old man's body slumped on the ground, his arms splayed.

No one moved.

Kristy felt her eyes fill and she pressed them shut, spilling tears down her face. Who was this man? Where was his family? *What a lonely death.* Her heart ached for him.

"That is the worst thing I've ever seen," Sherry said, holding her belly. "I'm gonna throw up." She walked away, bent over, gagging.

Callan made a wide circle around the body to where the shotgun lay. He squatted, reached out to pick it up, and then pulled it back as though it might bite. After a moment, he kicked it toward the Jeep.

"Take a fucking minute, Callan! A person just died," Kristy said. Callan froze with a guilty look. "He might have had the virus and been sick but he was still a person. Have you lost your fucking humanity that quickly?"

"Take it easy. I was just retrieving the gun."

Her body trembled, and she wrapped her arms across herself.

Greg said. "Are you okay?"

She shook her head. "No." Greg curled a hand around her and she hugged him, sobbing. This was it. She couldn't *be* a doctor anymore. Death ravaged her conscience every time. One of the senior residents had told her she would know if it was for her or not. *Not.* "Thanks," she said, pulling away to rub her eyes.

Callan wiped the gun with an old t-shirt, which he then balled up, and stuffed in the back of the Jeep. "Sorry for screaming at you before,'" he said to Kristy. "I didn't know what he was going to do."

"Forget it."

Sherry returned, wiping her mouth. Greg said to her, "You wanted to know what would make me take life seriously? This. I'm taking this very fucking seriously."

Sherry said, "I'm glad, although I wish we hadn't found him. It scares the shit out of me. What do we do with the body?"

"Nothing. We don't touch him," Callan said.

Kristy said, "We can't leave him there. He needs a proper burial."

"Do you wanna risk infection? We don't know how this thing is contracted."

"Look at his boots," Dylan said. A worn patch of sock showed through the sole. "He's walked miles in those things."

"He could have come from any farmhouse in the area," Callan said. "There's a ton of them."

"Get me out of here before I completely lose it," Kristy said. "I don't want to drive anymore."

"Greg, you sit up front with me," Callan said, passing the pump action over. "I want you at my side."

They piled in and Callan put the Jeep into first gear then let the clutch out, easing them around the body and back onto the highway.

Greg said, "We ain't got much ammo left. Maybe a handful of shells. We shouldn't have pissed it all away shooting at beer cans."

"Yeah, it was a laugh at the time, but doesn't seem so funny now." Callan shook his head grimly.

Whatever optimism Kristy felt leaving the lake had disappeared. All the familiar feelings of doubt had returned and her stomach twisted into knots of apprehension. The man had almost certainly been infected by a virus, and likely the one on which the paper had reported. *He killed himself so he wouldn't become too sick.* What had he seen? Coupled with the abandoned gas station and the dead couple, his actions pulled a dark and foreboding sense of uncertainty over her. She wished they could turn around and head back up to the lake.

She shuddered, pushing in closer to Dylan.

"You okay?" he asked. She shook her head and he placed a hand over hers. Any other time it would have been thrilling, but she couldn't shake the feeling of despair.

Nobody spoke as the car sped down the highway, edging closer to home, passing more rolling paddocks and long patches of wild scrub. The air through the gap in Greg's window turned colder, and a mass of threatening grey clouds gathered in the west. In an effort to get home

34

more quickly, Callan decided on an alternative route, leaving the main highway.

They hit the brown gravel and the Jeep relayed a mild vibration, soothing Kristy. Her eyelids grew heavy. Eventually, she dozed. When she woke, the others were climbing out.

"Toilet stop," Dylan said.

The dirt area contained a small brick structure, several galvanized metal rubbish bins, and a couple of wooden slabbed tables and chairs. Beyond the small clearing, dense scrub spread for miles in every direction. Above, a grey sheet of cloud had drifted over. Kristy stretched as the boys disappeared into the toilets. The place had an unusual silence, lacking the pretty bird melodies to which she had grown accustomed over the past month.

Sherry hung back. "That was the most disgusting thing I have ever seen. I wish that guy had killed himself back wherever he came from."

Kristy stared. *Classic Sherry insensitivity*, she thought. *You might be better off without her, Cal.*

"Do you think it's bad at home?"

Kristy said, "I don't know. Trying not to think about it yet."

"What's going on with you and Dylan?"

"What do you mean?"

"Has anything happened? Are you ever going to do anything?"

"No. Not yet. I mean, we've chatted *a lot* but nothing else has happened."

"Really? Not even by the fire after we'd all gone to bed? I don't believe that."

Kristy scrunched her nose. Maybe this was her chance to ask Sherry for advice. "I don't want to scare him off."

"You'll scare him off if you *don't* make a move."

"I suppose." Greg walked out of the toilets in their direction. "I like him so much. I don't want to screw it up."

35

"You won't," Sherry said. "Take a chance."

"What about Greg though? I think he might like me too."

Sherry's eyes widened. "So?"

"Well, I don't want to hurt him. He's like my brother."

"Fuck him. Figuratively." Kristy's mouth fell open. "He's a big boy. He'll get over you. Besides, he's liked you forever and if he hasn't done anything by now, he never will."

Kristy stared. She knew Sherry could be blunt, but this was cold. The discussion made her more depressed. She had to change the subject, and recalled her conversation with Callan. "Remind me not to get on your wrong side. What about you and Callan? You two have been distant this whole trip. Is everything okay?"

Sherry considered this. "I know you're his sister and all, but…" Kristy raised her eyebrows. "I just feel like we've drifted apart. We want different things now."

Damn it, Kristy thought. Callan had suspected right. "Have you told him?"

"No. Not yet. I was going to talk to him when we got home."

"What's changed? And when? I always thought you guys were rock solid."

"He's just… different now. So am I."

"I think you should talk to him, tell him how you feel. You owe him that. Surely you can sort it out."

"I will. I don't know."

Greg approached. "Who's hungry?"

In a low voice, Sherry said, "Don't you tell him. Let me do it."

Kristy felt a pang of concern for how Callan would react to the revelation; he adored Sherry. "I won't. But don't wait too long." Sherry shrugged and walked away.

"Hungry?"

"Yes," Kristy said, pushing her lips into a smile as Greg arrived. "Starving."

She tried to shake off the conversation. Insensitivity was part of Sherry's personality and they all accepted it, but this went deeper. She seemed genuinely unhappy. The idea of them breaking up was shocking. Kristy would give her a day or two to speak to Callan before talking to him herself.

Greg passed her a cup of coffee from a thermos they had prepared at the lake. "Thank you," Kristy said with a smile.

She marveled at the change in him over the past four weeks. While he still burped, swore, and drank too much beer, he had shown a side uncommon in men— uncommon to her, anyway. Greg had shared the burden of chores and followed her instructions without complaint, including washing clothes, dishes, and cleaning up. He had also killed and cleaned their meat catches, afterwards cooking and serving them with a palpable sense of satisfaction. Whenever he had made food or acquired a drink, he always offered some to others, especially her. She had known for some time that Greg liked her. He hadn't made it obvious, but something Callan had said at a party awhile back made her aware. She was flattered, but having known him since she they were children, she considered him a brother, rather than a potential lover.

"Nice?" he asked.

She nodded, sipping. "Yeah."

Since they had found the old couple at the gas station, Greg's frivolous nature had vanished. "You're not making jokes or playing around anymore? I don't remember seeing you like this."

He shrugged one shoulder. "Something's not right here. I've got a bad feeling about this one." He considered his next words. "To be honest, I'm scared."

"You? Scared?" The idea twisted her stomach. Greg was what Callan called *country tough,* a man who had fought bushfires and floods, toiled for days on end without rest, and suffered injuries working on the land that would have sent lesser men to the hospital. Kristy had never known him to be scared.

"Losing your parents makes you different. It's not something you can control. You're vulnerable. You can be tough, fight hard, and never give in, but still lose. My grandparents are all I have left, all I've really known. If they're gone..." He glanced off into the bushes. "I don't know what I'd do, but I'd be alone."

Kristy flushed with sorrow. It was a huge contrast for a man who had never seemed to take life seriously or have a worry in the world. She realized that the rest of their problems were faint compared to his suffering. Greg was an electrician, spending his days wiring houses around Albury and Wodonga. He worked hard, enjoying football and his mates. Kristy had never seen him so serious, despite the challenges he had overcome. She felt a sudden admiration for him and wished she could ease his concern.

"No you won't," she said, taking his free hand. "I don't think that will happen, and I pray it doesn't, but if it does, you'll have us. Callan and I, we are your family. We've always been family." She thought about the next sentence, but she couldn't stop it. "I've always thought of you as a brother. You *are* my brother."

He creased his brow. "A brother?"

Regret filled her. "We've known each other since we were, what—I must have been six?"

He chuckled. "I used to pull those long, blonde pigtails of yours."

Kristy laughed. "You did. But you also beat up any boy who tried to hurt me."

"Yeah, I nearly broke Brad Taylor's arm when he tried to kiss you." They both laughed.

Kristy remembered the incident. She had suspected Brad liked her, but he spent days chasing her around the schoolyard, calling her names she didn't know existed. Eventually, Kristy had grown sick of it and faced him. Brad had grabbed her shoulders and tried to plant a kiss on her lips, but she had fought him, screaming and kicking. Greg had leapt on the smaller boy, pinning his arm behind his back until, through tears, he had apologized. "Nobody bothered me again."

"So that means… as a kind of brother…"

A sickly feeling reared, and her mouth curled down at the edges. She tried to explain, but only shook her head and said, "No. Not that. I'm sorry."

"That's cool. Cal would probably kill me anyway."

"Yeah," she said, knowing the truth.

His face looked flushed and one finger curled around his necklace. She scratched for a subject change. "What's that?"

"This? It was my father's," he said, thumbing a silver medal on the end of the black cord.

She frowned. "I haven't seen it before."

"Nah, just put it on today. I wore it the first day but didn't want to lose it in the lake. My grandmother found it while she was cleaning out some old boxes. It's a service award from the Vietnam war."

"Your father was in Vietnam?"

Greg smiled. "Yeah. He did two tours."

"Wow. I never knew that."

His mouth firmed and he looked off into the distance. "Grandma says that's why he was so fucked up. He came back the second time with gunshot wounds, got hooked on the painkillers, and then moved to the grog. She said he could never get over the shit that happened there. You know he died choking on his own vomit after drinking for three days straight?"

Kristy was speechless. They had known the death of Greg's father had been alcohol-related, but the circumstances horrified her. She felt a deep sadness. Just then, the others appeared from the toilets.

"If you can keep this to yourself, I'd appreciate it."

"Of course," Kristy said. "Greg, I'm so sorry. The rest of us take our parents for granted. What your father must have gone through… and then you not having him as part of your life. It makes me so sad."

He nodded. "Me too."

Kristy visited the bathroom under a cloud of melancholy, and then sat on a faded table eating a packet of potato chips as boiling grey clouds crept across the sky. A cooler, moist smell had drifted in on the breeze, promising rain. Callan and Greg secured the Jeep's cover as the girls sought jackets to curb the touch of the dropping temperature.

"We're about two hours from Albury," Callan said. "This might sound a bit crazy, but I'm gonna use an old back road my dad used to take me on that runs alongside the Murray River, rather than stick to the main highway. We'll meet up with the Hume Highway just below Holbrook. Come into town from Table Top Road."

"Why?" Greg said.

"It's quieter. Less people. I don't want any more confrontations like the one we just had."

"No towns along those roads," Dylan said.

"Just a tiny gas station my dad used to stop at. It's probably a little quicker, too."

"There are farms all around here," Sherry said. "Should we stop in and see if they can tell us anything?"

"The old man came from one of those farms," Callan said. "They might be infected. He mentioned someone getting his wife. Sounds dangerous. Could be looters about, too."

"What about going to the police?" Sherry said.

Callan said, "Nothing out this way, but it's a good idea and we should head there when we arrive into Albury."

"I agree," Dylan said. "You know we should be prepared for the worst. If this thing has gotten into the town, there's a fair chance some of the people we know might be infected, or worse."

"Let's not get presumptuous," Callan said.

"He's right," Sherry said. "The newspaper said millions were dead on the East Coast."

"Doesn't mean Albury is infected."

"That was three weeks ago," Dylan said.

Kristy said, "The old man said the symptoms started yesterday, which indicates the virulence is high and it moves quickly."

"Will they be working on a vaccine somewhere?" Greg said.

"Maybe. Do you remember the H1N1 virus a few years ago? It took a few months to formulate a vaccine."

Callan laughed. "You're dramatizing it. Flu strains come and go every few years. Who knows if that guy wasn't just crazy?"

"Just be prepared," Dylan said, walking off to stretch his legs.

3

They stopped at another gas station nestled in heavy scrub. Callan wanted to keep the fuel tank full. It was no more than a dilapidated shack sprouting an ancient bowser bearing the faded MOBIL logo. Two cars sat out front, and dust clung to the windows in a thick film. Although the place appeared deserted, Greg decided to look inside. Kristy needed to stretch her legs, so clambered out to join him.

Sherry had fallen asleep and Dylan couldn't be bothered with moving, preferring to sit and consider the circumstances with greater thought. This happened whenever he felt nervous or stressed, and wouldn't cease until the issue was resolved. He thought it might be a long time before that happened. He opened the window and the strong smell of gum leaves filled the car.

Sherry opened one sleepy eye. "Where are we?"

"Another gas station on some dirt road in the middle of nowhere." He thought about joining Kristy. He wasn't fond of Sherry, although she seemed compelled to unload her problems on him and had done so a number of times on the trip. She and Callan had been distant over the past five weeks, and Sherry had griped to him more than once. He felt bad for Callan having to put up with her bossy, obnoxious ways. Sherry was never happy, no matter what Callan tried. His obsequious efforts gained little thanks. Dylan recalled an incident she had referred to a few days ago. It had roused his curiosity.

"Great. Another delay."

Dylan added "unrealistic and impatient" to her list of flaws. "The other day, when we were talking near the swimming hole, you mentioned an incident that had happened before the trip."

Sherry watched Callan pump gas. Kristy was standing in the doorway of the shack, talking to Greg, who was inside. Sherry let out a big sigh. "I cheated on Callan," she said.

Dylan's mouth fell open. It was the last thing he had expected her to say.

"You're not gonna say anything to that?"

"To be honest, I couldn't think of an appropriate response. Are you joking?"

"No. No joke."

"Why haven't you told him? You obviously haven't, or he'd be majorly pissed."

She shrugged. "I will. When we get home."

"Shit. This whole time you've been carrying that around."

"I know. It's been difficult."

"Not for you. For him! You've been pretending to love him."

"I stopped doing that a while ago."

"Oh, fuck me. Why are you telling me this?"

"You asked, and I've got nobody else."

"Why did you come on this trip?"

She rolled her tongue over her lip. "Guilt. And I wanted see if there was any love left."

Dylan closed his eyes and lowered his head. Callan wouldn't think so, but he was better off without Sherry. What a mess. Nobody deserved this. The guy was hapless with girls. Dylan thought back to grade ten. He knew Callan still blamed him for his breakup with Emma Sandhurst. Dylan had barely spoken to her. She had chased him and he'd been as confused as everyone else as to why she'd done so. It wasn't his style to pursue an attached girl. Emma had fed Dylan lies and he'd gone along with it, probably making it seem worse to Callan. They had been peripheral friends until that point. A shocking thought formed in his mind.

"Who was it? And don't you dare fucking tell me it was Johnny."

Sherry looked away.

"Noooo. No. Come on, Sherry. One of his best mates? He loves Johnny. Are you trying to fuck him up completely?" Tears ran from the corners of her eyes. "Anyone but *Johnny*."

The door opened and Callan jumped in. Dylan's heart froze.

"What'd you say about Johnny?" Sherry wiped at the tears. "We were just talking," Dylan said, his heart thundering, "about who might have survived. We think Johnny surely would have bunkered down somewhere safely."

"You bet," Callan said. "No chance that he's sick. He's too smart and tough. Are you okay, babe?" Sherry took his hand. "It's okay. Johnny will be fine. Our parents will be fine."

Dylan turned away, suppressing disgust. He was ready to explode. He hated knowing secrets. He had a bad habit of inadvertently making them known.

Greg and Kristy returned empty-handed. The place was deserted, no phones or newspapers, little food. No dead people in the house out back, either. They drove away, Dylan feeling the secret like a lump of ice in his stomach.

He checked his phone again, but there was still no service, not even the "SOS Only" message. He needed to talk to his father. Dylan was certain he would be tracking the virus, collecting papers and making notes. He'd never let him down and would have a plan for staying safe. Survival. He loved his father. He loved his mother too, but he was closer to his father, the same way his sister, Lauren, was closer to her. The man had been there every day of Dylan's life, coaching, counseling, providing. He ran a hugely successful business, although Dylan had rarely suffered his absence for it. He had long encouraged Dylan to follow his dreams and pursue whatever made him happy. His father always supported him unconditionally. He thought about their last conversation; funnily enough, it had been about Kristy.

"So you like her, then?" His father had a wry smile beneath a trimmed moustache which was showing the first flecks of grey.

"Ahhh. I don't know."

His father had laughed. "Just like me at your age. I bet you *do* like her. A lot. It's complicated, isn't it?"

Dylan had frowned. "Yeeeahh."

"See. Let me guess. Her brother. He doesn't like you."

Dylan narrowed his eyes. "That's easy. You know the whole backstory. You're *part of it.*"

Bob Cameron shrugged. "Don't let the thoughts and feelings of outsiders affect this, Dylan. It's between you and Kristy. If you like her, do something about it." He walked over and put a hand on Dylan's shoulder. "Mate, your mother and I just want you to be happy. We'll deal with anything or anyone, as long as you're where you want to be."

"Thanks, Dad. I *do* like her. A lot. But a few things worry me and I'm just not sure how to approach them."

"Well, either of us are here if you need to talk. But take a risk. I wouldn't have this amazing family or the business if I hadn't taken plenty of risks."

Dylan thought about never seeing him again, and tears blurred his vision. He tightened his jaw until it hurt. *I hope you're okay, Dad.*

He shut away the thoughts and gazed at the scenery through the window, reminiscing about the time at the lake. The rain came soon after leaving the stopping area, pattering the windows in long bullets. Overhead, dirty clouds bubbled, creating a feeling of impending dusk. No one spoke. Dylan knew they were all turning different questions over in their minds. Answers would be difficult to find. Some would emerge when they reached Albury and their respective homes. He tried to bury the secret Sherry had told him by assuring himself that it would sort itself out. Callan had never shown any concern for him, so why should he worry?

They spotted the checkpoint about fifteen miles out of Albury, just north of Table Top Road. They hadn't seen a single vehicle traveling in either direction. Callan stopped the car on a roadside patch of gravel and cut the engine. On their left, a thin creek flowed in lazy green eddies, surrounded by more tussock grass leading to fences and undulating paddocks beyond. About half a mile along the blacktop, two Army trucks touched noses at angles across the highway. In silence, the group surveyed the scene. Through the thin mist of fine rain, they couldn't see any sign of soldiers.

Dylan felt rumblings of concern. An Army blockade meant things were truly bad. Either they would have to turn back altogether, or soldiers were inspecting citizens for signs of the virus before letting the uninfected pass.

"We could ram it," Callan said.

"Don't even joke about that," Kristy said.

Sherry said, "We're not infected, though. They'll have to let us through."

Callan said, "What if they don't? What if the *town* is infected and they won't let us go back?"

"I doubt it." While the old man had scared Dylan, too, that one incident didn't mean the world had gone to hell just yet. The Army would know what was going on and they would have a suitable plan. They would tell them exactly what had occurred along the East Coast, and more importantly, in Albury. The newspaper they'd found was weeks old. Surely the government had control of the situation by now. "They've probably cleaned up Albury and just want to make sure nobody brings the virus back in."

Callan said, "We'll see. Just remember there are forty-five thousand people in Albury and another thirty-five thousand in Wodonga. That's a lot of people to get sick."

Kristy bumped Dylan's leg. "Sorry," she said, but one finger remained resting against his hand.

He smiled and looked away. He had to consider her now. Despite his father's advice, he had promised himself nothing would happen while Callan was around. *Technically*, it hadn't. They had never even kissed, but his feelings had developed into a deeper affection. She was irresistible; smart, kind, a wonderful listener. Despite the danger, he'd admired how she had rushed to help the old man, deferring her safety for the welfare of another. She was selfless. Such a contrast to his ex-girlfriend, whose self-interest had been her predominant trait. In hindsight, he didn't know how the relationship had lasted. Perhaps it had been the companionship. He hated being alone. That was one of the reasons he had agreed to the trip. His roommate was traveling overseas and Dylan detested coming home to an empty house.

"Let's see what they have to say," Greg said. "The worst they can do is turn us around."

Dylan noted the absence of humor in Greg's voice. Until their roadside episode, he would have bet money that Greg was incapable of being serious. It added to Dylan's anxiety. When the joker stopped joking, it was time to worry.

Sherry said, "If they turn us around, we can try another way."

"What if they arrest us?" Callan asked.

"Why would they do that?" Kristy asked.

"I dunno. Just a crazy thought." He turned the key and the engine rumbled into life. "Let's do it, then."

The car crept along at forty miles an hour. Callan turned the windscreen wipers to full speed. Greg laid the Remington beside the seat, out of view, and passed the shotgun to Dylan, who placed the weapon in the back compartment.

As they approached, Callan slowed, waiting for a soldier to exit a truck and greet them. He stopped twenty yards short and let the vehicle idle.

"Doesn't look like a standard Army blockade," Greg said.

"How the fuck do you know?" Callan asked.

"From the movies."

"Maybe they're stretched a little thin," Dylan said. "This is all they can afford."

The trucks were identical, about twice the length of the Jeep, with large, treaded wheels and a square cab for the driver and passengers. The chassis and bed wore a mix of light green, dark green and tan paints, while the canvas canopy covering the rear showed a more detailed camouflage pattern. A thick black snorkel for underwater driving ran from underneath, up above the roof where the front window and driver's door met. The truck on the right was a bit slanted; both wheels facing the group were flat. Between the noses of the trucks was a table covered in equipment, including several desktop computers. Beside that stood an upright device that reminded Dylan of an x-ray machine at the airport. On either side of each truck were barricades to prevent cars from driving around. A large white sign topped a pole and said: DO NOT PROCEED BEYOND THIS POINT WITHOUT AUTHORIZATION.

"Should I press the horn?" Callan asked.

"No," Greg said. "Don't. It might piss them off."

Sherry pointed to the gap between the noses of the trucks. "Can you squeeze through there if we move that table?"

Greg said, "You don't want the Army coming after you for breaking their blockade."

Callan made a pinched face. "Doubt it. Not with the boat on, unless I smash it up."

"What about driving around the trucks?"

The left edge fell away to a steep embankment and sloped down to the river. Tall grass filled a rainwater gutter on the other, leading to another ridge and beyond, a small hillside.

"Looks a bit risky."

"What's on the table?" Sherry said. "And what's the funny thing standing up?"

"It measures body temperature," Dylan said. "A few years back, when the bird flu struck Asia, my dad and I went to China; they had a similar thing at the airports. As long as your body temp wasn't too high, they let you in."

"So they're here to check for the virus," Kristy said. "Fever must be a symptom."

Dylan felt his heart beating faster. "I don't like it. Two Army trucks parked in the middle of the road with nobody about. Surely they would have heard us?"

"Maybe they're in the back," Greg said. "Keeping out of the rain."

"We're gonna have to find out," Callan said.

"No," Kristy said, touching his shoulder. "Don't get out."

"We can't wait here all day. If they've left for some reason, we'll have to move a truck. Dylan, grab the axe out of the back, will you?"

Sherry asked, "The axe? What are you going to do, chop someone up?"

"We've only got a little ammo left. We don't know what's out there. Just a precaution."

Dylan unbuckled his belt and reached over the back seat. He had to move a couple of bags to find the bladed handle. They had all used it with regularity, getting a decent workout each day as they shared the task of splitting wood.

"Greg, you take it—"

"No," Dylan said. "I'll go." He cursed himself, but Greg had gone to Callan's aid with the old man. They had to share the load, even if it was a simple check. Callan already hated him. The only way to win credibility was to show some mettle.

Callan nodded. Greg took the pump action and passed it to Callan.

"I'm sure you won't have to use that thing," Kristy said, squeezing Dylan's arm. She narrowed her eyes. "Be careful." Suddenly he didn't want to help. He wanted Kristy to beg him to stay inside, but she said, "And you too, Cal. Just run if… you know."

Callan nodded and checked the gun's chamber, then opened the door. "Have the shotgun ready," he said to Greg. "Shoot first and ask questions later. Climb over the front, Kristy, and be prepared to punch it through that gap in the middle. We'll move the table."

"I thought you said we wouldn't fit?"

"In a choice between our lives and the boat, I don't give a fuck about the boat. But let's make sure before we smash it to smithereens."

They climbed out, shut the doors, and stood beside the car as the rain fell in thick drops, splattering off their faces. Dylan spat water from his lips. In the distance, thunder rumbled. He could barely swallow, so he tipped his head back and opened his mouth, but his eyes caught more water. He shook his head to clear them.

They each took an end of the light timber table and lifted it aside, then did the same for the upright device.

Callan said, "I'll go first. We go through the middle and take a quick look around the back, see if anybody's inside either truck, okay?" Dylan nodded. His tongue was stuck to the roof of his mouth. He tightened his grip on the long axe handle, holding it in position like it was a baseball bat.

The rain made softer tapping noises on the canvas bed covers. Behind them, the repetitive swipe of the wiper blades sounded. Dylan noticed an unfamiliar scent through the smell of rain and grass. It became stronger as they crept between the heavy vehicles.

"You smell that?" Callan asked quietly, scrunching up his nose.

"Yeah. What do you think it is?"

"Blood."

A cold tingle ran up Dylan's spine. He shifted the axe. "Shit. Are you sure?"

"I've skinned enough animals over the past month. I have a bad feeling about this. Just be ready to run."

Callan tipped his head toward the right lorry, then quick-stepped around and lifted the gun to his sight. Several flies buzzed near the doors. Dylan watched his impassive face, lips pressed tight.

The Remington wavered, and then Callan dropped it. "Padlocked."

Dylan felt a pounding pressure in his chest. *Jesus,* he thought*, can a heart really beat this hard?* He swallowed again and his throat cracked. *Toughen up*, he told himself. *You can always run.*

Callan nodded at Dylan, then tipped his head toward the second truck, where the doors were open. Dylan lifted the axe. He hated this shit. He wasn't the macho type looking for action. He had never even had a real fistfight. In grade nine, he had wrestled Stephen Goeby to a draw by administering a fluky headlock, and that was the extent of his fighting career. But he had no choice. If he ever wanted to win Callan's approval, this was the route. He counted in his head, *one, two, three,* then stepped around the tailgate.

An icy spear pierced his heart.

Flies buzzed about inside like a squadron of mini-fighter planes. Slaughtered soldiers lay over the floor among a spread of automatic machine guns and cases of exposed ammunition. Red streaks covered the walls and roof. Blood had run on the angle into a pool at the back of the truck, spilling over the edge and onto the bitumen. One man sat hunched over another, his head buried in his colleague's stomach. The rotted eye sockets of numerous victims stared at them.

Dylan opened his mouth to scream. He let the axe fall to the road with a clunk and glanced at Callan, whose face was slack, his mouth an "O". Callan raised his pump action but its long barrel smacked against the back of the truck.

The feeding soldier looked up.

Red, swollen eyes glared at them from a sweaty face. He wore a standard-issue uniform, green Army shirt and pants. A dark stain covered his neck and chest. He licked his bloody lips and a chunk of flesh fell from a mouthful of broken teeth. He snarled, made a low growling noise, and stuffed another lump of flesh between his jaws.

"Sh… sh… shoot it, man!" Dylan said.

The soldier stood, hunched over, and walked toward them.

Callan lifted the gun and fired. It thundered and Dylan flinched, feeling a sharp pain in his right ear. The soldier's entire left arm exploded. Blood and muck sprayed the wall. Callan loaded the chamber and the Remington roared again, but the shot missed, shattering the cabin window.

The soldier kept coming.

Dylan groped for the axe but all of his strength and awareness had fled. *Oh, shit.*

Callan leapt forward and grabbed the right side gate. "Shut it! Shut the fucking door!"

Dylan took the left side and swung it around, meeting Callan in the middle. They twisted the plate and jammed the lower bolts into the bed.

Both boys leapt away. The doors shook as the soldier screamed in rage, pounding on the gate with successive blows.

"Fuck, man," Callan said. "That was close." The truck rocked. "I haven't missed a shot like that in a long time."

"I can't believe I dropped the axe."

The lorry bounced as the soldier continued to flex the doors. He made a low growling sound, like an angry dog.

"He's an unhappy fucker. Did you see his arm explode? He just kept coming."

"He's sick," Dylan said. "Much worse than the old man."

"Jesus, I've never seen anything like it. You think it's the virus?"

Dylan felt his pulse racing. "What else? Rabies?"

"Did you see the guns and ammo? We need that."

Someone called out from the Jeep. Callan tilted his head in their direction.

Greg was hanging out of the passenger side with the Stevens shotgun leaning on the door.

"What? What's wrong?" Callan asked as they approached. He could hear the trapped soldier still banging on the gates.

Kristy leapt out the driver's seat. "What's *wrong*? The windscreen exploded and we heard yelling. And what's that banging?"

"We locked one of them in the back of the truck."

Sherry leaned forward in the back seat. "One of what?"

"It's much worse than we thought," Callan said.

"It's infected," Dylan said. "One of the soldiers. There must be fifteen dead guys in there."

"No bullshit," Callan said. "It's fucked up."

"Fifteen dead?" Sherry said. "Are you sure?"

Callan said, "One hundred percent, babe. It looks like a butcher's shop."

"How did they die?" Kristy asked, walking toward the truck.

"No," Dylan said, stepping in front of her. "Don't go there."

Callan glanced at Dylan. "I'd say the soldier killed them. He's… *it's* like a rabid dog."

"What?" Kristy asked. "What do you mean?"

Dylan took a deep breath and spoke in a low, controlled voice. "The soldier was feeding on one of the other soldiers."

A long pause followed his words.

Greg broke the silence. "Say again?"

"That's it."

"That's ridiculous," Kristy said, laughing.

"Do you think it was the virus that made him like that?" Sherry asked.

"Viruses can't turn people into cannibals," Kristy said.

"I don't know," Callan said, "but we both saw it."

"I need to have a look," Kristy said. "If you guys are bullshitting—"

"Kristy!" Callan yelled, grabbing her by the arm. She twisted free of him.

"Leave me alone. I want to see." Her eyes were glassy.

"No," Callan said, pulling her away from the lorry.

"GET OFF ME!" Kristy screamed. Tears fell to her cheeks.

Dylan moved toward them. "Don't fight."

Callan shook her. "LISTEN TO ME! The soldier might have this virus. It is eating people. This is not a fucking game; it's real, and you have to accept it." He pulled her to him and hugged her as she wept.

"This can't be happening," Kristy said. "It just can't be."

"It is, babe. I don't know how or why, but it is."

Dylan rubbed his temples. Things were falling apart. Kristy's reaction was understandable. Doctors helped people, and he knew Kristy had struggled to accept the realities of death. She had seen the dead couple at the gas station and saw the old man kill himself. Now her brother spoke about a truck full of cannibalized dead soldiers.

The lorry shook violently. Bulges appeared in the canvas covering, as though the soldier was trying to punch its way out.

"It knows we're here," Callan said. "We have to move the truck."

"Could it break through the canvas?" Greg said.

Dylan said, "I don't know. Maybe."

The rain grew heavier, slamming against the hood of the Jeep as thunder cracked in the distance, rumbling across the hills. Water dripped from their saturated hair onto their faces, and their clothes had darkened.

"Dylan, check the wheels on the other side. If they're flat, it won't roll out of the way and we'll have to barge through."

Greg stepped out of the front seat and swung the shotgun up into position, his blonde hair colored dark by the rain. "I've got you," he said, following Dylan.

He felt comfortable with Greg at his side. The man was reliable, honest. Around town, his word was a binding contract, and Dylan had never known him to break it. He had been around guns the longest and had killed the bulk of the game that fed them at the lake with impressive accuracy. Dylan considered Callan's plan as he went around the back of the lorry. He wondered whether they could remove the key items from the boat. It would save fuel and get them home faster, but they would have to leave half their supplies behind. Callan was right, they might need those.

They stopped at the rear of the truck. Both wheels were intact.

"How bad is it?" Greg said, glancing at the silent cover.

"I've never seen anything like it. They all look dead, except the one whose arm Callan blew off. It didn't even flinch."

"I got a feeling Albury's gonna be in a bad way."

"Me too."

"We gotta look after the girls, make sure nothing happens to them, okay?"

Dylan wondered if he specifically meant Kristy. "Sure." He hesitated, then asked, "You like her, don't you?"

Greg shrugged. "Kind of."

"Have you told her how you feel?"

Greg shook his head. "I know she likes you. I've... accepted that."

"I'm sorry, man."

"It's cool."

Dylan nodded and they emerged at the front of the truck. "We're good," he said to Callan. Kristy was in the driver's seat again. Dylan wished he were sitting beside her.

"There are weapons in with them," Dylan said to Greg. "Automatic machine guns and a load of ammo."

"We need it. We're down to our last few rounds."

A ripping noise sounded and Dylan jumped back from the lorry. A fist and forearm thrust through the side of the cover, the soldier's bloody fingers searching for a victim.

"We gotta move!" Greg yelled. He raised the shotgun and took aim. It was best suited for small, speedy game where the shot would disperse into pellets, but at five feet, it was a lethal weapon no matter the prey. He fired the gun with a noisy report. The soldier shrieked and fell back into the darkness. "Take that, fucker." Greg pumped the next shell into the chamber.

Callan stepped up onto the lorry and opened the driver's door. The lifeless body of another soldier fell to the bitumen with a dense thud. A gaping wound in his neck glared at them with crimson fury. Dylan felt his stomach rise into his throat.

"Jesus!" Callan screamed. He hurried into the cab and fiddled with the controls. The truck began to roll backward toward the embankment with painful sluggishness; Callan leapt from the doorway.

They converged on the Jeep, zebra-striped clean and dirty by the rain, and Greg resumed his place as the front passenger. Dylan opened the back door as Sherry shuffled to the far side, allowing Callan to get in first.

Kristy stepped out of the driver's seat.

"No, you drive," Callan said, slipping inside. "We don't have time."

"I can't, Cal. I'm shaking."

Behind them, the soldier screamed as he rushed the side of the lorry, exploding through the canvas in a shocking rip of thick fabric. He landed on the road

56

headfirst with a sickening thump, and blood spread across the bitumen.

"It's escaped!" Greg screamed, winding up his window. "Hurry!"

Kristy was halfway around the front of the Jeep, leaving Callan no choice. He pulled himself out, passing Kristy as he circled the hood, and slipped into the front seat.

The soldier climbed onto one knee and shook his head, spraying blood from the split in his skull. He sprang to his feet, then ran toward them like an angry gorilla, grunting and slobbering, his red eyes focused on Kristy. A second gunshot wound had blown a flap of his shoulder away, leaving a bloody crater.

Kristy clawed her way to the rear passenger door, yanked it wide open, then froze when she spied the monster in her peripheral vision.

In the background, the truck rolled down the embankment with a thunderous crash.

Kristy screamed and fell back against the door. The soldier grabbed for her throat.

She shrieked hysterically. "GET HIM OFF ME!"

Dylan wrapped an arm around Kristy's waist, but the monster's grip prevented him from pulling her into the Jeep. Panic swept over him. He couldn't get past her to help; if he pushed Kristy, she would fall further into its deadly grip.

Greg kicked the front passenger door open, knocking the soldier aside, and sprang from the car. He stepped away and swiveled, drawing the shotgun into position. "YOU WANT ANOTHER ONE?"

The soldier groped and pulled, inadvertently dragging Kristy into the firing line. Greg flipped the gun around, taking it by the barrel, and struck the wooden butt down onto the back of the soldier's head.

It staggered.

Dylan swept Kristy aside with his right hand and kicked out with both legs, pushing the monster away. It teetered backward, shaking its head and growling.

Greg took aim and fired. The shotgun roared and the top half of the soldier's head disintegrated in shocking ribbons of crimson. His limp body collapsed in a pool of blood and brain.

Screaming, Kristy swiped at her face and neck. Dylan leapt out of his seat. He drew her to his chest and she fell against him, sobbing and shrieking.

The acrid smell of gun smoke hung in the air. Dylan leaned away from her, his heart pounding. "Did it get you? Kristy? Did it get you?" Kristy shook her head, gasping, close to hyperventilation. "It's okay," Dylan said, pulling her close again. "It's okay."

Greg dropped the shotgun and bent over, fists on his knees. His face was red, his messy blonde hair disheveled. "I couldn't get a line of sight until Dylan kicked him away."

Callan put a hand on Greg's back and, in a soft voice, said, "Nice work, man. Quick thinking."

Kristy's breathing began to slow, and she pulled back. "I don't think it got me." Smears of blood and tears covered her cheeks.

"Are you sure?" Callan asked, inspecting her.

"Yes. I didn't feel it scratch."

"Take off your top."

"What?"

"We need to be sure."

Dylan and Greg turned away. Dylan felt his body stiffen. He felt sick at the idea that Kristy might be infected. *Could you kill her if she attacked you?* He shut the thought out, rubbing his eyes.

"Let me just check your neck and shoulders," Callan said. "Pass me the water bottle."

Kristy gasped as he tipped water over her upper body. "Sherry, have a look, see if you can find anything."

58

Dylan glanced at Greg, his brow furrowed. It was happening too quickly. What if Kristy had been infected? Would they lock her up? Shoot her?

"I thought I was going to die," Kristy said.

Sherry scrutinized, wiping Kristy's golden skin with a towel. "I can't find anything."

"Are you certain? Check properly," Callan said.

Dylan said, "Come on, man. She's clean."

"I want her to be okay more than anyone," Callan said. "But we have to be sure."

Sherry tipped the remaining water from the plastic bottle onto Kristy, who shuddered. She probed her skin, looking for tiny red lines. "She's good. I can't find anything," Sherry said.

Dylan let out a breath, not realizing he had been holding it. He covered his face with his hands and promised himself he wouldn't think about what might have been.

"Zombies," Sherry said, to nobody in particular. "It's like a bad horror movie."

"It *is*," Callan said. "I've seen so many movies with these things in them. We know everything about the bastards. How to kill them. What happens if…" He trailed off. "The idea that they're real though, it makes me feel like I'm going crazy."

Dylan knew what he meant. It was difficult to get past a fictional thing suddenly being real. If someone had told him of their existence without him seeing it, he would never have believed. "Yeah, well, we know they're real now."

"And we're out of ammo," Greg said, loading the shotgun back into the Jeep.

"Shit," Callan said. "I almost forgot. The back of that truck is full of weapons."

The three boys walked over to the embankment. The truck's nose stuck out of the creek like a partly submerged log. Through the broken windshield, they saw a pile of bodies floating on the water line. The smell of death floated up to them, and they each made faces of disgust.

"Fuck it," Callan said. "It'll all be wet now."

"What is that?" Greg said, pointing at the truck. "One of them is still alive."

An arm on one of the bodies moved, scratching at the wall as if trying to climb out.

"They were all dead when we looked in the back," Dylan said.

Callan said, "Let's move. He ain't going anywhere, and there's nothing more here for us."

4

The rain had stopped, leaving the road dark and slick. Although it was just after five o'clock, sooty skies made it appear later. They all tried their phones again but there was still no service, which could only mean that all the networks were down. An unpleasant smell wafted from behind the locked doors of the second truck; nobody suggested opening them. Callan checked the cab and found a magazine of shells for a 9mm handgun, but no weapon, and an inbuilt two-way radio he couldn't pry loose. Fresh black skid marks at the rear of the lorry indicated someone had fled the scene. They decided to do the same.

No one spoke. Kristy lay against Dylan's shoulder, her eyes closed. He had one arm around her, watching the paddocks roll by. Callan felt a spark of irritation but let it go. She deserved and needed comfort.

They had been lucky. Alternative scenarios made Callan uneasy; he had to think of other things to push them from his mind. Realizing what they were up against now, he knew they were in real shit. The Armed Forces, people paid to protect civilians from harm, were infected. Callan guessed the Army had been deployed to guard the roads into major country towns like Albury and Wodonga. What would happen if the Army couldn't stop this thing?

It was no longer just a virus. The infected appeared to turn into some kind of violent cannibals. He almost laughed at the idea. It was absurd, but he had seen it with his own eyes. They had beaten one, but what if there were five, or ten? A hundred? How would they possibly survive? As they edged closer to home, Callan wasn't sure they were prepared for what they might find. He still hoped their families were safe, but doubts crept in.

It had been almost four hours since they left the lake under cloudless blue skies and a steady, enjoyable heat. The gas station had been on the Tooma Road, and from there they kept a steady speed along the curves of the Murray River Road, crossing the Murray River at Wymah Ferry Road and taking Bowna Wymah Road all the way to the Hume Highway. Callan didn't want to enter Albury from the north. Instead, he opted for the east after taking Table Top Road, where he could use back streets to access his parents' house on the western side of town.

He felt a sick desperation to see them. His father was often traveling, and he might even be away now. He needed to make sure his mother was safe. He didn't think he would ever love another person the way he loved her. She had been a constant source of strength and inspiration, protecting them, raising them while his father worked long hours in the truck. He recalled the night a burglar had broken into their house when his father was away. Callan must have been eight years old.

Kristy and Callan had been allowed to stay up late, watching Star Wars on television. Their mother had armed them with ice cream cones, a bowl of popcorn and soft drinks, and went upstairs to finish chores. The man broke the lock on the laundry door and entered the family room where the kids sat watching TV.

"Who are you?" Callan had asked. The intruder had a balaclava pulled over his face and a shotgun pointed at them. Kristy creamed. Callan clamped a hand over her mouth.

The man growled at them. "Shut up, or I'll kill your mother."

Callan didn't move, afraid he might wet his pants, but he also felt a deep stirring of anger. What had they done to the man? Why had he chosen their house to burgle? Callan didn't know that their father had collected a large payment for a shipment he had just transported along the East Coast. The cash was sitting in a drawer upstairs. *Somebody knew.*

Their mother had appeared at the base of the stairs moments after Kristy's scream.

"Don't hurt my children," she said, stepping in front of them.

"Just gimme the fuckin' money."

She tipped her head up toward the second floor and said, "In the main bedroom. Bottom drawer on the left side of the bed."

"I'm takin' one of the kids with me," he said, putting a hand out toward Callan and Kristy.

"No."

He raised the gun as if to strike her, but she did not flinch.

"If you lay a finger on either of them, you will be sorry. I promise you that."

The gunman hesitated. He snarled at her, lowered the weapon, and stalked past, disappearing quickly up the stairs. His heavy footsteps thudded as he explored the second level.

"What do we do, Mom?" Callan had asked. He had an arm around Kristy, who had begun to cry.

"Nothing. We wait. Don't cry, darling. It will be over soon."

The man returned with a beefy plastic bag. "Don't even think about callin' the cops. Or I'll come back another time and take one of the kids."

Debra Davidson looked at the burglar for a long moment. "Get out of my house." He laughed and exited through the laundry room.

The memory still made Callan's blood boil; he felt an immense love for his mother for protecting them the way she had. A weaker person might have let the man take Kristy or him, and who knew how that might have turned out? She set a wonderful example and made him want to be a better person. He would die protecting her.

"The plan is still to go home, make sure Mom and Dad are safe. Then we can check everyone else's property."

"Are you still backing that horse?" Dylan asked. "It's a silly idea. My house is closest and it has everything we need."

"We're not going to your house. I still think it's just as safe to go to mine."

"But it's not. It's crazy. We have guns. My dad will be on top of this thing. He might be able to tell us more—"

"Than my dad? Why? Things have changed, Dylan. For all we know, there's no one left in Albury."

"Please, Cal," Kristy said.

Dylan said, "We'll be safe at my house. It's up on the hill, and we have electrified fences."

"No electricity."

"We have a good store of guns and ammunition."

"We all do."

"We've got no ammo left, though. What you propose is that we put ourselves at greater risk by going to your house. What if we come across more of those infected soldiers? We can't hack them all to death."

"It's not longer." Callan couldn't argue with the second part, however. All they had left to use in a fight were the axe, a tomahawk, and a chainsaw. None of those provided him with any confidence. They were all weapons that required close fighting, and he wanted to avoid getting close to one of *them*. A firearm allowed them to strike from a distance. They needed shells *and* more guns.

How could he tell Dylan that his mother was more important, that after the burglary he had promised he would always protect her and never let harm come her way, the same as she had done for him and Kristy? "I don't care. I'm not changing my mind."

Sherry said, "We all want to go home, Callan. But maybe going all the way to your parents' house isn't the best idea."

"I can't and I won't. Don't you get it? I don't think it's safer going to Dylan's house, and I need to know Mom's okay. Once I do that, we can go wherever you guys want."

The first abandoned cars appeared on the side of lower Table Top Road. *Leaving town*, he thought. Callan peered ahead into the first vehicle, a navy blue Ford, and saw the dark shapes of several bodies. He sped up and watched the road ahead. The tightness of fear rose higher in his chest. He closed his window as a rotten smell drifted in on the wind.

They turned right at the Riverina Highway and crept past Munga Bareena Island and Reserve. The grey sheet of sky smothered the last of the day's glow; the Jeep's headlight sensor thrust rays of yellow ahead onto the rough bitumen. Callan took a right at the next street and then slowed the vehicle to a crawl as they approached the first in another line of cars.

"Jesus," he whispered.

Shattered glass lay across the blacktop like confetti after a parade. Both the roadside and rear windows had gaping holes; hanging out of the driver's window, with broken glass cutting into its torso, was a headless body.

Callan rolled alongside and saw blood pooled on the road.

"Don't stop," Sherry said. "We've had enough delays."

Callan braked, briefly wondering what had happened to the owner's head, then accelerated, the tires crunching and popping on the glass. Most of the cars had been pushed off the road, and he wondered if the Army or somebody else had come through to clear them.

They drove several miles, crossing the Hume Highway past a dozen more forsaken vehicles, a bus with shadowy windows, and a dark mall. A sooty plume of smoke rose like a leaning skyscraper into the blackening sky. The odd vehicle sat in the parking lot. The five travelers could see a hint of orange light through the towering windows at the entrance to the mall.

"I'd hate to think what's inside," Callan said. A thought formed, of them hacking their way through a supermarket in search of food. The idea left him cold.

"It's so quiet," Sherry said. "Where has everybody gone?"

An explosion sounded from the mall, flames spilling through a side window. Several blackened forms fell out through the flames, still alight.

Callan turned away. "Dead. Or walking around as zombies."

They made a right turn, then another onto an unpaved road, and saw a long stretch that eventually curved around to the left, flanked by lifeless streetlights. They moved slowly as gravel crunched underneath the tires, watching the headlamps vanish into the murky depths beyond. There were no cars parked at the curb, although a few sat in driveways.

Shadows beckoned from the houses. Such a street should have been ablaze with light, but there were no porch lamps greeting visitors, no cracks of light from between lounge room curtains, no flashes of television screens. Back at the lake, they had welcomed the absence of electric light, marveling at the speckled blanket that sparkled down on them each night. Now, Callan wished for the orange and yellow glow of the town.

"What's that?" Greg asked, sitting forward.

"What?"

"There. A light. I saw a light."

Following Greg's finger, Callan squinted into the darkness on the left side of the street. "Shit, man, you've got good eyes."

"I see it," Kristy said. "Up there."

Callan peered low through the windscreen, straining to see ahead, when he felt the vehicle slow and the trailer pull to one side. "*Fuck.*" He knew instantly what had happened.

He stopped the car and jerked the stick into park, then ripped the handbrake on. "We could have a problem." He shut the lights off and climbed out, slamming the door with a thud, then turned in a circle, surveying the road in all directions. The smell hit him as if he'd opened a

AFTERMATH: INVASION OF THE DEAD

rubbish bin, and he knew that there were more than four or five dead people in the town.

Greg arrived at his side, his face twisted in similar disgust. "That smell is fucked up. What's happened?"

"Flat tire, I think."

Callan removed the thick-handled flashlight from the back of the Jeep, then hurried to each wheel on the trailer and kicked, feeling for air pressure. His boot rebounded off the first three with a jarring thud.

When the fourth softened, he squatted, cupped his palm around the top of the flashlight, then switched it on. As he had feared, the steel rim touched the ground on a bed of flattened rubber; the trailer slanted toward him. "Shit." He saw glass fragments stuck in the tread and a larger jagged piece embedded deep into a rut.

Greg said, "We gotta change it, unless you wanna leave all the stuff behind."

"No." The fuel and extra food might be critical at some point, and Callan would fight for it. But if they were going to do this, they needed to be ready for a quick getaway if they were under threat. "Let's think about this. What are our options?"

Greg considered the question. "Unhook the boat. Have Kristy sitting behind the wheel with the car running."

"That's good. Very good. But still risky." He peered over the boat. "Where did you see that light?"

Greg pointed into the darkness about twenty-five yards away. "There."

Callan focused. After a moment, he saw a faint shade of yellow against the back of a white weatherboard house. "Okay, let's try that. We ask if the girls can wait inside while we change the tire. They might even be able to tell us more about this mess."

"That's if they even open the door."

Squatting in the driver's side doorway, Callan explained the plan to the others and made Kristy sit behind the steering wheel with the engine idling. Dylan took the axe and stood ready.

The rain had passed, and a warm breeze touched Callan's cheek. What were they doing? The madness of it all threatened to derail his plan, but he pushed it away, focusing on what needed to be done. He hoped there would be time later to reflect on all that had happened, and on what lay ahead. *That* worried him the most.

Greg led them through untended grass toward the house. They crept without the flashlight until they reached the front yard, and then Callan activated the beam. Tall weeds grew in clumps around several dead and dying shrubs. Wooden edging outlined what once may have been a beautiful garden, now overgrown with green wildflowers.

They followed a series of cracked, unstable paving stones onto a wooden porch, where loose boards creaked and twisted under their weight. A heavy wire security door was firmly latched in front of a solid wooden slab.

"Let's be quick. I don't want to leave them too long," Callan said. Greg rapped on the door with the side of his fist. They waited, listening for movement.

"Please. We have a couple of girls with us and mean no harm. Our trailer has a flat tire. Can the girls stay with you while we change it? It'll only take five minutes."

"Fuck off," a muted voice said. "There's nothin' here for you 'cept lead poisoning."

"Please," Greg said. "Just give us a minute."

"Get your ass off my porch right now."

"You won't help us?"

"No."

"You don't care if a couple of girls die right outside of your house?"

"No."

"You don't have to open the door."

"Piss off. I've had your kind before and it ended badly—for them."

"Look, mate," Callan said, "we've been camping up at Lake Eucumbene for the last month. When we originally left town, this… virus was barely making news. Earlier today, we stopped at a gas station out bush and saw a newspaper, but it was three weeks old. Then…" Callan trailed off, considering how to describe it. "We've gone through a lot of shit to get here, and if you're locked up inside, you've seen it too."

Behind them, bats chirped, gliding through the air.

"We just want my sister and my girlfriend to be safe while we change the flat on the boat trailer. My name is Callan Davidson. My sister Kristy is with us. My dad is Keith Davidson. He works at the abattoir. My friend here is Greg Harding. We have Sherry Vandenberg and Dylan Cameron, Bob Cameron's son."

There was a pause. "Bob Cameron's kid. Where's Bob? Is he okay?"

"We don't know, but we're trying to find him. Please, just tell us what the fuck is going on."

A lock clicked and the chain slid back. The inner door opened and a tiny light from a cell phone illuminated a disheveled face and sagging red eyes. Thick black stubble flecked with grey covered his cheeks and neck. He groomed his moustache with thumb and forefinger, eyeing Greg and Callan with suspicion. "I have a Remington 308 bolt action here that'll turn you into mince if you give me any trouble. And I ain't opening that door, girls or not. I've got my own females to protect."

"No trouble," Callan said, holding his palms up.

"You shouldn't have that flashlight on," the man said in a raspy smoker's voice. "They'll see it. They're attracted to light."

Greg switched it off and asked, "Who?"

"*Don't be dense.* The fucking zombies. The dead. Or *undead.* Whatever you wanna call 'em."

Callan felt his skin chill. "They were infected with the virus, weren't they? It turns them into that."

The man licked his lips. "Some of them just die. It's bad. They're everywhere. You're crazy standing out there after dark."

Callan swallowed, but his dry throat caught and he had to cough to clear it. "Is there … anyone alive? Hiding? Like you?"

The man shrugged. "Maybe. Most of 'em are dead, though. Dead or turned into zombies."

"All of them?" Greg blurted out. "Not everyone can be dead?"

The man wiped his nose again. "Son, on the last news report ten days ago, they estimated 75 percent of the country had the virus. Nearly everything had shut down. Banks, supermarkets, hospitals. People were dyin' like the plague. Hell, it *is* the plague! Once you've got that virus, you're either dead... or you come back." He hung his head, and then looked up at them. "If you survive until tomorrow, be prepared for what's happened to this town. It ain't a sight you've ever dreamed of seeing."

A long, high-pitched scream sounded from a street or two away.

Callan jerked around. "What was that?"

"Leave," the man said. "Leave town and go back to where you came from. I'm sorry, but I can't help you." The door crashed shut. The lock clicked, and the chain slid into place.

"Shit," Callan said. "We should have just changed the fucking tire. We'd be done by now."

"Let's do this. Fast. No flashlight."

They ran in short strides down the steps and onto the broken pathway under a crack of moonlight. Callan aimed for the crooked pavers, leaping from one to the other as they sped across the dead lawn. Twice he missed and felt the pointed edge of the stones. Reaching the curb, he spied the dark shape of the Jeep along the road.

"Shit!" Greg yelled from behind. "Shit! Shit! *Shit!*"

70

Callan halted and his friend hopped into him. "What is it?"

"My ankle. I rolled it on the edge of the fucking pavers." He stopped, holding his right foot off the ground. He tried to take another step. "Oh, *fuck* that hurts."

"Grab on," Callan said, leaning into Greg's shoulder. He braced his legs as Greg leaned on him.

In the distance beyond the Jeep, a terrible moaning noise sounded. Callan froze. Greg stood, foot raised. "What the fuck is that?" he asked, his voice a pained whisper.

Callan shook his head. "I don't wanna know. Let's move. Slowly, no noise. The Jeep's just over there." He wished they had brought the axe or tomahawk.

They made short, difficult steps along the gravel. Another groan sounded, followed by an angry grunt and several cries. Callan took Greg to the passenger side, where the injured man fell against the door. They both knew that, the moment they opened it, the internal light would alert anything in the vicinity to their location, and they still had to change the tire.

He tapped on the window, pressing his knee against the door so Kristy couldn't open it.

The window slid down.

"Where have you been?" Kristy said.

"Shh. Trying to keep you safe. Greg hurt his ankle. Flick the switch on the roof so the lights won't come on when we open the door." Two clicking noises sounded. "Dylan, I need your help to change the tire."

"Fuck the boat," Sherry said. "Is it really that important?"

"Yes, babe. It has all our fuel and most of the food. We might need it."

Dylan said, "Couldn't we get more from town?"

Callan shook his head. "I don't wanna take the chance; there might be nothing left."

"What about your life?" Sherry said.

"It won't come to that."

Greg fell into the front seat and Callan closed the door with gentle pressure. He nodded at Dylan. "Let's do this. You hold the flashlight. And bring that axe." He whispered to Kristy, "Keep the engine running, no lights, and be ready to punch it."

They unhooked the trailer, prepared for a quick getaway, then unloaded the gear in the back of the Jeep and removed the tire iron and jack.

Crouching beside the flat, Callan said, "Okay, now turn on the light, but keep the beam low to the ground." Dylan complied. "Good. That's perfect."

Something grunted, perhaps fifty yards away, and made a high-pitched shriek.

They froze and looked at each other. Dylan glanced at the axe that lay beside him. Callan took a deep breath and then proceeded to place the jack under the trailer chassis.

He pumped the handle and the trailer slowly lifted. He had changed a good number of tires in his time and now unscrewed the wheel nuts with practiced speed.

"What's the story with you and my sister?"

Dylan snorted. "Nice timing. You'll feed me to the zombies if I give the wrong answer?"

"Maybe."

"No story yet."

Callan grunted as he lifted the wheel off the axle and dropped it on the road with a thump.

"You like her?"

Dylan seemed to consider this. "You wanna talk about this *now*?"

"Yeah. I do."

"I like her."

A cry pierced the night, like a person in trouble, followed by growling, and then—sudden silence.

Dylan passed the flashlight to his left hand and picked up the axe. Callan moved faster, unbuttoning the spare wheel from the chassis under the shaking light and lifting it off. He slipped it straight onto the axle and the trailer shook. With trembling fingertips, he tightened the nuts.

"You know Greg likes her, too."

"Yeah. We spoke earlier."

Callan picked up the wheel spanner and began to tighten the locks. "I don't think it's the best time to be starting a relationship."

"I don't even know if she—"

"She does. As much as it pisses me off, I've seen it, and she likes you."

"Why—" This time, the noise sounded more like the growing murmurs of a protesting crowd. "That *does not* sound good," Dylan said. "It sounds like there's a group of them."

"Shit," Callan said, tightening the third nut. A chilly shiver touched his spine. He felt exposed, expecting at any moment to feel the cold grip of the undead. In the otherwise silent night, they heard the unmistakable sound of movement: feet crunching along the road.

Dylan stood, keeping the light focused on the wheel. "Can we do this any faster?"

Callan rattled the spanner onto the final nut. "I'm going as fast as I can."

"Please do. I don't know what's gonna happen with Kristy. I don't know why her liking me pisses you off so much, and I'm sorry about Greg. I didn't know he liked her until today."

Callan inserted the square end of the tool into the jack and twirled the lever. The trailer started to drop. "Let me just say, if you hurt her, you'll have two angry fuckers to deal with."

The trailer settled back into place. Callan snatched the jack out from underneath. "Let's move." He opened the Jeep's rear window and tossed the jack and spanner into a pile of bags. "Leave the flat. We'll get another one."

"You smell that?" Dylan said, twisting his nose in disgust.

"I'm trying not to."

As Dylan guided the flashlight, Callan lifted the trailer head onto the tow ball. It resisted, but he pushed harder and it clunked into place. He slipped the chain over the hook and plugged in the electrical adaptor.

Kristy knocked on the window, signaling that she was now in the backseat.

Callan yanked the driver's door open and then jumped into the chair, clipping his head on the doorway. Pain exploded in his skull. *No time for that.* He took the headlight switch between shaky fingers, his heartbeat racing, and turned it.

Shock rendered him immobile.

"Get going, man," Greg said.

Sherry gasped. "Oh my God."

He had imagined what a group of them might look like, young ones and old, but his creative side had always been limited; he could never have imagined the terror that stood before them. *We're gonna die. We're all gonna die.* "Pull your fucking head in," he said under his breath.

In the twin cones of light, dozens of dead people stretched along the street, wandering in random patterns from around the corner. Men and women, old and young, their faces bloated and bloody, their eyes listless, their pale, flat aspects shining in the golden light. Their dirty, tattered clothes hung from their bodies; some were shoeless, others wore one or both. They squatted in the gutters, chewing on the deceased, blood dripping from their chins and hands. Several fights took place, the combatants punching and biting until only one remained standing; a horde converged on the fallen. Their movement was unhurried, patient, as though they had a lifetime to feast at the buffet, and the crowd was edging toward the Jeep.

"He was right," Callan said. "I thought he was full of shit."

Greg said, "They're all dead. All fucking dead."

"Is that Mrs. Baker?" Sherry asked, sobbing.

Callan squinted. "I think so. And that might be Frank Carter getting attacked by the tree."

"You have to drive through them," Greg said in a slow, disbelieving voice.

The lead zombie was twenty yards away and closing with a slow gait. Others were following, drawn to the headlights, while more stood on either side, lost in their own madness.

"I know," Callan said.

He reached out and moved the stick into gear but still couldn't accelerate. A month ago, he might have spoken to some of these people in the street. Now they were dead. Not just *dead*, but…. He had a premonition that this was only the beginning, that what they witnessed tonight, or tomorrow, or the next day (if they survived that long) would make *this* seem mild. *What if Mom and Dad are like this?* Would he be able to kill them? He closed his eyes, thinking about the camping trip, wishing they were there now.

"Callan?" Kristy was wiping away tears. "Please go. I don't want to stay here any longer."

He opened his eyes. "Okay."

Something banged against the driver's window. Callan jumped.

"Shit!" Sherry screamed. "What is *that*?"

One of them, Callan thought, staring at it, although not the vague, indifferent kind that stood in the headlights. Bright, blazing eyes glared in at them, its cheeks puffing in anger, as though *they* had done this. It still had a full set of bloody teeth, and when it opened its mouth and snapped its jaws shut, the sound carried through the window. Saliva trickled from its lips, and only a few long strands of hair remained on a grey, parched scalp. Bleeding hands climbed the glass, leaving smears; the thing pried its fingers between the window and doorjamb.

"GO, CALLAN!" Sherry shrieked.

The thing slammed its fists against the glass, and Callan punched the accelerator to the floor, screaming like a kamikaze pilot. The engine revved and the car bolted forward.

The undead turned toward the vehicle, their infected bodies slow and bungling. *We won't make this*, Callan thought. *This might be the end*. He urged the car on with gritted teeth, swerving to strike the creatures as if he were playing a video game. The others with their hungry faces fell like daisies under a lawn mower, thudding against the fender and disappearing underneath the car. It bumped and bounced; Greg's head hit the roof amidst the girls' screams. The Jeep smashed into a creature with a solid thump, splitting its body in half. The upper part spun across the hood and rolled up the glass, leaving a trail of red gore.

As the last one within range fell, they reached the bend and Callan jammed on the brakes, throwing them into a slide. The boat pulled hard to the right and he thought they were going to end up around a tree. He gunned the engine and the car swept side to side, then straightened. He felt like he was going to puke.

"Whoooaaaa," he said as the last one disappeared in the rearview mirror. "That was close." He cackled, fighting back the hysteria. "Greg, buddy, did you see that?"

Greg sat rigid, his fingers pressed against the door. "Good driving, man."

In the rearview mirror, Kristy clutched Dylan's hand in a double grip. Callan looked away. Sherry had a trembling fist over her mouth, her eyes large and skittish.

"You okay, baby?" He wished he could comfort her.

She gave him a cold, hard look and slumped back against the seat. "No, Callan. No, I'm fucking not."

"Jesus Christ, people, we just made it out of hell!" He had thought they were trapped, that the zombies were going to line up and block the way, then mob the car and turn it over and pull them all out, clawing them to death.

His heart was still hammering. *Get a grip.* Dylan and Sherry were wild-eyed, and he probably was too, but he felt relieved that they were still alive. The number of zombies wandering along the road was staggering. Why were there so many? What had happened to cause it? Had everyone turned into a zombie? They knew so little about everything.

His relief faded as he thought about the next choice. Which direction? He had skirted the city center, hoping to avoid trouble, but if the zombies were everywhere, what did it matter? He decided to push through the main street and take the most direct route home. They were still fifteen minutes away.

"Little change of plan," Callan said. Dylan sat forward, hopeful. "We're driving straight through the center of town."

"We're stopping at my parents' house?" Dylan asked.

"No," Callan said. "We've been through this. I'm going home."

Sherry said, "That's just crazy. We need to stop. I need to get out of this fucking car, Callan. You brought me on this stupid trip, so you'd better take me somewhere safe."

"I will, babe, I will. But I need to know if Mom's okay."

5

Callan's stupidity infuriated Dylan. He had to think of something else to stop himself from inciting another argument. Callan's house was too far. They would have to drive through another five mobs like the previous one, and next time they might not be so lucky.

The situation was worse than they had imagined. Survival rates would be low. The idea that he would never see his mom or dad again left him with an overwhelming feeling of panic. He felt like throwing up and briefly considered fleeing the convoy and trudging home to find out if they were dead or alive. He understood Callan's desire to investigate his house first, but it put the group at greater risk. They had to stick together though. Alone, they wouldn't last five minutes.

The car burned down East Street, turned the corner and hurried along Main. Dark shops crowded the road on both sides, and they could see straggling zombies at the fringe of the headlights. More cars sat parked at the curb, their windows shattered.

They chased the bend around Jameson's Park, where shadows promised fresh horrors. Dylan grabbed the front passenger seat as Callan brought the car to a sudden halt, the tires chirping in protest.

Ahead, milling at the intersection of Lauren and Jackson Streets and far beyond, were thousands of them. A cold fog crept over him. If their previous encounter had seemed dangerous, this would surely mean death. The bulk of them wandered about the road, turning in small circles, bumping into each other. The odd one stood gnawing on the neck or limb of an ignorant victim. It was one enormous zombie party. Bodies lay on the street in lifeless layers, some dead, others moaning. Even in the sparse illumination of the headlights, they could see the blood splashed across their faces and clothes. Several shops were ablaze and glass lay shattered over the bitumen. He felt sure that one of their parents had to be in the group. The odds of all surviving seemed infinitesimal.

The Jeep sat a hundred yards away and, so far, the horde hadn't noticed the headlights. Dylan was certain they wouldn't get through to Callan's house in this direction. Back to the Riverina Highway was the only option, if Callan insisted on his original plan. Dylan's home was a five-minute drive away. His parents lived in a double-story house on a hill, and an electrified, barbed wire fence surrounded the property. It might not stop a thousand hungry corpses, but it would prevent individuals from strolling in.

Pointing this out to Callan would only cause trouble, though. He needed to figure things out for himself, to see the wisdom in Dylan's request. Dylan thought he might be close.

"I don't like our chances of making it through that," Callan said.

"There's too many of them," Greg said, shuddering.

Callan smashed a fist against the steering wheel. "Fucking FUCK!" He lay back against the seat. "I can't win. If I drive on, we'll die. If I don't go home…." He glanced at them. "What if we go home and they're in trouble and because we went *there*, we saved them?"

Kristy opened her mouth to speak, but Dylan put a finger to her lips and shook his head. He knew Kristy and the others agreed with his plan, but her brother was close to the same deduction.

In a softer voice, Callan said, "I've tried to make the right choices today. All the decisions have been about safety. Going home was supposed to be the least risky move. I really thought that."

Dylan wanted to tell him it had always been risky.

"But that…" Callan glared at the mass of zombies. "That's madness. This entire *fucking thing* is madness. That last one that pounded on the window, who tried to get in… there was something different about him. He was scary. If they had all been like that, we'd be dead."

"What are you thinking?" Greg asked.

"How far is your house, Dylan?"

Dylan sat rigid, controlling his hopefulness. "You go right at the next turn, along Gillam and onto Starling, then all the way out to Silvan Road. Ten minutes, tops."

Callan considered this. "Let me be clear. As soon as it is safe, I'm going to my parents' house to check on them. Alone, if I have to."

"I'll come with you," Greg said. "Soon as we get some more ammo."

"All right. I ain't driving through *that*."

Several zombies looked up toward them and began a slow trudge in their direction.

"They've seen us," Sherry said.

A commotion occurred about fifty yards ahead, below a sign that read: SIRELLI'S PIZZA. They had all eaten pizza from Joe Sirelli's shop. Orange flames appeared at street level, reaching out through the front windows, and smoke rose in a grubby trail. One of the zombies moved unusually fast, bouncing from one foot to the other.

"Is that a person?" Dylan said.

"Yeah," Callan said. "I don't think—"

"Two of them," Kristy said, as another chased.

They had burst from the flaming pizza shop in a desperate escape, running toward the Jeep.

"They've seen us," Kristy said. "They need help. Drive closer, Cal."

Zombies lurched at the desperate couple, blocking their way with gangling limbs. They had made it about fifteen yards. Callan rolled the vehicle forward.

"Don't be stupid," Sherry said. "Where are they going to fit?"

The man led, waving his arm, shoving the undead aside with desperation, and calling out in a muffled voice.

"They can sit in the boat," Greg said. "If we pull the cover back they'll be able to hold on until we get to safety."

"Go closer, Cal. We have to help them. I think it's Serena and Joe. They must have been in the pizza shop for weeks," Kristy said.

"It's them." Callan let the brake off a little more, edging the car forward.

Serena fell first. One of the zombies feeding on the road turned toward the commotion and tripped her. She went sprawling onto the bitumen in a heap. Others aborted their ignorant wanderings and fell onto her. A shrill, piercing scream chilled Dylan's skin.

"No," Kristy said. "We have to do something." She unclipped her belt and flung off her three-hundred-dollar pair of Dolce and Gabbana sunglasses.

Dylan grabbed the buckle. "We can't."

"He's right," Callan said. "We'll die."

Kristy seemed poised to argue, but said, "Please, Greg?"

Greg watched, unmoving.

Joe Sirelli had gone back for his wife, throwing his heavy build at the monsters like a football blocker to keep them away. They milled around her, fighting to get at the fresh meat. He swung wild roundhouse punches, and the rotting zombie heads snapped rearward. Others groped for him, and when his fists would not work, he kicked at them and they fell into each other, collapsing in an awkward tangle. Finally, he reached his wife, but a pack of undead fed on her, and as Joe desperately clawed at them, others converged on him in overwhelming numbers.

Kristy sobbed. Sherry looked away.

"*Fucking bastards*," Callan said. Joe disappeared from view as the zombies fed.

"There," Greg said, pointing at the throng.

"What?" Callan said. "Is that a…"

At the edge of the massacre, a dog appeared, barking and growling.

"It's a Heeler," Greg said. Blue Heelers were famous for droving cattle. They nipped at the heels of the cows, driving them in the required direction for herding. Stocky and tough, they generally had black pointed ears and a predominantly bluish-white coat.

"Get 'em boy, get 'em," Callan said. "Tear some fucking heads off."

Several zombies lurched at the dog, but he was quick, zipping between their legs in figure eight patterns.

"Don't get caught, doggie," Kristy said.

One undead staggered after it, clawing repeatedly at fresh air, unwilling to quit. It shoved aside the others, biting into the neck of one in another failed attempt. The dog scuttled to the edge of the mayhem, turned, and barked. *You can't catch me,* it said.

"Go buddy, go," Dylan said, pumping a fist.

The zombie screamed. The dog turned and ran off into the night.

"That's one of the crazy ones," Callan said. "They're different."

The Jeep gave a violent shake, and Greg reached up for the handle above the passenger door.

"Shit," Dylan said. Several zombies banged on the back window of the Jeep. "Just drive. We can't help the Sirellis."

He turned to see if there was another of the crazy ones, but their blank, impassive expressions confirmed they were the normal type. *Fuck, I'm classifying them now,* Callan thought. He flicked the switch down to parking lights, accelerated the twenty yards, and turned right onto Gillam Street. Stragglers from the mob were still thirty yards away.

"They're gone," Dylan said.

A soft orange glow spilled onto the road in front of them, offering poor visibility, but it would ensure their stealth through the streets.

In the darkness, Kristy took Dylan's hand again. Her skin was soft and warm, and he closed his eyes, knowing that his feelings for her had grown beyond a curious liking. Perhaps it was the situation embellishing the sensation—he didn't know—but the feeling existed in his belly, sweet and enjoyable, fighting against the constant nervousness and fear.

She sniffed, fighting tears, and Dylan put an arm around her shoulders, pulling her close. What could he say? There were no words. They all knew the Sirelli family. The emotional impact was greater than it had been with the old man or the soldier. If they had been living in the beginning of a bad dream before, now they were in a full-fledged nightmare.

It took a little more than ten minutes to reach Silvan Road. Dirt greeted them and the car slowed. They had left the city borough. Thick brush lined the roads, and cows and horses roamed extensive paddocks.

Callan twisted the indicator to full headlights.

Dylan asked, "Should we do that? They might see us."

"You know what it's like out here. The roads are narrow and there are potholes everywhere. We might end up off the side."

The road narrowed to one lane in the places where feeder creeks cut their way through snarling trees and lush vegetation to join the mighty Murray River further out of town. Dylan's parents had talked about forming a paying coalition to have the road paved, but it hadn't happened, and probably never would now, he realized.

They reached Dylan's property where a wide and heavy steel gate loomed, odd against a backdrop of paddocks and trees. Years ago, an unhappy employee broke in through the garage and confronted Dylan's mother, so his father had hired a security company to outfit the estate. Wire fences ran along the boundary, the upper section barbed. Under normal circumstances, they would be electrified, but

Dylan suspected the electricity was out. They might be able to get the generator running, though.

Callan turned the Jeep into the small section of space in front of the gate and let the car idle. The lights painted the entrance and the stony driveway beyond. The house sat huge and shadowed in the distance. Three enormous gumtrees towered over the dwelling in different locations, as if protecting it. Dylan had expected darkness. If his parents were inside, they wouldn't be advertising it.

"You don't have a remote for the gate, do you?" Callan said.

Dylan chortled. A coil of nerves tightened around him. "I wish." Kristy squeezed his hand. "There's a lever that changes the gate from automatic to manual. Won't take a moment." He unlocked his seatbelt.

"Take the axe," Callan said. "You never know."

Darkness beyond the murky yellow headlights appeared peaceful, innocuous. It might have been any other night, coming home from a friend's house or the movies. *Tell yourself that.* He had no choice. He had argued for the refuge of his parents' house and now he almost had it.

"Good idea."

He took the axe from the storage area in the back. It was a familiar tool. He had spent countless hours splitting timber for his parents' wood fire. Out camping, they had shared a roster for the essential jobs: firewood, clean water, dishes, and washing. He had grown to know the axe like a friend and it felt comfortable, but he prayed he would not have to use it.

"Be careful," Kristy said, placing her hand on his arm. "I couldn't deal with it if…"

He thought about kissing her for good luck. A peck on the cheek, or maybe the lips. What if he never got the chance? What if he was killed or maimed so badly he couldn't function? *You'd be a zombie then and wouldn't remember anything.* He knew Callan would be pissed though, and Greg would be heartbroken. "Thanks."

"You want a co-pilot?" Greg asked from the front seat.

Yes, he thought. *That would be fucking great.* Greg *was* a good guy. If Dylan had learned one thing on this trip, it was that. It sucked that he liked Kristy too. He wouldn't risk anyone else, though. "Thanks man, but I'll take this one."

Sherry said, "Hurry. I hate being out here exposed."

Stepping outside, he closed the door. The day's heat remained, covering the land like a warm blanket. The ground was dry, as though it hadn't even rained in Albury. He inhaled through his mouth, bunching his nose in disgust at the rotten scent. *Death.* It was close.

Dylan hurried to the fixed section of the gate where the sliding part closed. The lever sat on the other side, and he needed to lean through the bars and pull it to release the connection. He turned in a circle, widening his eyes and attuning his ears to the night.

The town was dark, except for the odd lick of orange flame. He heard them, far off, goring and grunting, feeding, killing. *We can't stay here.* It wouldn't be long before they overtook the town, if they hadn't already. They would find them up here on the hill, eventually.

He leaned the axe against the fence and squatted, reaching through the railings. His fingers groped, finding weeds and the bulky motor casing. He felt around but couldn't locate the lever. *Damn.* He didn't want to have to climb over. It was too high for him to scale without a boost from one of the others.

Straining with effort, he reached between the bars and touched a thin, flat metal rod. He clasped his fingers around it and pulled, feeling the mechanism dislodge. He took the axe and walked to the heavy gate, then leaned into it, pushing with his thighs.

The gate moved a couple of inches and stopped.

Once it gathered momentum it would roll all the way to the other side, but he didn't have the strength in one arm. He would have to put the axe down.

His heart skipped. He looked around once more just to be sure they weren't waiting for him inside the property. He laid the axe on the ground and stood at the end of the gate, then pushed, getting his shoulders and legs behind it.

The gate slid open, picking up momentum. He gave it a final shove and it coasted to the other side, leaving space for the Jeep and trailer to enter. He heard the muted sounds of clapping from inside the car and gave a thin smile.

Picking up the axe, he stepped aside and waved them through.

The Jeep spun its wheels on the gravel, found traction, and then rolled past, rising slightly as it crossed raised ground under which a concrete pipe ferried rainwater from the roadside gutter. The brake lights of the boat glowed as he stepped into the gateway, preparing to pull the barrier shut.

The boat cover was partially off. Dylan halted.

The shadows moved and two zombies sat up in the bottom of the boat, sniffing the air with vigor. Chunks of animal flesh hung from their mouths.

The rabbits.

They were eating the meat Callan had stored in the boat fridge. The smell must have lured them. The zombies dismissed their curiosity and returned to the feast. With their heads down, it was impossible to see them in the dark.

Dylan's guts shriveled and he fought the urge to run. He had known such a fight was coming, eventually. Did he call the others? No, it would alert the zombies. He had the advantage of surprise and might be able to kill one easily.

Holding his breath, he stepped toward the boat. *Could he really do this?* What if it was someone he knew—one of his parents, or a neighbor? They were no longer who they had been in their previous life, he reminded himself, and they would kill *him* without hesitation. If the town was as infested as they suspected, killing these things would become normal. And if he didn't kill them, there wouldn't be any kiss with Kristy, only death.

He tightened his grip around the axe handle and raised it.

The first zombie looked up. Dylan swung sideways as if cutting into a tree. The blade dug into the soft flesh of its neck, and its head jerked sideways. Blood spurted in jets, and Dylan felt wetness on his shirt. The zombie fell out of the boat with a thump. Dylan pulled the axe loose and stepped back for another swing as the other monster slid over the edge.

As it approached, a third zombie feeding in the bottom of the boat stood up, grunting. It started climbing out. *I can't beat three of them.*

The distraction cost his advantage and the second undead closed, sticking out its arms, clutching with curling, bloody fingers. Dylan felt slimy hands and swung the axe, breaking its grip and slicing its arm. The zombie shrieked but didn't halt. Dylan jumped back, then turned to face them on a steeper downward slope, gagging at their stinking smell, fear tugging at the stability of his mind.

They lurched at him as he raised his weapon, moving to secure his footing for a powerful swing, but his left foot slipped on the loose gravel and he lost his balance. They were on him in a moment, scratching at his clothes, and he felt their hot breath on the back of his neck. *I'm dead,* he thought. *I'm going to die.* He couldn't believe this was how it would end.

A dull thud sounded and one of the zombies fell aside, grunting. *Move,* he commanded himself. *Do something!* Dylan thrust upward with the thick back section of the axe, connecting with a head. He swung again and hit the monster's torso, knocking it backward onto its ass.

Greg stood to the side with the shotgun turned upside down, drawn back as if waiting for a pitch. The zombie crawled toward him, begging for more, and he swung again with one of the sweetest actions Dylan had ever seen. The result was a thick, almost damp thump, like a stick striking leather. The side of the monster's head caved in and it folded to the gravel.

Two down.

Dylan stood, drawing the axe into position. "Thanks," he said, breathing heavily. He had thought he was as good as dead, writing off Kristy, making it home, and finding his parents. Euphoric joy flooded him and he wanted to shout, but he knew they weren't finished.

The monster Dylan had knocked over looked from one to the other, hissing. It chose Dylan and lumbered toward him. Invigorated, he re-enacted his first swing and the axe dug into its bony neck but did not sever the head. The undead staggered and Dylan swung again, this time knocking it to the rocky patch of ground as stones kicked up. It lay with savage wounds to the neck and shoulder, its mouth opening and closing like a fish out of water. He thought of how close he had come to dying, and he raised the axe and thrust it down, tearing through the zombie's neck in a clean cut, separating its head. Inky blood spurted onto the gravel in short sprays until the undead horror lay still.

The zombie with the crushed head kept trying to stand, but the damage had ruined its balance and one leg kept failing. Dylan passed the weapon to Greg, and in one motion, he spun around and drove the axe through the meaty neck and into the gravel with a clunk. The body twitched once, then stopped moving.

They stood, surveying their efforts, breathing heavily from exertion and adrenaline. Dark stains covered the gravel in random blotches.

"I'm glad I can't tell who they were," Dylan said. "I don't think I could kill one of my old school teachers."

"You might have to, soon. Don't think about it, though. I didn't kill a soldier at the checkpoint. I killed a fucking animal trying to hurt Kristy." Greg paused, considering. "Think of it like this. If you don't kill it, you'll end up one of them."

Dylan couldn't stop himself from thinking that he would, eventually. The others, too. "Thanks, man. For helping. Again."

"Sure," Greg said, touching one of the heads with the toe of his boot. "Anytime."

Greg raised the axe again and detached the first zombie's head. "Just to be safe." Together, they drew the gate across, and Dylan locked it in place, securing them inside the perimeter.

Back in the Jeep, Callan asked, "Where did they come from?"

"They tore the cover back and climbed into the boat, probably when we stopped on Main Street. They were after the rabbit meat."

"We have to be more careful," Kristy said. "These things are everywhere."

The car edged up the winding incline. The broad yellow beams revealed a large, two-level house with surrounding rock gardens and manicured lawns.

"Greg saved me," Dylan said. "I slipped on the gravel. I must have walked over it a thousand times before, half the time blind drunk. Without him, I'd probably be dead."

"I think Greg gets the 'Zombie Killer of the Day Award'," Callan said. "I'd be scared if I was one of them." He put up the palm of his hand and Greg slapped it lightly.

Kristy smiled and squeezed Dylan's hand. "I'm glad you're okay."

Dylan felt stirrings of desire. He *had* fallen for her. He took her hand, lifted it to his mouth, and pressed his lips against the velvet skin, feeling electricity suffuse his limbs and torso. Kristy's eyes widened, then her face softened and she smiled. They looked at each other for a long time and then lay back in their seats, their bodies close and comfortable.

6

Callan guided the Jeep onto a flat area topped with crushed rock beside the main veranda, and followed the outer boundary in a circle until it pointed away from the house. He cut the lights and darkness rushed in, broken only by a sliver of moon.

"Flashlights?"

"In the boat. Pink bag," Kristy said. "With the batteries and rope."

The day had been an emotional roller coaster. If she thought about the dead, she lost control and cried, sympathizing for those who had suffered, and wondering when it would end. She couldn't recall crying so much before and wished she were emotionally stronger, able to deal with it the way Sherry had, even if it meant being a bitch. She needed a distraction, something to take her mind from the darkness.

Dylan was that something. The fingers of her left hand remained entwined with his. She wanted to prolong it, sit there all night. Until now, he had been coy, at times removed. The odd instant between them had kindled the flame, but beyond a few words or the briefest touch, she had made all the investment. What had changed his mind? Right now, she didn't care.

"Let's move, then," Callan said, turning to Dylan. "Which way into the house?"

Dylan snatched his hand away. "Front veranda. If it's locked, there'll be a spare key hidden."

"Good. Greg, you get the flashlights. Dylan, lead the way, and you girls go straight inside, just to be safe."

With the exception of Greg, they walked across the gravel parking area. A giant gumtree stood beside the house, and for a moment, its strong smell of eucalypt took Kristy back up to the lake; she felt a pang of longing. Four wooden steps preceded a long merbau veranda edged by a three-tiered rail. Dylan led them down the decking to a set of wide glass sliding doors reflecting the sparse moonlight. He paused, then turned the handle.

Locked.

"I'll find the key," he said, squatting to feel the underside of a potted plant.

Kristy noticed the grass was long and scruffy. She had visited Dylan's house before, and it had always been pristine. She doubted the gardener had been around of late. A moving shadow caught her attention further off in the darkness.

"What's that?"

"Got it," Dylan said, holding up a small key.

"Where?" Callan asked. Kristy pointed toward the lower paddock. An invisible spider ran over her skin.

"Inside or outside the fence?"

"Inside, I think."

Dylan touched her arm. "What is it?"

"I don't know. I thought I saw something move down there."

Beyond the rocky garden with its rough outlines of plants and shrubs, the moon cast a wan silver hue upon the lower paddock.

"We've got a few sheep," Dylan said. "Could be one of them."

"Let's get inside," Callan said. "I won't be comfortable until we're behind locked doors."

Greg arrived with two flashlights and a box of supplies. Dylan opened the door, pushed apart heavy curtains, and stepped inside, poking one of the golden beams through the blackness. He held the drape for Kristy and she entered. She wanted to hold his hand, reignite the magic that she had felt touching his skin in the car, and to comfort him as he prepared the news about his parents. She didn't know how long she would be able to stay away from him. Callan would have to deal with it. She felt bad for Greg, too. Aside from the rough, beer-guzzling edge, he was sweet and caring.

The sliding doors led into a family area where two long couches joined at right angles beside two armchairs. A coffee table sat in the center of the room, and a large television hung bolted to the wall. Dylan walked across a soft rug to a junction. Left and right led to other rooms. Ahead was a wide timber kitchen with a large island bench as its centerpiece.

Sherry and Callan stood near the couch. Greg placed the box on the table.

"Well, we made it," Dylan said. "I didn't think we'd get here."

"For now," Callan said. "But we still don't know if our families are safe."

Greg moved toward the door, still favoring his ankle. "I'll bring the rest of the stuff in."

"I'll be there in a second," Callan said.

"Mom, Dad?" Dylan called out in a loud whisper.

He swung the beam over the room. It looked neat and orderly. Several plastic containers sat on the bench beside a notepad with a list. A blind extended over a large window above the sink, where a wire dish rack sat filled with plates, cups, a bowl, and utensils. Dylan walked to the fridge and opened it to darkness, confirming the power was out.

"They're definitely still alive," Dylan said. "There's a bit of food. Vegetables, some leftover meat. No milk, though."

"You got a veggie garden?" Callan said.

"Yep. Wait, there is milk. In a jug."

"Cows?"

"No. The Henrys, our neighbors, have some. There's a bowl of water at the bottom. Probably ice. Melted by now."

"So somebody's been here in the last day or two," Callan said.

Dylan went left into the formal lounge. A grand fireplace had been cut into one wall, and now stood, black and cold. More plush couches settled in a square pattern around a low table. In this area, though, piles of newspapers and notebooks lay spread about.

Dylan picked one up. "Holy shit, it's a newspaper from two weeks ago."

"What does it say?" Sherry asked.

They heard Greg drop a box of supplies in the family room.

Dylan said, "Eleven and a half million dead along the East Coast and there's still no vaccine." He looked up, mouth open. "Jesus, this is beyond bad. That's half the population."

Callan picked up a notebook and turned the pages. "Someone has written down a load of information. This details the... what they refer to as 'the plague'." He followed his finger across the page. "There's stuff about the infection. What to do to avoid it. How to protect yourself." He put the book back on the table and looked across the other pages. "This is amazing."

"Has to have been your dad," Kristy said.

"I told you he would have it covered." Dylan dropped the paper and ran to the stairs, calling his parents' names. Kristy followed, but Callan said, "Let him go. I don't think anybody's here."

A few minutes later, Dylan returned. "They're not here. But they've slept in their room and there's a pair of old leather pants and a jacket on the bed."

"You were right," Callan said. "This is a good place, much better than mine. Up on the hill we'll be able to see from all directions. We have vegetables, maybe even some fresh meat, and milk. And this stuff... your dad's done an incredible job."

"What about your parents?" Dylan asked.

"We'll take a look first thing tomorrow. I hate to do it, but driving around in the darkness is too risky for me. We can start at my house, then make sure everyone else's family is okay."

Kristy felt the first sliver of relief. Despite the circumstances, they had reached a destination and found some kind of refuge, at least for the night. She thought about what they had gone through, and who had literally and figuratively driven them most of the way. She smiled and said, "Hey, Cal, thanks for getting us here."

"Yeah," Dylan said. "Thanks, man."

Callan nodded, a flash of surprise on his face. "I'd better help Greg."

Dylan said, "When you're done, we'll take a look out back at the generator. If we can get that working, we can electrify the fences and help keep them out."

"Sure. Collect all the ammo and guns you can find. We'll need it."

Callan disappeared through the curtain folds, and the girls gathered in the kitchen. Dylan carried the boxes Greg had left in the family room over to the island bench.

After he dropped the first lot, Kristy grabbed Dylan by the shirt and pulled him to her. She took his face in her hands and said, "Kiss me, please."

"What about Greg and Callan?"

Kristy shook her head. "They're not here right now."

With his eyes open, Dylan leaned forward slowly and parted his lips. Kristy tingled as they met, feeling waves of pleasure roll through her neck and breasts. It seemed to go on and on, and she felt herself drifting away to another place where nothing but the electricity of their touch existed. When their lips finally parted, she hugged Dylan and felt the warmth reciprocated as he pulled her to him. "Finally," she said, beaming over Dylan's shoulder at Sherry.

"About time."

Callan stumbled through the curtains holding the axe, searching the family room and kitchen with large, wild eyes. "Is Greg in here?"

Dylan drew back from Kristy. "No."

"I can't fucking find him."

"What do you mean?" Sherry said.

"He's not at the car, or on the veranda. I called out to him but he didn't answer."

Dylan said, "Could he be playing a prank? You know what he was like before today."

Callan shook his head. "No way. Not now."

"Gimme a minute to grab another flashlight and I'll come—"

"No. Stay here. I'll find him." Callan disappeared through the folds of the curtains.

"Don't go out there," Kristy said.

"I have to help find Greg. He saved my ass."

A tapping noise sounded from the lounge room.

"What was that?" Kristy asked. Her entire back tingled with terror.

"It's those two playing tricks," Sherry said.

"I don't think so," Dylan said. He passed the flashlight to Kristy and took a knife from the drawer.

They gathered near the entrance to the lounge room, Dylan leading the way, Kristy holding the flashlight, and edged forward down the steps until they stood beside the table.

Tap, tap sounded on the window. Kristy shrieked.

Dylan's face drew into a mask of worry. "It's gotta be them." He stepped away from the girls, crept around the couch, and reached out a shaky hand for the drape. Intuition told him whatever was on the other side of the window wasn't good, that it might make what he had seen so far irrelevant. *Don't do it, man. Walk away and let Callan handle it.*

He grasped the curtain and paused, then yanked it aside.

Kristy screamed and the flashlight wobbled. Standing before them, one curled finger on the glass, was a zombie.

It was female, with long tendrils of dead grey hair hanging in patches from a dry, cracked skull. Its bloodshot eyes were sunk deep into its bony head. It opened its mouth, revealing rotted, gapped teeth. A long moan sounded, as if it was in pain.

It stared at Dylan, grimacing. He tried to speak but his lip trembled.

"It's your mom," Kristy said.

Part II

7

Callan almost ran into the zombie.

He paved the way along the veranda with the flashlight and didn't see it standing at the window until he had run past. He leaped over the side of the veranda, landing on the grass, watching the monster with wary suspicion.

The moment he shone the light on the thing, he knew it was Dylan's mother. She stood at the window tapping on the glass, begging Dylan to join her. He felt the tingle of pure terror dance over his skin. *They were going to have to kill her.* But not him. It was Dylan's call, the same way it would be up to him and Kristy if they found one of their parents in a similar state.

He had to find Greg. Dylan would have to deal with his mother. He walked beyond the end of the veranda, swinging the light in an arc over the driveway area.

"Greg?" Callan called in a loud whisper. "Greg? Where are you?"

He reached the Jeep and found it untouched, the back window zipped down, boxes of food and bags of clothing stacked on one side.

He swept the flashlight's beam across the boat and circled it, noting the splatter of blood over the motor and rear section. The gravel around it was clean, though, so he reasoned that it was probably from the incident at the gate. The storage chest was open and he peered inside, feeling his stomach churn at the sight of the decimated rabbit carcasses.

"Greg!" *Where did he go?* Panic amplified his voice. "Greg!"

The sound of clunking metal came from behind the house, toward the rear of the property.

"GREG!"

Callan ran, spearing the flashlight through the darkness with his left hand, gripping the axe in his right. He sprinted around the edge of the house. A landscaped area with a pool fence beyond was on the left; on the right sat a large green shed with two cream-colored roller doors.

He slowed, dropping the beam low, feeling his heartbeat jump up two gears. Greg lay just outside the entrance with both hands locked around the doorway, dragging himself toward it. The grotty corpse of a zombie stretched out behind him, reaching forward, one hand around his ankle.

He was still alive. In trouble, but still alive.

Callan started forward but something caught his foot and he went sprawling onto his knees. He swung the flashlight around and caught his breath. A dead zombie lay on the ground, its grey, decaying head severed from its body. A teenager, he saw, before turning the light away, with a mop of light brown hair that hadn't yet thinned. Lying three feet away was the tomahawk. Callan dropped the axe and picked up the smaller weapon, preferring its ease of use.

The zombie had its claws around Greg's feet. He kicked out, connecting with its head and breaking its grip. Greg rolled over and commando-crawled through the doorway, disappearing into the darkness. The zombie labored to its feet and staggered through the entrance after him.

Callan sprinted toward the shed, aiming the flashlight through the doorway. Just as he gathered speed, something struck him from the right and knocked him to the grass. His vision spun and the air rushed from his lungs. *Get up.* He rolled over and lifted the flashlight, revealing another zombie.

It grumbled something unintelligible then shambled toward him with its arms open. Callan poked the torchlight into its bloodshot eyes and it grunted, flexing bony fingers, opening its mouth in anticipation. It had once been a teenage girl of medium height, with long, thick hair, and a shapely body that hadn't shrunk with ruin. The soft face had turned to dead white flesh, riddled with dark veins and escalating rot. Callan felt his guts squirm as he moved backward, drawing it around toward the shed, the tomahawk raised.

He hadn't killed one yet. He'd shot the soldier in the shoulder, but Greg and Dylan had done the slaughtering. Now he wished he had. The first gunshot in the back of the Army truck had been premature, caused by his jittery thumb. These things were not random people from a distant farm or nameless soldiers from the Army. They were Albury citizens whom they had, in all likelihood, spoken to or encountered before.

The monster lurched toward him, slow and stupid, making a low hissing noise. Callan was quicker, though, dancing away, drawing the tomahawk above his head with his right hand. Suddenly the smaller blade didn't seem so potent. *Just kill it.* But he hesitated again. Shooting one was worlds apart from hacking it to death.

The clatter of hardware sounded from the shed, followed by a human cry. Callan turned and looked back. This gave the monster its chance, and it was suddenly on him, clawing for his juicy flesh, begging for a piece of him with its gibberish. Callan twisted away and swung the tomahawk side to side like a sword, hitting it in the face, halting it momentarily.

Greg screamed again and the chill of his friend's anguish drove Callan into action.

He waited as its cold, strong hands grabbed his arm, then drove the tomahawk into the side of its head, turning away at the last moment to avoid the spray. It felt like chopping soft wood. He pushed the ghoul off and yanked the weapon free, blood gushing sideways, his stomach pitching as the flashlight swayed over the sight. The monster stumbled and fell to the grass, gurgling.

But it wasn't dead. Climbing to one knee, its smashed head rolled to the side as it reached out a bony arm for him. Callan screamed through clenched teeth and swung the tomahawk underneath the zombie's jaw. It crashed to the ground as the flashlight fell to the grass. He leaped to its side in a half-circle of yellow light and hacked repeatedly, the body twitching and wriggling.

With the head severed, he stood back, panting, and wiped a forearm over his twisted face. His stomach turned again and this time he couldn't hold it down, projecting a load of vomit onto the grass. He stood bent over, hands on his knees, coughing the soggy remnants of lunch from his burning throat.

A tremendous crash sounded from the garage. Callan swept up the flashlight, stumbled over the dead thing and bolted, the light bouncing over the grassy stretch. "Greg! Greg! Fight it off!"

He reached the shed and burst through the entrance, thrusting the beam around. The structure was long and narrow, about two hundred square feet. Benches and perforated hardboard sat against the walls, stacked and hung with tools, containers, and myriad other items for household and garden use. A red lawn tractor and a bulky refrigerator sat in the far corners. A messy pile of larger power tools, oil drums, and hand tools lay on the floor.

The zombie lay crouched over Greg, its face perilously close, separated only by the wooden handle of a shovel, both sets of hands locked around it in a competition of strength. The tall female zombie, dressed in a dirty skirt and a grimy white shirt, moaned. Red streaks lined the corner of its mouth. Callan pointed the flashlight into its face and saw hideous yellow skin riddled with dark veins. One ear was missing, leaving a mutilated, bloody hole, and its long mane of hair had become dull and lifeless.

Greg cried out as the monster forced the shovel away and grabbed his throat. He pushed at its arms, then punched its chest, but the zombie leaned forward and opened its mouth.

Callan realized he risked covering Greg in blood if he stuck the zombie with the tomahawk, so he grabbed a fistful of hair, shivering at the touch, and pulled it backward. Screaming, he thrust the weapon down with every measure of his two hundred pounds behind it, and drove the metal blade into the back of the zombie's neck. The weapon dug deep through soft flesh, spraying blood in sideward jets. The thing screamed and arched its back, twisting to get free. Callan hacked again as the zombie moved, hitting the base of its skull near the ear. It fell backward, blood washing the floor, and slumped to the ground.

Greg crawled away screaming, "The head! Cut off its head."

Callan eyed a mark on the top of its skull and swung, fighting to keep the light on his target, but the zombie lurched forward, screeching, and took the blow on the arm. He lifted the tomahawk again, but the monster sprung up and knocked him backward with the point of its bony shoulder. Callan tripped over a paint can and the guarded head of a brush cutter, fighting to keep his balance.

He did, though, feeling his legs trembling, his heart hammering. It lunged at him, teeth bared, hands clenching. He realized then that it just wanted flesh and blood and wouldn't stop until it had obtained such. *They live to feed. Feeders.* He wondered how the brain beyond those dead, lifeless eyes could possess any coherence.

Lying against the side bench, Greg stuck the shovel out, tangling the monster's feet; it fell into a heap.

Callan swung down in a powerful arc, burying the blade in the top of the zombie's head with a jarring crunch. It split open, spilling a mess of grey, bloody gore. He gagged again and grabbed the bench for balance.

He stood over it, chest heaving, and dropped the tomahawk, amazed at the amount of blood. *I'm alive.* He couldn't quite believe it. He had killed a woman and a teenage girl. His sanity teetered on the edge of madness, processing what he had seen and done. In that moment, he might have gone either way, but Greg moaned and drew his concentration.

He placed the flashlight on the bench, maximizing the spread of light, then went to Greg, who still sat against the left side of the shed.

"Are you all right?" Callan asked, eyeing the blood-soaked section of jeans on his lower leg. Splatters covered the rest of his clothes, and Callan noticed them on himself. "Did you get bitten?"

Greg grimaced, shifting his right leg, and said, "No, but I fell on the axe and cut my leg open."

Pointing to Greg's shin, Callan said, "Is that your blood?"

"I don't know. I hope so."

So did Callan. He didn't know much about the transmission of the virus, but he suspected that if zombie blood got into your bloodstream you were in big trouble. They needed Kristy. "Can you walk?"

Greg reached down and touched his foot. "I think I've sprained my ankle worse, too. They came at me from outta nowhere, and I fell and twisted it."

Callan grasped his friend underneath the armpit and helped him onto his feet. Greg leaned on his shoulder, and with tomahawk in hand, Callan put an arm around his waist. "Slowly." They started off hopping at first, before Greg got the hang of it. Callan snatched the flashlight from the bench and poked it into the darkness. "Now tell me what happened."

Greg closed his eyes as they shuffled along. "I saw it trying to get into the shed. I thought I could take it so I crept up with the axe, but the other one came from the right side out of the darkness. Knocked me over. That's when I fell on the axe and fucked up my ankle."

"You were lucky," Callan said.

"As far as I know."

8

Don't cry, man. Don't you fucking cry.

His mother stood at the window. No longer his mother, but rather, but the carcass of what was once a beautiful, loving mother and wife. It was easy to tell. Her skin had turned a cold, lifeless grey. Her eyes regarded him as nothing more than food. He understood in that instant that *she* was no longer. The virus had killed her. Or was it a bite from another? He didn't know. What he did know was that he would never wrap his arms around her again, never kiss her goodbye, or goodnight, or wish her a happy birthday. The advice she had so appropriately given him for the last twenty-eight years had ended. The thing ogling him through the window was a monster, and he would have to kill it.

He broke, his face folding into lines of unbearable sadness. He fought tears, but they trickled out like sparse raindrops down a window. He sobbed, made a hitching sound as he tried to squash it, and finally looked away, pressing his eyes shut until they hurt.

"Dylan," Kristy said, fighting tears of her own.

"I have to do it," he said, wiping his nose. "Before it hurts Callan or Greg." He looked at the knife in his hand and thought about sinking the long silver blade into his mother's head. He shivered. "It's not her anymore." His voice trembled. "It's not." Still, he wouldn't be able to do it. He would engage her and raise the knife with the best of intentions, but at the last moment, her memory would sabotage his actions and *she* would kill *him*.

He let the drape fall and stumbled backward, falling onto the sofa.

"Dylan, wait," Kristy said. "You don't have to do this."

He pushed to his feet, holding the knife. "Who's gonna do it then?" She looked away and he pushed past, his vision blurring. Kristy followed, shining the light ahead.

Dylan turned into the kitchen and rustled through one of the boxes on the bench until he found another flashlight.

"Stay inside." Kristy and Sherry stood in the center of the room. "I won't be long." He rubbed away the tears with white knuckles, then headed for the door with the flashlight in his left hand, the knife in his right.

He stood at the curtains, breathing deeply. What choice did he have? She was sick. *Beyond sick.* She had become a monster, like the ones they had killed at the gate. Whose mother or father were they? Did she deserve the right to live any more than them? He could ask every question about her entitlement to remain, argue all the wonderful things she had done as a mother and a person, but none of them would stand against the horrible truth. She had to die. To let her live would prolong an injustice to her memory, and risk them all.

Dylan pushed the curtains aside and stepped out onto the deck. He swung the light around to the window, but she was gone. He turned the other way and poked the yellow beam along the decking toward the rear of the house. His hand shuddered and his teeth chattered, despite the warmth. Empty.

He tiptoed toward the driveway and saw her standing at the bottom of the stairs against the brick house. He sucked in a breath and whimpered, unable to shine the light directly on her. Instead, he inspected her at the edge of the beam.

She looked toward the town, tendrils of patchy hair falling around her grey, parched face. Torn clothes hung from a bony frame that shuffled from one foot to the other. Her hands twitched and her head rolled in small circles. Dylan couldn't move. One more step would draw him closer to the inevitable. When she opened her mouth and revealed a hyperextended jaw, he jammed the fist with the knife handle into his mouth as he sobbed. That was it. *Kill or be killed,* Greg had said.

He stumbled forward, lifting the blade high, waving the cone of light in her face. She turned and hissed, the blackness of her eyes touching a place in him that shrunk his testicles. He cried out, sobbing, and staggered down the steps.

He swung the knife in a weak arc, missing by a foot. She clawed for him, but he could have moved in slow motion. *Stab her in the head.* He poked the weapon out, pushing her backward, pulling it short, but then her arm clashed with the blade and she shrieked.

"Dylan!"

He broke down, sobbing. "Mom, I'm sorry," he said, withdrawing the knife. The feeling of cutting her flesh made him nauseous. "I didn't—"

"Dylan!"

Somebody was calling his name. He threw the light to his right and saw Callan helping Greg walk.

Cold fingers gripped his left arm. He smelled her hot, fetid breath and realized she had been eating something rotten, something dead, and the paltry contents of his stomach rushed upward. Dylan brushed her off and turned aside, gagging, the knife and flashlight falling to the ground.

Kill her. He couldn't do it. He couldn't murder his mother. In that moment, he was certain.

She struck him and they fell backward, hitting the soft ground, the impact knocking the breath from him. Gulping for air, he held her back, surprised at her weight. She felt like a barbell rigged with only a couple of small plates. She hung over him, moaning, and he wondered if it wouldn't be easier to let her. *You won't remember any of this,* he thought.

But a stronger voice said *move* and he rolled away, seeing Greg standing against the house beyond the cone of light.

She grunted, groping for his neck, and he knew he had to move quickly or she would be on him again.

"I'm sorry, Dylan," a voice said, and when he turned over he saw Callan looking down with a sad, reluctant posture, the axe drawn high and ready.

Dylan crawled away, tears blurring his vision, pressing his face into the grass. He wanted to call out for Callan to stop, that his mother *might* be saved if they could find a treatment or a cure. Surely, someone was working on it *somewhere*.

His mother moaned and he heard her shuffling about, trying to stand. Dylan heard the thick, mushy whack of the blade. Callan grunted and repeated the action.

Silence. A long, terrible silence. Dylan was holding his breath.

"It's done," Callan said. "I'm sorry."

Dylan lay there for a long moment, unable to believe they had spoken their last words. He let out his breath slowly. He would never rid his mind of that despicable image, the monster she had become, ignorant to him, searching for the sweet nourishment of his flesh. His body shuddered and he bit down on his knuckles to hold back a cry.

"Wait there," Callan said. "I have to take Greg inside. He's bleeding pretty bad. We killed three of them up the back."

"My father?" Dylan asked, as he sucked in a sharp breath.

"No. An older female, a younger one, and a teenage boy."

Dylan remembered to breathe and found his nose congested. He nodded, unsure if Callan could even see him.

Callan's footsteps faded. Dylan heard him helping Greg up the stairs with a bump, along the decking and with help from the others, through the sliding doors. Dylan's flashlight sat on the grass, poking yellow light against the brick wall, illuminating the spot where he had seen her in her wretchedness.

His mother had been a quiet, reserved woman, in many ways like Dylan, and she observed more than she let on. She was kind, caring, and always capable of providing sound advice. He thought of the time he had a stupid argument with some kids at school about whose family ran a better business. One of the boys' fathers had won an award and spent the day spouting off about it. Dylan had contested the boy, knowing his family's business was more successful. Dylan had quizzed his mother about why his father hadn't gone for the award to prove his ability and success.

"Why does it matter?" his mother had asked.

"So everyone will know he's the best," Dylan had said, still standing in the kitchen with his schoolbag slung over his shoulders.

"But why does *that* matter?"

Dylan had grown perplexed. "Doesn't he want everyone to know how good his business is?"

She had tousled his hair and put an arm around him. "It doesn't matter what others think of you. The most important person that knows how wonderful and talented and successful you are is yourself. As long as *you* know, that's all that matters."

He had lived with that shrewd advice ever since, deflecting unfriendly comments about his supposed inadequacies, knowing the truth. Such comments had never gotten him down again.

"Dylan?" a voice called out for him in a loud whisper. *Kristy*.

Footsteps clunked on the decking, then shuffled across the grass toward him, and paused. He would have to face her eventually; he steeled himself not to cry. He wasn't brave and manly like Callan or Greg, and he didn't want to give her another reason to think he was soft. The glow of the flashlight leapt off the lawn and into his eyes.

"Dylan?"

Even in his devastation, her voice raised a single butterfly in his stomach. He sat up and put a hand across his brow to shield his vision. Kristy moved the light from his face. "Yeah."

"I'm so sorry. Callan told me." She flicked the light to the left, paused, and pulled it back with a gasp. "Oh Jesus." The light shook for a moment, and then she turned it off.

Kristy squatted beside him, dropped his flashlight onto the grass, and put a hand on his back, pulling him close. His body convulsed again, and he was instantly sobbing. *So much for steeling myself.* But he didn't really care. If he couldn't bare his inner feelings in front of Kristy without her judging him, then she wasn't the one. She stroked his back and hugged him tight, kissing his hair. "I'm so sorry."

"Kristy! We need you."

Kristy lit the flashlight and speared the yellow cone at the sliding doors. "In a minute."

In a hushed voice, Callan said, "He's bleeding everywhere."

"Okay."

Sniffling, Dylan said, "What happened?"

Kristy soothed his back again. "Greg's been hurt. Callan said he fell on the tomahawk, and there's blood all over his pants. The wound might be contaminated."

"Go. I'm okay."

She kissed his cheek and glanced about into the darkness. "Come inside."

He nodded. "In a minute."

She trailed a hand over his back as she went. Dylan watched the beam of light cross the lawn and climb the stairs. Callan waited at the door, holding the blinds for his sister. He cast a narrowed gaze out into the darkness, then disappeared inside.

Dylan let out a long breath and felt for his flashlight. Part of him wanted to turn it on and look at her, to see if she really was dead, but it would only cause more heartache. He had to bury her, though, and the idea left him feeling weak. Maybe he could ask Callan to do it.

He cursed himself, knowing he should have been prepared for such an outcome. The chances of survival were slim, for all of their friends and family.

As he climbed to his feet, Dylan heard the angry ones in the distance, fighting among themselves. Where was his father? Was he dead too? At the thought, Dylan pushed away a tight feeling in his chest. His father would be somewhere, riding it out, staying low. His sister, Lauren, was at university in Melbourne, living on campus. He hoped she was safe.

Dylan trudged toward the decking, wiping his eyes, fighting to not look back.

Greg lay on the sofa in the family room groaning, his face a mask of pain. Kristy had inspected the wound and then checked his other vitals. His ankle had begun to discolor and swell. A definite sprain, and she had no ice to help reduce the inflammation.

They had a candle on the table in the middle of the room, and another on the kitchen bench. "Get me some warm water," Kristy said, "and towels. We have to clean him first."

"There's no warm water," Callan said. "We don't have any power yet."

Kristy guided the flashlight around the room, looking for her medical case. "Check the stovetop. They should be on bottled propane." She spied it in the corner near a pile of clothes bags Greg had brought in from the Jeep.

Callan whispered, "How bad is it? Could the zombie blood have gotten inside the wound?"

"I don't know. Once I clean him up, we'll know more. Sherry," Kristy said, "I saw some candles earlier. Grab half a dozen, find a couple of tables or chairs we can rest them on, and drag them over to the sofa. I need some light around me."

"It's working," Callan said, standing at the stovetop, one of the burners glowing with blue flame. He snatched a kettle from the back burner and began to fill it with water from the tap. "Water tanks are still going too."

Dylan appeared in the doorway. Kristy felt her heart leap and she gave him a warm, relieved smile, which he tried to return.

"How is he?" Dylan asked.

Greg lay back with his eyes closed. Kristy said, "We're just about to start washing his leg. We have gas in the burners, though."

Dylan said, "We're on bottled propane out here."

Callan said, "And there's tank water, too." He placed the kettle on the burner and it made a low whirring sound as the tin began to heat.

"We also have a septic tank, so the toilets will flush."

Dylan walked toward Greg as Kristy opened her medical bag. She reached out a hand and he took it, squeezing lightly. She tried to think of something comforting to say, but gave him pouted lips and a furrowed brow to convey her sadness. Even in the dim light, his eyes looked red and puffy. She just wanted to sit and hold him in her arms, comfort him, tell him they would get through it together. He seemed determined to push on, though, and she was proud of that.

"What do you need?" Dylan asked, peering at Greg.

Kristy slipped on disposable latex gloves and said, "A garbage bag. We'll need to burn his clothes. Callan, did you wash your hands after bringing him in? We can't take any risks until we know what we're dealing with. And put some gloves on. You too, Sherry."

"Just a rinse under the water."

Kristy shook her head. "Not good enough. Dylan, can you bring soap *and* anti-bacterial hand sanitizer, if you have it?" Who knew how this virus was transmitted? What if Callan had a cut on his hand and blood from the zombie got into the cut? The idea gave her a flutter of panic. "Actually, we need as much of the anti-bacterial sanitizer as we can find. I want us all using it regularly." Dylan activated his flashlight and disappeared toward the lounge room.

Sherry set chairs at the head and foot of the sofa, and one in the middle, then placed candles upon them. She ignited the wicks and a warm glow enveloped the small space.

Kristy stood over Greg, surveying his condition. Blood splatter covered his shirt and jeans, and the laceration below his knee looked gruesome, even through the rip in the denim. She took a tight, controlled breath, hoping it hadn't been contaminated, and opened her medical bag. Gore like this had never bothered her. She pictured the injury in her mind and thought about how she would repair it. In this case, she had to clean Greg's leg, sterilize the wound, and close it up. Simple enough under normal circumstances, but these circumstances were nothing like normal.

"I need you to hold the light for me," she said to Sherry.

On the table, she placed a pack of thread, a packaged needle, scissors, gauze pads, bandages, and a bottle of antiseptic lotion. "How's that warm water? I don't want it boiling."

"Almost there," Callan said.

"How are you feeling?" Kristy looked at Greg.

Greg nodded. "I'm okay. My ankle hurts more than the bloody tomahawk cut."

"Not much we can do for that at the moment. I put some cream on it, but ice is what we really need. Just keep it elevated and try not to move it."

Dylan returned with the promised items, including a bunch of towels, soap, sanitizer, and a large black garbage bag, which he laid open on the floor beside the sofa. Kristy's mouth curled up at the edges, and she said, "Thank you." A smile touched the corners of his eyes but it disappeared. She couldn't imagine his suffering.

"You should put some of these on," Kristy said, holding up a box of disposable gloves. Dylan pulled two clear rubber gloves from the pack. "We'll need to burn the clothes and anything with their blood on it. All of us."

Callan arrived with a pot of water. "Do you have any local anesthetic?" Kristy shook her head. "Ouch."

Greg said, "What choice have I got?"

With the scissors, Kristy cut away sections of Greg's jeans and passed each piece to Dylan, who placed them into the garbage bag. She repeated this until the entire section of his leg from the thigh down was clear of clothing. "Help lift his leg for me, Cal. I need to lay towels underneath." Callan took Greg's boot and lifted while Kristy spread the white linen over the sofa.

"Well?" Callan asked. "What do you think?"

The wound was four inches long, a gash revealing red, bloody flesh. It was clean and straight, definitely a result of a knife or sharp blade.

"It doesn't look dirty. I'll clean it as best I can and..." She glanced at Greg. "Hope."

Callan asked, "How long before we know?"

"I don't know that."

"What do you mean? You're a doctor."

"I don't know anything about this virus. Clearly, it's nothing that anybody has seen before. Just let me sew him up, okay? Forget about the virus for now. I need to clean the wound. Given what you said about him crawling over the grass and through the shed, there's a chance it will probably get infected, anyway, but the longer I leave this open, the greater the chance it has of becoming that way. Grab me a bucket or some kind of tray to put under his leg so I can wash the wound. Then a jug of water." Callan disappeared.

Kristy had sewn up worse in her time in the ER, but never one so vicious in a damned lounge room. *Nothing changes. Focus.* She envisioned the checklist from med school. Wash, sanitize, sew, and dress.

"Wait," Dylan said, then left.

Kristy scrutinized Greg's ankle again, pressing the flesh in several different places. On the third touch, Greg hissed. "Sore? Looks like you've strained your calcaneofibular ligament."

"What the fuck is that?"

She touched a section of skin running from the side of the ankle to the heel. "It connects your fibula to your heel bone. Did you roll your ankle inward?"

Greg furrowed his brow. "I might have."

"You need to keep your ankle elevated," Kristy said, placing a pillow under his foot. "And stay off of it until the swelling goes down." Greg frowned.

After taking a towel and dipping it into the bowl of water, Kristy made long, gentle strokes over Greg's leg until the white fabric had turned a dark, dirty pink. She tossed it into the garbage bag and took another one from Dylan, who handed Greg a bottle.

"Johnny Walker Black," Greg said. "Not bad. I'm a 'Red' man, myself, but I won't complain."

Kristy doused the second towel in warm water and began wiping, working her way closer to the gash this time, careful not to touch the raw flesh.

"I've seen you suck the liquid from alcohol swabs," Callan said from the kitchen, "and you didn't complain about that."

Greg turned the bottle up and took three long gulps, then pulled it away with a swish, grimacing in pleasure. "Whoa, that shit is *good*."

Callan returned with a plastic tub from beneath the sink. He placed it under Greg's leg, then handed Kristy a jug of water. She poured it over the wound, washing away the remaining streaks of blood and dirt. Using a towel, she patted it dry, careful to avoid the gash.

"This is going to hurt," Kristy said. "I'm sorry I don't have any anesthetic." She took a needle from its packet and attached the thread. With a steady, practiced hand, she punched the barb through Greg's skin at the end of the gash.

He jerked, sucked in a sharp breath, and said, "That's not... nice."

"There's more." Greg chugged the Scotch down again. Kristy poked the needle through the other side, and closed the gap by pulling the thread. "One down. Fifteen or so to go."

Dylan walked to the sliding doors and peered between a slit in the curtains.

"What is it?" Callan said.

"I thought I heard something."

Kristy looked at Callan and raised her eyebrows. She suspected Dylan wouldn't want to leave his mother's body out on the grass for too long.

As if hearing her thoughts, Dylan said, "I need to bury my mother."

"I'll take care of it," Callan said.

"Thank you."

By the time Kristy had sewn up the wound, Greg had consumed the remaining Scotch. She applied the last of her antiseptic lotion, then took the flashlight from Sherry and inspected the dressing from various angles. It was neat, clean. She didn't think she could have done a better job in the ER. The only differences were the sterilization of the wound and her tools. Finally, she covered it with a gauze pad, then circled his leg with a bandage and tied it off with a safety pin. All she could do was hope that an infection didn't take hold.

"Brilliant," Greg said, slightly slurred. "Thanks. What now?"

Kristy realized she had completed the entire procedure without once questioning her ability as a doctor. The idea filled her with surprise and relief.

"Nothing for you," she said. "Rest up on the sofa. Do not walk on that leg, hear me?" Greg nodded. "I'll give you couple of paracetamol for the pain. Take some more in the morning to help with your hangover."

"How long before we know if he's sick?" Callan asked. Greg shifted in his seat.

"It depends on how quickly the virus works. For now, we just wait."

10

There was little food left in the pantry. Under candlelight, Sherry cooked up the eggs from the fridge in a frying pan; they ate them in silence, between slightly stiff slices of bread. When the bread ran out, Callan devoured his third egg straight from the pan. Despite eating little since breakfast, he wasn't ravenous; the day's events and the anxiety about what lay ahead left him feeling slightly nauseated.

Dylan sat on a stool in silence, his brow furrowed, flipping through pages of one of the notepads his father had left in the lounge room.

"What's it say, man?" Callan asked.

Dylan shook his head slowly, as if unable to believe it. "It's a journal. My father wrote an entry every few days."

Kristy asked, "Like a diary?"

"Yeah."

"Can you read some of it out loud?"

"It's basically an account of what happened. Get comfortable." Dylan slipped off the stool and sat on one of the sofas. He thumbed the notebook, cleared his throat, and started reading from the beginning.

"*My name is Robert Norman Cameron and I'm adding this foreword a week into this 'event'. The point of it now has become about leaving a record for myself of what has occurred, or for others, if anything should happen to me. If you are reading this, I hope I am being a little paranoid, that matters at hand have been resolved, and those who have survived until this point (Day Six) are safe and healthy. What lies in these pages are the thoughts and observations of a man with sound mind. I think…*"

"*Day 1, December 29, 2013: Another flu epidemic is apparently on the way. My 'silly hobby' as Margaret calls it, starts again. I was looking back at some of the notes I made during the swine flu pandemic in May 2009. That was scary. This one hasn't had the build-up, though, having had only modest reporting over the last few weeks, but the online articles and newspaper reports are*" *saying it's going to get a lot worse. Let's hope it doesn't. I'm starting this as 'Day 1', but I'm hopeful it doesn't really go anywhere."*

Dylan turned the page. "Not much in day two," he said before continuing.

"Day 3, December 31, 2013: This thing is starting to get a little hairy. The news is reporting it to be a new strain of H1N1, comparing it to the Spanish Flu of 1918, but I think there's more to it than that. Thirty percent of the workforce called in sick today. Okay, it is New Year's Eve, but I put on a bit of a bash for them and they get to leave early and I still pay them for it. We had to stop sections of the factory and could only dispatch half the orders. The local hospital is crammed with people. Apparently, there is no vaccination against this strain. The CSL is working on one, but says it will be months before it is available for distribution."

"Maybe there *is* a vaccine," Sherry said, pulling her mane of red hair into a ponytail.

"I doubt it, babe," Callan said, standing up. He went to the sliding doors and peered through a gap out into the darkness. "Besides, there's nobody left to use it."

Dylan turned the page. *"Day 5, January 2, 2014: Seven of my staff died today…"*

"Fuck *off*," Greg said. Kristy gasped.

Dylan glanced up and Callan saw pain in the lines around his eyes. Nobody spoke. Dylan started slowly. *"I'm shutting the office for a few days. Almost everyone has called in sick or hasn't called at all. Something is not right with all of this. I was in town for most of yesterday and people are scared. The government isn't saying anything. They haven't even made a statement. The newspapers are saying it's big in the US and Europe. I'm going to get some supplies from town and keep Margaret and myself away from it all. We have plenty of gasoline and propane. The water tanks are full. Just until this thing blows over."*

Dylan looked away in thought. "Maybe that's why they lasted so long, because they stayed away." He turned back to the book. *"Day 6, January 3, 2014: Ian McKenzie is dead. He called in yesterday morning with symptoms, and when I went by his house this afternoon to see how he was doing, his wife said he had passed. Thirty-two years I've known the man and then he catches the flu and… They still don't really know how it started."*

"I knew Ian," Dylan said. "Nice guy."

"Lots of nice people have probably died," Sherry said. Dylan nodded.

"Day 7, January 4, 2014: I got hold of Lauren in Melbourne today and told her to go and buy water and food and to stay in her apartment in the city. She said the place is empty. New Year's Eve was very quiet. Streets are bare and most people in her apartment building are staying put. None of her flatmates have gotten sick so far, but she said several people she knows have died and plenty are sick. It was all over Facebook in the first few days but the posts have started to dwindle. I told her not to move until this was over. As for Dylan, he's up at Lake Eucumbene camping, and may not even know this is happening. I pray he stays up there as long as he can, at least until things are better down here…"

"We're so lucky," Sherry said. "Sooo lucky."

"God, I wish we had stayed up there," Kristy said.

Callan thought back to the moment they drove away from the gas station. He had considered the idea of going back, but the need to know if his parents were okay was too strong. He felt like a failure for not getting there, but knew they had made the right choice coming to Dylan's house. In hindsight, he didn't know how they had made it. He closed his eyes and felt the pull of exhaustion. They hadn't stopped since rising early at the lake to pack up camp.

"What else does he say?" Callan asked. "I want to try and turn the generator on before bed."

Dylan looked at the next entry and read. *"Day 9, January 6, 2014: The phones are down. I spoke to Lenny Carter this morning, but since then I haven't been able to get cellular service and the landlines are dead. The Internet is still going, though. Lenny told me some things I am finding difficult to write down. I assume he's made a mistake. He said that some of the sick are recovering but… they're different. Not themselves. They still <u>look</u> sick. Some walk the streets as though they've lost their way. Others are quite aggressive.*

There has been widespread fighting and a number of robberies. I decided to take a drive after I got off the phone with him, just around the edges of town, and I saw the only remaining police officer, Roger Tarbitt. He told me that he's had no contact with Melbourne or Sydney in the last twenty-four hours, and the last time he spoke to either center they were down to their last few available officers because most had gotten sick or died. I saw several people wandering about but didn't go too close. And finally, the power went out this afternoon. I've started up the generator and have plenty of fuel to run it for a week or so."

"Day 11, January 8, 2014: The government has issued a warning, rating the virus a category 5 on the CDC Pandemic Severity Index chart. Everyone seems to be sick. Hospitals are closing down. All major airports are shut. No phones. The streets are empty. All the television stations except ABC have stopped broadcasting, and ABC's is only a brief news bulletin twice a day, updating people with little information. I never thought it would get this bad. I'm seriously worried. I won't go into town at the moment. There's just too much unrest. People are taking items from some of the shops. Regardless, this will go down on record, if records still exist when this is all over, as the greatest catastrophe in human history. I don't think the Australian government has been incompetent so much as incapable of handling such a scenario. Who can prepare for such an unrealistic situation? I doubt any of the other countries' governments have done better. Newspaper reports said that every continent and major city in the world had been affected. The death toll from the initial virus in Australia is in the millions, probably more. Nobody has the infrastructure to handle 25 percent of their population becoming fatally sick within a ten-day period."

"Jesus Christ," Greg said.

Dylan went on. *"Day 19, January 16, 2014: I haven't made notes for eight days now. There have been gunshots from the town, car horns blaring, and a few fires. The internet died four days ago. No more ABC. The only communication we've had is with our immediate neighbors, the Henrys. Marg wants to leave, but I figure we're safest here for now. Nobody really knows we're here, and I haven't seen any of the crazy people out this way. I drove partway down Silvan Road yesterday morning just to check out some of the houses. There were a couple of families who came out, and we spoke, but they didn't know much more than us. They said the Army might be sent in soon to clean things up. If we can hold on, wait it out, these H1N1 virus variations tend to taper off as quickly as they arrive. Might take a couple of months, but we can last."*

"The handwriting on this entry is messy, as though he's got a problem with his hand. *"Day 21: 18th of January, I think. The generator ran out of fuel this morning and all the cans are empty, so I had to go into town to try and scavenge some. Marg wanted to come, but I wouldn't have it. What I saw still makes me uneasy. My hands are still shaking. The first two gas stations were empty. The third had one pump that still worked but I had limited time and could only fill six of the eight five-gallon cans. There was a mob of people, men and women, trashing shops, and they saw me and started walking toward the station. I've never been so scared in my life. They didn't look normal. They were slow and lumbering. They had blood on their hands and arms, and on their faces, as though they'd been eating fresh meat. One or two of them ran after the car, throwing rocks at it. I thought I was gone. But it was the last bit I saw that sends chills up my back. I looked up into the rearview mirror to make sure I had outrun them and saw one of the big men turn to another in anger and bite into his neck, and then others leapt on him and he disappeared under them."*

Dylan put the notebook down. "Right up until then, he mustn't have known what they were."

"He stayed away," Greg said, shifting his position on the sofa. "That's why. They were smart. We should just go back up to the lake and leave this place behind."

Sherry said, "Maybe he's right. Maybe getting out of Albury is the safest option."

"No," Dylan said. "I don't believe that. We're safe here. We have heaps of water and propane, and once we get the generator working, we'll have electricity and fences to protect us."

"It might stop a few of them, but what about a mob?"

"We could go on about this all night," Callan said. "I don't know if there's a right answer just now. I do know we could use some sleep, though. How many more pages?"

Dylan sighed and turned to the last page. "Just one— *Day 23: One of them climbed through the fence and wandered up from the lower paddock.*" Dylan glanced up with an expression that said "Don't say it."

"*We didn't see it until it was almost at the garden. I shot it from the rocks with the .22. Took half a dozen rounds, and it wasn't until I put a few in its head that it went down. Jesus… I was shaking like I'd been out in a blizzard. I dug a hole up the back near the tennis court and buried it. I drove around again before dusk, mostly along Silvan Road to see if there were any more of them wandering around, but it got dark and I came home. They seem to be moving north from the southern end of town. The entire southern section has been destroyed. I can't help but think that, sooner or later, we'll be in their way.*"

Dylan lay back against the sofa, staring at the notebook. It was time for Callan to apologize. He had criticized Dylan for comments about his father knowing what had transpired. But Dylan had been right. *More than right.* What they had was an account of the disaster as it had unfolded. Without it, they would never have known exactly what had happened. "I'm sorry, man, for being such an ass today. I was… worried about getting everyone back here. About my parents. Not knowing if they were okay or not."

"It's okay. I get it." Dylan ran his tongue over dry lips. "I just hope he's… alive."

Callan felt Dylan's desperation, and his longing to know. Callan had almost convinced himself that his parents were dead. It was better that way; he could gradually accept the loss. He hoped they hadn't turned like Dylan's mother. Anything but that.

"Don't give up on him yet," Callan said. "From what I've seen, he's got more of a handle on this than most. If anyone's got a chance, it's him."

##

"We have to get those fences electrified," Callan said, dumping the last pile of dirty clothes in the laundry. "I'm not washing these by hand. Will you?"

"Do you have to do that now?" Kristy asked.

"Aside from all that washing, I thought you'd want a warm shower," Callan said. "The hot water service runs on electricity, doesn't it?"

"Yep," Dylan said. "Too expensive to run on bottled propane. If we get the generator going, we can power the fridge, some lights, and pumps for the water tanks."

"I need a warm shower," Sherry said. "If you don't turn it on, I'll go out and do it myself."

"It's okay, babe, we'll have it on soon." He promised himself to work harder at making Sherry happier.

"I'll come with you," Greg said, swinging his legs off the sofa.

Kristy was beside him before he could stand. "No you won't. You're not moving until the swelling on that ankle goes down. Doctor's orders."

"Anyway, you've done your share," Callan said. Turning to Dylan, he added, "There's one other thing."

"My mother." Callan nodded. "I know you said you'd take care of it, and I appreciate that, but I need to help."

"Are you sure?"

"You don't need to do that, Dylan," Kristy said, putting her arms under his.

Callan felt his teeth grind. *Get hold of yourself.*

"No, but I do. I couldn't kill her. I tried and I fought it, but in the end, I just couldn't shut off the light in her eyes, as dark as it was. Callan had to do that for me." Tears flowed, and Callan found it had been easier to kill Dylan's mother than see him cry. "I haven't said it, but I appreciate that, Callan. I really do. She's my mother and I need to bury her, but I could use your help." He wiped his tears and nose with the back of his hand, and pulled Kristy close to him; she lay against his chest, talking in a muffled voice.

Callan felt bad for him. He, too, would have battled with killing his own mother, but he didn't think he could handle himself as well as Dylan. The sadness of the moment suppressed his ongoing anger, allowing him to watch them, to see Dylan and Kristy as people, rather than as his sister and the boy who'd stolen his grade school girlfriend. Kristy seemed taken with him, and, other than that one problem, Dylan had always been a respectable man. Intellectually, they were similar, and he knew Kristy enjoyed their discussions, something she had found wanting in other partners. Callan looked over at Greg and saw his head hung low, eyes down. His fingers were still locked around the empty bottle of Scotch. His heart ached for his mate. He knew the feeling of longing. Greg had liked Kristy for years, and it had taken him that long to divulge his feelings to Callan. And now, after finally disclosing this to Kristy, Greg had to watch another win her heart. Sometimes life wasn't fair.

Dylan glanced at him and then turned back to Kristy. She planted a soft kiss on his lips.

"Let's get this done," Callan said. "Where are your dad's guns?"

"There's only one left. A rifle. He must have taken the others. There's plenty of ammo for the both Remington's, though."

"That's okay. One of us holds the flashlight, the other holds the rifle."

Dylan disappeared, then returned a few moments later with a Winchester .30-30. He handed the rifle to Callan, and then embraced Kristy again before swiping a set of keys off the bench.

"Be careful," Kristy said. "No heroics."

"We'll get the generator started and dig the… grave," Callan said. "Forty minutes, tops. Where are we digging?"

"The front garden. There's a patch in there between some of her favorite flowers."

A cold shiver crossed Callan's neck, and he couldn't help feeling as though he might need to make a similar decision soon.

Armed with the tomahawk and flashlight, Dylan led Callan through a side door off the kitchen and into the laundry. A dead-bolted backdoor barred their way, and he turned the latch slowly, holding his breath as the heavy pin clicked out of place. He went down two steps and held the door for Callan. They stood in the darkness beneath a spacious covered area where his parents once entertained friends at barbecues and parties.

"Turn on the flashlight," Callan said, lifting the rifle into position. His heartbeat raced. Would they be standing before a waiting, hungry mob? "You did load this, didn't you? And how many rounds?"

"I did, and five."

Yellow light flooded the area, revealing cream-colored paving stones and a square wooden table surrounded by eight chairs. Beyond, a stainless steel barbecue sat on a rock partition, and beside it, a bar fridge had been fitted into the wall. Three large ceiling fans hung from timber beams overhead, and on the right, at the edge of the patio, sat a three-seat rattan sofa.

Dylan waved the beam about, at the edge of the seating, and underneath the table. "I thought one of them would be here for sure."

"Me too. They won't be far, though. Let's not wait for them."

Dylan led him along the back wall with the flashlight low. They passed a broom, several potted plants, and a car battery. It took them twenty seconds to reach the end of the house.

"You've got a massive house. Is the second level as big as the first?"

"Almost."

Dylan turned right, away from the dwelling, and walked fifteen yards before stopping at a wooden structure. "Dad built the generator out here away from the house. The cables run underground and the timber walls keep the noise down, although it's pretty quiet, anyway."

"He's thought of everything."

Dylan took a key from his pocket and opened the padlock with a clunk, then swung the door outward. The bulky monster was illuminated in the gleam of the flashlight.

Callan whistled. "Nice. Looks brand new."

"Yeah, I don't think it's been used until recently."

Dylan passed the flashlight to Callan, then stepped inside and shuffled along the wall. He felt around, clicked several switches, then reached down and pressed a button.

The motor gave a lethargic whir, then stopped. He tried again without result.

"Gotta be the fuel," Dylan said, stepping forward. He unscrewed the fuel cap and they peered inside the tank. A bit of fuel puddled in one corner. "Empty. There might be some in the shed. My dad usually keeps a five-gallon can in reserve."

"We got some from the gas station."

"The shed's closer."

A noise sounded from the dark yard beyond. Their eyes met. Callan twisted toward it, carefully levering the round into the chamber, then lifting the rifle into place.

Dylan stepped out of the generator box and, taking the flashlight back from Callan, swept its beam out beyond the immediate garden. Something moved in the shadows.

"Shit, what was that?" Callan asked, stepping forward. His finger feathered the trigger. He was ready to go. Dylan brought the flashlight back and the beam washed over a pair of glassy eyes. "There."

The rifle exploded. The shot cracked through the silent night and rolled across the town, alerting the world to their presence.

Dylan leapt away. "Relax, mate, it's just a kangaroo. Take it easy." Gun smoke wafted between them. "They bounce around here at night."

Callan lowered the rifle. "Sorry. It just looked like something else. Can you put the flashlight back over there?"

Dylan directed the light to their left and saw the departing form of a medium-sized Eastern Grey kangaroo bounding off into the darkness. "Good chance if there are 'roos around, there won't be any zombies."

"Let's hope."

They passed through a garden bed and the flashlight revealed a shiny black fence surrounding a pool, the green water still and clear. Dylan moved the beam in an arc across the grassy yard, prodding the shadows for surprises. Ahead, the green steel shed beckoned; outside the doorway lay bodies with their severed heads nearby.

Dylan aimed the light at the closest one and held his breath. "That's Allan Henry from next door. He's in... was in high school. Just started." He walked around the body, probing it with the light.

"The other one is over there."

He swung the flashlight around and froze it on the second form. "She's bloated, her skin has changed color, and some of her hair has fallen out, but I'm pretty sure that's Karly, Allan's sister. Karly was older than Allan." His shoulders and face went slack. "She was a gorgeous girl. Beautiful and happy. My dad used to say he was going to adopt her as his own." Callan could read the sadness in his face. "If the one in the shed is female, it's probably Mrs. Henry."

Callan looked around and pointed past the shed to the dark shadows of the trees. "Their house is over that way?" Dylan nodded. "How far?"

"A hundred and fifty yards. Most of the properties up here are fifteen or twenty-acre blocks. Ours is twenty. There are not many houses out here, and that probably kept Mom and Dad safer for a bit longer. I wonder what happened to Mr. Henry, though?"

"Could he still be wandering around?"

"I don't know. I guess." Dylan fanned the light over a thick section of trees separating the properties. "See that little gate?" He pointed at a break in the fence and saw through into shadows, then deeper, to the large brick house where dark windows flashed.

"It's open." They stood waiting for something to appear. "We should close it."

They walked slowly, approaching the gate. Dylan swept the beam along the shadowy fence line. Callan was on edge after the kangaroo incident. His heart thumped and his mouth had gone dry. "Keep the light right on it." With the rifle poised, he stepped up and reached out, waiting for the attack, his skin prickling with terror.

His fingers clasped the cold metal. He pulled the gate shut with a soft slick, slid the bolt across, then stepped back.

"Let's go," Dylan said.

They walked away with slow, cautious steps, Dylan glancing back every five yards as though Mr. Henry might come rushing after them. A trail of blood led into the shed, and Callan entered first with the rifle ready, Dylan lighting his way.

"That's Mrs. Henry," Dylan said. He walked around the rectangular room, kicking objects aside with his foot, lifting others from stacks. From a shelf over the workbench, he took two pairs of heavy-duty leather gloves, donned one, then tossed the other to Callan. He picked out a white shovel with a large tray and stuffed it under his left arm, then took a long-handled type with a narrower head. "No fuel cans. You see any?"

Callan shook his head. "Let's get the fuel from the boat, then. I don't want to be out here any longer than we need to be."

"Good thing you didn't leave the trailer behind."

"Yeah, but I almost regretted it."

With the light at their feet, they crossed the grassy area toward the Jeep.

Callan said, "We should do something with the bodies tomorrow. They might attract others."

"Good idea. We have no idea how they sense things like that."

"Will the electric fences run once we get the generator working?"

"Everything will. Instead of running power cords, Dad installed a transfer switch, which links to the circuit board, and the generator connects to that."

"Brilliant," Callan said. "I'm impressed."

At the boat, they emptied the remaining items, placing three five-gallon cans of fuel out on the gravel against the house.

"Leave two of these here for now."

Dylan placed the tomahawk under his arm, took the fuel in one hand and the flashlight in the other. Callan fumbled with the rifle and two shovels. If they were ambushed, they would need to drop everything to fight.

In the distance, toward the town, a high-pitched cry sounded, followed by gunshots. They both stopped and looked out into the darkness. After a long moment, they continued onward to the generator.

11

"I need some more booze," Greg said from the sofa, his feet stretched out, a pillow underneath his head.

Sherry sat in an armchair reading one of the newspapers from the lounge room. "This is terrible," she said. "The newspaper claims the government tried to suppress details of the epidemic."

"You sound surprised," Greg said.

He slurred the last word. Bloodshot, drowsy eyes peered into space. Kristy wondered if it was the booze, the surgery, or the events of the day. She was reluctant to serve him more alcohol.

"I can give you some more pain-relief tablets," she said.

"Nup. Had three. They aren't doing any good. Need some more Scotch."

Kristy glanced at Sherry, who looked back at her with an apprehensive expression.

Sherry stood up and said, "Let me see what I can find." She held Kristy's stare, conveying that she didn't think it was a good idea, either.

Kristy sat at Greg's feet. "How do the stitches feel?"

"Okay."

"You were brave. Callan would have squealed." He gave a thin smile. "The ankle?"

"Sore, but I could still be out there helping the guys."

Kristy tilted her head. "If you don't rest it, you'll end up on crutches. They won't help you run away from zombies."

"Yeah, but that might not be such a bad thing," Greg said.

Sherry returned holding a bottle with a splash of Chivas Regal. "That's all I could find."

Greg scoffed, snatching the bottle away. He unscrewed the lid and drained it in one gulp, then dropped the empty on the table. It rolled off and clattered onto the hardwood floor.

Kristy stared. Greg closed his eyes and lay back. The behavior was unlike him. Usually, he became happier when a little drunk.

"What's wrong?"

"Nothing."

"I don't believe you."

"Okay. Don't."

Kristy felt a lump in her throat. Greg had never spoken to her like that. She glanced at Sherry, who raised her eyebrows and stood.

"I'll be back in a minute," she said in a low tone, and disappeared.

Kristy laid a hand on his arm. "There *is* something wrong. Tell me."

"I'm fine. Just tired."

Instinct told her to push it. "I don't believe you."

He opened his eyes and sat up. "Stop saying that. I don't *care*."

"Yes you do. You can't go from saying what you said today to…"

His eyes narrowed and heavy lines crossed his forehead. "Forget what I said. I'm stuck in here while your boyfriend is out there with my best mate. That's what I'm pissed about." He slammed his head down and rolled over, exposing his back.

Of course, Kristy thought. *You stupid woman.* "I'm sorry. I wasn't thinking."

"Just leave me alone."

She had no experience dealing with Greg in such a mood. He was normally so easy going. She felt his pain and it made her uneasy. She stood, contemplated saying more, then turned and walked out of the room.

Sherry had sensed Greg's mood too, and Kristy wondered what she thought. The flushing toilet drew her through the lounge room to a powder room at the base of the stairs. A pink candle sitting atop an antique buffet cast shadows on the wall. Sherry closed the bathroom door, wiping her eyes.

"What's wrong?"

"Nothing."

Kristy had just experienced what "nothing" really meant. If Sherry hadn't been crying, she had suddenly developed a bad case of the sniffles.

"Please, tell me. Whatever it is..." Maybe it was starting to catch up to all of them. It had been an incredibly emotional and challenging day. Their world had changed and no one, aside from Dylan, knew if their parents were alive or dead. Kristy had ended up in tears multiple times. Sherry hadn't cried yet. In fact, she had only ever seen Sherry cry once, after she had discovered her father screwing his secretary at his office.

Her cheeks glistened in the soft candle light, but her mouth remained closed. Kristy put a hand on her shoulder; Sherry stiffened, but she kept it there. "Come on," Kristy said. "I know today has been difficult. I feel like crying now. Is it your parents? Don't give up on them yet."

"It's not that," Sherry said. She took a deep breath. "I think I'm pregnant."

Kristy's hand fell away. "What? How? I mean, what makes you say that?"

"I'm late."

"That doesn't necessarily—"

"I'm *never* late. I'm on time every month, without fail."

"*Every month?*"

"I've only been late once before and that was when... I was pregnant."

Kristy's stomach dropped. "You were pregnant once before?"

"My father had it fixed. There was no way my parents would ever have let *that* happen."

"I can't believe Callan didn't tell me."

She looked away. "It was before Callan."

132

"Oh, sorry. That's none of my business. How long are you overdue?"

"Two and a half weeks."

"How do you feel?"

"Moody. Although I'm sure nobody has noticed anything different there. I've been a little nauseated in the mornings over the last few days. It's real. I know it. I can feel it."

"Were you having... sex around that time?" Sherry's face went red. It was the first time she had ever seen it happen. "Don't be embarrassed. Just because Callan's my brother—"

"Okay, I get it," Sherry said in a humorless voice. "Yes. Six or seven weeks ago."

Kristy rubbed her forehead. "Well, we need to get a pregnancy test from the drugstore."

Sherry nodded. Her face scrunched and she sucked in a quick breath. "Oh shit, Kristy. This is such a mess."

This time, when Kristy put a hand on her shoulder, Sherry didn't stiffen. On the back of what Sherry had told her today, it *was* a mess. Couples in a relationship crisis shouldn't have babies. But part of her felt joy. She was going to be an aunty and her brother would be a father.

"What sort of world will we be bringing a baby into?"

"Who knows what it will be like in nine months? Maybe things will have changed. When are you going to tell Cal?"

"Tonight. And I'll ask him to get me a pregnancy test when he goes into town tomorrow."

Kristy put an arm around her. "Come here." They hugged, but she knew that, for Sherry, it didn't feel normal.

12

The light bobbed alongside the back of the house, over neat garden beds speckled with ornamental rocks and stout plants. Dylan probed the flashlight into the darkness, looking for unexpected visitors.

They reached the generator and Callan let out a long breath, as though they had found another safety point. Every second brought the possibility of meeting another zombie, and only when they were safely inside again would he truly relax. They had waged this battle for just one day, and Callan didn't know how they were going to survive the emotional fatigue of worry, let alone the physical demands. Their lives had already been risked multiple times. He couldn't stop thinking about his mom and the notion that she was already dead. When he looked at it logically, that result came out every time.

Dylan lifted the can and guided the nozzle into the fuel tank opening. "It's a six-and-a-half-gallon tank. Should last a while."

When it had gurgled itself empty and the vapors had drifted away, Dylan shone the flashlight up close and pressed another switch. "Circuit breaker has to be off when you start it. Then you turn it back on when it's warmed up. Cross your fingers."

The engine whirred and then rumbled into life, hopping and jigging on the spot as it purged the cold.

"It's quiet," Callan said.

"Even quieter once it's warm and the door is shut. Give it a minute."

Callan realized he had spent more time with Dylan today than any other in his life. He no longer seemed so strange. He had done some handy work at the Army blockade, and again later, helping with the tire change. Like Callan, he had been scared, but he had hung in and finished their task. Callan admired that. Kristy had deep feelings for him too, and he trusted her judgment. Maybe

Callan had been wrong. Admittedly, part of his dislike revolved around the situation with their fathers. Aside from that, Dylan was proving to be a surprise. One issue remained unaddressed, though.

"Tell me what happened with Emma Sandhurst. No bullshit. Put it all on the table, right now. Clear the air."

Dylan smiled. "You're serious?"

"Fucking oath. I loved that girl."

"Sure. But I didn't, and I had no idea why she liked me."

"You didn't chase her?"

"*No.* I didn't have the balls to speak to her before then."

His response seemed honest, and it was true that Dylan had never been one of the cool kids in high school. He had spent most of his time studying.

"Why did you go out with her, then?"

"She was hot and she asked me. I thought I'd won the lottery." Dylan raised his eyebrows, his eyes wide with surprise. "Look, we've never been friends. You were good mates with Johnny and I hated him. I had no allegiance to you, and as far as I was concerned, you two had broken up. "

Callan suppressed the urge to defend Johnny. He couldn't think about him yet. It was all true, though. Callan had picked his friendships, and Dylan owed him nothing. Callan nodded. "Okay. I get that. And that's the truth? That's everything?"

Dylan hesitated. Concerning this incident, it was, and if he peddled that line, he felt he wasn't really lying. "I swear to you, that's exactly what happened with Emma."

"Okay." He stuck out his hand and Dylan gave a little smile, then shook it. The generator hummed peacefully beside them. "Will the fences be working now?"

"They run on the mains, so now that we have power, they should be."

Armed with the digging tools and weapons, they walked around the far side of the house, through another garden bed where the earth rose in a slight incline and flattened into a wide patch of lawn. Dylan stopped on the rise and waved the flashlight at the tennis court beyond, through the black chain link fence, and onto the trim grass surface. The white lines flashed in the glow.

He aimed for the corners and lifted the light high, pushing the yellow beam as far back as his height would allow. Callan felt his nerves stiffen, wondering if the flashlight would draw them, expecting to see a hunched over, lurching form materialize out of the shadows, or worse, one of the more savage ones with pulsing fury that would tear them apart before they could realize what was happening. He thought of the monster at the window with the blazing eyes, inspecting them as though they were meat in a butcher's shop.

They trudged along the side of the house, descending past the guest bedrooms. Dylan glanced in through the dark glass. As they approached the front of the house and saw the body lying on the lawn beyond the veranda, Callan stopped.

"What's wrong?" Dylan asked in a cautious voice.

"Are you ready for this? You don't have to do it. I can handle it." He looked off into the darkness. "Who knows, you might be asking me the same thing tomorrow."

Dylan drew in a deep breath. "No, I have to do it. I'll probably cry like a baby, but she's my mother, and she was wonderful and she deserves a proper burial."

Callan nodded. "Show me where to dig."

Dylan directed him to a spot in the garden between a large pink rose bush and a beautiful frangipani blooming with white and yellow flowers.

"These were her favorites," Dylan said. "She used to cover the frangipani in winter so the cold wouldn't kill it." He touched the flowers, deep in thought. "I helped her plant these when I was maybe... twelve. It was spring. I loved getting out into the garden with her. I think I saw how happy it made Mom, and I wanted that too." He stood with his nose close to the flowers, eyes closed, filling his head with the scent. "They smell so good. They even block out her odor if you stand close enough."

Callan stood aside, allowing Dylan the moment. His gut tightened, even though he had never met the woman. He put aside the thing whose head he had severed and listened to the memories and the love in Dylan's voice. In that moment, the two boys were closer than they had ever been. Callan knew that if it had been him standing there remembering his own mother, he would be a wreck. He admired Dylan more than he'd ever thought possible.

Dylan turned, wiping his eyes, and Callan saw his wet cheeks in the light.

In the distance, the flat crack of a rifle sounded. They both glanced up and looked out toward town, where several fires still burned. The sound repeated.

"Survivors," Dylan said. "Others like us."

"Yeah," Callan said with a slight grin. "Could be your old man. Might be mine." Dylan brightened. "Tomorrow's gonna be a big day."

"Let me dig first," Dylan said, picking up a shovel. He stuck the plate deep, loosening the dirt without removing any, and quickly fell into a rhythm until he had scuffed the surface.

"My turn," Callan said, stepping to his side. He dug the shovel deep and turned the first load of soil to the side of the hole.

They worked as a team, with Callan piling earth high until the ground was hard again, Dylan stepping in and loosening it. They set the flashlight at an angle so its beam shone directly on the grave, wasting little light beyond its boundary. Neither spoke, the pleasant silence of the night broken only by the occasional gunshot from the town center. When they were halfway done, Dylan took the flashlight and made a sweeping check of the garden and house. Callan saw more tears on his face.

He resumed digging, and Callan considered what to say or do, then realized that helping was what Dylan needed, and that no words could console him. He sent out more silent hope that his mother was safe and that the roles wouldn't be reversed soon.

In fifteen minutes, they had cut a deep enough hole. Callan stopped and peered back toward the body. "That'll do. I'll take care of this bit."

"Thanks," Dylan said, turning away.

Callan carried the flashlight to the body, trying to avoid looking directly at it. He took the legs and dragged it toward the hole. He stood with both feet aside and drew Dylan's mum into the grave until her dirty sneakers rested at the bottom. He laid her arms by her side and flattened her body onto the bed. He walked back to where the head lay, making note to wash the bloodstains off the grass tomorrow, then, holding his breath, picked it up and held it at a distance. In the grave, he placed it beside the neck, feeling the egg sandwiches rise and threaten.

When he stood up, Dylan was at his side, looking down at her and sobbing. "Thank you."

Without thinking, Callan clapped a hand on his shoulder. "Nobody should have to do this."

Dylan nodded. "I think there's a lot of shit we're gonna have to do that we shouldn't."

Callan took the shovel and mined a load of earth from the pile, then paused over the grave. "Okay to fill it?" Dylan pressed his lips tight and nodded. Callan emptied the soil over her feet, and began to load the grave from that end. Dylan turned away, still sobbing.

Callan spread the soil into a flat bed, covering her face. By the time Dylan turned back around, she had disappeared from view. With a lethargic motion, he picked up the long-handled shovel and dumped a plate full into the hole.

When they finished, Callan patted the top flat and asked, "You want to say a few words?"

"Wait," a female voice called out.

Callan looked up and realized the others had been standing on the veranda. Kristy led Sherry and a limping Greg along the decking and down the stairs to the grave. She went directly to Dylan and hugged him, burying her head beneath his neck. There was genuine affection in their embrace, and it broke the back of any belief Callan might have had about it only being a holiday romance.

He reached out for Sherry and she took his hand. Callan felt a tickle of pleasure, hoping it wasn't just the moment, and then his guilt washed it away, knowing Dylan's mother was lying at the bottom of the hole. They all stood in a line at the edge of the grave.

"I'm sorry, Mom," Dylan whispered. "Sorry you had to suffer like this, probably alone, without Dad, or me, or Lauren. You deserved better." He wiped his nose with his sleeve. "You were a wonderful lady. Sweet and caring, always putting others before yourself." He took a deep breath. "I miss you already." He reached down and took a handful of dirt from the small pile, then tossed it onto the grave. "Love you."

Callan felt pressure in his eyes. He grunted, took a deep breath through his nose, and then did the same. He regretted not knowing Dylan's mother. From his account, she sounded a lot like his own.

"We can make a cross tomorrow," Kristy said, sniffing away tears. Greg and Sherry followed.

"Let's go," Dylan said. "I just want to go to sleep and shut this all out for a few hours."

13

The clock read 8:52 pm. They had been awake for over fourteen hours, but it felt like a lifetime for each of them. The world as they knew it had ended, especially for Dylan. Greg had fallen asleep on the sofa after another round of painkillers; Kristy had covered him with blankets. The remaining four sat on the soft leather chairs in the lounge room under dimmed lights, thumbing through the newspapers and notes that Dylan's father had accumulated. The electricity ensured that the fridge, hot water system, and kettle all functioned. After taking showers, Kristy and Sherry had tied up their wet hair. The boys had followed, peeling their soiled clothes off and throwing them into another garbage bag for burning. Once they were all clean and in their underwear, Kristy had insisted they inspect each other for scratches or cuts. The girls checked each other, the boys vice versa, using Band-Aids to cover anything that looked like a nick.

"Is this really happening?" Kristy asked. "Is the world as we know it really gone?"

Dylan said, "For now, I guess. I mean, look at what my father wrote. Here's another section—day four. I missed it earlier. *People have stopped going to work. Only seventy-five of the four hundred and fifty staff turned up today. I had Gemma call some of them but not one person answered their phone. They're either sick or dead. We'll see how it goes tomorrow, but if it doesn't improve, and I suspect it won't, I'll have to shut the plant.*"

Callan read from one of the newspapers. "*We're working around the clock to make a vaccine, the Health Minister said today.* What a crock of shit. I doubt there's any fucking vaccine."

Kristy handed Dylan a new notebook. "I think this one is the continuation of the other."

Dylan opened the first page. "Oh shit, this is the last entry. *Today*," Dylan said, feeling a jolt of excitement. "*Heading into town to get some more fuel for the generator.*" He glanced up at Callan, who nodded. "*We've got nothing left and*

I can't wait any longer. Although we've only seen a couple of dozen out this way, I believe the electric fences turn them away, so I can't leave them off for long. Have to check on the Henrys next door when I get back. Haven't seen Rob for a few days now, and I know he went into town on the weekend." Dylan looked up again. "That answers our question about Mr. Henry."

"Maybe it was him," Callan said. "Maybe he got infected and came back and passed it on to his wife and kids."

"There's a bit more,' Dylan said. *"Margaret will stay at the house. Last time I took her, I was too busy worrying about her to concentrate on keeping myself safe. I know she will fight it, but here is the safest place for her.*" Dylan bit his lip. "That's one thing he was wrong about." He closed the notebook and laid it on the coffee table. "Kristy, how does it happen, then? Can we still get the virus?"

"You don't get bitten," Callan said. "That's a good start."

"It's hard to say, not knowing what kind of virus it is. I think the most important things are that we keep covered up with gloves and thick clothing and even go as far as wearing face masks if we have to kill any more of them."

"That's a good idea," Dylan said. "Stop ourselves from getting blood splatter in the face. I think there are some of those full-faced ones in the shed. My dad used them with the brush cutter."

"I think we should all get some sleep," Sherry said, standing. "My eyelids keep closing on me."

Callan put the paper down and pushed to his feet. "Good idea. We can read some more in the morning."

"Take one of the guest bedrooms up that way," Dylan said, pointing toward the back section of the house beyond the kitchen and family room.

"What about you and Kristy?" Callan said.

Dylan laughed. "I'll be in my own bed upstairs, and I'm sure we can find somewhere for Kristy."

Kristy said, "Give me a break, Cal. I'm not your daughter. It's none of your business where I sleep."

Callan pressed his lips together. "Fine. Let's use candles for now." He and Sherry disappeared into the hallway.

"You were right about your dad," Kristy said. "I'm glad we ended up here. Of course I want to make sure Mom and Dad are okay, but I don't think we would have made it there."

"I'm glad Callan saw reason in the end. This is the safest place to be. We're a long way out of town, and we have electricity, weapons, food, and clean water."

She looked at him with an unwavering gaze, and after a moment, Dylan looked away, as though she might see through him and discover he wasn't as wonderful as she seemed to think. "What's wrong?"

She stood, walked over, and sat on his lap. "How are you?" Her palm cupped his cheek. "How are you even handling this?"

"I think if my mom had died in the normal world, I wouldn't be coping the way I am. But because everything is so messed up… it hasn't really allowed me to stop and grieve."

"I'm sorry for that. It's not fair. She deserves—"

"No, no, I'm glad in a way. It kind of makes it easier for now. It doesn't mean I loved her any less because I'm not a wreck. I've cried for her and I'll probably cry some more. It's hard to accept because I haven't seen her. That thing that attacked me wasn't really her."

Kristy rubbed his back, and nestled into his shoulder. "You're very brave."

"And very tired."

"Me too. Where can I sleep?"

Her face was impassive. Dylan wanted her to stay with him in his bed, but she might get offended. After all, they had barely gotten out of the starting blocks. He decided to play it safe. "There's a spare room upstairs, not far from mine."

She nodded. "Okay. That sounds good."

Dylan began collecting the paper and notebooks into piles. Kristy grabbed his arms and pulled him close.

"Don't be silly. I thought you'd want me to stay with you, in your bed."

"I… of course," Dylan said, feeling his face flush. "I just didn't want to pressure you. But if that's what you want…"

"There's no pressure. We won't be having sex *tonight*, anyway. I just want you to hold me."

"Sure," he said, smiling. "Fine by me." And he was, for now. It had been the worst day of his life and he didn't want to spoil their first time. The idea of sleeping with Kristy both excited and scared him. She was far more experienced, and her expectations would be higher. Her charms had worked their way around his heart and with every hour, he found himself falling deeper for her. That meant the risk was greater, too, and he didn't want to mess it up.

He led her up the stairs by candlelight, her soft hand in his. They crept down a carpeted hall and into his bedroom, where he closed the door. There was a queen-sized mattress covered with a thick quilt, resting on wooden slats surrounded by four posts. Kristy fell onto it as Dylan placed the candle on an old wooden desk that had been his great-grandfather's. He adjusted the curtains at the edges to keep in the light.

"Ohhhh," she said, eyes closed, feigning sleep. "That feels sooooo good. I can't tell you how sick I am of that airbed. And a sleeping bag, too." Dylan sat on the edge and slipped his shoes off. Kristy rubbed a hand over his shoulder. "Lie down."

Bending forward, Dylan pulled his socks off and slipped his pants down, revealing boxer shorts. Kristy did the same, and they pulled the covers back and slid under, nestling into each other's recesses. Kristy put an arm over his chest and lay her head on his shoulder.

"I heard some good news before," she said. "Well, it depends on whose perspective you look at it from."

"Oh? We could all do with some good news." He pushed closer to her and tightened his arm around her body.

"I think Sherry is pregnant."

Dylan felt the air sucked from him. "What? Are you sure?" A barbed thought struck him.

"I know, it's a bit of a surprise, and the timing is terrible, but Callan will be so happy."

"Are you sure, though?"

"Based on what she says, it's plausible, but only a test will confirm it. I'm going to be an aunty."

Dylan tried to stay relaxed. This was bad news. Sherry had said she didn't love Callan any more, and that she was ready to break up with him. She had cheated with Johnny. What if the baby was Johnny's and not Callan's? He had acquired more of a liking for Callan today, something he never thought would happen. "The world is a changed place… probably not the best place for a baby."

"I know, but let them enjoy the moment for what it is. I know Sherry and Cal have been a bit distant of late, but this might bring them closer together."

You don't know the other half of it, Dylan thought.

He lay there for a long time thinking of how much their lives had changed in one day, wondering how they would ever get back on track.

14

Callan woke to the sound of Sherry vomiting. He sprung out of bed and rushed into the bathroom to find her hunched over the toilet bowl, heaving dry air.

"Are you all right?" She nodded and pitched again. "Do you want me to get Kristy?"

"No," she choked, raising one hand. "I'll be okay."

Callan feared seeing loved ones sick. His mother had contracted an unknown virus when he was young and he watched her suffer for weeks, until she eventually ended up in the intensive care unit. He immediately suspected something more sinister. "Was it something you ate? How long have you been feeling like this?"

Sherry coughed, flushed the toilet, and then stood up, wiping her mouth. "Only a couple of days. I'll be fine." She lurched to the edge of the bed and turned on the bedside lamp.

Callan drew the curtains open, throwing grey light into the room. Maybe Sherry was getting sick from the virus. What if she had caught it from the old guy or the soldier? He rubbed at his temples. "I'm gonna get Kristy. Throwing up isn't normal. I don't—"

"Sit down here," Sherry said, tapping the bed. "I've got something to tell you."

Callan didn't move. His skin prickled. She didn't look worried. Why wasn't she worried? "Not sure I like the sound of that." She gave him a weak smile. "Tell me it's good, after yesterday." He sat beside her and she took his hand in hers.

"It is." She smiled one of those soft, magnetic smiles, showing her beautiful white teeth and perfectly sculpted lips. "I think I'm going to have a baby," she said. "I think *we're* going to have a baby."

Callan couldn't breathe. A baby? *A baby.* They were going to have a baby. He had always wanted kids. His mother's maternalistic gene had passed to him, missing

Kristy. He reached out and squeezed Sherry with such force that she grunted.

"Go easy," she said with a smirk. "You'll squash the baby."

Callan let go immediately and drew back, looking at her stomach. "Shit. Sorry."

"It's okay. I don't know for certain yet, but I'm pretty sure. I'm never late. Not even two days. But I'm weeks over, this time."

Callan stood and walked over to the window, looking out at the spacious yard. This was not just good news—this was great. Sherry wasn't ill; she didn't have the virus. She had morning sickness. He had always imagined having kids with Sherry after they were married, little reddish-blonde haired girls to look after him when he was old. Although the timing was off, in one motion, this irrevocable bond had resolved the problem of their relationship falling apart. *Two for one,* he thought. What a relief. He dropped down onto the bed and started hugging her again. "I am so happy."

She smiled. "I can tell. But let's keep it quiet until I get a test, okay? I meant to tell you last night but... Kristy found me coming out of the toilet crying. I was a little upset by it all. The thought of..."

"No. Don't think like that. We'll get through it. I promise, I'll look after you guys. The both of you. You don't have to worry about a thing."

"Can you get a test from the drugstore? That will confirm it." He hugged her again, then she pulled away. "I've been a bit strange lately, Cal. I know that, and I'm sorry. I've been moody, distant. Even a bitch, at times."

He shrugged. "I've been worried. I won't lie. But doesn't pregnancy play with your hormones or something? Maybe that's the reason."

She smiled. "Maybe. To be honest, I didn't really know what I wanted. But this. *This* is what I want. You're going to be a great father. You're a good person and, although I don't think I deserve you, I know you'll take care of us."

Callan hugged her again and placed his lips softly against her smooth cheek. "Don't say silly things. I promise I'll take the best care of you and... the baby."

Downstairs, Callan found Dylan standing at the kitchen window with a pair of binoculars, peering out across the back lawn toward the shed and swimming pool. Despite the gloomy skies, it was mild and a little muggy—t-shirt weather, and in another life, they might have had a swim in the afternoon.

"What is it?"

"Just checking things out," Dylan said. "No kangaroos this morning. Come with me out onto the front veranda."

They passed Greg snoring on the sofa and slipped through the sliding doors onto the decking. Callan had to keep reminding himself to be quiet about Sherry's pregnancy. The excitement made him want to bounce around, and when Dylan gave him an odd look, he realized he *was* bouncing from one foot to the other.

Dylan stood at the corner of the balcony and scanned the lower section of the property. "Can't see anything besides sheep and goats." He rotated his gaze, covering the entire green paddock to the front gate.

"Any ideas about what to do with the dead ones?" Callan asked.

"I know my father buried the one he shot, but I'd rather burn them. There's a pile of brush down the front. We can leave them on there for now and light it later when the wind dies down."

"Okay. Then we head into town."

"I ain't looking forward to that."

They left the veranda and walked around the front of the house, past the Jeep, and across the grassy strip to the shed, where they found some leather gloves, the plastic face protectors, and the wheelbarrow. They lifted the first body and its head into the barrow, then rolled it down to the front paddock where Dylan's father had gathered a pile of tree branches and leaves. Normally, once the weather turned cold, he would burn the stack on a dark winter's night while family and friends stood around watching the bonfire. Callan made a space in the middle of the brush and Dylan tipped the zombie out into an awkward heap. They climbed the slope and did the same with the second and third zombies, piling spiky branches over them until they could no longer see the cracked skin or wispy hair of Mrs. Henry.

They dropped the wheelbarrow back at the shed and then walked past the tennis court to the northwest corner of the property. The corner abutted the Henry property and that of their other neighbors, the Roussos, a Greek family who had made their living producing small quantities of premium olive oil since the 1960s.

Beneath the shadows of a massive pine tree, they saw the grassless patch where Dylan's father had dug the grave. It should have been rough and lumpy, but instead, it was a gaping hole, with piles of dirt around its rim; as they peered into it, Callan felt his skin tingle. They glanced at each other, but neither seemed capable of finding the words.

"Where is it?" Callan asked. Dylan shrugged. "Could it have dug itself out?" The idea draped a cloak of anxiety over him. He thought of Dylan's mother.

Dylan said, "Maybe that's what got my mother."

Callan glanced around. "We should really be carrying a gun."

"That's a good point."

They turned away from the grave and started back toward the house. Talk of guns reminded Dylan of the shooting in town the previous night. "You know, we're not alone in this town. The gunshots we heard last night… others will be fighting for supplies, too. Dad only left a little bit of ammo. I hope Shaw's hasn't been cleaned out."

Inside, Callan went to check on Greg, who was still on the sofa with a blanket over his head. He peeled it off and asked, "You awake?" Greg groaned. "How's the leg?"

"Sore. I got up to take a piss before and almost collapsed. Got any more booze? It's the only thing that makes it feel any better."

"You wish."

Kristy walked in and went straight up to Dylan, giving him a hug. Callan felt himself tense. He hadn't asked Dylan, but suspected they might have slept together. He tried not to think about it and focused on Sherry and his good news.

"Morning," he said.

Kristy slipped Greg's sock off and inspected his ankle. "Still heavily swollen. You really have to stay off it, Greg. Keep it elevated."

"But I'm bored lying here all the time."

"There's no other choice. Until the swelling goes down, you can't put weight on it. I'll put some more cream on it to try to bring out the bruising." She slid the leg of his pants up and grimaced when she saw the stitches.

"What is it?"

"I don't like the look of this, either."

Callan joined her. "What's wrong with it?"

"Nothing yet, but it looks a little red. Dylan, do you have any antiseptic cream in your medicine cabinet? I used all of mine up at the lake."

Dylan disappeared for a minute and returned empty handed. "Nothing. I'm sorry."

Kristy continued inspecting the wound. "Whoever goes into town today will need to get some cream. How do you feel?"

"Shithouse," Greg said.

"What about… flu symptoms? Any aches and pains? Trouble breathing?"

His eyes narrowed. "A bit warm."

They gathered on the seats around the kitchen bench while Dylan made a breakfast of baked beans, tinned spaghetti, and poached eggs. They ate with plates resting on their knees. Orange juice from a plastic bottle in the cupboard and freshly crushed coffee beans, brewed in the kettle, washed it down.

"We have enough food for another day," Dylan said. "Unless we can find some stuff at one of the grocery stores."

"So what's the plan?" Sherry asked. Callan had his arms wrapped around her from behind. "And who's going?"

Callan had not stopped thinking about his parents and the probability of their survival. On the trip back, he had insisted on checking their home first, certain that any delays in reaching them might add to the peril. But the more he learned, the more he grew to realize that the chances of them surviving were slim. In all likelihood, all of their relatives and family were dead. Until he knew, though, he retained that minuscule chance of the opposite, and therefore couldn't yet grieve. Today, he would find out.

"I guess I made such a big deal yesterday about going home first that we should start off there. Then check each of our families, see if anybody is still alive. But I don't think we should all go."

"I'm not staying here," Greg said. "I wanna know if my grandparents are all right."

Callan put his hands up, palms aimed down. "Hold on, mate. Under normal circumstances, you'd be the first person in the world I'd want with me. But your leg is fucked. What are you gonna do if we get attacked or chased?"

Greg shrugged. "I'll shoot the fuckers."

Callan smirked. Typical Greg. He had no doubt the big guy would do it, too, but the risk was too much, for all of them. "I know. But I think I have a better idea. I propose just Dylan and I go—"

"Hang on," Kristy said. "What if you find people that need treatment? Wouldn't it be good to have a doctor with you?"

"Yeah. It would be great, but what if we find three people who we need to bring back with us? If you come along, we only have two seats left. This is primarily a check on our families to see if anyone is still alive. If Mom and Dad are alive, we bring them right back, then go to the next house."

"What about relatives?" Sherry asked. "I'd like to know about Grandma. Even my auntie and uncle."

"I don't know, babe. I don't think we have the luxury of time or safety to be checking too many places at this point. Maybe just our parents first, or in Greg's case, his grandparents." Sherry looked away and Callan rubbed a hand on her back.

"I need some more supplies from the pharmacy," Kristy said.

Sherry nodded. "Me too." Callan smiled.

"Greg stays here with you and Sherry. He's the best with a gun. Dylan's father has a Winchester we'll leave with you. We'll take the two Remington rifles, but we should stop by Shaw's Hunting Store. Hopefully, whoever is running around out there hasn't taken all the ammo."

"I don't like it," Kristy said, looking at Dylan. "So far we've done everything together, as a group. We've survived like that. All this driving around, stopping at places. It's risky."

Dylan took her hand. "It is, but these are things we need to do. Once they're done, we can fortify ourselves here and have a better chance of surviving for the long term."

Greg climbed off the sofa and tottered on one leg, testing his balance.

"I just told you to stay on the sofa," Kristy said.

He sneered, and shuffled a step. "I have to piss again. Besides, if you're leaving me here, I'm gonna need some more grog. I'm not gonna lie on that sofa all day twiddling my thumbs." He shuffled over to them with little steps. "Dylan, where's the booze cabinet?"

Dylan pointed toward the lounge room. "On the far wall."

They all watched him leave, Callan raising his eyebrows. "Let him go. He's dealing with shit."

"We all are," Sherry said. "What makes Greg so special?"

Kristy said, "If the wound has an infection, he'll be feeling unwell."

Greg shuffled back into the room holding up a fresh bottle of Johnny Walker Red. He broke the seal, unscrewed the lid and threw it on the table, then turned the bottom up and gulped down a shot of Scotch. He let out a satisfied breath and fell into the sofa.

"Don't go too hard on that stuff," Callan said. Greg shot him a look he had never seen before.

"My fucking leg is killing me. I'm supposed to sit here all day and do nothing?"

He had never seen Greg so pissed. Perhaps leaving him alone with the girls wasn't the best idea. Greg took another swig, looking out through the sliding doors onto the garden and lawn. He wore a scowl and his eyes were red.

"Okay. But the girls might need you—"

"How? I'm fucking useless, aren't I?"

Callan felt a stab of tension. Their relationship had always been one of fluent agreement. They had rarely clashed. He felt uneasy, nervous. Their friendship was part of his being. If Callan had a brother, he wouldn't have been closer than Greg. He glanced around at the others and nodded his head toward the lounge room. They slowly left.

He sat on one of the armchairs. "What's wrong, mate?" Greg narrowed his eyes and frowned. "Are you for real?"

Callan opened his mouth but wasn't sure what to say. After a few moments, he said, "I'm your mate. I genuinely want to know what's wrong." Greg's mouth pressed into a thin, tight line, but that didn't stop his top lip from quivering. He rubbed his prickly cheeks.

"Aside from the fucking obvious, I've killed four zombies that were people a few days ago. By my calculations, my grandma and grandpa are dead, and the girl I've loved since before I knew how to swear has hooked up with another bloke. I've sprained my ankle and can barely walk, I fell on the axe and split my shin open, and I'm probably infected with a virus that will turned me into a zombie like the ones I killed while saving everyone's ass. I suppose it doesn't matter, though, because if I am infected, I'll be dead in a day. Have I missed anything? Oh yeah, and my best mate has replaced me with his future brother in-law."

Callan rocked back in his seat, eyes wide. "Whoa, man. Whoa. First, you're not infected."

"But you don't know that."

"Well, I don't think you are." Greg looked away. "Most of the blood on your jeans was your own. We got you inside pretty quickly. Kristy did a great job cleaning it up. Who better to have on hand than a doctor? You're not infected."

"Are you saying that to calm yourself or me?"

"Me. And you. But I fucking believe it mate, I really do." Greg took a long breath, let it out, and then swallowed another mouthful of Scotch. The bottle was already a quarter empty.

"Man, you should go easy on that stuff. I don't know how well it goes with the painkillers."

"Who gives a fuck? Everything is hurting. This stops it."

"But surely—"

"I don't wanna drink. Honestly." His bloodshot eyes grew glassy. "I still remember my old man throwing up on me when I was a kid. But he wouldn't let me clean it up until I got him another bottle." He gnashed his teeth. "I fucking *swore* I wouldn't be the same. *Swore it* to myself. And look at me. I'm…" He paused, swallowing to gather the words. "I'm a disgrace." Callan pressed his own lips together, fighting emotion. Greg continued. "I wonder what hope I had, though. You know how old I was when I had my first drink?" Callan shook his head. "Eight. He made me have a sip and I pretended I liked it, and then I had to drink a six-pack. Fuck, was I sick."

Callan grimaced inside. "I'll be honest; I don't know how you've done it. How you've stayed so normal, and reliable. I admire you so much for even making it to where you are." Greg nodded in acknowledgement. "As for the other stuff, I'll never replace you, even if you hate me, and if you've liked Kristy for that long and didn't do anything about it…"

Greg looked down, and gave a curt nod. "Fair enough."

"We'll check your grandparents' house today, and if they are alive, we'll bring them back. I promise you that." Greg took another swig, then set the bottle on a side table. Callan needed something else to shift Greg's attention. He paused, then leaned forward and said in a hushed voice, "We're pretty sure Sherry's pregnant. You're going to be an uncle, mate."

For a second or two, he thought Greg wasn't going to react. A cold look gripped his eyes, a look that spooked Callan. Then his rocky face cracked and a sweet smile unfurled. "No shit?" Callan shook his head. "Good job, man." He reached out a long arm and opened his hand. "Congratulations."

Callan shook it with a firm grip. "Thanks. But keep it quiet. I have to get a pregnancy test from the pharmacy so she can confirm it. She sounds sure, though." Greg nodded. "You good to go?"

"Yeah. I'm okay."

15

Kristy and Dylan embraced by the lounge room window, looking out at the garden and paddocks beyond. So far, she had only seen kangaroos and rabbits.

"I wish we didn't have to go," Dylan said. "But nothing is going to keep Callan away from your parents' house, and we need supplies."

"I can't even think about my parents at the moment." She glanced up, grimacing. "Sorry. You're incredibly brave to keep going like you are."

"I'm trying not to think about it. Everything that's happened has been so bizarre; part of me still doesn't believe she's dead." He shook his head. "I know she is, though, and at some point I'm probably going to lose it. But if I stop and get lost in that now, I won't be of any use."

They hugged again, a soft, warm embrace that turned into a clingy squeeze, Dylan trying to convey his feelings: his appreciation for Kristy's concern, and maybe even love. The night had been sweet, comfortable, no sex, but they had lain cuddling through the depths of their sleep, waking in the same position.

"I'll be fine," he said.

"I'm scared, though. Really scared."

Dylan had felt anxious since waking. The prospect of facing hordes of zombies terrified him. Three had been frightening, but what if they came across a mob like the ones they had seen the previous night? He couldn't think about it, the same way one didn't think about the inevitability of dying one day. He was committed to helping Callan check his parents' house, and since the others were staying behind, checking on their families, too. "Just focus on what needs to be done here. Keep an eye on Greg. Be his doctor." She nodded. "You could make this place a bit more secure, too."

"Like what?"

"Maybe board the windows? There are some old fence palings in the shed. Plenty of hammers and nails."

"We'll turn your house into a fort."

"Exactly. I think this is the safest place for us now. We've got everything we need right here."

They looked into each other's eyes, then Dylan tasted the familiar sweetness and texture of her lips, his head swimming in delight. He wanted to kiss her all day, to savor it. Being with Kristy felt *right*. Better than anything he'd experienced before. When they broke apart, he tightened his arms around her again.

"I just have to run upstairs," Kristy said. "Meet you in the kitchen?" He nodded.

"So what's the plan?" Dylan asked, entering the family area.

"Simple," Callan said, loading both Remington rifles. "Sherry's house first. We bring them back here. Then we go to my house, and then Greg's, which is probably the furthest away."

Dylan expected that they'd find the houses empty, but tried to suppress the pessimism. "And then?"

Callan shrugged. "We need more ammo and food. Sherry is making a list. I have to get some stuff for her at the drug store, too."

Dylan's stomach turned. He watched Callan stuff an arm into one of his father's leather jackets. *The poor bloke*, he thought. Part of him wanted to tell Callan, but he knew it wasn't his responsibility and would be badly received. They might be forming a relationship, but they weren't mates yet. Only Sherry could tell him the truth.

Sherry appeared from the walk-in pantry with a notepad and pen. "Anything you want, tell me and I'll add it to the list."

"Booze," Greg called out, still resting on the sofa in the other room. He seemed to have dragged himself into a more content mood since his discussion with Callan. "And some food."

Callan disappeared toward Greg. Dylan watched Sherry making notes.

She glanced up and said, "Don't look at me like that."

"What a mess. What a *mess*, Sherry." His voice became quiet, constrained. "How did this happen? Is it even Callan's kid?"

With gritted teeth, she said, "Shut up. I told Kristy not to say anything."

"Why did you even tell me about Johnny?"

In a rush, she said, "I don't know. I wasn't sure I was pregnant yesterday."

Dylan rubbed his temples. "Are you sure about it?"

"Yes, but Callan is still getting me a pregnancy test from the drugstore."

"You better hope you're wrong."

Sherry placed the notepad and pencil down on the bench. "Fuck you, Dylan. The world has changed, in case you haven't noticed. Callan has always wanted children. There might not be anybody left on the planet who can do that for him." She stiffened and raised her chin. "I know it's not right, but I don't feel as guilty about Johnny, giving him this."

"You keep telling yourself that."

Sherry turned away, and a burning anger rose in him. He had to force it down by clenching his jaw. He hated secrets. Working beside Callan and knowing such life-changing things meant he could never drop his guard, else he inadvertently say something. He walked away and veered into the laundry.

Hanging on a plastic hook beside the back door were the black gloves his father often used to handle split wood. Dylan took them down and examined the thick, impervious material. He recalled his father buying this pair because he'd always get splinters. He had said nothing could get through the material.

In the family area, he showed the gloves to Callan. "What's this material?"

157

Callan felt the material. "Kevlar. It's a synthetic fiber. They use it to make all sorts of armor, sports equipment, even tires. Where did you find them?"

"The laundry. Dad used them for moving wood."

"Got another pair?"

"I think he had another pair, but I'm not sure where they would be."

Sherry came from the kitchen with the notebook and pen. She opened it to a page thick with writing. "It's got what everyone said and whatever else I could think of. Bottled water, in case we have to travel at some point, any tinned food like baked beans, canned meat—"

"Canned meat?" Greg asked with a pinched face. "That shit's filthy."

"It's also highly processed, which means it will keep for a while, and is full of protein," Kristy said.

Sherry continued. "Even stuff like tins of corn, beetroot, basically anything in a metal can. Energy bars, cereal bars, health bars, multivitamin tablets. There should be containers of them. The multivitamins will supplement our lack of fruit and vegetables."

"What about the orchard out near Cabramurra?" Greg asked. "I've driven past it a hundred times in the last few months on the way to the Army base and back. It has heaps of fruit. And the fields out near Palmers Road. They've got vegetables."

"We could probably drive out there," Callan said.

Sherry continued. "Any non-perishable meat. Beef jerky, even hot dogs. They need to stay cold, but they keep for months and have already been cooked. Peanut butter, nuts, sultanas, and candy. As much candy as you want. Great for energy."

Kristy chuckled. "Then we'll need toothpaste to brush our teeth even more."

"What about non-food items?" Callan asked.

Sherry nodded, brushing a strand of auburn hair from her face. "I've made a separate list for that." She opened a second folded sheet. "Candles—we'll run out of them soon—matches, any extra flashlights, batteries in every size, preferably lithium, but see if you can find one of those chargers *and* the batteries that go with it."

"What about two-way radios?" Kristy asked. "We might be able to pick up a broadcast. And first-aid kits; they sell them in little packs you carry in your car. I've still got some supplies, but you can never have enough of that stuff."

"That's good," Callan said, turning to Dylan. "We need to check out Shaw's Hunting Shop. Besides guns and ammunition, knives will help, and I need some of those Kevlar gloves."

"What about leather clothes?" Dylan asked. "Pants and more jackets if we can find them."

"Hang on," Callan said. "Motorbike clothing is made from Kevlar. What about the motorbike shop on Young Street?"

Sherry's pen sped over the page, trying to keep up with the ideas. She stopped, shook her hand and asked, "Anything else?"

Callan shook his head. "We might need a bigger car."

"What about the boat?" Sherry said.

Dylan said, "It's too noisy. Maybe we should think about a bigger vehicle." Callan frowned, his deep-set eyes narrowing. "I mean, if everyone is dead, we can pretty much take whatever car we need."

Sherry lowered the notepad and let out a long sigh. "So this is it? We're making a survival list. Is the world as we knew it really finished?"

"That happened last night for me," Callan said. "When the Sirellis died on Main Street. That was the end."

"Yeah," Greg said. "That was bad."

For Dylan, it was all of it—from the gas station, to the old man who shot himself, the soldiers, and the zombies on the streets. It had been like a nightmare, horrid and surreal. But seeing his mother had been the tipping point.

They had buried the old world with her in the front garden, and they could never get it back. "Mom," Dylan said. "That was it for me."

They all hung their heads.

After a moment, Callan stood. "We should go. If we don't make it back before dark, close all the curtains and only use a few candles."

"Why wouldn't you make it back?" Kristy asked.

"I'm sure we will. I'm just saying."

"I don't care if you come back empty-handed, as long as you come back."

Callan said, "We will. We won't risk anything." Sherry tore the paper from the notebook and handed Callan the two lists. "We need the other notebook too, the one with all the information about the zombies."

Their departure was swift and uneventful, as though making a bigger deal of it might jinx them. In the family area, Kristy wrapped her arms around Dylan's neck and kissed his mouth with full lips. It aroused him and he had to pull away. She leaned forward and whispered in his ear. "I promise you, there's a lot more of that if you come back safely."

Dylan smiled because he felt the tightness rising in his throat, the kind that carried tears. He turned away, glancing at Callan and Sherry who embraced softly. The secret jumped into the forefront of his mind. He had to drive it away, knowing the knowledge of Sherry's cheating ways could undermine the operation.

Callan shut the sliding door behind them, giving the others a curt wave, and then it was just the two of them, the gravel crunching under their feet as they headed for the Jeep, which was now unhooked from the trailer. Callan pulled the back seats forward, creating a larger storage space for whatever supplies they might find, and then jumped in the front, his leather jacket squelching.

"Did you get those face masks?" Callan asked.

"In the back."

160

The engine kicked over and Callan accelerated down the driveway. There were no problems at the gate this time, and both boys pushed it open and locked it back in place. Dylan checked the electric fence with a quick touch and received a mild shock through the Kevlar gloves.

"Dad always kept the grass and weeds short under the fence; otherwise, it grounds out and won't work. We'll have to keep the grass trimmed."

They drove at a reduced speed, eyeing the paddocks and roadside vegetation. A slate sky stretched above, but showed no clouds to signal rain.

They were halfway along Silvan Road when they spotted it in the long grass to the side of the dirt strip. It knelt over a cow that had broken loose from one of the paddocks; its head was buried inside the large carcass. As they rolled past, the thing withdrew and turned toward them. Its thick brown hair had started to thin, and blood covered the pale, dead flesh on its face, dripping in thick, viscous gobs. Dylan thought of his mother's own gory expression again. Had his father suffered the same fate? He would be looking out for signs of him or his car.

Callan pulled the Jeep into the long grass. "That's just too fucking close to the house for me. It could walk there in ten minutes." He lifted the Remington .308 bolt action from beside the seat and handed it to Dylan. "Show me how it's done, mate."

Callan took the axe from the floor and they swung out of the Jeep.

They crept along the gravel road toward the zombie, which once again had its head stuck in the cow. Dylan stopped about twenty yards away. He hadn't used the .308 since early on in the trip, preferring to use the Savage shotgun for rabbits. The zombie's head jerked and writhed as it fed, then it perked up, sniffing the air before burying itself again. He thought of the others he had battled with the axe and didn't feel the same level of discomfort and apprehension. They were no longer human; if he didn't kill them, he'd be turned into one.

He lifted the rifle and lined the sight, touching his finger to the trigger.

"In the head."

When the zombie's skull centered on the sight, Dylan gave the trigger a gentle squeeze, maintaining his tight grip, anticipating the recoil. The rifle exploded, stinging his ears and jerking his arms high. To the right, a clump of weeds behind the zombie exploded, kicking up dust and grass.

"*Shit,*" he said. "That was pathetic."

The zombie sat up again, its mouth open and hissing. Turning toward them, it grunted and began to rise. Its lower jaw appeared to be gone, revealing bone and gore, dripping blood. "Jesus," Dylan whispered, frozen. It stood, smelling them with its upturned nose. It wore a navy blue police uniform and was undoubtedly male, perhaps taller than Greg, with a solid chest and torso. They would both have a problem if it got hold of them. It started forward with a shuffle, scratching its tattered shoes on the dirt road.

"Come on," Callan said.

Dylan felt the seed of panic reach up from his gut. He engaged the bolt, raised the gun again, and sighted on the shambling monster. *Easy does it. Just like* Call of Duty. *Don't anticipate the recoil before it happens,* he reminded himself. The gun boomed and the zombie's left shoulder jerked backward, blood bursting from the wound. It staggered, tottered, and slowed.

He levered the next round, clenching his jaw.

Callan swung the axe up into a baseball grip. "Come on, don't make me use this."

The moaning zombie shook his head, sending blood flying off in flecks, then leaned forward and broke into a shuffling run.

Dylan's heart raced now, thundering in his chest. He recalled his father telling him many years ago to *be* the bullet and watch its course in his mind before the shot. He did this now, flying from the barrel of the gun and torpedoing through the air, hitting the zombie in the right eye and puncturing its brain. "Just a little higher, and a little to the left," he said, squeezing one eye tight.

A loud crack sounded and the gun recoiled. The right side of the monster's head exploded, flesh and blood bursting outward like the rotten spoil of soft fruit. It grunted, spun off balance, and collapsed backward to the dusty road with a crunch.

"Yes," Callan said. "Nice one."

Dylan let out a long breath. The zombie groaned, and one heel kicked at the road in an attempt to stand. "It's not bloody dead."

They crept forward, Callan with the axe raised, Dylan with the rifle in position. The zombie's googly eyes stared up at the sky; one hand twitched, as though groping for something. Dylan raised the gun and took aim.

This thing wasn't human. It wasn't even an animal, with feelings and thoughts. You couldn't keep it as a pet, and none of the virtuous human characteristics remained. In the hierarchical structure of organisms on earth, this thing had no position. No importance or function. Dylan pulled the trigger, and this time he struck the zombie in the eye. Its head exploded, painting the road with crimson stew.

16

They rode in silence for a time before Dylan opened his father's small notebook. "Have you read any of this?"

"A little." Callan had glanced through it. There were general notations about things Dylan's father had seen, limited at first to distant observations and comments from those he had spoken with in town who had witnessed more.

"He calls them 'feeders'," Dylan said, "not zombies, although he believes the ones that come back in this state have technically died. Says here that Doug Edwards from the hunting store saw someone die in the final stages of the virus. They actually died. No pulse. But within minutes, they were awake, alive, walking around. He said you wouldn't have known."

"Jesus."

"I think maybe the old guy was in this state, the one who killed himself. Dad also says, from what he can gather, the blood and flesh of other living entities keeps them alive, that it satisfies the fundamentals of the virus."

"All they care about is feeding. Feeders." It sounded appropriate.

"According to my father, there are three types. The basic level that has zero mental faculties. They eat, and when they have consumed everything, they look for the next thing to eat. They will even eat themselves if desperate enough for food."

"Like the ones we saw last night in town, fighting each other."

Callan braked the car at the intersection of Silvan and Starling Road, and glanced both ways. He almost didn't see them. "There." On the left, wandering aimlessly around the front lawn of a wide property was a small pack of zombies. They might have been from the crowd they'd seen outside Sirelli's. Shirts open and torn. Hair thinning.

One of them held an arm or leg in its hands, gnawing at it as if it were a big chicken wing.

"Do we kill them?"

If they stopped for every zombie, they might never reach town. These were a good hike from the property and, even if they shambled up Silvan Road, Callan thought he and Dylan would beat them back. "No. If they head toward home, we'll catch them on the way back."

He found humor at the notion of calling Dylan's house "home," but the reality was that they had nothing else. He didn't expect to find much in town. Although he was closer to knowing if his parents were safe, the idea made him uneasy. He had argued for going home since the beginning, but that had been before they'd known anything. Now he almost wished it wasn't imminent, that he could delay it further and avoid the knowledge. The truth scared him. He was certain they were either dead or diseased. Dead was probably better.

They pulled away from the zombies and accelerated down Starling Road. Dylan opened the notebook again.

"Dad says, *In all likelihood, they will decimate the food source and then move on to the next location where food is available.'* Does that mean they're going to eat everything in town and then move further out, looking for more?"

Callan nodded. As if on cue, they saw two feeders hobbling along the footpath. Three houses further, another stood in a front yard, drooling as it stared into a drying shrub. "I guess that makes sense."

More zombies appeared as they navigated along the streets toward Sherry's house: men and women, even children, with their bloody, torn clothes and thinning hair. They were stuck in front gardens, wandering in driveways, and out on the road. Callan didn't try to mow them down, but wasn't swerving to miss, either. The occasional car sat discarded in the street, and once he had to take the Jeep up onto the curb to get through a pileup. Among it was another Army truck, lying on its side, the bed empty.

They took Groves Lane out past the football field toward Old Gap Road. Dylan continued reading, thumbing the pages back and forth. "The other classes sound a lot worse. He says the second type is more aware of its existence than the first. They can fight back and sometimes carry a weapon, but they're still slow and can't really chase. You can still kill them fairly easily."

"What about the third type?" Callan thought he knew what the explanation might be.

"I think this is probably the one we saw at the car. He says they're smart, calculating. Insane. '*If you see one of these, run.*'"

"He looked like a scary motherfucker."

Dylan said, "I feel like I'm walking around in a dream half the time. It's like I'm in another person's body, in another world. It isn't what I had planned for my life."

Callan understood the feeling. "I know. What did you wanna be when you were growing up?" Dylan gave a puzzled expression. "Kristy and I used to play this game when we were kids. It was a fantasy thing about what we were gonna be when we were adults. Hers was always the same. A doctor." He drifted off in thought, remembering them as children.

"What was yours?" Dylan said.

Callan smirked. "A policeman. I always wanted to be a cop. I thought protecting people and putting the bad guys away was the most honorable thing in the world."

"What happened?"

"I guess my father tainted that image. His opinion of the law was pretty low, probably because they nabbed him for breaking it so many times. I've learned a thing or two over the last few days about my father's perspective on life. What about you?"

"A video game developer." Dylan laughed. "*My* father wasn't too impressed with that. He had me running the family business by the time I was twelve. Anything else was a fantasy."

"That'd be cool."

"Maybe one day, when the world gets back to normal, you could be a cop."

"Let's hope I have that chance."

The roads leading to the court in which the house was situated were almost empty. They pulled into the vacant driveway and filled their pockets with ammunition. Callan took the Remington .30-06 pump action and Dylan stuck with the bolt-action rifle. "What do you think we're gonna find? Not just here, but the other places?"

"Hopefully nothing. Sherry's parents were wealthy and connected. They might have fled to one of their holiday homes before the virus took hold. Greg's grandparents were elderly. I think they probably got sick early on. I'm trying not to think about my parents, but if I'm honest..." He glanced at Dylan. "I just hope they're dead.

Sherry's house was empty, except for the note from her parents telling her they *had* gone to their holiday house in Byron Bay, and that she should follow them the moment she found the letter. Callan debated leaving it there and not telling her but decided against it, reasoning that they must all be free to make their own decisions in such a crisis. He didn't think Sherry would be silly enough to want to chase after her parents, but she'd want to know they might be safe.

As they slipped back into the Jeep and flipped their facemasks up, Dylan saw two zombies in the side mirror, lurching down the middle of the road. They turned slowly, observing.

"Where to?" Dylan asked.

"Home."

As they drove the long way around to 33 Graham Street, Callan kept tightening his hands around the steering wheel. He'd been chasing this moment for the last twenty-four hours. Now that it was upon him, however, he didn't want it. He knew the answer. Knew it in the pit of his stomach. *Knowing* it, though, might send him over the edge.

He thought about sending Dylan in first. If it was bad, they could drive off and he would live with the knowledge, but his memories would remain intact. What he found at home might define the rest of his life.

His parents lived in a four-bedroom single-story place on the outskirts of the town center. It was a quiet street where Callan had grown up playing football and cricket with the other kids on a daily basis. Most of the neighbors had known each other for thirty years, had shared Christmas parties, New Year's Eve, and Australia Day barbecues. Some of them gave birthday presents to each other's children and received wedding invitations. They had fought bushfires together, floods, and council members. Some had died of terminal illnesses, others had divorced—but now, as Callan turned down Graham Street with his heart beating a stiff drum in his chest, none of that mattered. It appeared that the residents of Graham Street shared something else entirely.

Callan stopped the Jeep seventy yards from the house. Up and down the road, they gathered in small groups, eating, fighting, crawling, and trashing. A body lay on the front lawn of a house that boasted a tall, yellow and white 'FOR LEASE' sign. Eight or nine zombies crawled around it, jostling for position. The ones at the front gorged themselves on bloody entrails. Callan could not distinguish if the "food" was human or zombie. Farther along, three or four of them stood outside of the Mitchells' wide front widow, staring into the house.

"You think they're looking at something inside?" The unnerving thought that Richard and Sarah, the middle-aged couple whom Callan had known since he was five, were still within, chilled his skin.

"Drive," Dylan said. "Don't hit any of them, though. It will draw attention."

Callan navigated the Jeep slowly along the road. The Davidsons' house stood toward the end of the street where few of the feeders had gathered. A lone figure wandered past as Callan turned the car into the driveway, but it seemed disinterested. A modest, faded red brick house stood before them, its orange-tiled roof speckled by mold and dirty brown bird droppings. Once-white windowsills were now chipped and peeling, revealing withered grey wood beneath. The front lawn looked like a paddock, unmown for a month at least, and the sight formed a knot in Callan's chest. He swallowed and had to cough to clear his dry throat.

They watched the front and side mirrors as others ambled past in random, lurching movements. When the last zombie had disappeared from view, Callan glanced up and down the street. "We're good. Get ready." He cracked his door open enough to slip his foot onto the pavement. "We go over the side fence and around the backyard, through the laundry door." Dylan nodded, adjusting the rifle. "You realize we could get into some shit leaving the car here?"

Dylan shrugged. "Shit here, shit there. We'll be in some shit wherever we go." He flipped his facemask down and said, "Let's go."

The fence was five feet high and eight feet wide, a strip of palings between the house and the property line. Callan went over by leaping hard against it with a smack and lifting his foot up onto the flat board across the top until he was sitting on it. He slid his right leg down the other side and swung his left leg over, then using his hands to balance himself on the top, dropped the two feet onto a pathway made of small white pebbles. Dylan handed him the two guns and copied the move, glancing back over his shoulder to an empty street.

Callan's heart raced. He needed to piss and thought it was probably just his nerves getting to him. The stones crunched beneath their feet as they trotted along the side of the house until they reached the door. Callan peered into the laundry room and saw a pile of dirty linens on the square, patterned tiles. Glancing in either direction, he took his car keys from his pocket and singled out one silver piece. It took him two attempts, but he got the door open, swinging it too hard and snatching at the handle to stop it from hitting the wall. He waved Dylan inside and then closed it behind them with a soft click.

They stood in the laundry, grasping their guns in readiness. Callan stepped to the front with the pump action raised and poked the door open with the barrel. He couldn't believe the time had arrived. In a few moments, he might see his parents. Part of him wanted to call out, tell them he was there, that he had come to save them. He had been building to this point since the discovery at the gas station. Now, after the horrors they had seen, it seemed an anti-climax.

He stepped through the doorway into the kitchen, where brown laminate covered an island bench. No one was visible there, or beyond in the family room. On the counter lay a scattering of photos. Callan picked up the closest one and felt a cold shiver skitter up his back. The first had an amber hue, reminiscent of images from the 1980s, showing two young boys and a girl standing beside a swimming pool in the bright summer sun. It was he, Greg, and Kristy, and the memory filled him with sadness. His childhood had been such a carefree time.

There were hundreds of other photos of his family; some were taken as a group, and some were individual shots. He touched them with a weak hand and wished he could sit and reminisce. How long since he had looked at such happy memories?

"Callan?" Dylan's voice sounded strange behind the plastic.

He shook his head. "Sorry." He took the photo and stuffed it into his back pocket.

They swept the large family area. Two brown suede sofas sat at right angles in front of a wall-mounted flat-screened television. The sink and floors glistened, and the tables were clear of magazines. *It looks like they've gone on a holiday,* Callan thought. They crept down a long hallway toward the front of the house. Bedrooms lay on either side of the passage, revealing empty shadows in Kristy's room, the study, and the spare room. Dylan ducked into the bathroom.

"Empty," he said, reappearing.

Callan reached the front bedroom, where a set of closed double doors adorned with a rectangle pattern greeted them. He stopped outside and touched the muzzle of the pump action to the wood, then glanced at Dylan. "This is the last place they might be," he whispered. "If they're turned..."

"Let me do it," Dylan said, adjusting his grip on the rifle.

Callan had dreaded this moment, dreaded it since the thought had first squirmed its way into his mind. *Can I kill them?* He had doubted it. Now that he was here, the question burned in his mind like a headache. *No. I won't.* He could not shoot his mother through the eye and see her head explode across the wall. He could not blow his father's face off, the same face that had kissed him goodnight when he was a child. "Okay," he said in a rough voice. "You do it. But if you have to, please make it quick."

Dylan clicked the bolt into action.

Callan put a hand on the steel door handle; its cool touch soothed his warm, shaky hand. His heart drummed faster than he thought possible. With a turn, the mechanism squeaked. He pushed the door open and stood back with the gun aimed as Dylan shuffled forward with rifle locked and loaded.

A mess of clothes lay scattered across the bed. Two empty blue sports bags sat in the corner beside a short teak bedside table topped with a teardrop-shaped lamp. Dylan skipped around to the walk-through closets and stepped forward into the bathroom.

"Clear."

Callan let out a deep, unsteady breath. They were gone. Had they gotten out in time? He hoped so. Part of him wanted to know what had happened to them, had sought an outcome so he could move forward minus the stress of the unknown. In a way, part of him had wanted them to have died peacefully from the virus so he could bury them and get on with life. Surely, even if they had escaped, they couldn't have survived.

"They might have made it," Dylan said, as though hearing his thoughts. "That's what I tell myself about Dad."

A sudden feeling of relief pervaded Callan. He dropped the pump action onto the bed, took his mask off, and ran his hands through his sandy blonde hair. "I really thought they'd be here. I thought they'd have turned."

Dylan lifted his mask and said, "Let's check the cars."

A battered white utility vehicle sat idle in the twin garage, and beside it, black oil spots stained the grimy concrete. Callan squatted and ran a finger through the mark. It was dry.

"Maybe they did get out. Seems like there hasn't been a car—"

A loud noise rocked the garage, and Callan flinched. Something crashed against the door and they both jumped back. The sound of moaning floated in from outside; the culprit slammed against the flap again.

Dylan glanced at Callan. "We might have to shoot our way out."

"Might?" The wide door buckled in multiple places. The zombies growled and grunted, begging for their dinner. Callan realized they were in real trouble. "What do you think?" Dylan shook his head. "We could open the door and go out shooting?"

Dylan scrunched his face. "Depends. If there are one or two, we can probably shoot through them. Any more and we might be better to sneak out another way on foot."

"I'm not giving up the Jeep."

"I thought you might say that. We can't open the door, though. We could get trapped."

Dylan was right. If they opened the garage door and a horde rushed at them, they would die. "What about the front door? Could we sneak out that way?"

Dylan tipped his head from side to side. "Maybe. Let's take a look."

They went into the main bedroom and took a window each, peeling the curtains aside just enough to observe the mayhem. A pack of zombies loitered in the driveway, roaming in varying states of decay. Some had thick heads of hair and pale faces, while others had lost sections of flesh and the only remnants of their hair were patches of stringy fibers. Their clothes were dirty and torn; one wore a police uniform, which was flapping open; a dead boy staggered about in grimy shorts and a bloody t-shirt—one woman even wore a bikini. The one commonality between them was the fresh redness on their blood-smeared faces. *They've all fed*, Callan thought. A handful banged against the garage door. A group had surrounded the Jeep and slung weak, ineffective fists at the doors and windows. Others ambled around the garden with their noses high, trailing the scent of the two fresh humans. Callan saw a lone zombie stroll along the road with a greater intensity than the others. It seemed focused. Ice rushed through his veins. *It's one of the crazy ones.* The others bumbled about as it moved toward the house, shoving them aside. Reaching the garage door, it slammed a heavy fist down on the metal sheeting and the house reverberated.

Callan swallowed with a dry throat. "Shit."

"Do you have a remote for the garage?"

"I think so. There's usually one attached to the sun visor in each car, and we keep a spare in one of the kitchen cupboards."

"The power's off, though."

"We've got solar panels on the roof." He turned and saw the red LED alarm clock. "See?"

"Grab the remote."

Callan sped from the bedroom and back into the garage where the noise from the pounding on the door made him wince. His father normally left the old utility unlocked, maintaining it contained nothing worth stealing, and he was grateful when the door opened. He slipped the green remote control from the visor and ran back to Dylan.

"We wait in the little alcove outside the front door, then open the garage with the remote and hope they run inside."

"Then we close it and trap them."

"Hopefully. You got everything you need out of here?"

He didn't, but he could have spent all day searching the cupboards for things he could take. That wasn't practical, though. Their lives were on the line, and survival was the priority. "Yeah. Let's just do this."

Callan felt his nerves stiffen as his fingers touched the cold handle. He pumped a shell into the chamber and then, moving painfully slowly, he unlatched the chain on the front door and turned the deadlock with a heavy clunk.

The door opened with a creak and Callan cursed himself for the number of times he'd ignored his mother when she had asked him to oil the hinges. He slipped through the entrance and pressed himself into the brick wall of the tiny alcove. Dylan pushed in beside him and they both pulled their face protectors down.

From several yards away, they heard the slobbery grunts and moans of the undead, sounds of fists beating against the flimsy garage door, hands sliding over the Jeep's windows, and feet denting the hood.

"Ready?" Callan asked. Dylan nodded, his expression grim and pale.

Glass shattered and Callan knew they had broken a window on the Jeep. He held the remote control out, touched his finger to the top of the button, and pressed.

17

Twenty minutes after the boys departed, a lone zombie appeared at the bottom gate. It began walking along the width of the heavy steel entrance, from one side to the other, at a casual pace. It stopped where the mechanism locked onto the fixed section, and stared.

Greg had taken another dose of painkillers and seemed content to be sleeping. Sherry and Kristy were out on the veranda securing boards to the wooden window frames. Once they fixed the boards over the front windows, they would attempt to roll the empty trailer into the garage.

They wore jackets as Callan had insisted, but the temperature was heading toward the mid-nineties. Sherry had collected a pile of the old timber fence planks, and from the shed found two hammers along with a nail belt. They had fixed covers over three windows along the westward facing side of the house looking out toward the garden and front gate when they ran out of nails.

"Check the garage," Kristy said. "Might save you a trip back to the shed."

"Good idea."

A few moments later, when Kristy heard Sherry's rapid footsteps crunching over the stones, she knew something was wrong.

"There's a zombie at the gate."

"What?" Kristy said, laying the hammer down on the veranda as she walked toward the steps. "How is that—" But the words faded as her stomach began to shrivel.

They walked across the stones and stood side-by-side in the circular area at the top of the driveway, staring down toward the gate at the thing in the green jacket and dark pants. Neither of them spoke for a minute. Kristy felt a flash of annoyance. They would have to wake up Greg and he would have to hobble out on his bad leg and shoot the thing.

"What's it doing?"

Sherry's hand shielded her blue eyes from the glare, and wisps of her strawberry hair danced in the tender breeze. "Looking at the gate, I think."

"It can't get in, though?"

"I don't think so."

"I'm not going down there to kill it. It can stay there for now."

"I suppose. While it's not moving."

"It's not hurting anybody at the moment. The boys will be back soon. They'll take care of it."

What if they weren't, though? What if it climbed through the wire and started up toward them? Kristy went back to hammering boards across the front windows, glancing back down the driveway every few minutes to ensure it hadn't moved. Sherry did the same.

But the unease wouldn't pass. Although the zombie hadn't moved, Kristy slipped back through the sliding doors and into the kitchen. She hated guns, hated the devastation they caused, and the last few days had fortified that belief. But she could handle one, and her father considered her a better shot than Callan. At fifteen, they had both entered the skeet competition in the Albury Royal Show, where Kristy had placed first in her age group and second in the women's, overall.

On the bench lay the Winchester .30-30 with a box of rounds. She picked up the gun and turned it in her hands, then opened the chamber. Empty. Although the wooden butt gleamed, it felt dirty. The weapon killed living creatures, and Kristy felt her job was to save lives. *The world has changed, though.* Everything was different now. She knew she must suspend some of her beliefs and reset others to cope with the changes. Yesterday had altered her. She was accustomed to death, but what she had seen on the return trip from the lake was beyond the realms of normal. Besides, those *things* weren't alive.

A sudden, cold despair overcame her. In that moment, she wondered how any of them could survive this... plague, and the zombies. Even if they were lucky, how would they last a week, or a month? Did they have so little future ahead of them? *Snap out of it.* Such depressing thoughts were unhelpful. A person couldn't exist worrying about the *when* of their death. She had known countless terminally ill patients who didn't have years to live; their management of short-term timeframes were lessons.

Passing back through the family area, Kristy saw Greg sprawled on the sofa with one leg hanging off the edge. The blanket covered his head; the section over his chest rose and fell in a slow, consistent rhythm. The pain relief tablets contained a mild sedative, which seemed to be working. She would have to ensure he stayed off the alcohol, too.

Kristy returned to the decking and placed the rifle near the sliding doors. Sherry stood in a difficult position, stretched high against the window struggling to nail a board in. Kristy reached up and took hold of it.

"Thanks," Sherry said. "I was thinking. I saw an excavator up behind the shed. Maybe we could dig out a channel behind the fence when the boys return and put stakes in the bottom. That way if they get through, it might stop some of them." Kristy's eyes widened. "What?"

"Great idea. What made you think of that?"

"If a zombie climbed through the fence, they could walk right on up here. If we're going to survive this thing, we need to start thinking about preservation." Sherry waved at the half-finished window. "Maybe that's the only way to survive in a world where you have to board up your windows so things don't know you're inside."

"Wow. You're right." Kristy let the surprise wash over her. Maybe this was a turning point for Sherry. Of course, she was intelligent, but her narcissism generally overshadowed her better qualities. Or maybe it was the thought of being pregnant that had jolted her from the selfish perspective they had all come to expect.

"You've changed."

"Maybe. I've been thinking about it more. I guess I have. A lot has happened in the last twenty-four hours."

"I think we all have, in a way. Changed."

"In the past, I didn't really care what anyone thought." She climbed down off the ladder and stood before Kristy. "Yesterday I told you I didn't care for Callan anymore. That was me trying to... justify... things. What I've realized is that he'll love me no matter what, and I might never find that again. He's a good person. I'm... lucky."

"I'm glad. He is. I know he's my brother, but he worships you and believe me, that's a difficult trait to find in a man." They shared a contented smile. "Is the zombie still there?"

"Last time I looked."

Kristy walked to the end of the veranda where the garden wouldn't obscure her view. Her stomach lurched. "It's not there."

Sherry joined her. "It was there a moment ago."

Kristy said, "Let's take a look."

"Should we wake up Greg?"

"No. At least not until we really need him. I don't think he got much sleep. Hopefully it just wandered off down the road, or onto one of the neighbors' places." Kristy knew she should take the gun and search the property, but couldn't bring herself to leave the porch. Without seeing the danger, it was easier to ignore. "Maybe—"

The distant sound of crunching gravel reached them.

Kristy went down the stairs and took two steps before skidding to a stop on the stones. The zombie from the gate was three-quarters of the way up the driveway, less than fifty yards from the porch. They hadn't been able to see because the trees obscured their view. She knew instantly it was one of the more aggressive types.

"Get the gun," Sherry said.

It didn't possess the vacant, illogical look of the town zombies. It walked with control and purpose, lacking the awkward amble of others she had seen, and it carried a stick or length of pipe in its right hand. It peered back at them with its inflamed eyes sunk deep into a pale face. Its thick, dark hair had not yet begun to thin, nor its flesh crack, but its Army green jacket bore dark splashes of what was probably blood, and its black grin chilled Kristy to the core.

"Move!" Sherry said. "The gun."

Kristy bounded up the stairs and scooped up the rifle. The monster started walking faster as it reached the large circular area that led to the stairs. *The gun.* She lifted the rifle into her sights as a moment of uncertainty gripped her. She couldn't hit it from here. She hadn't shot a gun in years. The rifle wavered, and her finger pressed lightly on the trigger.

"SHOOT IT, KRISTY!"

Twenty yards.

Sherry's footsteps rattled across the decking, and then the doors slid open. Kristy clasped her fingers around the rifle, her trembling legs threatening to betray her. The monster grunted like a bull as the gravel crunched underfoot. She knew she had made a mistake not running.

She fired.

The bullet zinged past the zombie's head and blew up dust from the driveway. It was ten yards away when she saw its burning eyes. It raised the length of pipe and began to scream.

18

The garage door rumbled and clunked as it climbed toward the top of its arc. Callan peered around the corner of the brickwork and saw half the mob run inside, including the savage. Six or seven still clung to the car, banging on the roof and hood, while one crawled through the shattered windscreen. He pressed the button and watched as the door jerked, then started down again.

"Go. Side by side so we don't shoot each other."

Both guns roared as they fired at the remaining zombies. Callan didn't think he would ever get used to the loudness. The first shots from both weapons were direct hits, exploding brain and blood from the backs of decaying heads. One was the female with fibrous hair who had smelled them first; the other was a fat man dressed in shorts, his large white belly covered in bloody gashes. They thumped to the ground and two more tumbled from the car to replace them.

The garage door was almost down, but the maniac zombie recognized the ploy and slid down underneath, attempting to escape. As the heavy steel frame reached the final foot, it stuck its legs out through the entrance, jamming the mechanism. The gears moaned and crunched, then gave a loud clunk and stopped. The zombie roared, pulling at the door, but it didn't move.

Callan pumped the Remington to reload the chamber and lined up the head of an oncoming zombie. Its skull disintegrated, gore splattering over the Jeep's side windows, and it fell backward, crashing into another. On his right, the rifle cracked and another of the undead collapsed, minus the top of its head. He pumped again but before he could swing the gun around, one of them was on him, lurching and grabbing at his arms, snapping its rotting teeth. He swung the butt at its ashen face, swishing air, then brought it back and clouted its rubbery neck, knocking the monster aside. He made two shots, missing once, then killing another with a bullet to the face. The zombie died for the second time with its mouth open. *Move,* he told himself. *Get to the Jeep.* Another shuffled toward him with open, loving arms. Callan twisted the rifle around and shot it in the neck. Blood splattered his facemask and he wiped it away with a leather glove, dirtying his vision.

Dylan shot another, which gave them a momentary respite as three zombies were still working on the back of the car. Callan yanked the empty magazine out of the gun, then snatched a replacement from his pocket, jamming it in with a metallic clunk. He saw Dylan on his right, fumbling with the same problem.

"IN THE CAR!" Callan screamed. He remembered the crazy zombie who was trapped inside the garage, and glanced at the door. It had squirmed halfway out, grunting heavily, the roller mechanism groaning and scraping as the barrier lifted an inch. "It's coming! Move now!" Callan ran for the Jeep and ripped the door open, kicking to his left as one of the undead slid along the side of the car toward him. The thing tumbled to the ground. Callan jumped into the driver's seat, lay the rifle on the center console, and stuck the keys in the ignition.

Several of the zombies had lost interest in the boys, preferring the carnage. Dylan finally made it to the other side but ran straight into a teenager with patches of long scruffy dark hair and dark red blotches on its pasty face. It hissed like a cat and stuck out two long arms, clutching for his throat. He ducked and the monster clunked into the window. Dylan sprung up and drove it backward with his shoulder, like a linebacker.

The garage door banged and shook. The maniac zombie had slid his entire body, excluding his neck and head, out of the intended trap. Callan contemplated driving the car forward and running him over, but a second zombie rushed at Dylan from the neighbors' property, swinging a short shovel. *Since when did they use weapons?* Dylan reached the passenger door and raised an arm, holding the front of the rifle to protect himself. The metal tool clunked into his elbow and the gun clattered onto the concrete driveway.

He roared in pain, clutching his forearm. The zombie dropped the shovel and went for him, wrapping its bloody fingers around his throat. Dylan's head thumped against the window, his face pressed on the glass, gasping for breath. The monster opened its mouth and moved forward to bite him.

He was going to die. Callan saw it all unfold in his mind. The monster would rip into his neck and tear out a chunk of bloody flesh. Callan couldn't save him. By getting back out of the Jeep, he exposed himself to certain attack. The crazy zombie was almost out of the garage. He just needed to reverse out of the drive and the monsters would fall away. *He'd* be safe. Kristy would be devastated.

Callan turned the key and the engine grumbled to life. He shoved more ammo into his jacket pocket, then leapt out of the car, clunking the rifle on the doorway. He ran around the hood, raising the gun and sighting the zombie. "DUCK!"

Instead of repelling the attack, Dylan drew himself downward and curled his hands over his head. Callan stepped up to the zombie and shot it through the ear. Blood sprayed over the Jeep and onto his facemask, obscuring half his vision. The monster stumbled backward with part of its head missing, then fell sideways, hitting the concrete with a heavy thump. Dylan collapsed to the ground. They had cleared the vehicle, but other zombies ran along the street, drawn to the sound of gunfire and the smell of blood.

"Quick, you gotta get—"

Callan felt himself lifted off the ground by the back of his jacket. He hung ten inches off the concrete driveway, and then he was sailing backward through the air. He hit the garage door with a thunderous crash, the breath slammed from his lungs, the rifle knocked from his grip. It clattered to the side and he rolled over, gasping for air, pressing his eyes shut, tensing his body against the pain. When he opened them, he saw the mad zombie standing over him, the ripped denim of its blue jeans before his face. Callan glanced up and saw a pasty torso bunched and rippled with muscles. *It could rip my head off,* he thought. Its lips drew back from sharp teeth as it reached for him with steel hands. He scuttled backward, but it locked its fingers around his ankles and dragged him forward with ease. He was hanging upside down, his arms pinwheeling, and he thought, *this is it.* The thing swung him around and slammed him against the garage door again.

He landed with another almighty crash and rolled forward, pain exploding in his head and back. Fighting giddiness and nausea, he responded to instinct, like a cat, and rose quickly to his feet. He saw others coming for them with decomposing faces and soulless eyes, but the thing with all the power just waved them off. It thundered forward, enraged, and lifted one clenched fist. Callan saw as it shot toward him with inhuman speed. Pain lanced in a dagger through his face as the knuckles cracked his nose, snapping his head back. The thing growled, and Callan stumbled, feeling himself spin again, and then it had him by the throat and he thought of Sherry, and the baby, and Kristy and his mother. The pain disappeared; he knew it was the end. How stupid they had been, thinking they could survive in such a world.

A gunshot yanked him from thought. He felt himself falling and then he hit the driveway, choking for air, pain flooding his senses in rushing waves. The monster collapsed next to him and Callan saw that the back of its head had exploded in a bloody mess. A hand took him by the shoulder and dragged him to his feet.

"Move."

Absolute incoherence. He could only follow Dylan's lead as he ran ahead, holding both rifles under one arm, pulling Callan by the shoulder. Callan knew he should be dead, had expected it, but Dylan had saved him. He tried to speak, to thank him, but his mouth was dryer than the outback and all he managed was a grunt.

They ran up the middle of the street as zombies lurched toward them from the side road, moaning as if calling to each other. Dylan handed Callan's rifle back and kicked an elderly feeder aside. It fell back like a frail invalid. It was only then that Callan realized they were leaving the Jeep behind. He broke Dylan's grip and spun around, looking back.

"The Jeep."

"Fuck the Jeep, man. It's gone."

The undead swarmed over it, climbing in through the windows, pulling at the cover. They moved in a throng up the street, drawn by the gunshots and blood and death. Some were walking toward the boys with a slow gait. Dylan levered the bolt action and shot the closest one in the neck. Blood spewed out like rusty water from a tap and the thing fell onto its knees. Its head hit the road with the sound of two bowling balls clunking together.

The shot distracted those gathered around the Jeep, and several looked their way. A few started toward them—a couple of teenagers and an elderly man who walked as though he'd had a hip problem in his previous life. Incredibly, a handful of them were fighting over the body of the maniac who had almost killed Callan. A tall, thin zombie wearing a white Nike t-shirt and blue boxer shorts stood its ground, fending the other two off. When they relented, it stopped and began to feed on the dead zombie's head. Callan felt his empty stomach convulse.

"I'm gonna be sick," he said, looking away.

A scream sounded from down the street. The mob on the road outside Callan's house parted as another crazy barged its way through, knocking its brothers and sisters flat with powerful punches. It saw the scene near the Jeep and rushed over to the car with frightening speed. With one powerful motion, it ripped the head off the zombie feeding on the savage Dylan had killed.

"Oh my God," Callan said. He watched as it got down on one knee and placed a hand on the dead thing's back. "It knows."

The first of the zombies reached them with their groping hands, and Dylan said, "We gotta move."

Callan stood still, fascinated by the appearance of the new monster. They were a special breed of zombie. Intense, aggressive, and *smart*. He realized with a bolt of fear that if it ran after them, they might not be able to outpace it.

He turned away and settled into a jog at Dylan's side. They were running like infantrymen with their rifles, leaving the approaching dawdlers behind. Zombies wandered about front gardens and doors; Callan thought he recognized neighbors, but he looked away, closing his eyes in an attempt at ignorance.

Eighty yards down, Dylan led them onto another street, along the white line in the center of the road. These were roads on which Callan had grown up, lugging his school bag over his shoulder, scraping his knees and arms skateboarding on the curbs, and pedaling his bike back and forth between his mates' houses. He passed a white weatherboard where he had spent the night many times and felt the sting of nostalgia. A gold number "2" hung beside a rickety screen; he recalled his good friend Jimmy Stephens answering the door to Callan's request to come out and play. Callan had attended kindergarten with Jimmy, and they'd gone on to share several different years in school. While they were no longer the friends they had been as children, they still managed a courteous "g'day" when they happened upon one another. Where was Jimmy now? Probably just another name on a long list of people who had either died from the virus or returned as the living dead.

The pale sun had broken through a patchy section of white clouds, providing them with their first perception of time. Callan suspected it was close to late morning. If so, they had been gone several hours and the others would be worrying. They appeared to have left the undead behind for now, and only the odd car sat parked on the street. It might have been a normal day, aside from the silence.

Dylan led them along the footpath under the cover of curbside trees. The intensity of it all crawled through Callan, rendering his movement clumsy, and suddenly he felt the parchedness of his throat. He staggered onto the weedy front lawn of a house, laid down his rifle, and turned on the water tap. Dylan stood, panting, looking back down the street as Callan filled his cupped hands with cold water and drank, letting it sooth the back of his throat. His belly quickly filled. "Go," he said, leaving the tap running.

As Dylan drank, the first zombie appeared at the corner with balding head and pinkish face. It lurched along, waving the stump of its left arm. Its ankle had been broken, and its foot trailed along like a wheel on a toddler's toy.

Clearer thought returned—of Sherry, and of the baby growing inside her. If they lived long enough, she would one day be heavily pregnant, and he wondered how she would outrun the zombies in that condition. He had to protect her, to make certain she and the baby were safe at all times. It was up to him, as the father, to embrace this responsibility, and he felt deeply that he was ready, that he had been waiting for this moment to show everyone he was capable. He would take care of them both by providing safety, food, shelter, and love, but was Albury the place for all of that? The evidence was mounting against it. They would have to consider their long-term survival in the town.

"We gotta move, man," Dylan said. Other zombies had joined the leader, who had crossed the curb of the property, reaching for them.

"This shit's never gonna end, is it?"

They ran.

19

Kristy cried out as the gun flew from her hands. She snatched for it until she saw Greg's feverish, hulking form holding the rifle. He nudged her aside and she fell against the wall, clawing backward as the zombie drew to within five yards.

Greg spun the gun around with a speed that caught her breath, pulling the sight to his eye before she could blink. The blast forced Kristy's hands to her ears as the zombie's cheek exploded. It staggered forward, then fell. It placed one hand on the gravel to balance itself, then rose again. Its remaining eye stayed locked on Greg as it gathered its momentum. Greg's hand did its magic reloading trick. *Five yards. Four. Three.* The gun cracked again. The bullet blew a hole in the monster's face and knocked it backward and down to the stones.

Kristy held her breath, afraid to move a single muscle. Greg hobbled to the railing and leaned against it.

Sherry crept up between them. "Jesus, Kristy, have you forgotten how to shoot a gun? We could have all been killed." Blood seeped out from underneath its head onto the white stones.

"I'm sorry. I haven't shot a rifle in years." She glanced up at Greg, now holding onto the rail, his left foot hovering. "Are you okay? You look terrible." Sweat licked his brow and his face twisted into pain.

He nodded and said through clenched teeth, "*I'm* sorry. I know you tried."

It was a shot she would have made with her eyes closed when she was younger. She climbed to her feet. "I panicked. Thank you. Again."

Greg put a hand on her arm, then turned on his good leg, laid the gun down on the wood, and began hobbling along the veranda. "I need to lie down. I don't feel so good." Sherry reached out for him and he leaned on her shoulder, shuffling back through the sliding doors.

188

"Thank you," Kristy called out. She felt like a fool. It had taken a sick man to save them. She had been lucky. If not for Greg, it would have reached her and she'd be one of them now. The thought gave her a shiver. She needed to be tougher and re-learn to shoot.

Sherry returned and they both stood looking at the body. "How did it get through the fences?" Sherry asked.

Kristy looked out past the parking circle. Beyond sat the boundary fence, which wasn't electrified. They hadn't spied the zombie until it was near the top of the driveway, and Kristy had assumed that was because of the trees along its edge. Perhaps it had come from the property on the other side, though. "Are those fences electrified?"

"I don't know."

"Maybe it—"

"Went next door and got into their property and climbed over that fence. I think you're right."

They had focused on the front boundaries and figured they were safe because the roadside fence was electrified. This new exposure worried her. They simply couldn't cover every flank of the property. Another point to discuss when the boys returned.

"I forgot to mention," Sherry said, "but there's a trailer in the garage, packed with lots of supplies. Looks like Dylan's father was preparing to leave."

"What?" Kristy started for the garage, keeping well clear of the dead zombie. That explained some things. Dylan had been surprised by the lack of food in the house. Now his idea about staying there and fortifying their position was called into question. He had been adamant the best place for them was his home, but if his father had been planning to leave... it didn't bode well.

The trailer was neatly packed with boxes of food, camping equipment, water, batteries, and several small propane bottles. A tarpaulin had been secured around the edges and thrown back, presumably waiting for the final items to be added.

Sherry said, "They were ready to go."

"This really goes against what Dylan was thinking."

They had all begun preparing themselves mentally for a long-term stay at the property, except for Callan, who wasn't convinced. Boarding the windows had been the first step in making the place less visible, concealing their existence. Kristy wasn't sure how to proceed from here. Dylan would be surprised by this; it might change their plans.

They left the garage and reached the veranda. Kristy said, "We need to move this thing."

"Cal said they took the other bodies to a pile of brush in the paddock."

"That's the least we can do."

With care, they each grabbed a dirty sneaker. The laces of one shoe were undone, and Sherry had to tie them so it wouldn't slip off. With stiff expressions, they started dragging the zombie over the stones and into the grass, leaving a thin trail of blood. The exit wound on the back of its head stared up at them.

The smell hit them before they made it around the front garden.

"What is *that*?" Sherry asked.

Kristy knew it well. It was the smell of decaying flesh. Seemed the undead dead were no different than the human dead. "The dead bodies. Breathe through your mouth if it gets too bad."

They tossed the body onto the pile of brush and Kristy wondered about the strength of the scent. Would it would attract other zombies? They should burn it once the day cooled down.

"Do you think the guys will find anyone alive?" Sherry asked as they walked from the pile.

"No. I've said my own goodbyes to my parents. I just hope they died quickly and didn't turn."

"Wow. In some ways, being a doctor has given you some sharp edges."

"If there's one thing I've learned, it's that we all have to die one day. My job, as I see it, and the thing that gets to me, is trying to prevent that death for as many people as I can, for as long as I can. When I fail at that… I question things. This is out of my control, though."

They reached the garden level, where dirt had once been piled up to form a twelve-foot high embankment to hold the lawn and landscaped area, now fortified by large boulders and shrubs that had set their roots deep into the dirt. Kristy climbed up onto one of the big rocks and looked out across the paddocks and beyond. The view was panoramic, revealing sparse properties snuggled within the bush all the way to town.

Kristy went on. "The reality is that very few people in this town could have survived, especially those living closer in. My parents probably had no hope."

"I'm not giving up on mine yet."

Kristy turned with a confused look on her face. "You barely speak to your parents. You argued with them constantly, at least since I've known you. And you trash them whenever their name comes up in conversation." Sherry didn't respond. She kept looking out at the view, and Kristy realized then just how much of a front her personality really was.

"Since yesterday, I've started to question some of my behavior. Yeah, my parents can be anal and demanding, and their expectations are ridiculously high. But they have always looked out for me. They always thought they had my best interests in mind. You know, they told me not to go on this trip. That was part of the reason I agreed to come. Maybe they saved my life."

"It's natural to start feeling guilty. You—"

"I don't feel guilty. I just can't think it's fair if they've become zombies, or died. They are good people."

They climbed down off the rocks and started through the longer grass toward the house. The plan had been to bar the windows and all doors except the front and back,

191

but Kristy now had her doubts. Discovering the trailer and realizing not all boundaries were secure filled her with uncertainty. She wanted to discuss it with the others. She supposed they could finish barring the front windows.

She passed the sliding doors, heading toward a pile of planks, when something caught her eye. She leapt back and opened the door; what she saw made her heart jump. Greg lay unconscious in the middle of the lounge room floor.

20

They sprinted away from the water tap, Callan reloading his rifle, Dylan doing the same with the bolt-action. Their boots slapped the road, drowning out the grunts and groans as more zombies turned onto the street. Thanks to the physical demands of their camping trip at the lake, both men had increased their endurance. Dylan was grateful for all the wood chopping and swimming they had done, as they now ran for their lives. He kept thinking of getting home to Kristy, keeping her safe. He had hated leaving her, and felt a new sharpness of separation as this "quick mission" spiraled into disaster.

As they approached another junction, Dylan saw one of the streets filled with the undead. On his left was another road, flanked by dark, silent homes. The two men took it without thinking, sprinting across the grassed curb and along the edge of properties, where trees grouped in shaggy clumps. An ancient memory of running this same footpath surfaced and Dylan forced it away, urging his mind to find a solution for their predicament.

They ran along the bitumen in long strides, searching for signs of life, for a place where they could take refuge. Callan tried several vehicles but found the doors locked.

Dylan kept wondering how they were both still alive. Back at the Jeep, he'd been certain the zombie would bite his throat. He'd thought Callan wouldn't be able to save him. He supposed the favor had been returned, though; without his intervention, Callan would be dead.

Hitting Spencer Street, they saw a mass of cars with their windows smashed, as though there had been a pile-up. They kept away from the vehicles, close to the gutter, pushed back as much by the smell as the awareness of danger. Most of the vehicles were empty, but in one, a pair of zombies fed on a fat man whose head lay back against the seat, a dried gash on his forehead. Dylan thought about killing them, but the remaining bullets were too important.

They had a couple of handfuls of ammo, and who knew what lay ahead.

They passed a laneway and doubled back, using it to access Young Street. It ran parallel to Spencer Street and beyond to the Hume Highway, which took traffic all the way to Melbourne. *Used to,* Dylan thought. Young Street had been one of the busier motorways in Albury, with many shops along its length, including a gas station. They were close to them now and had their best chance of finding a usable vehicle.

"Which way?" Callan said between breaths.

"The gas station," Dylan said. They turned right and headed south.

It felt like an early Sunday morning, when most traders had yet to open. They jogged past a bakery and then a motorbike shop whose front window had a large hole in the glass. The usual line-up of new motorbikes for sale lay sideways in a sprawl. Several appeared to be missing.

Dylan paused at the broken glass, glanced around, and asked, "What about a motorbike?"

Callan ran on a few steps and stopped. "I suppose. What about the leather bike gear?"

"Kevlar. Some motorbike gear is made from that. Let's take a look."

With careful steps, they entered the motorbike shop through the front window, glass crunching underfoot. Bikes in a multitude of colors and variations stood in rows: trail, road, quad, and farm bikes in red, blue, green, and yellow, striped and accessorized with black, white, and silver. Beyond, racks and shelves held helmets, gloves, stickers, spare tires, and clothing. The boys took a section each and started browsing.

They quickly found the Kevlar gear and began piling items for each of the five of them onto the carpet.

Dylan chuckled. "You're not gonna insist on paying something for this?"

"No. I've learned my lesson. Two pairs of everything should be enough."

Using a Kawasaki equipment bag, they packed pants, jackets, gloves, and boots. Callan had to sit on the bag while Dylan pulled the zipper closed. They tried to start several bikes, but none appeared to have gasoline, and they abandoned the idea.

Callan slipped on a new pair of Kevlar gloves, then led them out over the broken glass with the bag in his left hand and the rifle in his right, glancing either way along the street. They hurried along the pavement toward the Shell gas station, where both of them had filled their cars with fuel countless times.

There were no vehicles stuck at the pumps, but two sat parked in the section outside the shop window where propane bottles and firewood were stacked in cages beside the big refrigerator boasting "ICE" in blue lettering. The electronic doors were open and a glance inside the store revealed a chaotic mess of stock strewn across the floor. The smell of gasoline made Dylan scrunch his nose and feel uneasy.

"You smell that?"

"Yeah. I think someone got trigger-happy at the pumps. We don't wanna hang around here too long."

Dylan checked one of the vehicles, a beaten up red Toyota sedan, while Callan checked the other, a lime green Holden station wagon. Both were locked.

"Any chance the keys are inside?"

"Maybe."

As they stepped toward the doorway, they heard a strange moaning sound coming from the distance. Dylan stopped, turning his ear toward the street. The first zombie hobbled right past the gas station and kept moving. A second and third followed, wandering with their noses pushed up high, as if chasing a scent.

"Move," Dylan said. "No shooting, either. We'll probably blow the place up."

Callan picked up the Kevlar pack and his rifle, then passed through the entrance and squatted behind a row of shelving that had once held magazines and newspapers. Broken milk containers and other bottles had been pulled from a small refrigerator near the door and lay on the floor. Dozens of bags of candy had been knocked from racking—chocolate bars, nougat, peppermints. The freezer containing ice creams lay on its side, and the melted contents had poured out through a broken glass lid. Near the counter, all the small chocolates and candy bars designed for impulse purchases were spread across the linoleum.

Dylan poked his head up and looked out over the bottom of the window, careful to keep his head behind a rack of sun hats. A mob had followed their scent. Dozens wandered along Young Street in a kind of pack. Everything the boys had witnessed so far indicated that their pattern of movement was fueled by one primary goal: feeding.

"There's heaps of them. Maybe thirty or forty that I can see."

"We'll have to wait here. If they catch our scent or see us, we're fucked."

"I don't think they'll smell anything around here but gasoline fumes."

"You might be right. We'll just have to sit tight until they pass," Callan shrugged as he whispered.

Dylan ached to get home. He couldn't handle the thought that he might get killed without ever seeing Kristy again. It wasn't so much the idea of his death that bothered him; rather, now knowing how she felt about him, he couldn't bear the thought of leaving her.

The horde would pass eventually, and while they waited beneath the empty racks and littered stock, the boys found another bag and filled it with candy bars, potato chips, and any other processed foods they could find. Callan found a bottle of neutralizing spray called Apeel. The label stated it

196

was derived from citrus fruits and that it would neutralize any odor. It warned against overuse, but they sprayed the mist liberally onto their clothes, faces, and hair.

"We need wheels," Callan said, after peering out and finding that the immediate threat had passed. "I want a new Jeep."

"We can have any car on the street, pretty much. You want to go all that way?"

Callan nodded. "Yep. And you'll see why."

It was a mile to the Jeep dealership on Hume Street. They used the backstreets: Swift onto Olive, right into Dean, left into Kiewa, hiding in doorways, behind parked cars, even lying beside a dead body here and there when the feeders wandered too close. They were lucky and clever, and the only time Dylan thought they might be caught, they simply outran their assailants, thankful that none of the crazy zombies were around.

They passed the Coles supermarket on the corner of Smollett. All the front windows were shattered; parading around the store were dozens of zombies. Several had fallen out through the front window, and one had skewered itself on jagged glass. It provided the feast for a dozen undead who tore into its body with fingers and teeth, distracted from the two passing humans.

"We might have a hard time getting any food in there," Dylan said.

A battered police car sat up on the curb further along from the supermarket. Dylan turned away when he saw blood on the steering wheel and driver's seat.

Zombies wandered along the shopfronts with their blank, purposeless expressions, but there was no mob. They crossed the road when a walker drew too close, but compared to other sections, the roads on Kiewa Street were empty, and the zombies seemed disinterested. Dylan wondered about the impact the neutralizing spray might had made.

They passed a drugstore at the bottom of Kiewa Street; Callan stopped and peered in through the broken glass.

"What is it?" Dylan asked, following his gaze. The place looked strange, both unfamiliar and normal, the contents untouched. Shelves were stocked, and displays of razor blades, Revlon makeup, and body lotions remained upright just beyond the doorway.

Callan let out a long breath. "I'm not supposed to say until it's confirmed, but," he smiled and shrugged, "Sherry thinks she's pregnant."

Smile. Just smile. "Wow," Dylan said, pushing up the corners of his mouth. "That's… amazing."

"I know. It was a big shock for me, too. Not the best time to be bringing a kid into the world, but hey, what choice have we got?"

"Do you know for sure?"

"That's why I need to get a testing kit. She's pretty certain, though."

"Congratulations, then!" But all Dylan could think of was how the kid might look when it was born. Would it be light and fair like Callan, or dark and olive like Johnny?

Callan stepped through the entrance and collected a plastic basket from a stack, then disappeared down one of the aisles. Dylan moved inside the door, hunching out of sight and watching the street. He couldn't shake the sadness he felt for Callan. The more time they spent together, the more Dylan realized he wasn't such a bad guy. He had faults, as they all did, but his heart was decent and he was reliable. He wondered how the problem was going to play out. He didn't know how long he could continue keeping such a secret. In his experience, people always discovered the truth. He suspected that day would come, and when it did, Callan would be devastated.

Callan returned ten minutes later with a plastic green basket overflowing with pregnancy test kits and painkillers. Dylan felt some of the tension in his shoulders and torso dissipate. "That was quick."

"It helps when there's nobody else shopping *and* you don't have to wait to be served."

Dylan had gathered himself, and as Callan slipped the packages into the bag, he said, "I'm happy for you, man. It seems like you really want this."

"I do. We need it."

"Then I wish you the best of luck." He stuck out his hand and Callan shook it with a firm, appreciative grip. They had each saved the other's life, more than once, but it was the most genuine connection Dylan had felt yet between them. He only wished it had been under thoroughly honest circumstances.

They reached the dealership with a clear run along Hume Street. A throng of vehicles sat behind the usual heavy black fencing. A small section of the fence had been removed and thrown onto the road, however, a clear space allowing cars from further back to exit.

"This is too easy," Dylan said, glancing around, expecting something to appear from the shadows of the dealership.

"That's it," Callan said, pointing to one of the many vehicles sitting outside the showroom. "That's the one. Right there."

He had picked a brand new Jeep Grand Cherokee in black, a mid-sized SUV. "I looked at them a few months ago. Dreaming of upgrading my older model. It was never going to happen, though. Unless... the world ended."

Any guilt he'd harbored yesterday about taking things without paying had disappeared. Life as they knew it was over, and if you were one of the lucky ones to have survived, you had to utilize everything available to remain that way. Dylan got it.

Though the area seemed empty, they approached the office with caution. Callan pulled at the door, mumbling the license plate number, while Dylan aimed the loaded rifle. The door swung open, unlocked, and they knew in a moment that someone had been there before them.

"They might be still here," Dylan said, moving the barrel around the room.

Without hesitation, Callan strode across the floor toward the office. "We need that vehicle. It'll tow a trailer and fit us all comfortably. Plus, it can convert to a seven-seater after the baby comes."

A wide, lockable grey cabinet hung open on the wall. Rows of car keys hung from tiny silver hooks. Each set had a license plate label. Callan inspected the numbers and after a few seconds, snatched a set and said, "Here we are."

They tossed their gear into the back and slid into the leather seats. Callan twisted the key, and the engine hummed a gentle vibration they could barely feel. He lowered the parking brake, then reached forward and pushed the automatic transmission into drive. The revs increased slightly, and he began to lift his foot off the brake when Dylan saw a moving object in his peripheral vision.

"Wait." Driving along Hume Street was another vehicle—not just any vehicle, but a black Jeep Grand Cherokee, identical to the one they were sitting in. "Do not move."

Crouched beside him, Kristy placed her hand on Greg's forehead and felt the warmth of a strong fever. "Greg?" She rocked his shoulder gently. "Greg?" He mumbled and his eyes fluttered. "Greg, wake up."

Standing over them, Sherry asked, "Is he okay?"

"No, he feels hot. I think he fainted."

"Is it the virus? Is he sick from that?"

"I don't know. He has a fever. The cut on his leg could be infected. Greg, can you hear me?"

Greg rolled over and made a face twisted in pain. "Ohhhhh. Callan. Get the guns. They're coming."

Hallucinating. Not good. "Greg? *Greg?* Can you hear me?"

He flinched and squinted at her. "Huh? We're all gonna die."

Kristy rubbed her temples. *Get control. Think.* She imagined him twenty-four hours from now, either desperate for their flesh or close to death from an infected leg. If he was hallucinating, it meant his temperature was likely above a hundred and two, and that made her think it was probably a local infection, unless it was a symptom of the virus. She hoped it was the former, although he would need antibiotics and that would provide its own challenge.

"We need to get you into bed. Help me, Sherry."

They each tucked their hands underneath his armpits and lifted, grunting at the weight. At first, they were unable to move him, but he seemed to gather some coherence and understood the idea, pushing with trembling legs. Once they had him on his feet, the girls each got an arm around their necks; they shuffled toward the bedroom with Greg's head lolling.

Once he was on the bed, Kristy went to her medical bag and returned with a thermometer. She placed it under his tongue and waited for the reading—it was almost a hundred and two. She bit down her concern and said, "I'm going to give you some ibuprofen. That should make you feel better. Do you think you can take a few tablets?" Greg made a face and groaned. "Find a cloth and run it under cold water," she said to Sherry. "I'll get the tablets. Be quick."

She had a difficult time getting him to swallow the pills. He drifted in and out of consciousness, talking again.

"Don't go—Dad. Don't—leave me." Kristy had goose bumps. A lump formed in her throat. "Don't leave me, Mum. Dad left…"

Sherry returned from the laundry with a wet washer. "I couldn't find any cloths, so I took one off the hanging line outside."

Kristy folded the soft material into a rectangle and laid it across Greg's forehead.

"Kristy… love her…" He reached out and grasped at her hand. Kristy snatched it away. "Not Dylan… me."

Sherry stepped in front of her and took Greg's fingers. "Shhh. Shhh, Greg. It's okay." She placed his hands on his stomach and took a blanket from the floor, then spread it out over him.

Kristy watched with a grim expression. The fever had bitten deeply into him. She hoped the tablets would quickly take effect. Ultimately, though, if it was an infection from the axe wound as she suspected, he would require antibiotics. She went to the doorway and waited until Sherry had joined her, then closed the door carefully.

A soft creak sounded from the family room. Kristy froze with her hand on the gold doorknob and rotated her head to Sherry. She mouthed the words "What was that?" Sherry shook her head. *Don't know.*

A loud thud sounded and both girls jumped. "Did you close the back door?"

Sherry looked away. "I think so."

Kristy crept along the hallway toward the family area, Sherry following. She stopped in the doorway and took hold of the frame, then peered into the open area. It was empty. Her chest thumped.

She stepped out into the room and felt a draft touch her cheek. The door to the laundry was open. The banging noise sounded again; this time she only flinched. It was the back door. She glanced around for a weapon but saw nothing nearby. Suddenly, she felt exposed.

She had stupidly left the gun out on the decking. Where was the axe? She couldn't recall. Her darting eyes locked on a wooden knife-block on the bench near the stovetop. She went to it and lifted the largest blade from its slot, a wide fin about ten inches long. She tightened her fingers around the handle and turned back to the laundry.

Sherry hung from the passageway doorframe. She pointed to the laundry and Kristy nodded, slow steps taking her across the tiles toward the small room. She didn't like this at all. Sherry had forgotten to close the back door, and now there might be a zombie inside with them. They hadn't seen any zombies roaming the property, but that didn't mean one hadn't climbed through the fence along one of the other boundaries. A sudden thought hit her and she stopped, looking at Sherry, her brain extrapolating the outcome. Callan and Greg had killed the infected family next door, except for the father. Had he wandered over from the other property?

Sherry stepped out of the passageway and around Kristy toward the kitchen. The door to the backyard squeaked again and Kristy felt the breeze. A moan came from the other room, causing a sharp intake of air. *Greg.* She waited, listening to him moaning, calling out something unintelligible. She wanted to go to him, wanted to comfort his pain, but her nagging intuition wouldn't let her.

The laundry door swung open with another creak, and Kristy arched her neck to see around the corner. Empty. Her nerves settled and she loosened her grip on the knife. Greg called her name now, but she hurried into the laundry and yanked on the handle, closing the heavy external wooden door with a thud. She let out a long breath, feeling a moment of reprieve. Maybe it had only been the wind.

As she turned, invisible spiders crawled up her neck when she saw a shadowy figure behind the internal door. A scream rose up in her throat, but before it could escape, a piercing shriek sounded from the other room.

As her eyes focused, she realized it was just a raincoat behind the door; she rushed out of the laundry and into the family room with the knife thrust out. Sherry had fallen back against the kitchen bench. Mr. Henry had his tall, wiry body pressed against her. His eyes bulged and scraggy hair hung over his blotchy grey face. He gurgled as though he had a mouth full of blood. Dark veins in his hands protruded as he pulled Sherry's thick red hair, exposing her neck. He leaned forward with his mouth open, teeth bared.

22

The boys sat in their new vehicle as the identical Jeep passed. Four shadowy figures moved within.

"You don't want to go after it?" Dylan asked.

"Nah. I know it's being paranoid, but we don't know who they are. The law doesn't exist anymore. Until we know for sure if another party is safe, I think it's best we stay clear."

They waited five minutes, then drove in the opposite direction, stopping to fill the gas tank at a service station near the Hume Highway.

Greg's grandparents' house was situated north of Albury, just west of the gas station, and they made good time, pulling onto the street less than ten minutes after placing the nozzle back into the pump. Either the zombies hadn't been up this way, or they hadn't effected the same carnage, because most of the properties appeared untouched.

Callan pulled the car up about thirty yards from the house, glancing around to see if they had missed anything. "Last stop, then. I'm a bit worried about doing the driveway-parking thing again. I'd park in the street, but if a horde of them come strolling along we'll have further to run."

"Driveway or street, it probably won't matter if they come after us again."

"Yeah. The fuckers are like bees; they move in a swarm and appear out of nowhere. Look at what happened last night while we were changing the tire."

"Let's just do it. Maybe one of us can stay in the car and keep it running while the other one goes in and checks?"

Callan laughed. "You're normally the smart one. What happens when a mob arrives? You drive off and leave me? You'll have no choice."

Dylan supposed he was right. Their teamwork had saved their lives so far.

The car rolled up the short driveway and Callan cut the engine. It was another brick property with a flat tin roof. Three windows peered at them from the facade.

"It's small," Callan said. "Three bedrooms, a kitchen and eating area, plus a tiny lounge. Won't take us long."

Dylan nodded. "Let's hope they're not here."

"Yeah. Hope is all we've got left."

They jumped over a tall, padlocked gate, using the boundary fence palings for a boost, then walked along the remainder of the driveway to another gate that connected the corner of the house and the edge of the detached garage.

"You don't have a key, do you?"

"No," Callan said, pointing up at a window along the side of the house, "but we can climb in there." The pane sat an inch out from the frame. Someone had left it open.

Callan pulled the window outward, then pushed on the flywire screen until it fell forward into the room. Callan swung a leg over the lower pane, bent at his waist, and eased down into the room. Dylan handed him the gun, then did the same.

Inside, the house smelled a little musty, but otherwise free of unusual odors. *That's a good sign,* Dylan thought. Most of the curtains were closed, making it dim, like early morning. Callan took them left down a short hallway, then left again into a tiny bedroom with a desk in one corner. On it, papers and boxes were piled high. The room was empty. The third bedroom, directly across the hallway, contained a double bed covered in a frilly spread. Antique furniture decorated the rest of the room: two bedside tables, a small wooden chair, and a dresser at the end of the bed.

They cleared the remaining rooms and ended up in the kitchen, where three heavy suitcases sat in front of a large sliding door. Beyond, a fern-filled garden surrounded a paved area on which a white table and two chairs sat.

Goosebumps tingled on Dylan's skin. "They never made it."

"Doesn't look like it."

The sink gleamed under a crack of light from beneath the blinds. No drying dishes. The stovetop was polished. The benches were clear except for a single envelope.

Callan glanced at Dylan, then reached out and picked it up. He unfolded the flap and slid a single page out, slowly opening it. His face softened and he let out a long breath.

"*Dear Greg. If you are reading this, then we are grateful and happy you are alive. We are not so fortunate, and I am sad to tell we have not survived this… plague, or whatever it actually is. The sickness has crept up on us and now we are both riddled with symptoms. We know we have a day, perhaps less, before the end. The government has been less than forthcoming in providing us information, and Herb suspects they don't know so much themselves. There has been much speculation throughout the town about where it came from and what it might be, but mostly people have either left or died. Many of our friends have succumbed to the horrible sickness. We thought we might be immune, and we even considered packing up and heading north toward your camp, but we didn't have the courage to leave. There have been other reports of things happening in the town. We're not sure, ourselves, and sometimes gossip grows legs, but be careful Greg. What a blessing your trip was and hopefully it has saved you from this horrible mess. We have lived a good life, anyhow, and are grateful for that. Don't be too sad. Move on with your life and beat this thing. Don't give in, and as we have always told you, be the best man you can. Lord knows you have overcome so much to be where you are today. We love you, Greg. Very much. You have been the most wonderful grandson, as wonderful as any of our children (much more so than some) and we thank you from the bottom of our hearts. With all our love from heaven, your grandparents, Herb and Nancy xoxo.*"

Callan's voice cracked on the last line. He threw the letter on the bench and gritted his teeth. "Fuck it."

Dylan glanced at the letter and saw the neat cursive writing common in that generation. His nana had written him countless birthday and Christmas cards in similar script. He sympathized with Greg. He would soon face the same kinds of feelings Dylan had experienced the previous night. He knew the truth of his mother's death hadn't hit him fully yet, but somehow he'd been able to push it aside and keep moving forward.

"I'm not gonna give him the letter," Callan said.

"What do you mean?"

Callan put his palms out as if it was obvious. "He'll fucking lose it. He can't handle this."

"You can't not tell him."

"Yes I can. I'm not. And neither are you."

Dylan opened his mouth to respond, but the words fell away. Was he any different, not telling Callan of Sherry's treachery? How could he be such a hypocrite? He looked out into the backyard, beyond the paved sitting area, and gasped. He held his breath and stepped toward the door, raising a finger. "Look."

Callan followed and his eyes grew wide. "Oh shit." Standing on the circular back lawn near the garden bed was a pair of zombies, male and female.

"That's them, isn't it?"

Callan nodded. The female wore a long, flowery dress, the kind that a woman in her seventies or eighties would wear on a summer's day. The male had a tuft of white hair along the back of his head, a green cardigan, and brown slacks. They walked in random patterns with slow, unsteady steps, similar to how they had probably been in life. They bumped into each other, then shuffled aside as though they were trying to pass in their kitchen. They had died and come back to life, but they were still old. Old zombies.

Callan put his hand out, and Dylan handed him the rifle. He unclicked the lock on the door and the right one glided open. The smell of rot and death drifted in and

Callan turned his nose. "I'll never get used to that. I don't think they'll be any trouble."

Dylan said, "I can do it if you like. I didn't know them. You were pretty close."

"I've known Herb since I was six. He used to give Greg and me horse rides at the same time, one on each knee." A smiled formed at the corner of his mouth. "I should do it."

"I'll wait here."

Callan nodded, passing through the doorway and beyond the table setting, loading the chamber and raising the gun into position. By the time he stepped onto the lawn, they still hadn't noticed him. When he reached a distance of three yards, their backs were still turned. Dylan held his breath.

Callan lifted the Remington and took aim at Herb's head. Dylan waited. The gun wavered, and then Callan slowly lowered it. Dylan wondered if he might have to handle it. The old zombie turned and spied Callan for the first time.

He started walking toward him; Callan stepped backward and raised the gun. The old guy took little steps, from which a child could have run away. He wasn't going to catch anyone. Dylan thought it was a wonder he had survived so long.

Callan stopped, but the thing that was once Herb kept coming in its slow gait. It raised long bony arms and curling fingers, then opened its dark, bloody mouth. Callan pulled the trigger. The zombie's eye exploded with a gush of red. It fell onto its knees, then slumped forward into the grass.

His wife turned as though someone was calling her from the house. Callan took two quick steps forward and shot her in the same place. Blood and brain flew in a jet across the pink flowering bushes. She fell back, hit a hydrangea bush, and rolled off into the bark, swallowed by the garden.

Callan stood motionless, looking from one to the other as though he couldn't believe what he'd done. Finally, he turned back. As Callan approached, Dylan saw his top lip quivering and his eyes pooling. He didn't meet Dylan's gaze. "Let's go." He took the note from the bench, folded it, and stuffed it into one pocket.

At the lounge room windows, they peered out onto the street and Dylan felt a shiver of relief that not one zombie was in sight.

23

Kristy ran forward, screaming. Regardless of her feelings for Sherry, Callan loved her, and Kristy would do all she needed to protect his interests. In that moment, she also saw her unborn niece or nephew under threat. It ripped away her fears and injected the most powerful emotion of all into her actions: love.

The zombie turned, alerted by the noise, and watched as she lifted the knife and rushed at it. She thrust the blade down and stabbed it through the eye, feeling soft, spongy flesh yield to the steel. Blood and fluid gushed down its cheek and onto the thin white business shirt, now grotty and stained with a thousand markings. It fell away from Sherry, who was also screaming, and slumped to the tiles with a wet thud.

Kristy dropped the knife and held out her hands. The blade clattered to the floor and Sherry fell into her, sobbing. They hugged, rubbing each other's back, tears streaming down their faces. It was the first thing Kristy had ever killed.

Finally, they pulled apart and looked at the corpse of Mr. Henry. Greg had stopped moaning, but Kristy drew away to check on him, turning on the hallway light. In the shadowy room, he lay silent, his breathing short and thin. She stood over him for a minute, waiting for him to stir. She put the back of her hand to his forehead, frowning at the heat baking off his skin. He needed real medicine, antibiotics. Ibuprofen would have to do for now.

In the family room, Sherry sat on the couch, her hands shaking. "That was… horrible."

Kristy rubbed a hand on her back. "It's okay. We're safe now."

"Until when? We're never going to be safe here. That's the second time we've been attacked in thirty minutes."

"I just meant we're safe. Until the next time."

"I think we should leave this place," Sherry said. "Dylan's father obviously had that intention. We should just pack up and go somewhere else."

"Where?" It wasn't only that Dylan wanted to stay, but she wondered if they would ever be completely protected in any place.

"We could just drive," Sherry said. "Drive away from here. On the way back from the lake we were safe."

"That's a discussion to have when the boys return."

Sherry stood, waving the residual shock from her hands, and said, "Can we get this thing out of here?"

This time, using gloves, Kristy took its arms and Sherry grabbed its legs. They staggered out through the sliding doors onto the veranda, resting for a moment on the gravel at the bottom of the steps. Kristy wondered if she should be inspecting the corpse in order to learn more about them.

They rolled him onto the edge of the growing pile of brush and bodies, noting the smell by scrunching their noses. It was getting worse. Surely, it would attract more of them.

Sherry saw it first and groaned, turning to face the road.

Kristy followed her gaze and felt her stomach tighten. In the lower western corner of the paddock, a zombie stood at the fence in the familiar vegetative stance, slightly stooped, arms hanging by its side, unmoving. She realized Callan and Sherry were right. They would never have any relief living here.

"It's not doing anything, but we should keep an eye on it."

They stood there for a long time, watching it, waiting for the zombie to make a move. When it didn't, Kristy turned and led them inside, hoping the boys would soon return.

212

24

They reached the Safeway supermarket on Swift Street and saw it wasn't in as bad a state as the Coles on Kiewa Street. Half a dozen cars sat unmanned in the parking lot. Several zombies wandered outside the glass doors where shopping trolleys had been stacked in a long row, ready for customers that would never return.

Callan stopped at the edge of the lot. "What do you think?"

One of the zombies noticed them and started toward the Jeep in a slow gait. "I'd run the prick over, but it would dirty the car."

"The back entrance," Callan said. "This has to be our last stop."

"We really need the stuff?"

"We've got nothing."

"We need ammo, too. I don't like having only a few dozen rounds."

Callan accelerated, swinging the Jeep around to cruise alongside the front windows. Dylan peered into the supermarket. It was shadowy, no lighting, but he could see a world of mess. Shelves had been knocked down, and stock lay scattered across the floor. Wires hung from the roof. A lone zombie poked about the cash registers. If they went inside, there was going to be risk.

They needed more supplies. Sherry had made a huge list for their ongoing survival. If they were to survive at the house, they needed provisions. Without them, they would have to leave, and he would do everything he could to avoid that.

Callan released the brake and took off. "Let's go take a look out back."

Dylan felt his nerves start to tingle. They were going inside. He could sense the tension in Callan's voice. They had at most a couple of dozen rounds between them. That could disappear quickly. "Maybe we should track down some more ammo first."

"We're here now. In and out."

Callan guided the Jeep around to the rear car park, where a double sliding door provided access. He parked parallel to a brick wall about five yards from the entrance, with the back facing the opening for a quick getaway.

They sat with the Jeep idling, and they both emptied their pockets.

"One full magazine and two rounds left in the old one," Dylan said.

"Five, ten, thirteen." He put the full one in and stuffed the half empty in his pocket. "Make 'em count." Callan's face twisted with worry. "Listen, if we get separated… if one of us can't get out, just run, okay? If it goes to hell, just get the fuck out of there."

Dylan nodded. "That goes for both of us."

They exited the Jeep, fitted on their facemasks, and walked to the rear entrance. Callan shoved the doors open and they saw straight through to the front of the store. The place was gloomy, lit only by splashes of grey skies through the front and rear windows. The cash registers sat in a line ahead of them, front to back of store, with twenty or so aisles of merchandise off to the right. They heard the random clatter of the zombie poking about up at the front. A rotten smell hit them and Dylan turned away, screwing up his nose. Callan made a pinched face. "That's fresh."

"Rotten food. Smells like the compost at home."

Dylan asked, "How do we do this? We'll need a trolley. One pushes, the other one shoots?"

"Sounds like a plan."

"I'll push."

With his gun in the basket, Dylan guided a trolley backward out of a short stack and wheeled it after Callan. He led them through the entry gates to what was once the fresh fruit and vegetable section. It was now a big contributor to the smell. Stacks of tomatoes, pumpkins, potatoes, onions, and capsicums lay spread across the floor. Most had lost their bright colors and were a horrible black, spotted with the lime green of mold.

Dylan pushed and pulled the cart through the mess, fighting to avoid the squashed produce, but in the end, he went through it, the wheels leaving tracks on the floor. Callan slipped on a pile of rotten tomatoes and looked like he might fall on his ass, flailing about. Under other circumstances, Dylan would have cackled.

They reached the other side of the vast produce section, where the bread racks began. Callan held up a palm at the end of the shelving, then stepped around the corner and checked the walkway. He turned back and stuck up one thumb, then reached into his pocket and pulled out a piece of paper. Reading from the list, he then arched his neck back and looked up at the signs listing the main contents of each aisle.

They stopped at the first aisle, designated as personal care, medicine, and oral hygiene. Callan started forward, then stopped suddenly. Dylan knocked the trolley into him. Ahead, crouched over a dead body about halfway along the aisle, were three male zombies. One wore a firefighter's suit. Dylan realized that from the back entrance, their view of the aisles had been restricted and their assumption of the limited number of zombies had been false.

Callan swung the pump action around and started forward.

"Wait!" Dylan said. Once they engaged the zombies, more would come.

The rifle burst with a loud metallic blast and the lead zombie's neck exploded. It slumped to the floor as the other two ceased feeding and watched in fascination. A second climbed gracelessly to its feet and stepped forward. The gun roared again and its head kicked back with a spray of the now familiar gore splashing a range of shampoos and conditioners. It fell back in a stiff, straight pose and sprawled on the floor. The fireman stood and moved toward Callan, dragging a deformed foot and leaving a trail of bloody goo. Callan pumped another bullet into the chamber and took a step backward, surprised at its speed. He pulled the trigger; the bullet hit the fireman in the shoulder, twisting it around. It maintained balance and spun back toward him, but Callan was ready, pumping the fourth round into the chamber and stepping to within a foot of its decaying body. Callan fired again and turned away as its head exploded, bloody grey brain coating the floor.

Silence. Callan stood, chest heaving, watching the scene he had just created. He turned to Dylan with blood spray all over his facemask and jacket. "Let's go."

Elsewhere in the store, glass shattered and something shrieked. Dylan's skin crawled with goose bumps. "They're coming."

They continued down the aisle with their rubber soles squeaking on the shiny floor, grabbing pain relief tablets, women's personal hygiene items, and deodorant. Dylan passed toothpaste and toothbrushes, and remembering that they had been Kristy's suggestion, grabbed handfuls of both. Callan took a dozen bottles of multi-vitamin tablets.

"That smell seems to be getting worse," Dylan said.

"I don't want to think about it," Callan said, reloading his rifle.

Callan led them around into the next aisle at a fast walk; Dylan had to jog to keep up. They filled the trolley with water and soft drinks, then biscuits, cereal bars and health bars from the next aisle. The fourth aisle contained canned vegetables, baked beans, and spaghetti that they tossed into the trolley with metallic clunks. As they turned into the clearway at the end of the aisle, the stench hit them.

"That's worse than the fruit and vegetables," Callan said.

216

Dylan felt the contents of his stomach rise. Just ahead was the delicatessen, full of stinking, wretched meat. Callan scuttled back. A number of zombies rose from behind the counter. Dylan stepped closer and looked over the glass casing. Dozens of them fed on the rotten meat: kabana, ham, chicken, bratwurst, sausages, and whatever else had been forgotten by the sick and dying. Several zombies began climbing over the glass cases, enticed by the idea of live meat.

Callan raised the rifle and fired, hitting one in the eye and spreading blood over the back wall in a symmetrical pattern. It fell forward, resting on the glass. A bloody trail dribbled onto some of the decaying meat in the trays. A desperate colleague leaned down and took a bite from its shoulder.

Two more zombies came swiftly toward the boys, and before either of them could move, the feeders were between them, groping and scratching. Dylan swung the trolley around and knocked one aside, then backpedaled the way they had come. Shopping was done. They needed to get out of there.

The pump fired again and one of the monsters shrieked. Dylan heard the soft shuffle of their footsteps behind him. They had stirred a hornet's nest, and for now, had been separated. He remembered Callan's words. *Just run.* He did.

25

Callan jogged along the clearway and turned up the first aisle, glancing back over his shoulder as a trio of feeders chased: a store employee and two middle-aged females. He stopped, fired, and hit one of the females in the chest, knocking it backward into the others, briefly halting their advance. He cursed himself, though, knowing a head shot to the brain was the only thing that would end their existence. He noticed a smoky haze in the upper reaches near the front of the store, and then a voice called out, inarticulate, but definitely human.

Glass shattered and something exploded. He cursed himself for insisting they stop. He would be with Sherry now, if they'd kept driving. In the safety of the house, confirming her pregnancy. They needed the supplies, though. Without them, they didn't have enough to survive.

He reached the end of the aisle and stopped, peering around the corner. A dozen more feeders had infiltrated the supermarket. Automatic gunfire split the air, causing him to flinch. There were other people in the store. Other humans. It was getting worse. Aside from the threat of zombies, they now had to contend with gunfire.

He glanced back and saw that the zombies were almost on him. Which way? Not toward the front. He fired off another shot and pinged the store employee in the cheek. It fell back, clasping its face. The two women ignored it and charged on. *Left, go left.* He did, but ran into another one, a big beefy guy wearing an open checkered shirt revealing a bulging, pallid stomach riddled with dark blood vessels. Callan gasped and jabbed the muzzle into its face, drawing blood and knocking it backward. Beyond, he saw more of them staggering toward him.

Retreating, he turned and ran toward the front of the store, but more gunfire rattled off and he cut right down the next aisle. It was devoid of zombies. Smoke had drifted in and he could hear the crackle of flames. He coughed, clearing his throat as the burning residue began to surround him.

Gotta get back to Sherry, he kept telling himself. Loud noise clanged in every direction, and he wondered what in the hell the newcomers were doing. Flames reached for the ceiling and he realized they were burning the place to the ground. He had to get out. He reached the end of the aisle and glanced in either direction.

Farther along, in the direction of the delicatessen, a fallen partition blocked his view. He knew the feeders wouldn't be far, though. Behind him, the big trucker he'd stabbed with the gun ambled along with a streak of blood down his face, several more allies following like diligent soldiers.

Where was Dylan? He'd fled toward the back of the store. Callan hoped he'd made it out. More machine gun rounds chattered behind him, closer now, perhaps near the cash registers, and he ducked instinctively, his decision about which way to proceed made for him.

On shaky legs, he pushed through the fallen partition and ran toward the delicatessen, filling empty spaces in the magazine with rounds. He had to get to the Jeep. A sprint along the back aisle and he was almost there.

But the pack who had been feeding on stinky deli meat seemed to have abandoned that in light of the sweeter-smelling flesh. At least twenty of them had clambered over the counter, falling, sliding, and leaping over the glass refrigeration units. Half had wandered toward the rear of the store, chasing something else, while the other half spied Callan and decided he looked tasty.

The others were closing from behind, and he had nowhere to go.

26

Dylan ran past the delicatessen and toward the fresh foods section, fighting the trolley for control. There were only three aisles to go, and he wasn't giving up the groceries until his life depended on it. There must have been twenty zombies in the deli, fighting and eating, climbing over the refrigeration cases as others tried to pull them back. He felt his stomach roll and then tighten in terror.

He glimpsed the fresh foods section, but two zombies slid out of the last aisle and stumbled into his pathway. Far behind, automatic gunfire sounded, the rapid *chat-chat-chat* like something out of the movies, and Dylan knew they were no longer alone. A faint haze of dirty smoke had spread through the supermarket.

Gritting his teeth, he rammed the first feeder, who was wearing Army clothes, and the metal trolley shuddered. The zombie fell onto its back, groaning. The second one, wearing a white smock and covered in blood, moved with dexterity, latching onto Dylan's forearm with a firm, dogged grip. It only had one arm; the other had been ripped off at the shoulder. Its mouth twisted in mockery, blood and juices dripping from its lips. Dylan had to let go of the trolley.

He did, then twisted himself around to fend the zombie off, shoving its chest. It was like pushing a wall. Where was his rifle? The zombie pinned him with a strong hand and drove him backward into the end of an aisle. Stock fell over them and crashed to the ground. They fell, rolling in a hellish embrace.

Dylan smacked his face on the floor. The mask cracked and blinding pain shot through his skull. He shook his head and felt the cold grip of the feeder's solitary hand on his neck, pushing him into the hard tiles, turning his head to the side. Dylan reached back with one hand and tried to push it off. He saw more of them emerge from the delicatessen, crawling over the glass casing with their blank, bloated expressions. Some fell down the concave barrier and landed on their noses, while others lay scrambling on the ground, attempting to stand. Several made it to their feet and began lumbering toward him.

He twisted his body and dug his other hand into the monster's chest, pushing to save his life. Even with one less arm, the thing was stronger. Was this it? Would he die like this, surrounded in the Safeway supermarket he had frequented hundreds of times? He thought of Kristy, waiting back at the house, growing ever more worried for him. They had only touched on their potential for love. She was *it*, someone with whom he could envision spending the rest of his life. Could he give that up, or deprive her of it?

Gunfire chattered behind him, the rapid pops of an automatic weapon, followed by the sound of a heavy weight hitting the floor. He turned to the side again and saw a single figure in Army fatigues wearing a facemask and holding a machine gun. It prattled again and Dylan heard the zombie's head disintegrate, spraying blood over the broken mask. The monster fell sideways and he helped it off with a hardy shove.

Crawling onto all fours, he looked up to where he had seen the figure, but a swarm of pursuing zombies had filled the space. Others lurched toward him and he knew he had to move. He stood, feeling a wave of giddiness, and put his arms out to keep balance. On unsteady legs, he staggered to the trolley and shoved it forward, glad for the support.

The area had filled with murky smoke and he began to cough, his eyes watery.

"CALLAN?"

A heavy crash sounded from another aisle, then booming gunfire. They were in trouble, no doubt. Complacency had been their undoing, but he had been dealt a full house and he intended to use it. *Only if you go now.* Callan's words lingered. He was out of options, and he hoped Callan had reached the same conclusion, too.

Dylan jogged alongside a wide bay of large freezers, where boxes and packets of frozen food had defrosted into mucky oblivion. A watery stink beckoned, but he saw the open plan of the fresh food area ahead and pushed harder.

A zombie wearing a soiled green Safeway shirt and black slacks appeared from behind the last row of shelving. *Not again.* A second bumped into it, nudging it forward, its body twisted in an incurable pose of zombiism. When a third and fourth joined them, Dylan felt sure his heart had stopped. He turned back and saw that some of the meat zombies had shambled to within fifteen yards.

He swiveled, looking for a way out. Three male walkers had wandered down the last aisle and Dylan realized he had no choice but to shoot his way out. He lifted the rifle from the trolley, then pushed the cart forward. It glided into a shelf with a bang, and the heavy end swung around perfectly, blocking half the lane.

He hadn't taken a shot yet and still had rounds in his pocket. Could he make it out? He drew the rifle up, walking toward them. Thicker black smoke spread across the room and into his aisle. The three zombies stopped as it circled them, confused by the veil.

Dylan danced around the trolley and lifted the gun into position. He shot one through the side of the head at point-blank range. It fell onto the other two, and they all went sprawling across the floor.

He reached back for the trolley with his left hand and pulled it hard toward himself, then spun it around and drove it over their legs with a crunch. He tried to leap past, but one of them stuck out a hand and caught his shin and he came down awkwardly, the trolley and gun spilling free. His palms slapped the floor, and he crunched his chin, biting his tongue. Pain shot through his mouth and jaw, but he was beyond a little pain, and he turned, scampering backward as a tall, balding supermarket attendant in a white shirt and tie grabbed for him. He swiveled again, crawling for the gun, which was still two yards away. His survival instincts compelled him, and he ignored the pain in his knees, reaching for it with the tips of his fingers, clutching it in his hands. The zombie's raspy breath fell on him and he rolled onto his back, raised the rifle, and fired, off balance. The bullet struck the zombie's right bicep, opening a bloody circle. As the zombie fell back, it struck out with its left arm and connected with the gun, knocking it from Dylan's hand. He watched, dumbstruck, as it flew into bags of rice and rebounded, clattering to the floor.

His lungs burned, but there was no time for deep breaths. The zombie climbed onto its knees, hunched forward, and reached out for his ankle. Dylan paused, waiting for it, then pulled his leg back and kicked with the heel of his boot, striking the monster in the face. It fell away, shaken, and lay still. The other climbed over its boss with the same compulsive intent. Dylan was out of breath and his limbs were exhausted. If he didn't move quickly, he was gone. He leapt to his knees and snatched up the rifle, slamming the bolt into action. He took aim, screaming. The top of the zombie's head disappeared. Before it had fallen, Dylan leaned over and shot the other one in the top of the skull, its brains splattering wetly across the aisle.

He stood, gasping, the pain of fatigue in his gut, unable to believe he survived. Emotions fought for their place, but the one overwhelming sense was relief—he was alive.

As if coming out of a daze, he heard a mix of automatic and rifle gunfire. There was shouting, too, but it was impossible to know from whom. He recalled Callan's exact words: "*If it goes to hell, just get the fuck out of there.*" A fit of coughing curled him over. Spittle flew from his mouth. He thought he might vomit but he pressed it down and took a long, deep breath. "I'm sorry, man." He grabbed the trolley and ran for the back entrance.

27

Callan ran, firing, pumping, firing again, hitting them in the head with an accuracy he could only have dreamed about. They fell aside, crumpled, spun around, blood, bone, and mucus flying through the air like confetti at a tickertape parade. There was a moment where his speed surprised him, but the thought was abruptly ended by the click of an empty chamber.

When he slowed to unload and reload, they kept coming, and he kicked out, pushing them aside with stupid ease. He was running low on rounds, but had almost reached the fresh food section, and then his path to the back entrance was clear. *Jesus, where was Dylan?* Smoke hovered up at the roof, stinging his nostrils, and he could hear the flames crackling as they grew, the shadows dancing on the ceiling. Gunfire popped and crackled, mixed with shouts from the others.

A fresh wave attacked and he blew them aside, elbowing and shouldering the ones he couldn't shoot. A clear space opened and he sprinted to the fresh food section, oblivious to potential occupants in the other aisles.

He hit the mess they had negotiated in the beginning, slipping and sliding over layers of squashed and ruined food. A large, wooden display box, once heaped with apples of various kinds, saved him as he hooked a hand onto the corner, regaining his balance. A flash of movement caught his attention. Dylan steered the shopping trolley toward the back entrance and Callan whooped with delight.

Toward the front, more gunfire echoed off the walls, and an explosion rocked the building, vibrating through the floor. Callan reached Dylan's side and they converged on the exit, neither looking back.

Dylan guided the trolley through the opening. Callan followed, the glass doors shuddering as he knocked his shoulder, and then he was outside, sucking the air down deep, unable to believe he had made it. Breathless, he held up his hand, palm flat. Dylan released one edge of the trolley and smacked it.

They kept moving toward the Jeep.

Dylan said, "I thought I was dead for sure."

"Fuck man, we look like crap." Dylan's face was grimy, caked in blood and smeared with black soot.

"Your face is cut."

Callan touched a hand to his cheeks and pulled it away. Blood covered his fingertips. "Just a scratch." He had no idea when it had happened.

They reached the Jeep and began frantically unloading the groceries into the back. Smoke had drifted out through the glass doors. They emptied the final items and Dylan pushed the trolley away. As they ran for their seats, the glass doors to the supermarket crunched and shook as the horde tried to flee. A zombie slipped through and into the daylight. Smoke drifted from its body and it made a mewling sound. It stumbled toward the Jeep, unaware of their presence. Callan started the car and put the stick into reverse.

The initial ecstasy of their survival had dissipated. Callan felt weariness slither over him, along with the desperation to get home. He debated running over the monster, but Dylan convinced him otherwise.

"Let's just go, man." Another loud explosion sounded, reverberating through the vehicle. "They're gonna rip the place apart," Dylan said. "Maybe that's what they mean to do."

"I think so. Those guys were leading them inside to kill them off. Maybe our timing was just bad."

More zombies jostled to escape. One ran through the doorway with flames leaping from its skull like a fire hat. Callan edged the car backward, spun the steering wheel until the Jeep faced the other way, then took off.

"What a waste," Dylan said. He closed his eyes and leaned his head back against the seat. "Take us home."

Callan glanced up in the rearview mirror as they accelerated toward the street. The undead poured into the laneway. There must have been fifty or sixty of them, all bumbling forward with their twitchy, erratic steps.

"This town is finished," Callan said. *And we should get out before it takes us down with it,* he thought.

Part III

28

Kristy heard the Jeep rolling up the gravel driveway first and felt tears in her eyes. She couldn't recall waiting more desperately for anything in her life than the return of her brother and Dylan. She rushed out through the sliding doors feeling a moment of anxiety, hoping they were both safe and uninjured. Given what she and Sherry had experienced since their departure, she suspected the boys would have found similar trouble.

On the veranda, her gaze went straight to the fence along Silvan Road and she was relieved to see the walker had disappeared, although they would have to be wary, given that the earlier one had done the same thing and then appeared on their doorstep. She led Sherry off the veranda and down the steps as the Jeep circled the parking area and pulled up beside them. It took Kristy a moment to realize it was a different vehicle, still black, but brand new, probably the latest model. She wondered what had happened to the other one. Even through the windscreen, she could read the exhaustion in their expressions and postures. Dylan had the seat angled back at sixty degrees.

They slid out, their movement slow and beaten. Their skin was grubby, as though they had been fighting bushfires under a blazing sun, and was flecked with the blood of untold monsters. A realization came to her that life was never going to be easy again. Wherever they went, the dead that had invaded the land would provide a formidable challenge and seek to kill them at every chance.

Dylan came to her and they embraced, his arms reaching around her and pulling her hips close. They kissed softly and Kristy felt her skin tingle, the dramas of the day washing away with the silky touch of his lips.

"I've missed you," he said. "*God, I missed you*. I didn't think I was going to make it back at one point."

She pulled away, catching her breath. "I'm glad you're back. We had our own trouble, too." She stroked his cheek. "Are you okay?"

He nodded. "Lots to talk about. Let's get the stuff inside first. We're here now; that's all that matters."

Callan left Sherry and gave Kristy a quick hug.

"You gave up your car?"

"How could I resist this?" He sighed. "Nah. We lost it. Long, *long* story. How's Greg?"

"Not good. His fever is still high. He's been asleep for the entire day. Well, most of it, anyway." She glanced around, making sure the missing zombie hadn't approached from another direction. "And we had a visitor." Callan snapped his head around. "A zombie attacked us on the porch. There have been two standing at the fence. We don't know where the other one is." Callan looked around. "We'll tell you about inside," Kristy said.

Callan opened the back door and began handing supplies to the others. "What can we do for him?"

"I'll examine his leg in another hour. If it's worse, it means the wound is infected. He'll need antibiotics."

"Shit," Callan said, pressing his lips into a thin line. "We were at the drugstore. We got some more painkillers, but I didn't think to check for antibiotics."

"Let's see how it goes. I've given him loads of ibuprofen and paracetamol. He might be feeling better the next time he wakes up."

"You're sure it's not the actual virus?"

"I don't think so."

Callan's shoulders relaxed. "That's something." He handed a small box to Sherry and gave her a kiss. "Good luck, babe."

Her smile was weak, almost forced. Kristy wondered whether she actually wanted the baby. She couldn't blame her, though. It was no longer safe to bring a child into the world. Perhaps, in eight months, things would be different.

They all helped lug the groceries and other supplies inside and placed them on the kitchen bench. Sherry and Callan disappeared toward the toilet.

"Any sign of your father?" Kristy asked.

"No. Nothing. Although we did see another car driving around, but we don't know who was driving. We waited until it had passed."

Callan returned holding Sherry's hand. A wide, weary smiled graced his face. Kristy hugged him warmly. Dylan avoided looking at Sherry and watched them, appreciating the genuine warmth between siblings. Dylan could relate. He and his own sister, Lauren, shared a similar relationship. The thought of her flushed him with sadness. Where was she? Alive? Dead? He refused to consider the other option.

"Congratulations," he said, shaking Callan's hand. "Again."

"If only we had some champagne," Kristy said.

The boys peeled off their old clothes—jeans, the leather jackets, and boots—and washed under warm water. Kristy had to call out to Dylan to ask if he was okay, he stayed in so long.

"I was just savoring the moment," he said, poking his head out the door, wrapped in a towel. He looked like he couldn't believe he was standing there.

They each tried on their Kevlar motorbike gear; the sizing was almost perfect. "We all have to wear this whenever we go out," Callan said. "It might save our lives. The leather jacket stopped me from getting scratched today, but this stuff's even better."

The boys washed their plastic facemasks under warm water in the laundry, and then they sat in the family area on the sofas and discussed the events of the day. Kristy and Dylan sat with their legs touching, Sherry and Callan on the single chairs. Kristy had tended to a graze on the side of Dylan's head, covering it with numerous Band-Aids. She had inspected their heads, necks, arms, legs, and hands for any scratches, but the gloves and leather jackets seemed to have done their job. Callan sipped at a glass of bourbon, and Dylan did the same with warm Coke from a bottle they had taken from the gas station a lifetime ago.

"I feel relieved knowing my parents got away," Sherry said. "I didn't think I was so worried but now I'm just... grateful."

Kristy didn't want to say that it didn't mean much. Byron Bay might well be like Albury. Who knew if there was a single place in Australia free of zombies? "And there was no sign of Greg's grandparents, or Mum and Dad?" Kristy asked.

Callan averted his eyes. "Nothing. No sign." He glanced at Dylan, then looked away.

Kristy didn't quite believe him. He couldn't look at her. There was something more to it, something Callan wasn't saying, but she knew if he kept silent, there was a good reason. She would prod him later.

Callan looked in on Greg and returned with a grim expression. "He looks so pale, and the heat coming off his forehead is unbelievable. He seemed okay this morning. How did it get to this point?"

Kristy explained the cycle of an infection, and told them their story, beginning with the first walker that almost reached her, Greg's heroics, and him fainting. Callan grew angry, pacing the floor, while Dylan sat beside Kristy with a hand on her arm. She continued with Mr. Henry, and everything that happened up until the point of seeing the second walker at the fence. At the end, Callan and Dylan sat in contemplative silence.

Finally, Callan said, "It's worse in town. I don't think there's gonna be a town in a few days. And based on what you've seen here, this place isn't as safe and remote as we thought. We need to decide what to do next. Whether we stay or go."

Dylan said, "Hang on, hang on. Go? What do you mean?"

Callan shrugged. "You saw what it was like. The town is fucked. Soon there'll be nothing left for us. And this place is a risk. They're moving further out of town every day. There must have been ten of them along the roadside on the way back."

"Look, I've been thinking about this for most of the day. I won't say I haven't considered leaving, but I still think we need a base, a place to return to, with all the essentials. This house has everything. Protection, weapons, electricity, and... comfort."

"But it doesn't have the protection," Sherry said. "The first zombie got in from the side fence. They're not electrified."

"Then we rig it up. I'm sure Callan and I can figure something out."

Kristy said, "Sherry had a good idea. She suggested we use the excavator to dig a trench inside the fence line and put some weapons in it so if they do get in, they'll get hurt."

Dylan threw his hands up. "That's a bloody good idea."

"It's not gonna be enough," Callan said. Dylan frowned. "The zombies are moving further out, there's no question of that. They're ravaging everything in sight. Sooner or later, they'll hit the outskirts. How are we gonna keep a thousand of the bastards out?"

"Everything my father has done so far has been right. He knows what he's doing and he wasn't leaving. He thought staying here was the best option. You went against him once before. I don't doubt how much you've done for us, but he's been spot on... mostly."

Kristy's shoulders stiffened. She didn't like what she was about to do, but Dylan had to know. "There's something you guys should see," Kristy said. "In the garage."

Dylan called Kristy back as the others continued on. "You remember what he was like yesterday, so adamant about visiting his parents' place first? It's that all over again."

She hated disagreeing with Dylan. "I'm sorry, but I have to agree with him this time. This place is no longer safe."

His eyes widened. "You really think that?" Kristy nodded. She took his hand and pulled him toward the front of the house.

They entered the garage from the internal access door near the front entrance, Dylan reaching around through the doorway, feeling for the light switch. Sitting in the empty space where his father's car would normally sit was the trailer.

"Sherry found it when we were looking for nails to board up the windows."

Dylan stepped down into the garage and walked around it, running his hand along the side. He looked beaten. Two large tents, several sleeping bags, a gas bottle, and a bench top cooker had been packed with care.

"We found a notepad in the lounge room among the other papers," Kristy said. "There's a list of seven points with the heading 'DEPARTURE STRATEGY.' They were planning on leaving."

"That explains why there's no food in the cupboards," Dylan said, holding up a can of spaghetti. "I just don't understand, though. This place is... safe. Do you guys know how difficult it will be, staying on the move all the time? Staying in a different place every night? Imagine we find a good spot, set up, settle down, and then some zombies find us. We'll have to pack up and start all over again." Nobody spoke. Dylan moved items around, checking the inventory. "I don't know what to say," he said. "I'm surprised. Really surprised he would be thinking this."

Callan said, "I'm not. I think he must have realized the entire region wouldn't survive. Even if only a third of the thirty-five thousand people in Albury have turned into zombies, that's still a shitload of the bastards to feed."

"Did the notes say where they were going?"

Sherry said, "No."

They took supplies from the trailer and went inside to cook a late lunch. Sherry boiled rice in a pot on the stove, then fried eggs in a pan and added them to carrots, garlic, and capsicum in the wok. Half a bottle of oyster sauce flavored the meal and they ate at the kitchen bench with a bottle of Penfolds red wine from Dylan's father's collection in the lounge room.

Kristy checked Greg's leg. He stirred when she put a thermometer in his ear to check his temperature. It was a little over a hundred and one. The wound on his leg had grown red and angry. He needed antibiotics.

"You should have seen him today," Sherry said. "Kristy would have died if Greg hadn't taken the rifle from her and shot the zombie."

Kristy hated thinking about it. "I don't know what happened."

"It's okay," Dylan said, resting a hand on hers. "You came through on the next one."

"What did you do with the bodies?" Callan said.

"We carried them to the pile of brush in the front paddock, where you put the others."

He nodded and said, "We'll have to burn them tomorrow. They might be attracting others."

"They are definitely moving out of town," Dylan said. "On the way out, we saw one right up at the top of Silvan Road, eating a cow, and a heap more wandering about down the bottom, at the intersection of Starling Road."

"There was another one at the fence," Sherry said. "After Mr. Henry. We just left it…"

"It was gone when you guys got back."

"We need to think about this," Callan said. "Overnight. Decide as a group what we want to do."

They cleaned up and sat on the couches talking as darkness rolled in. Candles lit the room, and Kristy lay with her head in Dylan's lap. He stroked her hair for what seemed like hours. Despite the situation, she could have stayed there forever, feeling as content in those moments as she had in a long time.

"How are you today? About your mother?"

"I haven't really had time to think about it. I spent most of the day trying to stay alive. If I wasn't saving Callan's life, he was saving mine. I guess at some point I'll have to."

Sherry lay on Callan's chest, her eyes closed, and Kristy decided the baby was a good thing. It seemed to have brought them closer. She wanted to believe Sherry had seen the light. From what Kristy had witnessed, she appeared different. How quickly things changed, she thought. Would they all still be alive at the same time the following night? Was life now a day-to-day proposition? Yes. What was their next move? Who was right? Her eyelids grew heavy and she drifted, her thoughts a jumble of Dylan, Greg, and their lives at risk. An urgent voice drew her out of it.

"You hear that?" Sherry asked, springing to her feet, turning her ear toward the wide sliding doors. The others looked perplexed. "It sounds like a car."

They all climbed off the sofa. "Lights off," Dylan said, dowsing one of the candles between his thumbs with saliva.

Callan slid the doors open and they stepped out onto the porch, one after the other. Stars glittered in the cloudless, blue-black sky. Shadows filled their vision all the way to the horizon.

"You must have ears like a wolf," Callan said in a whisper.

Sherry hushed her voice and said, "I used to be able to hear my parents whispering with their door shut, and I was in the farthest room."

"What was it?"

"An engine."

Kristy squinted, trying to focus on the blackness for signs of movement. The trees murmured in the gentle breeze, which carried the scent of the town after weeks of death and feeding. It hadn't been so bad yesterday, and Kristy wondered whether they'd be able to walk outside in a week without gagging. They'd probably get used to it. But for now, outside of town, where the fresher scents of the country hadn't yet been completely tarnished, the smell of the old world was still fighting for its place.

Kristy saw it then, on the dirt road, just past the gate. A flicker of light. "There. Moving away down the road."

They watched the shadows in silence. After ten seconds, the trees and roadway toward the end of the dirt road were illuminated. Taillights glowed red, and Callan said, "That's a Jeep. Same brake lights as the new one."

Dylan said, "They're checking the area. Do you think they followed us?"

"Maybe."

There was a long silence. Finally, Sherry asked, "Do you think they know we're here?"

Nobody answered.

Callan lay facedown on the soft bed in the back room and eased his head onto the pillow. He closed his eyes, feeling a pleasurable sensation engulf his body, fighting away the aches and pains that had developed from the day's activity. Sherry straddled his back and began to tease the knots from the muscles on his bare back.

"Ohhhh that's good. Very good." She chuckled. "What have I done to deserve this?" He couldn't recall the last time she had done such a thing.

"Risking your life. Finding more food. Fighting for us to leave this hellish place."

"You think we should go, too?"

"We can't stay here. Albury's infected. They're already starting to wander out this way. Two today. How many tomorrow?"

Callan harbored similar impressions, and he trusted Sherry's judgment. He thought about an episode he'd seen on the National Geographic channel, about a pack of lions. Once they'd exhausted their food source in a particular area, they moved to another. The zombies were like that. They had started where the supply was most plentiful, but it would soon run out, and they would seek new sources. There would be people in the wider area, and a plentiful supply of farm animals, too. He had to convince Dylan they were in danger if they remained at the house.

"You're right. We need to persuade Kristy, though, and she will help us with Dylan."

"Why does he want to stay here so badly?"

Callan had thought about this, too. Maybe Dylan expected his father would eventually return. *Sorry mate, but that's not going to happen.* Unless Mr. Cameron was some kind of superhero, Callan doubted he was even alive. "His father, I guess."

The other immediate issue was Greg. He'd never seen his old mate look so bad. Kristy believed that antibiotics were the only thing that would make him better, and that meant going back to town. Whatever it took. It wasn't the same without Greg. While Dylan had saved Callan's life and done everything required, Greg was a whole other level of force. As a team, the three of them would be unbeatable.

Sherry finished her massage and Callan rolled over. She smiled, sucking the breath from him, and he couldn't help but respond with his own. His loins stirred. She hadn't smiled like that in ages. It was genuine joy, hard to fake. She began to unbutton her blouse and a momentary feeling of alarm pervaded him. They hadn't made love since before the trip. Countless nights he'd initiated contact, created an environment of intimacy, only to have her reject him again and again.

"Soon I'll have a fat belly and a chubby face," she said. "You won't think I'm so attractive then."

He frowned. "Rubbish. I can't wait to see you like that. I bet I love you even more."

She slipped off her top, revealing a black bra and modest fill, then dropped it on the carpet. Leaning forward, she kissed his lips, then took his top lip between her own, running her tongue lightly over it.

"Ohhhh," Callan said. "You're a tease."

She slipped off her bra and the playful smile turned into one of modesty. Callan's eyes glazed over, the magic of her body entrancing him. They hugged and kissed and frolicked like they hadn't since the beginning, when everything had been fresh and captivating. His manhood awakened from a six-week slumber, begging for her touch. He had waited patiently, his love never dented or doubted, and he had known the time would come when she would turn the corner and the flame would flicker again. *The baby*, he thought, grateful for life's wonders. They smothered each other's bodies with their mouths, reaching new levels of desire and intent, and Callan thought that, after the turmoil of the last days, this was exactly what he needed.

He soon lost his way, giving in to her sensitive delights, following her advice willingly, and in the end, when she called out his name, he drifted into a cloud of pleasure and wondered how it could get any better.

Afterward, Sherry lay in his arms, and Callan drifted off to sleep with the first genuine smile on his face in months.

Callan woke early and found Sherry bent over the toilet bowl again. It was worse than the previous day, and although he knew it wasn't a serious condition, he still felt his own kind of illness, seeing her in such a state.

"What can I do?" he asked, one hand rubbing her back.

"Leave me be for a while." Then she vomited again.

Callan dressed in his Kevlar gear in anticipation of the day ahead. He didn't want to use any of the supplies Dylan's father had prepared in the trailer, so against his better judgement, he climbed the fence to the Henrys' house and waded through the slaughterhouse that was the chicken coop. He took the last seven eggs supplied by the now dead chickens, then harvested a container full of tomatoes and zucchini from the vegetable garden behind the house. He returned to the kitchen and began frying eggs and tomatoes.

He thought about checking on Greg but decided to wait until Kristy appeared in case he woke him or did something wrong. He couldn't shake the concern for his old mate. Kristy insisted it wasn't the virus, but how could she be sure without a test? Even if it wasn't the virus, he was in trouble and needed stronger medicine than headache tablets. Whatever Kristy decided was needed, he would find. Aside from convincing Dylan that they needed to leave Albury in search of a safer place, that was his mission for the day.

He hoped Dylan would see sense this morning. He wasn't sure what the car driving with its lights off on

Silvan Road meant, but in a place where survival was the priority every day, how long before they came under attack? In a post-apocalyptic world, most people forwent their ethics and morals in favor of survival. They had items of value and others might want and need them. The quicker they packed up and hit the road, the better for all of them. He liked the idea of the Army base in Wagga and felt that should be the first place they checked. If anybody had answers, it would be the Army, despite the state of their roadblock on the trip back from the lake.

Kristy plodded downstairs into the kitchen, her yellow hair bunched above her head and pinned with a brown clip that looked like a dinosaur tooth. "Morning," she said in a sleepy voice.

Callan knew she had slept up in Dylan's room, but the world had moved on. Such things were of little importance now. He squeezed her in a hug and felt proud that he could finally get past it. "How are you feeling?"

"Better. But I'm sure I'll be a nervous wreck before the morning's out. You going back into town?" She climbed onto one of the timber stools at the counter.

"Well, we need ammo. Does Greg need the antibiotics?" She nodded. "Then we're there." He poured brewed coffee into a mug and added a splash of milk.

"Don't be too long. I don't think I could handle another day here alone."

"What do you think? About leaving?"

She yawned and took the mug of coffee. "Thank you. I trust your judgment."

"You wanna tell Dylan that?"

"No. He'll work it out soon. I have to check on Greg." She took the coffee and swung off the stool.

Callan put the eggs on a plate and placed it in the oven on low heat, then went out onto the veranda. Three separate smoke columns rose up from the town center. Two were a dirty black color, the other a sooty grey. It was happening. How long before the whole place burned to the ground? They had already lost the Coles and Safeway Supermarkets, which probably equated to three-quarters of the human food supply. He suspected that whoever had saved them yesterday had set the place on fire to eradicate the zombies that had converged on the store. Nice plan, but why destroy all your food and supplies? There would be nothing left by the end of the week.

Inside, Kristy had a cloth under running water at the sink. "How is he? I wanted to check on him but…"

"Temperature is still a hundred and one. I've given him some more paracetamol but the wound is red. It's infected."

"But it's not the virus?"

She shook her head. "He's got no signs of respiratory problems. From all accounts, that's the basis of it. He's got a fever and he doesn't want to move. He feels tired and has no energy. It all fits."

"What do we do?"

"He needs antibiotics."

"And if we can't get them?" Kristy pressed her lips together. Callan said, "I'll get them. At the chemist?"

"Yes. I doubt the refrigeration will be working, so they'll be useless. See if they have some in pill form."

"We'll go now."

Callan woke Dylan and they prepared themselves for a return into the war zone. A lump of uneasiness filled his gut. They had been so lucky the day before. If they didn't have some more of that luck today, one or both of them wouldn't make it back.

Dylan moved like a man who was going to his death— quiet, lethargic, eating his eggs and tomatoes with slow, thoughtful bites. He and Kristy spent time in the lounge room, talking in low voices and embracing for long periods. Callan hoped Kristy was swaying his opinion about leaving.

Callan packed the rifles and the axe into the Jeep, along with the remaining bullets that suited the Remington models, leaving a box of shells for the Winchester .30-30 in case the girls and Greg had company again. As he closed the car door, he glanced down toward the front fence along Silvan Road and a spear of fright poked him.

Half a dozen zombies had wandered up the fence along the perimeter. "Oh fuck." Further down the road beyond the front gate, he saw the odd straggler. He ran inside and alerted the others, with the exception of Sherry, who was still upstairs, and they joined him in the parking area at the top of the driveway. He took the Remington bolt action from the Jeep and stood ten yards away from the others.

The first shot rocked the morning sky but missed a target, ending up in the trees lining the other side of the dirt road. The zombies didn't flinch. The second hit one of the fence posts, shattering the top of the wood in a shower.

"Don't use all our ammo," Dylan said.

The third shot hit a feeder in the chest and knocked it into the long grass. Callan waited to see if it would get back up, knowing chest shots were useless. Half a minute later, it rose unsteadily to its feet. "Bastard." He lifted the rifle and cracked off another shot, this time hitting the same monster in the neck. A ribbon of blood exploded and it tumbled backward down the rocky roadside, out of sight.

"This is a waste of time," Kristy said. "We should just leave." Dylan shot her a sharp look. "Do we have enough ammunition to stand here all day shooting at them? There were two yesterday. Now there are six. How many tomorrow?"

"I don't think you guys understand how difficult it's going to be on the move."

"At least we'll be alive," Callan said.

Kristy put a hand on his arm. "Your father knew what was going to happen. He was preparing to do the same thing."

"What if he comes back?"

Callan didn't think he was coming back. Dylan's father had to be dead. Nobody could survive several nights in that place. But Dylan wasn't ready to accept that. "We'll drive around and have a look for him. His car must be somewhere." Dylan nodded.

"Why don't we all just leave now?" Kristy said. "Pack up and head off together, stop at the drugstore on the way through, and look for Dylan's father at the same time."

Callan raised his eyebrows. "I suppose we could. Let me check on Sherry."

He ran upstairs, feeling like he'd won a victory. They had agreed to leave. Technically, they hadn't all agreed, but Dylan hadn't opposed it. Sherry lay against the bathroom wall beside the toilet, head back, eyes closed. A layer of bile floated at the bottom of the bowl. Callan flushed it. "Babe, how do you feel?"

She shook her head and said in a pitiful voice, "Sick."

He went back downstairs and found Kristy pulling supplies from the pantry. "You'd better check on her. I don't think she can go anywhere yet."

Callan finished piling food on the kitchen counter while Dylan picked from a plate of eggs. "We'll have to go on our own. The hunting store first, and then the drugstore."

Dylan put his elbow on the bench and rubbed a hand over his face. "Oh man, I really don't wanna go back there."

He felt the same way, but Greg needed medicine and nothing would stop Callan from trying everything within his power to find it. "I'd tell you to stay here, but the truth is, without you yesterday, I wouldn't be here."

"I think we're even," Dylan said, slumping back in the chair.

Kristy came into the kitchen. "You're right. She's in no state to move yet. Give her a couple of hours and she should have improved enough. I'll take some paracetamol up to her soon, but she'll probably just bring it back up."

"Let's go, then," Callan said. "Get out and back as quickly as possible and then just leave." Dylan nodded. "I just wanna check on Greg."

He crept into the bedroom and found Greg lying on top of the covers, eyes closed, a cold washer on his forehead.

He didn't expect Greg to be awake, but he said in a whisper, "Hey man, how you feeling?"

"Shithouse," Greg said in a deep, croaky voice. "Get back from me. I don't want anyone else to catch it."

At least he was talking now. "What do you mean? Kristy said your leg was infected."

"It is. Throbbing like a motherfucker. But I've got the virus, too."

"Nah man, Kristy reckons you don't. Dylan and I are going into town to get you some antibiotics."

"Don't bother."

Callan reached out and put a hand on the covers where he thought Greg's shoulder lay. "Just—"

Greg twisted himself and threw up an arm. "Get away, I said!"

"Hey, take it easy, mate." Callan stepped away. "I'll get your medicine. We'll be back soon."

Greg sat up and Callan drew back, feeling the sting of Greg's appearance. His face looked narrower, and even in the ambient light from beneath the curtains he recognized the face of a sick man, pale and washed out.

"…me up."

"What?"

"I said, tie me up."

"What for?"

"In case I'm sick. In case it's the virus."

"That's ridiculous."

"What if it is? What if I go feral and bite Sherry or Kristy?"

"No fucking way. Kristy says you're fine. I won't do it."
He backed out of there, watching Greg watch him, his eyes
full of sickness, and something else he couldn't place.

In the kitchen, Dylan had changed into his Kevlar gear.
Minus only the helmet, he looked like a motorbike rider.
Callan told them of Greg's comments.

"He hasn't got it," Kristy said.

"Just leave him. He'll be okay," Callan said.

He climbed the stairs and found Sherry still sitting on
the floor of the bathroom. He helped her to her feet, and
she wrapped her arms around him in a weak hug, Callan
holding her up. Despite this, he felt a stronger connection
with her, more than any other moment in months.
Memories of the previous night swelled his heart, and he
realized this was the breakthrough he had been craving.

"Look after yourself," Sherry said. "Don't play heroes.
I need you around to take care of this baby."

He flushed with pride. "Nothing will happen to me.
I've got Dylan at my side, and if you'd seen the shit he
pulled yesterday…"

"Funny, you didn't even really like each other a month
ago."

"I got it wrong. He's a good guy." They kissed lightly.
He could smell the sickness on her, but he didn't pull
away.

"Sorry," she said, when they had finished. "I'm not in
the best state."

Callan pulled her tightly to him, savoring her touch, the
smell of her hair. His belly ached with love. He didn't want
to leave. He should have been taking care of her, but time
was short. The quicker they left, the sooner they'd return.
Their hands locked, and as he drew away and they
separated, his skin tingled. He turned, keeping her face in
his mind's eye as he descended the stairs.

30

The Jeep crunched and popped over the gravel as it rolled down the driveway. They each had their trusty Remington rifles—Dylan the bolt action, Callan the pump. On approach to the gate, Callan slowed the vehicle, and the closest zombie left its post at the fence.

"And so it begins," Dylan said, pulling the bolt action across his lap. Callan nodded.

Five of the original six remained. The Jeep stopped before the gate and Dylan leapt out. By the time he reached the motor box, a zombie was there. He loaded the chamber and stuck the muzzle between the bars. Its cloudy eyes peered back at him, tongue rolling around an open mouth. Callan noticed his hesitation. Perhaps Dylan wondered who had owned the thick dark hair, the dirty navy blue jeans, and black Nike pullover before now. The man looked to have been in his early twenties, but was unfamiliar. Callan knew most of the younger people in Albury. A second feeder approached, a female, much older, with jowls around her neck and a beefy head of bleached blonde hair. *Freshly turned,* he thought. As if in agreement, she reached up to the man and tried to bite his neck.

Dylan turned the weapon toward her and pulled the trigger. Her head disintegrated and she fell into the grass. The male didn't even look at her. He gripped the bars tighter and kept on rolling his tongue. Dylan reloaded the chamber and prodded him away from the fence, then shot off the top of his head.

He adjusted position when the third approached, repeating the exercise, and dispatched it with a shot to the dead center of its skull. It leapt backward and landed on the female with a thump. The fourth and fifth remained in spots further along the fence, where it was electrified. Dylan unlocked the gate and rolled it open, looking back at the feeders as Callan drove the Jeep over the drain hump and onto a thicker bed of gravel. Neither moved. After he had pushed the gate back into place and locked it, he glanced at Callan, who nodded. They weren't leaving a live one this close to the house.

Dylan walked along the lumpy side of the road where weeds sprouted from tiny hills of dirt. Horse hooves and tractor wheels were the only things that usually moved along it. Neither monster noticed his approach. As he shot the second one in the side of the head, the wind lifted, and even sitting in the Jeep with the window down, Callan realized what had drawn them there. The smell of the other dead zombies filled his nostrils; he blocked his nose.

"Gets easier, doesn't it?" Callan asked as Dylan slotted the rifle into the foot well of the passenger seat and slipped in.

"Sadly, I think you're right."

They saw zombies in the neighboring properties, roaming the hill leading up to the house, feasting in groups on a sheep and two cows.

"We gotta leave Albury, man."

"I know. I just have to have one more shot at finding my father."

"It's gonna get worse," Callan said. "We need to leave today. By tonight, there will probably be a horde waiting at the gate."

Dylan flexed his fingers around the rifle. "Agreed."

The zombies weren't just on the move, they were *migrating*. Since driving up the dusty road late the previous afternoon, the population had exploded. Every property had zombie tenants. They wandered beside the road in ones and twos, feeding, fighting, some just standing, their empty stares scarier than a snarl or growl. Some carried sticks and other weapons, possessing a glint of recognition beyond the usual indifference, but most wore the familiar expression of incoherence.

They turned off Silvan Road and saw a continuation of what they had seen further out, which blanketed both young men in silence. There was no point in stopping. In some areas, Callan had to push the Jeep harder to avoid becoming blocked in. Zombie bodies flew from the front and edges of the SUV, bumping and banging the unspoiled paintwork.

"You think there's any place left in Australia where these things don't exist?"

Callan tilted his head. "I doubt it. But we'll find it, if there is."

David Street ran parallel to Young Street, where they'd found the Kevlar clothing in the motorbike shop the previous day. The front windows of the hunting store were among the few unbroken, but the fresh produce store beside it had been destroyed. Shattered glass and rotten fruit lay over the pavement. Through the broken windows, racks and boxes were visible, scattered across the floor. Under the shopfront canopy, a fat man with no shirt and a female with a bloated face and googly eyes fed on a body.

"Let's try the back," Callan said. "We might be able to slip in and out without them knowing."

"Yeah," Dylan said with sarcasm, "that worked yesterday."

Callan pulled on the steering wheel and did a U-turn, heading south back toward Wilson Street, where he turned right and pulled left onto a narrow cobblestone laneway.

"Gotta love that suspension," he said, smiling as the Jeep rode the rickety surface. He braked, noting a sign above a galvanized steel roller door that read: SHAW'S HUNTING & FISHING. He angled the car away from the entrance, then backed it up until he heard the sensor beep, indicating he was within a yard of a barrier.

The roller door wouldn't lift, and the handle on the smaller entrance, a heavy, wooden slab, didn't budge.

"I knew I brought the axe for a reason."

Callan took a swing and stuck the blade into the door about halfway up, feeling it shudder through his upper body. It bit deep, and he twisted until it pulled free, then repeated his action, smashing at each previous mark to weaken the wood. He kept at it, feeling sweat along the base of his neck. His shoulders began to weaken, but soon he had a hole in the door that Dylan was able to reach into, unlocking it from the inside.

The entrance led them into an empty receiving area where bright blue and orange Dexion racking lined both walls. They walked on through the doorway into the main shop. A counter ran along each wall for about half the length of the room. Behind each sat rows of rifles and shotguns, boxes of ammunition, and signage for the major brands of weaponry: Beretta, Remington, Browning, and others. No less than fourteen deer heads had been mounted and bolted to the wall, displaying the hunting prowess of the shop's owners. Some of the racks were empty, and below those spaces, there was no ammunition.

"Jesus," Callan said, walking to the middle of the shop. "Gun heaven." He felt a sudden, overwhelming feeling of power, as though they might now actually have a chance of protecting themselves in the longer term. "It's a pity we couldn't get hold of any semi-automatic or automatic weapons."

He stepped behind the right counter and looked along the wall for the most impressive rifle. Reaching out, he took a Sauer S 202 Yukon from the shelf. The price tag said $3900, but this particular model, according to the tag, had a Zeiss Victory HT 3-12x56 scope that would set the buyer back another $2600. The tag also said it used a 9.3x62 caliber, and had a capacity of three rounds. He made note to ensure they got some ammunition for it. They each took two long bags from underneath a shelf and began filling them with guns and boxes of ammo.

A particular handgun and its $1800 price tag caught his eye. He looked closer and saw that it was a Browning Hi-Power Stainless 9mm. He grabbed four and stuffed them in his bag, then added a couple of Glock and Beretta handguns. They filled the remaining space with rifles and shotguns of varying size, including a brand new FN Special Police Rifle (SPR) A5M.

Callan walked to the ammunition cabinet and spotted a rack of knives. "These will come in handy." He took four and secured them in with the guns.

With two loaded bags of weapons, they began stacking ammunition into several plastic baskets. They piled them near the counter and ended up with five, although it still didn't look like enough. He thought about driving from town to town, defending themselves against an army of feeders, perhaps unable to find more bullets.

They unloaded the contents of each basket into the back of the Jeep, then refilled them until the stock behind the glass cases in their various calibers grew patchy. Their movement in and out of the shop had attracted attention, though, and on the final run to collect the last baskets, Dylan spied visitors at the front window.

"Walkers."

Callan turned to see three zombies standing at the door, one holding a long weapon. He sidestepped behind a stand filled with fishing lures. Dylan spied a stack of fishing rods and did the same. "I knew it wouldn't last long." He peered around the edge of the stand and saw more zombies had joined the other three. "We're gonna have to make a break for it."

The group pounded against the door. There were several loud bangs as Callan scanned the shop for anything they might have missed.

Glass broke, crashing over the carpet at the front of the store. They had to move. Callan stepped out, glancing up at the doorway as he picked up one of the baskets, feeling the strain on his shoulder. One of the zombies had a pale arm through the broken glass door, feeling for the lock. He felt a strange comfort wash over him. *I must be getting used to it.*

Callan said, "Let's move. No point fighting. We've got what we need."

"I need a scope for the rifle. I'll meet you there."

Callan flipped his facemask down, then ran through the back section and out the door into daylight. He glanced toward the laneway entrance and saw a lone zombie lurching toward him. His first reaction was to shoot, but it was slow and bumbling, so he ran to the back of the Jeep and heaved the basket inside, then danced around to the front of the car with the rifle drawn.

The feeder had reached the shop exit, and a handful more appeared at the entrance to the laneway.

"Dylan! Stay in—"

But he burst through the doorway before Callan could complete the sentence, hitting the zombie with a slap of flesh. Both went down, the basket of ammo crashing to the concrete. The walker fell onto Dylan, and they began an intense wrestling match.

"Move out the way!" Callan stepped forward, looking for a clear shot. The other zombies loped forward, sensing fresh meat.

From the rubble-strewn area on his left, Callan saw a flash of blue and white near the edge of the driveway. His mind registered the image, but until the dog barked, he didn't realize it was the same dog they had seen attacking the zombie horde two nights ago. It was unmistakable though—same height, length, and pointy black ears.

The dog sprinted in and leapt onto the zombie's green pullover, snapping and growling, then fell back to the driveway. The feeder pulled away from Dylan and swiped at it, but the dog was quick, scampering backward to avoid its hand. Dylan kicked the thing away and crawled backward like a crab toward the newly arrived crew.

Callan shot the zombie in the neck and it toppled backward as blood gushed onto the pale concrete. The horde ran for Dylan, but he was quickly on his feet, dashing toward the Jeep. Several of them broke away and went for their fallen colleague. The dog diverted the remaining zombies with a frenzy of barking as it pushed its safety to the limit.

"Let's move," Callan said as he shot another.

Dylan found his feet and the dog yelped. One of the zombies had caught its leg. Dylan stopped, ready to defend the dog, but Callan ran forward, pushing one aside, and kicked the walker in the face, its jaw cracking. The dog broke free and zipped away, yelping. A second zombie shuffled in close and reached for Callan. He leaped aside, spun on one leg, and fired the rifle. A red cavity appeared near its collarbone and it fell, providing a critical moment. Callan pulled away and both boys ran to the vehicle and yanked their doors open.

The dog was safely away. Amidst the madness, Dylan laughed. "What a crazy dog."

"Saved your ass." Had it known they needed assistance? It sprinted down the laneway toward the road with its black pointed ears pinned back, leaving the zombies behind. It reached the roadway free of harm, then turned and barked at them.

Dylan slammed the door. Two undead reached the hood and began thumping on it. Callan inserted the key and twisted. The engine turned once, twice, with a metallic wrench, then kicked in, and Callan revved it. Grimy hands slid along the hood to the driver's window, smearing streaks of gore. An old man pressed his pallid, rotting face against the glass beside Dylan.

Callan slammed the accelerator, chirping the tires on the concrete as he bowled over the zombies. He went directly for the ones feeding on the ground, and the car bounced over the bodies, shaking and bumping. Dylan grabbed onto the handle above the door and pushed against the center console. Callan clutched the wheel with white-knuckled hands, his face twisted into a mask of rage and disgust. The last zombie clunked under the wheel and then it was gone, their ride smooth and calm again. The

Jeep skidded as he turned the corner and left the laneway behind.

Dylan looked at him, hair skewed, face red, eyes wide. "Fuck this. I'm over it."

"One more stop and then we're out of here."

31

They reached the drugstore through a twisted route of broken down cars, and parked at an angle facing the wide doors. Aside from the hunting store, the streets were quieter than the previous day. Smaller groups of zombies wandered about, but most of the shop fronts were empty, as though they had taken all they could and moved on.

Dylan had been thinking about what Sherry had told him on the way home. He had debated telling Callan, but felt as though they still didn't have the friendship to warrant delivering such news. Things had changed in the last few days though. They had both earned each other's respect. Now he felt more obligated to divulge what he knew but couldn't quite bring himself to do it. As the car came to a rest, Dylan asked a question that had been with him since the beginning of the trip.

"What is it about Sherry?" Dylan said. Callan frowned. "You're so loyal to her. Clearly you love her very much, but…"

"Why?" Callan said. Dylan nodded. "There's more to her than what you all see. She's… been through a lot." He looked out the window. "I'll only tell you this because it helps explain the way she is sometimes." Callan's eyes narrowed, his face tightened. "She was abused as a kid. By her uncle."

"Oh, fuck."

Callan's head bobbed in agreement, mouth twisted into a snarl. "The bastard used to stay with them, and he'd come into her room at night after everyone was asleep."

Dylan felt sick. He couldn't imagine how badly that would affect someone. Sherry had a right to be pissed AT the world. "I'm so sorry. That explains a bit."

The peg slipped into the hole. Suddenly *everything* made sense to Dylan. Sherry was probably more messed up than he could ever understand. Jesus, and he'd been so hard on her. Although it didn't justify what she had done to Callan, it colored his perspective and he felt a stab of guilt.

"Don't say anything, please," Callan said, "but maybe just cut her some slack at times."

"Yeah, sure. I'll do that."

Callan reached out for the door handle, and said, "Let's do this then."

Movement further along the street caught Dylan's eye. The second moving car they had seen in five weeks rolled along the bitumen toward them. For a long moment, he didn't move. Callan's mouth hung open. Then they both reached for their rifles and laid them across their laps.

"What's this?"

Callan said, "Let's just sit for a moment."

It was the same vehicle they had seen driving past the car dealership the previous day, a black Jeep Grand Cherokee. It came to a stop thirty yards away. Callan could see an object tied with a rope to the tow bar. For a long moment, nobody moved. Then the door clicked open, and a heavy brown work boot and blue pants slowly appeared.

"Oh shit," Callan said. They both knew the man and his mate, who stepped out on the other side. If they had wanted any two people in Albury to survive, these two would be the last.

"Had to be those idiots," Dylan said.

Callan swung the door open. "Stay alert."

They met between the two vehicles. The two newcomers wore blue jeans, checkered shirts, and baseball caps. Steve Palmer and Chris Smith were guys they had grown up around. They had been several grades behind the duo, but they hadn't escaped the older boys' sadistic torment in the schoolyard. They stayed clear of each other now, although Greg had thrown Steve out of a nightclub a year or so back, amid a stormy fight. Steve's father was also the man who had lost a finger in the machine incident at the factory.

"Well, well," Steve said, cigarette smoke curling from the corner of his mouth. "Nice car. You guys got lucky."

Callan tipped his head, tightening his jaw. "We could say the same for you."

"Heard you were up at Lake Eucumbene, fishin'."

"We were," Callan said. "Just got back the day before yesterday."

Steve laughed. "Big changes, huh?" Both boys chuckled. "Where ya holed up?"

Callan glanced at Dylan. "Around."

Telling these two where they were based was like saying "come and steal our supplies." Common belief held that Steve and his father ran some kind of thieving racket having to do with stolen cars. Steve's uncle owned a panel-beating shop, and the volume of business through that place was staggering. Dylan wondered if it had been their car on Silvan Road the previous night. Odds were good—or bad, depending on how you looked at it.

"Oh, come on. You don't trust us? Shit, we got all we need back at our place." Steve's tone grew firm and serious. "Besides, who do you think saved your asses yesterday in the supermarket?"

Steve's eyes were hard and unflinching. Dylan realized he wasn't bullshitting. He glanced at Callan, who looked sheepish. "We're grateful for that, believe me," Dylan said. "I probably wouldn't be standing here, otherwise."

"Well, we're pleased to have helped. You did us a favor, in a way, by drawing all those fuckers into the supermarket."

Chris laughed. "We got 'em though. Nothin' better than seein' 'em burn alive."

"What about all the food?" Callan said. "There was a shitload of stuff."

Steve said, "We got heaps. You should come by and grab some if you need it. How many of you are there? Four, five?"

"Five. Greg, Sherry, and Kristy."

Steve's face brightened. "You got a doctor? Handy. Your mate Johnny is with us, plus some other folks from Wodonga side that we found scratching around one of the shopping centers."

Callan stiffened. "Johnny Stavros?"

"Who the fuck else? Only one *Johnny* in Albury." He seemed to think about that and added, "Literally, now."

Stepping forward, Callan lowered his rifle. "What happened to him? How did he survive?"

"I'll let him tell you the story. We have to keep movin'." He turned around and started back toward the truck. "You should come on back and check out our place. It's cozy. Fully stocked. Lots of beer and booze."

"We might do that," Callan said, ignoring the look of concern on Dylan's face. "Where are you staying again?"

Steve stopped and turned back around. "The old Lyle farm out on the Riverina Highway, near Laboratory Lane."

"Of course. Nice place."

"It's a few miles out, but we haven't been bothered by zombies yet. We got the place protected pretty well. Come on out and have a look. We might be able to help with some food if you run low."

Dylan glanced at Callan, trying not to reveal his irritation. These guys weren't to be trusted, and even if Johnny was with them, Dylan didn't like the sound of it.

"We will," Callan said. "Tell Johnny we're on our way. Hey, what's that tied to the back of your car?"

Steve laughed. "A couple of *them*."

"Them?"

"Zombies. We caught 'em, snaked a rope around their necks and tied 'em to the back. Drag 'em along while we drive."

"Oh," Callan said.

Steve saluted them, then walked back to the vehicle and climbed in. He turned the engine on and revved it twice. He rolled past them, then accelerated, the tires screeching. The vehicle skidded sideways and Steve slammed on the brakes, the red lights glowing. He swerved around a battered vehicle and disappeared around the corner, gunning the motor again.

"What a bunch of fuckwits," Callan said. "Seriously, tying a zombie to the tow bar? He's got to be one of the slimiest, most conniving people in Albury. The number of times he's sleazed on Sherry is unreal."

Dylan suppressed thoughts of Sherry's behavior. "I don't trust them," he said. "If Johnny was alive, why wouldn't he have come looking for you?"

"Maybe he doesn't know I'm back."

"My father said Steve's family were the biggest crooks Albury had ever seen."

"That might be, but if Johnny is with them, I want to see him. He'll come with us if he knows we're alive. Maybe on the way out of town we can drop by and pick him up."

The appearance of the two men left Dylan uneasy. They were big trouble. Who tied a zombie to the back of their car? And the way they had taken off, screeching the tires, almost crashing into a battered vehicle. The image replayed in his mind and then something clicked. The brake lights. "The car we saw last night, it looked very much like a Jeep, didn't it?"

Callan frowned in thought, then his eyes widened in surprise. "Shit, you're right. It was *them*. Had to be. Do you think they'd drive to the house?"

"Not sure. As far as they know, Greg is there, and they'll know he's nobody to mess easily with."

Callan said, "Let's get what we need and head back, just in case."

"Agreed."

They entered the chemist with their rifles drawn, boots crunching on the broken glass of a thousand perfume bottles, containers of hand cream, hair cream, nail and foot cream. Almost all of the pain relief tablets, cough medicine, and other kinds of medicines for various aches and ailments were gone.

Dylan took an empty cardboard box from behind the counter and collected what remained—cough medicine, muscle inflammation cream, and several boxes of throat lozenges. Callan hurried around the counter and leapt up a step to the prescription-medicine section. He disappeared between rows of shelving.

On the far side of the room, near a messy pile of pamphlets, Dylan saw something that made his heart beat faster. He stepped over a fallen cardboard display for Panadol and reached down to pick it up.

It was his father's favorite cap, the famous blue peak bearing a white 'NY' symbol on the front. He turned it over in his hands, staring. A thousand questions burned through his mind. Did he lose it during his escape, or did it fall off as he was being eaten alive?

"Not one bloody box of antibiotics," Callan said. "Some bastard has taken them all. What's that?"

"My dad's cap. We went to New York when I was about ten and I got to choose a present. I picked that and gave it to him." He turned it over and pushed the tag aside, revealing the initials "R.C." Robert Cameron.

"Wow."

"He's still alive," Dylan said, stepping over the littered floor toward the broken front window. He spun back to Callan and said, "We gotta look for him." Dylan looked at the man who had once been his worst enemy. Callan wore an uneasy look of consideration. "Come on, man. He might be close."

"Okay. Let's go."

32

Kristy watched from the veranda as Dylan dispatched the zombies along the fence. When the new Jeep had disappeared out of sight, she felt a flash of overwhelming concern. What if more arrived? What if they broke the fence down and attacked the house? She felt jittery now that it was just the three of them, especially since neither Greg nor Sherry were in any condition to fight. *Toughen up.* She felt a flash of annoyance. The time for being scared was over. If she was going to survive, if she was going to help all of them survive, she *must* toughen up. She had proven herself yesterday by killing the zombie in the house. She thought of the ER and how she had stressed under those circumstances. She was a different person now.

Sherry appeared downstairs forty minutes after the boys had left. She looked pale and washed out, but the retching had passed, and Kristy gave her some paracetamol. It wouldn't stop the vomiting if her nausea returned, but it would make her feel better. Sherry ate a handful of savory biscuits and downed several glasses of water, then followed Kristy out to the garage. She heaved open the roller door from the inside and removed the bricks from the wheels, then lifted the front. Gravity edged it forward until it was outside the garage, where she jammed the turning wheel back into the ground and brought the trailer to a stop. Callan could back it up and hook it onto the tow bar when they returned. They had abandoned Callan's boat and trailer after a failed attempt to scrub the dry blood and gore from the aluminum.

They began filling leftover space in the trailer with other essential items like clothes and any toiletries they had brought back from the camping trip. Sherry suggested they take two cars to increase the amount of inventory and to have a backup in case one vehicle had an issue. Kristy thought it was a good idea.

Kristy checked on Greg several times, taking his temperature, feeding him a rotation of paracetamol and ibuprofen in an attempt to reduce his fever. A nervous knot formed in her belly, and the self-doubt that had plagued her before the trip crept back into her psyche like a bad dream. The wound was infected, and she couldn't help but feel responsible. What went wrong? The cleaning. She'd failed there, unable to get deep enough to remove all the bacteria. She didn't know what else she could have done, though. Now he was ill, and if the boys failed to find antibiotics, Greg would eventually die. She couldn't allow that to happen.

The next time Kristy checked the fence along Silvan Road, eight zombies had replaced the ones Dylan shot. She raced out onto the veranda and leapt off the steps, telling herself it couldn't be happening. Sherry followed at a slower pace, handing Kristy a pair of binoculars as she reached her side. Kristy looked through the special lenses with a flat expression, her jaw tight with concern.

A sheep wandering near the fence caught a whiff of one of the monsters and sprang away with a *baa-baa*, alerting his flock that trouble had arrived. Others scattered, moving higher up the slope toward the house.

Three more feeders appeared from a cluster of willow trees on the far side of the road. They hobbled across the dirt track toward the property and joined the others.

"None of them seem crazy," she said, raising the eyepiece. They were what Dylan's father had called "level one," but well advanced in their deterioration—pallid, chafed skin, almost complete hair-loss, sunken eyeballs, rotted teeth.

"What do you think?"

Sherry tipped her head and nodded. Kristy realized in that moment that Sherry was a stronger person than she, possessing a deep resolve, a steely confidence that couldn't be learned. "We shoot them. You stabbed one in the head, right? We can shoot them from this side of the fence. We can't leave them there."

Kristy swallowed. It was the right answer. It had to be like this now. There weren't going to be any more easy days. Almost every hour was a fight for survival, bringing a new test or challenge they would have to overcome. She could hide in the house and wait for the boys to return, or she could adopt some of Sherry's attitude, take the rifle, and go down and kill them. "I'll get the gun." She handed the binoculars back to Sherry and went inside.

Upon her return, they strode toward the lower paddock with their boots crunching in the parched, knee-high grass, the gentle breeze bringing the stench of their enemies and the dead zombies in the brush pile. The smell was horrifying; the girls buried their noses and mouths in the crook of their elbows. There were no birds chirping in the treetops. It should have been a pleasant, mid-summer morning, but instead, it was like a day in an alien world.

"Oh, that's really bad," Sherry said.

"The house must be upwind. I've never noticed it before." Kristy wondered if the smell had drawn the zombies from town.

As the girls approached the edge of the property, none of the walkers moved, as though they were hypnotized by the electric current running through the fence. Kristy glanced along the road, hoping to see the black Jeep, but knowing that the boys would be longer than an hour.

"Can you shoot this time?" Sherry asked. Kristy nodded. "Cause if you can't—"

"No. I'm fine." She needed to do this. She had failed dismally when Greg saved them yesterday. Today, she would find redemption.

One of the undead had its fingers wrapped around the electric wire. Smoke drifted from the edges of its hands. It looked at them with an open mouth, its eyes seeing nothing, its nose twitching in recognition of their scent.

"Just looking at them makes me feel nauseated," Sherry said.

Across the road, four more walkers shuffled out of the trees. One held a long machete. Kristy felt a pang of terror.

"That one's different," she said as it crossed the road, watching them. It had poise and control of its movements, things lacking in those which were closer to a vegetative state. Its skin was smoother, its hair fuller, and she could make out the thicker flesh around its neck and face.

There were now ten zombies spread along the fence line. Kristy said, "This is not good." She looked down Silvan Road, toward town, and saw a trail of them meandering in the direction of the property. There must have been a dozen spread out over thirty yards. "Oh shit, a lot more of them are coming."

The zombie holding the fence let go as the smoke began to shroud its frail form. Sherry pinched her nose, but to Kristy, the smell was no worse than some she'd encountered in the ER. The zombie lifted a clumsy leg and stuck it through the second and third rungs of wire, jiggling as its ragged shirt sizzled against the electrified section.

"Shoot it," Sherry said, stepping back.

Kristy took aim. *You can do this.* The rifle barrel wavered as the zombie tried to push the rest of its body through the fence. Its shirt caught on the barbed wire, then tore free as it fell forward and landed on the grass in a graceless heap.

Kristy stepped back, tightening her grip. *When it stands up*, she told herself. *It's not human anymore, and if I don't kill it, we'll both be dead.*

The zombie made a feeble attempt to stand, then turned its rotted grimace toward her. She clutched the butt and the forestock, held her breath, and stepped toward it, pushing the muzzle close to its head.

She pressed the trigger.

The rifle cracked, the recoil jerking her arms high. Kristy screamed as the sound rolled across the valley. The

262

zombie's head exploded and it toppled into the grass beside the fence.

Sherry said, "Good job."

Another zombie got down on all fours and began to gnaw on the dead one. A second joined it.

"You're disgusting," Sherry yelled. "Shoot them, too."

Kristy looked at the dead zombie's blank, cloudy eyes. The side of its head was missing. *They're not human anymore.* She reloaded the Winchester and stepped up to the fence, aiming the barrel between the wires. The feeder looked at her, a male, probably in his twenties, with dark hair and the semblance of a beard. It had no concept of its impending death. She couldn't shoot it in the face, though. She stepped around and shot it through the side of its head. It fell back with a stream of blood running over its shoulder. The other monster left the more challenging feed and went to the fallen undead.

Kristy took a deep breath. This wasn't so bad. As long as they stayed on the other side of the fence, she thought she could keep doing this. The idea of racing back to alert Greg had crossed her mind, but for now, they had control. She lodged the shell into the chamber with a jerk on the rifle bolt, and looked for her next mark.

The "type two" had moved toward the gate, looking for a place to cross. Beyond, down the road, more walkers had gathered, and some had climbed into the neighbors' property. A cold shiver touched her neck. It was starting to get dangerous. She could shoot the zombies along the front fence, but what if they start crossing from the other side?

Where are Callan and Dylan?

Maybe it was time to wake Greg.

33

Holding his father's cap, Dylan could feel the pulse of anticipation. He was close. His intuition sang a knowing tune. A lost cap might mean he had fallen into trouble, but sometimes, during a quick escape, things happened.

Callan put the cardboard box on the back floor and slipped into the driver's seat. He spun the car around and drove back slowly along Wodonga Place, scrutinizing every angle of the shopfronts and their shadowy depths beyond. They followed Kiewa Street all the way up to North, then went right onto David and zigzagged through the backstreets and side streets, past parks and motor inns, restaurants and the old community center. They had all been decimated, broken down by the will of the undead and whoever else remained. *Probably dodgy Steve and his crew*, Dylan thought. Once, near the Quality Hotel on Olive Street, Callan pulled the car over to the curb at Dylan's insistence. Dylan leapt out after spying a set of dirty legs at the bottom of a bus stop. He sprinted around the small weather-shield, only to find the lower half of an overweight body. He slunk back into the car and slammed his fist down on the seat, feeling stupid. Callan said nothing.

After twenty minutes, he began to think it was hopeless. The only thing he knew without doubt was that the town was finished. Beaten. A wasteland. Even since the previous day, it had deteriorated into a hellish mess. Not one glass shopfront remained intact. Staring into the store carcasses, they saw the moving shadows of chaotic zombies, tearing the insides apart, looking for the next feed. The footpath was covered with shattered glass all the way along Young Street. Callan had seen three fires the previous night, but now they counted eleven. Someone had to be starting them. It was as though they were trying to burn the undead away. He wondered if it was Steve and his crew.

The southern end, which they had avoided until then, was even worse. Sections of buildings had collapsed, bricks had turned into piles of rubble, and entire walls had folded.

"That's either grenades or heavy artillery," Callan said. "Somebody doesn't want this town to survive." Car pileups littered every street, some black and gutted, others pocked with bullets holes. "He won't be down this way anymore."

"Unless he's dead."

Callan eased the car to a stop on Hume Street across the road from Hovell Tree Park. They watched three zombies loitering beneath the shady elms in a place named after one of the early explorers of the region, William Hovell. The long grass covered the shoes of the trio, and at least three ruined corpses lay strewn around them like forgotten litter. Piles of rubbish dotted the children's playground.

"What do you want to do?" Callan asked.

Dylan pressed his lips into a thin line. "I don't know. You're worried about those idiots going to the house while we're not there, aren't you?"

Callan nodded. "I don't trust them. They don't have the same values as the rest of us."

Dylan turned the cap over in his hand. He wanted to keep looking. With each store they passed and every corner they turned, he felt the expectation of seeing his father. It kept them away from the house longer, though, and exposed Greg and the girls to potential danger. Maybe he was being selfish. The same way Callan had been selfish, wanting to go straight home to check on his mother. Probably. *Yes*. It was similar. For the good of the group, they should return home, pack their things, and leave. Even arguing to stay at the house had been selfish. He had debated with Callan on their drive from the lake about putting the good of the group first, and now he had done the same thing, not once, but twice.

"Let's go," Dylan said. "Home."

"You sure?" Callan asked. He nodded. "Okay."

He was doubly depressed knowing Johnny Stavros was still around. Even before the apocalypse, Johnny was at the bottom of Dylan's list of decent people. Now that he knew of Johnny's treachery toward Callan, he despised him more. Johnny had always been sneaky; discovering that he was now associated with Steve Palmer didn't surprise Dylan. The challenge was going to be keeping his mouth shut and communication cordial if Johnny did connect with them.

Callan circled the park and went by the drugstore again, then headed north along Wodonga Place in the opposite direction the other guys had driven. They went through the blank lights at Dean, and around onto Creek Street. There, in the middle of the road, lay the slaughtered body of a zombie. It wasn't any zombie though.

"That's the one they had tied to the back of their car," Callan said.

That meant the boys had travelled up this way, rather than west, toward where they were camped. "Oh fuck," Dylan said. "I just had a very bad thought."

"They've gone home."

They took the corner onto Englehart Street on two wheels, and for a moment, Dylan thought the Jeep was going to tip. The tires shrieked and he threw a hand up against the roof, but it touched down again. Turning right onto Victoria, Callan slowed a bit.

Please let her be safe, please let her be safe. Dylan didn't want to think about what might be happening at home. Steve and Chris had a good start on them. If they had gone directly there, they would have made it by now. Instead, he was watching the zombie migration up Jones Street, as if they were heading for some kind of event toward the north end of town. They chased Sackville Street, and as Callan guided the Jeep left onto a service road, past the

Jones Street Takeaway, where several feeders were piling through the front window, Dylan felt his breath catch.

Two men ran along the street chased by a group of zombies, several of which were faster than any Dylan had seen. One of the men was his father. An explosion of relief washed over him and he leapt forward, hands on the windows. "There he is!"

The men had a small lead, stopping and firing, then running on, but the horde of zombies trailing them stretched for a hundred yards or more. Dylan fumbled for the switch that would lower the window. His father looked like a homeless person, dirty, grey, his clothes torn, flapping as he ran. Dylan put a hand on the door handle and prepared to exit the car when the Jeep slowed.

But it didn't. He swiveled around. "What the fuck are you doing?"

"Pick one," Callan shouted.

"Huh?"

"Your father or Kristy? I choose Sherry, Greg, my sister, and my unborn child."

"What? Just stop the car and let them get in!"

"Steve and his boys will take everything we've got. Greg will try to stop them, and if the girls do, too, who knows what will happen."

"But my father—"

"I'm sorry. We'll have to come back for him."

Dylan sat with an open mouth, frozen in shock as his father disappeared from view.

"Let's go," Kristy said, starting up the slope toward the house. The moment she left, feeders began climbing between the wires, ignoring the zap. They had been kidding themselves that the electrified fence would hold them back. Their only luck until now had been that the zombies had remained away.

Sherry jogged to catch up. "Look," she said, pointing to the east boundary. Five zombies had breached the Petersens's front fence and ambled toward them. "This place is going to get overrun."

"I'm going to wake up Greg."

"I don't think he's going to be able to do much. There are too many."

Sherry was right. Kristy felt a knot of terror in her gut. *Think. THINK.* The BMW was in the garage. If they could find the keys, the three of them could drive away. They wouldn't have time to pack any more things, and they'd have to leave the trailer behind, but they'd survive. What if Dylan and Callan returned and the place was empty, though? If they hurried, perhaps they could drive into town and meet them on their return.

"We have to leave," Kristy said. "We can't stay here any longer."

Sherry's eyes widened. "How?"

"The BMW in the garage."

They passed the pile of bodies and brush, hands on knees as they struggled up the final fifteen yards of the steep gradient. They both reached the top, huffing and puffing, and looked back down the slope.

The feeders were coming from all directions. The front and side fences, the property opposite, the one next door, and along the road from town.

Sherry counted them out. "Twenty-three."

"Four," Kristy said as another appeared at the Petersens's front fence. "I'm not even sure there is enough ammunition left to kill that many."

They were halfway across the lawn when a sound from the road caught Kristy's attention. She glanced around and saw a black Jeep driving through a cloud of dust. It pulled up at the gate and Kristy felt the kind of relief you feel when you know everything is going to be all right. "Oh, thank God." She peered through the windows but they were tinted dark and she couldn't see clearly from the distance.

The vehicle paused, and she waited for Dylan or Callan to appear. Another dust cloud appeared down Silvan Road. A second and third vehicle rolled up to the first.

"Who's that?" Sherry asked.

"Don't know. Maybe they've brought someone to help."

The Jeep reversed away from the gate and stopped beside a large white SUV, a chrome bull bar twinkling in the broken sunlight. Something wasn't right. Why hadn't they opened the gate? "I don't like this," Kristy said.

The Jeep reversed slowly up Silvan Road as a number of feeders lumbered toward it, then spewed gravel and flew backward, running two over with a thump that reached the girls.

The white SUV spun its wheels on the rocks. Suddenly it shot forward and rammed the gate, creating a shrill crash.

"Oh my God, what are they doing?"

It reversed, then accelerated forward again. The gate twisted and bent over. The final attack tore it from the post. The white SUV drove a short distance up the driveway and pulled over, allowing the black Jeep to pass. Then it fell in behind, followed by the third vehicle, a bright red Toyota Land Cruiser, and they hurried up the hill toward the house, a throng of zombies trailing.

"In the house," Kristy said. "That's not Callan and Dylan."

They ran to the veranda without looking back. Gunshots cracked. Terror swarmed through Kristy. They needed to get to the car. "Have you seen the keys for the BMW?"

"Yes. They're in the car."

Kristy opened the sliding doors and they stepped inside. "Grab everything you need and wait for us in the BMW. Don't do anything silly."

"What about you?"

"I'll get Greg."

She put the rifle on the bench and headed toward the back bedroom, hearing the crunch of the internal door to the garage closing. She wanted to keep Sherry away from the action. Nobody would know she was in the garage, and if Kristy was quick, they could be out of there in minutes.

Who were the people in the cars? They weren't friendly. She thought back to Callan's comment the previous night when they had spied the vehicle driving by. He had said the taillights were the same as his new Jeep. This must be the same group.

She turned left into the first bedroom and listened for the sound of Greg breathing. She hated waking him, but this was life or death. The thought seemed stark, but a group of people had smashed down the front gate to gain access to their property, and God knew how many zombies were following. She estimated they had three minutes to leave.

The covers had been thrown aside in a disheveled mess. She felt a stab of panic.

"What happened?" Greg croaked. A shadow moved at the corner of the window. "I heard the gunshots." Another rifle boomed.

"Big problems. We have to get out of here. People are attacking us, and there are zombies all over the place.

270

They're through the front and side fences. I shot a few but there's a heap walking up Silvan Road."

Greg shuffled over to the chair and lifted a pair of jeans. "How many zombies?"

"*Too* many. I don't think we've got enough ammo to shoot them all. And by now there are probably another twenty or thirty." He pulled his jeans on and stood for a moment with a hand on the bed.

"People?"

"Three cars."

"Have we got any guns? Are you sure people are attacking us?"

"Yes. One of them rammed the gate and broke it down!"

Greg had pulled a t-shirt over his head and paused with it halfway down, his face showing through the neck hole. "They knocked the gate down?"

Outside, they heard the shouts and calls of men. Gunshots popped like firecrackers, one after the other. Kristy stepped over to the window and pulled the curtain aside. Greg put a hand over his eyes. She gasped, shocked at the image.

Zombies littered the upper and lower sections of the paddock, too many to count. Some fed on fallen comrades or sheep, while others wandered toward the house. A few carried weapons at their sides, and one looked like the crazy kind they had seen on the first night, in full control of a strong running action up the hill. Two unknown men ran behind them, shooting in all directions, felling the feeders with practiced ease. She let the blind fall. "We have to leave right now."

"Bad?" She nodded. Greg pulled his shoes on and stumbled forward into Kristy. "Sorry."

She led them out of the bedroom and up the hallway toward the kitchen, mentally running through a list of essential items they would need—primarily, water and food from the trailer. A rapid burst of gunfire sounded, shattering the wide sliding doors in the family room area. Kristy threw herself to the floor, grunting as Greg landed on her back.

"Sherry's in the garage. We can take the BMW." She climbed to her feet and helped Greg stand. He pulled her arm down as he struggled to gather his balance. "Can you make it?" His pale face went stiff for a moment and she thought he might totter over.

"Yep," he said, lumbering forward. "I'll be all right."

Kristy slid the Winchester rifle off the bench and they shuffled down into the sunken lounge room. She left Greg standing near an armchair while she crouched by the fireplace. She put two boxes of rounds into her pockets and thumbed loose bullets into the rifle. Greg trembled, his face flecked with pain and illness. When was the last time she checked on the wound? She hoped Callan had found some antibiotics. Even if they got through this nightmare, without those, Greg would deteriorate quickly.

As she stood, the front door burst open, cracking against the inside wall. She lifted the rifle and cranked the lever, her finger feathering the trigger. The last person she expected to see backed through the doorway, his handgun roaring its killing noise.

Johnny turned and, seeing them, said one word.

"Run."

35

"STOP THE FUCKING CAR!" Dylan screamed, glaring at Callan. His voice cracked on the last word. He twisted around and watched the distance to his father increase.

Dylan turned back to the front, then reached across and yanked on the steering wheel. The Jeep turned sharply to the left, skidding, and then the right wheels lifted. For a long moment, the vehicle drove like it was in a stunt-car show. Then it smacked back down with a chirp and Callan jammed on the brakes, fighting the wayward helm as he tried to keep it from running off the road. The tires screeched and Dylan fell forward, the belt pinning his chest before they came to a sudden, grinding stop.

"What the fuck are you doing?" Callan yelled. "Are you mental—"

Dylan kicked the door open, leapt out of the car and began running, holding the rifle in a tight grip.

His father had outpaced the zombies by twenty yards, but his face looked strained, his teeth gritted. Dylan didn't know how much he had left.

The other man had fallen behind and let out a piercing scream. Dylan's father stopped, twisting his body around.

"No, Dad! Don't stop."

Dylan ran toward them, watching the other man reach for his freedom as he crawled along the stony bitumen. Two zombies reached him and took hold of his legs. The man swung his shotgun and hit one of them on the head with a clunk. It dropped his foot and fell, but the second grabbed it back up and shuffled backward, pulling on him. Dylan saw his father race forward with the shotgun and swing the butt down on the walker's head like a baseball bat.

"Dad!"

The zombie shook off the blow and continued dragging the man away. Other feeders reached the altercation. Dylan knew that, in a moment, the situation would be hopeless. He sprinted the last thirty yards, feeling tightness in his lungs.

His father continued swinging the club from left to right, clunking arms and heads, pushing those close a step back, but his swings grew shorter and slower.

The zombie dragging the man away knelt on the road and bit through his shinbone. The guy threw his head back and shrieked. Dylan's dad tossed his gun and hit the thing in the forehead; the rifle clattered onto the road. Unmoved, the monster turned the man's leg around and chomped into the soft flesh of his calf muscle.

Dylan slowed and took aim, firing several times at approaching zombies, knocking two down with a throat and a head shot.

His father made one last effort to pull his friend to safety, cupping him under the arms, but others converged on their prize. Dylan's father had little choice and finally he began to retreat, staggering backward with a helpless cry.

Dylan took him by the arm and they ran to the Jeep. He helped his father into the back as several zombies started for the vehicle. Dylan slammed the door and then yanked the front open, but at the last moment, he saw a familiar flash of blue-white near the feeders.

The dog. It must have followed them from the gun store. Dylan stuck a thumb and forefinger in his mouth and whistled.

The dog's head stiffened and its ears perked.

"Here boy! Come here!"

It ran wide of the pack as many zombies, unable to get a piece of the action in the street, started toward the Jeep. But the dog was quick, sprinting along the bitumen well ahead of the enemy. As it approached the car, Dylan lifted the hatchback and the dog leapt up into the rear compartment. Dylan slammed the door and ran to the back, jumping in beside his father.

"Go, go, go!"

Callan turned the Jeep back onto the road as the desperate thumps of zombie hands hit the rear window, then accelerated away, the rear wheels spinning on the loose stones.

"The dog," Dylan said, breathless. "He must have followed us."

"That's Blue Boy," Bob Cameron said. "I found him about a week after it went bad. He's been staying out here with us, but then I lost him when I went into town the other day. He gets around, all right."

Dylan clamped a hand on his father's shoulder, squeezing to make sure he was real. A wide, irreversible smile cracked his face. He had accepted the loss, prepared himself to leave town never knowing what had happened. He braced himself against the sway of the Jeep. Callan swerved left and right to avoid zombies on the road. Without a belt, his father reached forward to hang onto the seat, his shirt pulling away from his neck. Dylan's smile folded. He glanced up and saw Callan looking at him in the rearview mirror.

"What is it?"

Dylan looked at the wound on his father's neck. "Dad? What's that?"

Bob looked into his eyes. In one second, realization washed away Dylan's happy heart.

36

Kristy didn't have time to feel surprise. The first walker ambled in through the entranceway and lunged for Johnny. In his attempt to flee, he tripped and fell backward with a cry, the gun spilling from his hand. The zombie bent over, reaching for him.

She fired the Winchester, stinging her ears, and blew its shoulder away. The thing spun sideways and hit the wall, then fell onto the bottom step. Johnny leapt to his feet and threw her a grateful look, then kicked out at the two that replaced the first and fired his pistol. The top of the front feeder's head exploded, blood showering the walls and roof.

They needed to get to the garage door, but more zombies kept coming through the entry. Johnny leapt over the zombie Kristy had shot, onto the second step and started upstairs.

"Up here."

Greg hadn't yet moved. Now he reached down and scooped up the tomahawk, but Kristy thought he was going to tumble right over. He tottered, latched onto the armchair, and managed to remain upright. She felt a mix of admiration and surprise when he stepped toward the stairway and swung the weapon at the lead zombie, pushing it back.

From the kitchen, another feeder appeared and turned toward her.

"Come on, Kristy," Greg said, having cleared a pathway toward the stairs. She could see Johnny's feet disappearing up to the next level.

She pulled the rifle up and ran toward the newcomer, firing at point-blank range into its face. Its head exploded, covering the wall behind in a thick stain of unfathomable gore. Even with her tolerance for blood, it turned her stomach. She sprang to the stairs and leapt over the original feeder, which seemed to be regaining its limited faculties.

"Up," Greg said.

But she paused on the step, looking toward the garage door. Sherry was inside, hopefully locked safely in the car. Was there a better place to be? Probably not. For now, anyway, they couldn't get to her. Through the open front door, Kristy saw that several of the men were engaged in battle with a swarm of zombies. Perhaps a dozen feeders had gathered in the parking circle, following those already inside.

"Come on," Johnny called from the top.

Kristy started up, glancing back to make sure Greg was following, but they were pushing at him. He thrust the tomahawk at their faces, then buried the steel deep into a zombie neck. It fell back and several clamored for its blood. Greg took his chance and climbed. Johnny had the pistol drawn, waving them on. Kristy had reached the halfway mark when a thump sounded and Greg roared in pain.

One of them had his foot.

"Down," Johnny said.

Kristy fell onto the stairs and thrust her hands over her ears. The handgun fired twice. She looked back; the two zombies had fallen away, one of them clutching Greg's shoe. He crawled upward using his elbows, his face taut with effort and pain. She reached back with her hand and he took it, pulling with force she hadn't expected. For a moment, Kristy thought she might topple forward, but then Greg found his footing and hobbled up the stairs, using the wall for balance. His bleached face locked in a grimace, his eyes closed; Kristy saw his hair and forehead slick with sweat. "Jesus, you're burning up."

"I'm fine. Get moving."

Kristy waited for him at the top, and that provided a view below of their pursuers. A chill of terror ran up her spine. Her arms and hands shook. She felt sick. Part of her wanted to find a place to hide. Among the clumsy, listless feeders, one stood out, pushing its way between them with fiery intent. It was bald, heavily muscled, and impatient. That was enough for Kristy. She said, "We have to get out."

"Here, give me that," Greg said, passing her the tomahawk. He took the rifle and she fumbled a handful of rounds from her pocket that he grabbed with surprising speed. "Get behind me."

"This way," Johnny said, returning from the end room. He led them into a bedroom that looked out over the driveway. Below it, the grey tin roof of the garage beckoned. "We go out through the window, and climb down off the roof."

Gunfire exploded in the hallway outside the room. Greg backpedaled inside, reloading the Winchester. "They're coming. We gotta go." Johnny slid the window open and pushed out the wire screen. It clattered onto the roof beneath. "Gimme a hand," Greg said, closing the door and reaching down for the wooden base of the bedframe. Johnny tucked his hands underneath and they lifted, turning the bed vertically onto its end. Grunting, they dropped it against the door as feeders banged on it.

"I'll go first," Johnny said, "make sure it's safe."

Typical Johnny, Kristy thought, self-preservation at its finest. He climbed onto the inside ledge, swung a leg out onto the windowsill, then climbed out onto the tin roof with a clang. Then he waved Kristy out.

Fists pummeled the door from the other side. It opened and the bed fell forward, but Greg leapt in behind it with his back against the mattress and squatted, pushing with the big muscles in his thighs. How he was still standing amazed Kristy.

"Go," he said in a tight voice.

"What about you?" The door began to inch open. Whatever was on the other side outweighed Greg.

"I'll follow."

278

"But they're coming!"

The door had opened a foot. Teeth clenched, Greg's face turned bright red. He lowered his head and pushed, but his feet began to slide over the floor.

"GO," he squeezed out.

She did.

37

Callan stopped the Jeep on the side of the road thirty yards clear of walkers. "What the fuck is that? Is it a bite?"

Dylan closed his eyes, cursing life. It was a bite. He'd seen the flicker of terror and acknowledgement in his father's eyes. Somewhere, somehow, a feeder had gotten its teeth into him. He wanted to ask, but couldn't get the words out.

Bob Cameron nodded. "Yep. It is."

"Out," Callan said. "You're fucking infected, like the old guy we saw on the side of the road. You're gonna turn into one of them."

Dylan grabbed onto Callan's shoulder. "Hang on a fucking minute. He's not *getting out*."

"He has to. What if he can't control it?"

"It is a bite," Bob said, and there was acceptance in his voice that filled Dylan with sadness. "Happened this morning. But I won't turn for another twenty hours or so."

With both hands pressed to his temples, Dylan asked, "Are you sure?"

"I saw it happen to Bill Henry. He was bitten in town. Came home. We spoke, said our goodbyes. He said he'd take care of it." He rubbed stubble Callan had never seen. His father had always been clean-shaven, dressed in a shirt and slacks for work every day. Seeing him like this, disheveled and wounded, cast a cloud over the whole thing, making it seem more unreal. This man was his father, but wasn't, at the same time.

"I think it starts as a virus, like a bad flu. It breaks you down and kills off your cells. Many of the townspeople caught this in the beginning. Some just died. They got sick and just died and didn't come back. Others... others come back after dying. But I suspect a direct bite means only one thing."

"But you don't know?"

"No, not for sure, but—"

"Then we don't know."

"I can *feel* it," Bob said. "I can feel it in my blood, working its way into my hands and feet, through my gut, and into my head."

"That doesn't prove anything—"

"That's bullshit," Callan said. "I'm sorry this has happened. He's done a lot for us with his diary and notes, but this is a risk to our survival."

"Callan, if those assholes are back at the house, we're going to need all the help we can to get rid of them. Dad can still fire a gun."

Callan tightened his hands around the wheel. The walkers on the road had almost caught up to them. Several trudging ahead had turned back to investigate. "I just think it's too risky. If he bites one of us, you can't take that back. Are you gonna accept responsibility for that?"

"Yes."

"Remember the other day when I was adamant about going to see my parents first? You tried to tell me, but I insisted. I thought I was right."

"Then you'll understand why I won't concede on this." Callan looked away. Dylan continued. "We won't be there for long. We're leaving, remember?"

"Fine. But he's your responsibility. Anything happens and it's on you."

"Of course."

"And the only reason I'm agreeing to this is because of what you've done for me over the past few days."

Dylan pushed back in the seat. "Thank you."

The tires groaned as Callan twisted the wheel and accelerated back onto the dirt. The zombies that had closed in on them threw up hands, begging them to stay. Callan clenched his jaw and watched the road ahead.

The moment was bittersweet. Dylan had accepted that his father had died or turned into one of the thousands of walkers wandering the streets, and although it might still

281

happen, to find him beforehand, to get a final chance to converse and to tell him how much he loved him, was worth much. He pushed the outcome down deep and concentrated on the moment.

"Where have you been, Dad?"

Bob Cameron sat forward. "Fighting to stay alive. Larry, the poor bastard. He kept me going these last few days. Without him I wouldn't be here."

"But where have you *been*?"

His forehead was slick with sweat, his face red. "Locked up in the storage room at the hardware store." He wiped a rough sleeve across his nose. "You made it home?" Dylan gave a slow nod. "Your mother? Is she... alive?" Dylan shook his head. Bob pursed his lips and nodded, understanding. "I thought as much." He looked out the window. "Did she suffer?"

Callan coughed, as if to clear his throat. "No," Dylan said. "She was dead already. We buried her, though."

He smiled and clamped a hand on Dylan's shoulder. "Good boy. Thank you."

The road turned in a slow arc as they drew closer to home. Dylan's nervousness increased as he worried about whether Steve and Chris had gone to the property, and the potential outcomes if they had. He saw Callan worrying too, folding his fingers around the steering wheel and biting his lower lip. Dylan cradled the rifle in his lap and filled the chamber with rounds, trying to concentrate on anything bar the risks to Kristy.

There were few zombies on the bitumen as they turned off Sackville Street onto Gap Road through Forest Hill Park. Dylan peered into the trees and saw ambling bodies drifting through the bush. He shuddered, turning back to his father. *They were everywhere.*

He took his father's hand in his. "I'm so glad you're back." Pressure grew at the back of his eyes and he sucked in a deep breath to stop tears. He glanced at Callan in the rearview mirror and saw him look away. "What happened, Dad? Why did you go to town in the first place?"

Bob settled back in his seat. "We planned on leaving. Everything was ready, but we needed a few extras like fuel and batteries. I went into the town as I'd done a dozen other times, but it went wrong thanks to the kids who destroyed the Coles supermarket. That was three days ago. I found Larry picking through the aisles. My car was destroyed, and we were chased out of there by zombies and those fucking guys." Dylan flinched hearing his father swear. He couldn't ever recall such. *The world has moved on.* "We've been fighting our way out for three days."

"You wouldn't be referring to Steve Palmer and his crew?" Callan asked.

"Yeah. Chaz's kid. What a screw-up he turned out to be."

"We spoke to them earlier. Maybe an hour ago, outside the drugstore." Callan swallowed, tightening his expression. "We think they've gone back to the house, knowing we're not there."

"Dad, this is Callan. There are five of us. Kristy, Callan's sister, who I might have mentioned before, his girlfriend Sherry, and Greg. They're waiting for us. We're planning to leave."

"Steve Palmer and his buddies?"

Callan nodded. "I'm worried. Really worried." The zombie numbers continued to grow as they drove further up Silvan road, packs of them, twos, threes, wandering, fighting, eating.

"Why are there so many up this way?"

"I think there are two reasons," Bob said. "They're following something. They have an acute sense of smell, so it could be all the dead bodies in the empty houses. They're drawn to the potential for food and they can track you for miles."

"We killed several of them and left them on the property," Dylan said. "It wouldn't be them, would it?"

"Might be. It's easy food. You've seen what they do when one of their own goes down."

"What's the other reason?" Callan said.

"The inner section of town is running out of food. They're insatiable eating machines. They eat a corpse and immediately look for the next one. Soon there won't be any bodies left in Albury."

Dylan threw an arm around his father's shoulder. "I'm glad to see you, Dad."

Bob put a hand on his son's arm and squeezed. "I'm sorry about your mother. It pains me... that she's dead, and you had to find her. I knew it would turn out like this. Hope is not something in big supply anymore."

They left the towering treetop canopy of the park and reached another estate where brick houses with manicured front gardens and two-car garages snuggled together. It was like Callan's parents' street again, and he gunned the Jeep around the odd wandering feeder, shifting in the driver's seat.

For several streets, Dylan thought the quantity of walkers had dwindled. The roads were empty, and he only saw one loitering at the front window of a dilapidated house. Turning onto Silvan Road, though, his hope fell apart. They were sporadic at first, the odd one rummaging in bushes, or wandering along the road. Callan swerved around them, preferring to protect the Jeep for their travels.

It became progressively worse, the stunned monsters gathering two and three deep along the roadside, turning to watch the oncoming vehicle. Callan had to slow the car to avoid whacking into them, although he clipped several and knocked them into the grassy gutter. They approached a handful of soldiers decked in full Army kit. Dylan felt hope rise when he saw their cropped hair from behind, but as they passed, the red eyes and blank stares squashed it.

They reached the upper section of Silvan Road, a place as familiar to Dylan as his own property. He had ridden his

284

BMX bike up this stretch from the time he was five years old, standing on the pedals and fighting the final climb that never grew easy. He had cursed it time and again, but now he wished he was back there, riding home to see his mother and father in another world.

Even from a hundred yards away, they could see the commotion through the trees. He had thought there might be a dozen or so along the fence, but knew immediately that expectation was too low. The fence was down in places, and as the car rolled up to the driveway and Callan began swearing, Dylan realized the gate had been smashed aside, too.

"They're here," Callan said. "They really did come back."

Zombies wandered everywhere, too many to count. They crawled over the grassy paddock, fighting each other and fighting with Steve Palmer's crew. Some fed on their fallen brothers and sisters, while others had caught sheep or goats. Several large packs fed on victims that Dylan couldn't see through the ring of bodies. He hoped it wasn't Kristy or the others. A mob hunkered around the pile of brush where they had left the bodies. Others ambled toward it, as if making a pilgrimage to their dead family. Three foreign vehicles sat parked near the top of the driveway, one a black Jeep Grand Cherokee, the same as Callan's. The crew belonging to these cars were scattered around the house, engaged in various conflicts with zombies.

Callan accelerated through the entrance, tires slipping on the gravel, clouting feeders as they stood about with vacant purpose. Several fell beneath the front, causing the car to jump and jive, but he forced it up the driveway and through others trapped in infinite ignorance. Guns popped and cracked, along with the rapid clatter of automatic gunfire.

"What's the plan?" Dylan asked, scratching around the back for guns and ammo.

Bob said, "I can help. Have you got a spare gun?" Dylan handed him a brand new Winchester .30-30 rifle.

"Can you see any of your friends?" Bob said.

Dylan scanned the mayhem. He saw half a dozen humans running around carrying heavy firepower. One stopped and fired rapidly, dropping three zombies, and then ran up onto the grassy section near the veranda. Another kept trying to shoot but the gun seemed to have jammed. He threw it aside and kicked at a walker's head, but missed, and another tackled him to the ground. No Sherry, Kristy, or Greg, though.

"No."

"You get them into the car and get the hell out of here."

Callan slowed the Jeep and guided it to the rear of the queue behind the other three. There were no zombies within twenty yards.

"Be quick," Bob said.

Callan jammed the brakes, jolting them forward. "Holy shit, is that Johnny outside the garage?"

Dylan saw Johnny standing there, looking up. Following his gaze, Dylan saw the faces of people in the window above.

38

Kristy laid the tomahawk on the brickwork ledge outside, then lifted her knee onto the internal windowsill and fell forward through the opening. Her stomach dropped and she spread out her hands, breaking the fall onto the roof. In the bedroom, she heard the crash and bump as the door slammed into the wall.

She scrambled to her feet and snatched up the tomahawk, feeling her balance totter. She hated heights. She turned back and grabbed for the window ledge. Zombies spilled though the doorway, crashing into each other as too many sought entrance through the narrow way. Leading them, though, was one of the crazies, with its thick neck and shaved head, elbowing the others aside, its flaming eyes locked on Greg.

Kristy held out her arm, tomahawk at the ready as Greg backed away from the door. Shooting was impossible in such tight space, and he wouldn't have enough rounds to stop them all. He leapt up onto the ledge as she stepped back, but the mad zombie was fast, taking a fistful of his jeans and yanking him onto the floor.

The gun spilled as Greg fell onto his palms. He rotated and thrust both hands up to protect himself. They wrestled, throwing each other sideways, backward, forward, and against the windowsill. Greg's red face glistened with sweat, his eyes large and frightened. Kristy wondered how long he could hold on. The other zombies spilled toward them, clawing for fresh meat, but with one powerful hand, the crazy knocked them into the wall. They battled, a big human riddled with fever, and a large zombie, infected with a rage and strength unlike anything Kristy had seen. They held each other at arm's length, faces taut with strain. Greg slowly turned the zombie toward the window, putting it between Kristy and himself, and drove it back several steps.

"Kill it," he said through gritted teeth.

Her hand flexed around the tomahawk handle and the monster's white face and vacant eyes turned to her. *Kill it, you have to kill it.* She anchored her feet on either side of the roof peak, and latched onto the ledge with one hand. She cocked the weapon, closed her eyes, and screamed, thrusting it forward, her arm jarring as the blade stuck into the bony flesh of its head.

Her eyes flew open as blood sprayed over the window and ledge. She dropped the tomahawk inside the bedroom and stepped away, gasping.

The crazy clutched its head and staggered away from Greg. He moved fast, snatching the tomahawk off the floor and leaping at it, his wrist snapping back and forward, driving the blade deeper, opening the thing's skull like a watermelon. It tottered, and Greg kicked it toward the waiting horde, where they dove on it with insatiable eagerness.

Greg dropped the tomahawk and scooped up the rifle as the remaining feeders shambled after him. He passed it through the window to Kristy, then sprang up onto the ledge and slipped over the threshold, landing on the angled tin roof. He began to slide, then caught himself, arms and legs taut with balance that belied his bulk and illness.

Two feeders reached the window and groped air, tongue out, teeth chomping. One attempted to climb onto the ledge, but knocked the other back. They both fell away, clawing at each other's faces.

Kristy shuffled along the roof peak to the edge and saw Johnny had dropped to the ground below. He waved his hands, holding both arms out.

"Jump! Quickly!"

But she had never been up so high, let alone jumped. She glanced around for alternatives, a tree or guttering she could slide down, but the wider view caught her attention. Along the driveway, in the paddock, and at the Petersens's house next door, hundreds of walkers lumbered about.

Rifle shots cracked and the tin roof beside her clunked.

"Someone's shooting at us," Greg said, squatting.

Kristy did the same and peered toward the garden. Steve Palmer limped toward the house, holding a rifle, his clothes splattered with blood. He sneered, then lifted the gun again and aimed it at Kristy.

39

"It *is* Johnny," Callan said, then ducked his head to look underneath the top of the windscreen. "And Kristy's on the garage roof."

Dylan said, "They must have gotten trapped inside. Greg's up there too."

"Where's Sherry?"

Callan threw the door open, feeling a hand of terror grip him. The joy at seeing his oldest mate was shattered by his concern for Sherry. Where was she? He had to find her. In the back of the Jeep, the dog barked frantically. Callan didn't want the mutt to get hurt, but he seemed eager to be out. He had survived on his own for weeks, and probably knew how to take care of himself better than most humans. He went to the back of the car and lifted the door. The dog barked and leapt out, then disappeared between the cars.

Johnny cracked a shot off from his rifle toward the garden. Callan couldn't see what he was shooting at, but a second later, a bullet clunked off the garage door. All over the property, gunshots peppered the air. Then he saw Steve Palmer leap out from behind a tree and fire off two more rounds. Callan responded, firing one, then pumping the rifle and blasting a second shot. Then he glanced over at Johnny.

"Good to see you, mate." Johnny nodded, smiling. "I thought you'd teamed up with him?" Callan said.

"I did. But the fucker's gone crazy. He was always on the edge."

Callan squatted behind one of the other vehicles, a white SUV, and peered around the corner. He glanced up and saw Kristy lying flat against the roof. They needed to get her down. "What's wrong with Kristy?"

"I don't know. She won't jump."

"Where's Sherry?"

Johnny shook his head.

Dylan and his father had crouched opposite behind the other car, both packing rifles. Dylan had his trusty Remington .308 bolt action, while Bob had the Winchester .30-30 they'd taken from the store.

Callan said, "We gotta get Kristy down, and I have to find Sherry."

Bullets whizzed through the air and clunked into the front vehicle with an iron *clang*. Johnny bobbed up, then down, returning fire, and Callan leapt up for another shot.

"I'll take care of Kristy," Dylan called.

Callan nodded. "I'll go in and look for Sherry."

"I'll come with you," Bob said.

"No, Dad," Dylan said.

Bob put a hand on his arm and said, "I'll be fine. This is what you need me for." He held the look a long time, and then Dylan nodded.

"Don't do anything stupid."

"Give me some cover," Callan said.

Dylan and Johnny sprung up simultaneously, each discharged a shot directed at the bushes. Johnny dropped, but Dylan remained standing and fired again.

Callan ran. As he passed by the garage door, he felt a pang of guilt for not staying with Kristy, but Sherry was his priority, and he knew Dylan would take care of his sister. He heard Bob's footsteps and heavy breathing behind him and felt relieved that Dylan had insisted on him coming.

As they reached the entrance, a zombie stepped through the door and Callan shot it in the face. *No indecision there.* Blood and brains sprayed over the brick wall beside the doorway and the thing fell into a rectangle rock garden beneath the front window.

Inside, gun smoke hung in thin clouds. Flies buzzed about, and the stench bit into his nose with fetid teeth. Callan scanned the room. Perhaps fifteen zombies were scattered about the lounge room and hallway in groups. Several fed, and Callan felt the contents of his stomach swim. Would he ever get used to seeing this shit?

"I'll check toward the back of the house," he said, wanting to make sure Sherry wasn't one of the victims.

Bob said, "I'll take the upstairs level," and his boots thumped on the carpet as he ascended.

"SHERRY?" Callan yelled, sprinting toward the first group, where he kicked aside one of the feeders. The other three kept their faces buried in their victim, certifying their primary interest in feeding. It fell backward against the wall, revealing a youngish man who looked vaguely familiar. Callan left them to their party, conserving bullets for more important needs.

The second group had eviscerated one of their own, and stuffed intestines into their bloody mouths like strings of unbroken sausages. Callan felt his stomach lurch again. He reached out for the wall and caught his balance, then rolled off into the kitchen and family area.

"SHERRY?"

Two zombies stood staring out of the shattered doorway in the family room but didn't even turn for him. He crept over to them and shot each in the back of the head. They tumbled forward out the door and onto the decking.

He went along the hallway to the first bedroom where Greg had slept, and stepped inside, pointing the gun into every corner. "Sherry?" A cold air filled the room, one that warned him to be wary. He touched the closet door handle and felt a chill on his neck. What if she had been bitten? Like Dylan the other night, he couldn't kill a loved one, especially not his girl, the mother of his baby. He shook it off and yanked the door open. Empty. She had to be in one of the other rooms, probably the one they had used, cowering under the bed or in the closet.

The crash of a door from the front of the house snagged his attention. He crept into the hallway and peered back into the family area. A loud thump sounded from upstairs, then several gunshots. He hoped Bob was okay, and he hurried along the passage toward the back quarters. "Sherry?"

He smelled its vitriolic odor before he reached their bedroom. His testicles tingled with fear. His breath caught in his throat, and he adjusted his hands on the rifle without comfort. A strip of light from beneath the curtains dimmed the darkness. From the doorway, he saw its bald head and grey skin on the other side of the bed, bent over, feeding. Callan's mouth opened but the scream was silent. When he finally inhaled, it was a jagged breath, and the zombie caught the sound, turning its head to reveal a face covered in blood and mince.

It slowly stood, stiff hands by its side, bloody fingers opening and closing, eyes like burning jewels, and growled like a wolf.

Callan swallowed fear down a painfully dry throat, and with a shaking hand, lifted the rifle and pressed the trigger.

Click.

40

Dylan pushed aside his feeling for Johnny and said, "Give me some cover while I try and coax Kristy down." Johnny nodded. In a squat, Dylan shuffled along behind one of the cars to the garage wall. Above, Kristy lay along the slope of the roof. As Johnny fired off several shots, Dylan stepped out and called up to her.

"Kristy? Kristy?" A blonde head appeared looking down at him wearing a pained smile. "Hi. Jump down. Just lower yourself off the gutter." She looked back toward Steve Palmer. The gunshots had stopped for the moment. "Come on," Dylan said. "You have to come down. We gotta leave."

Dylan poked his head up and peered about. There were still dozens of zombies engaged about the front of the property. Near the garden area where Steve Palmer was shooting, zombies ambled between the trees or squatted, feeding on bodies in the short grass. He didn't like the way one of them was looking toward the vehicles. In the lower paddock, they hung in clusters around dead animals, dead people, and their own deceased. The scenes reinforced to Dylan that their primary goal was the consumption of flesh and blood.

"Isn't there another way down?"

"I don't think we have time for that."

She peered over the edge and yanked her head back. She couldn't do it. He was going to have to help.

"I can't, Dylan. I can't jump."

He stood up, hunkered over with the crook of his elbow protecting his face, and ran to the garage. Bullets pinged off the brickwork and he realized stupidly his arm would probably not save him.

He stopped below Kristy and said, "I'll catch you."

"Okay." She turned the other way and spoke to Greg in a low voice. Then she rotated her body and swung her legs over the edge.

Rifle shots boomed. The tin roof clunked under gunfire. "Cover man, we need cover!" Dylan yelled.

Kristy screamed and her hands slipped off the guttering. She dropped like a rock onto Dylan, who hadn't set his footing or put down his gun, and he grunted as she knocked the wind and the rifle from him. They tumbled backward onto the gravel and rolled apart.

From the gentle slope of the backyard, a male feeder with a ring of grey hair and bloody saliva dripping from his lips strolled toward them. His bloated stomach protruded and he still had pieces of flesh on his hands.

"Move," Dylan said, scrambling to his feet and helping Kristy up. He ushered her away, then ran forward and scooped up the gun. A second zombie appeared further back, holding a short black fence stake. *Type two*. Dylan clicked the bolt and closed one eye as the other lined up the target. He fired the rifle and it jerked upwards.

The shot was true, though, and it flashed through his mind that his aim was improving. The zombie's arms flapped and it folded to the ground. The zombie with the weapon glanced down at his brother but kept on coming. While they all needed to feed, this type possessed a basic understanding of conflict; it was prepared to fight.

Dylan crept backward, maintaining his aim. The zombie trudged on. "Get in the Jeep, Kristy." He realized that, assuming Johnny joined them, they would require six places and the Jeep only had five. They would need the BMW, or if some of the other crew didn't make it, one of the three cars sitting in the driveway.

"What about Sherry? She's still in the garage."

"Callan's gone in to get her." He heard the door click open and then a gentle close. He glanced up at the roof and saw Greg crouched at the edge holding a rifle. Dylan kept moving backward. Another feeder appeared from the front of the house, bumping into the cars as it took small steps. It looked old and beaten, its blue woolen pullover full of holes and flapping on one side.

Beyond the type two zombie, three men appeared from the back of the house, carrying one of the big propane bottles, lifting it a yard at a time. They were dirty, as though they'd been crawling through mud, and two of them had splashes of blood over their white shirts. Concentrating on the heavy object, they were unaware of the scene unfolding ahead and kept walking.

Sensing this, the type two feeder made a beeline for them. Before they realized it, he attacked, biting the man at the rear on the neck. He began to scream.

Greg shifted to the edge of the roof and lined up the zombie who had come from inside. He fired and its head exploded, dropping it with a crunch onto the gravel. That alerted three zombies who had been feeding near the landscaped area. They left the carcass and ambled toward the driveway, drawn by fresh meat.

"We're gonna have company," Johnny said, scrambling away from his post near the white SUV. "On our left. And I'm outta ammo."

"Check the back of the Jeep."

Dylan sprang up, levered the bolt, and fired toward the threesome, grimacing as his ears stung again. One of the zombies took a belly hit, and it fell to the ground, clutching its stomach. The other two glanced at it but kept shuffling up the slope toward the cars, on promises of greater treasures. Dylan picked rounds from his pocket between unsteady fingertips and fed them into the rifle, surprised with his improving speed.

Greg slipped off the roof and hung in the air for a moment, contemplating the result of such a fall on his ankle. He dropped and let out a sharp cry, then hobbled between the cars, joining Dylan. Gunfire sounded from the back of the house. They sat low, peering around the vehicles. They saw the two men who had been carrying the propane bottle shoot the zombie and haul their friend aside.

"Man, you look in a world of pain," Dylan said. Greg's face was pale, his eyes red. Dylan could feel the heat coming from his face. Splashes of dark red covered his clothes.

"You could say that. But it ain't bad enough to lie down and die."

"Run into some trouble inside?"

"Yeah. Same shit, different day. We have to get out of here."

"That's the plan."

Dylan stood carefully. A voice called out, followed by two gunshots. Dylan swiveled toward the sound and saw two walkers lying on the ground, and Steve Palmer approaching. He veered away and made another shot, dispatching the zombie Dylan had hit in the stomach. Dylan knew what was going to happen next. Steve jogged toward them with his rifle aimed.

"We're gonna have a problem."

On his right, the other two had abandoned the propane bottle and now trudged their way. Dylan and the others were stuck in the middle.

"They're coming."

Greg said, "Let's try and talk our way out of this."

The boys stood, weapons drawn. Steve sighted Greg, and Greg did the same to Steve. Dylan turned the bolt action on one of the others, and saw they had also taken aim.

Steve slowed and began to laugh. "Well, if it isn't two of the top contenders on my 'People I'd Like to Kill' list."

Dylan stood straight and held his head up, switching his aim between the two propane boys.

"We can all walk away from this unharmed," Greg said.

Steve nodded. "Is that right, big man?" He adjusted his grotty hands around the gun. "See, I don't think that's necessarily true. Cos we got three and you only got two."

The others laughed.

Callan dug into his jeans pocket as he backed through the doorway. The zombie started forward, glaring at him, then ran into the base of the bed, falling on its face. Callan scuttled away as the window in the room on the right shattered and a horde of feeders forced their way inside, eager to join the banquet.

He ran down the passageway, making a feeble attempt to unload the empty magazine and reload a newbie from the store. He wondered whether he should just bail out the window and come back through the front door, but he could sense Sherry nearby. He passed the other bedroom on his right and saw more walkers trying to climb in another window. *Keep running.* He swung the hallway door closed and twisted the tiny latch to lock it, the thud of the crazy's footsteps reverberating through the floor. *Sherry.* He had a sudden, terrifying thought that she had already turned, and *she* would chase him. He stumbled back through the family area, but as he turned, he felt the impact of another body.

Callan thudded to the floorboards, tensing as pain swallowed his arm and shoulder. *Get up! Get up!* He twisted onto one knee and pushed onto his feet, swinging the rifle around.

It wasn't a zombie, but a short man with dark hair and a beard. Callan had never seen him before. A dozen zombies crammed through the sliding doors from the veranda after him.

"Help me," he said as a zombie yanked him backward by the shirt. Mouths opened and closed around his neck and back, arms and legs. His eyes grew wide and Callan reached out for his hand, but he fell from range, disappearing among the hungry.

Something brushed Callan's leg. Another feeder reached up from the floor and clasped his ankle. He kicked it away as the hallway door broke open to reveal the maniacal zombie.

Screaming, Callan danced backward, but the monster crashed through the splintered doorway and covered the distance with incomprehensible speed. Callan brought the gun around and tried to parry him away, but the thing brushed it off and shoved him in the chest. He tumbled backward, the gun clattering to the floor, sliding over the polished boards and into the wall. He had about three seconds. He turned onto all fours and scrambled across the wood, knees and hands clunking, chasing the weapon. He heard the zombie grunting, its shoes scuffing on the flooring.

"BOB!" Callan screamed. "BOB!"

He didn't know if Bob was even alive, but in that moment, Callan took back every bad thing he'd ever said about the guy and prayed for his help. Heavy steps on the first floor sounded through the roof. *Please, oh please.*

The gun still lay a yard away. He kept expecting to feel the cold grip of death on his legs or its dead weight land on his back. His only chance was to leap for it.

He did, stretching so much that he felt the muscle under his arm pull tight with pain. His elbow cracked on the floorboard and he skidded the last foot, locking his fingers around the metal barrel. He twisted, dragging the gun into a firing position, but it was long and awkward. Surly, harsh noises closed fast, so he dropped the rifle across his body and created a simple barrier. The zombie dived over him, kneeing his testicles and he shrieked, feeling pain explode from the region. He pushed back with the gun as though he were performing a bench press at the gym.

It lay over him, boots and legs scratching at his, forcing the gun toward his chest. The smell of its breath made him gag and he turned away, straining enough to flare pain across his brow. He was as close to death as he had ever been.

Footsteps sounded on the stairs but he wouldn't look, instead concentrating on channeling all his strength into his shoulders and arms to stop the zombie from biting his face. It was much stronger than he had expected. He felt like he was trying to hold up an impossible weight. Its mouth moved closer, and he could see the gory remains of flesh within.

"Hold on, Callan!" Gunfire roared from the lounge room.

"Hurrryyy!"

But the zombie was too strong. Born from a genetic mutation spawning supernatural strength, it drove the gun into Callan's throat, cutting his air supply. Callan watched its mouth open, teeth bared, and began a soundless scream.

There was a bark nearby, and then a growl near his ear. The blue dog leapt up onto the zombie's shirted back, snapping at his ear. The feeder released its pressure on the gun and sat up, swatting at the mutt.

Before Callan could react, the butt of another rifle connected with the side of the zombie's face. It tumbled off with a thud, and Callan rolled away as Bob fired the gun. The zombie fell, bits of its skull plastered on the wall.

Callan watched the blue dog scamper away through the crowd of walkers. "Thank you," he stuttered as he snatched the rifle and sprinted toward the entranceway. "Sherry? SHERRY?"

He slowed near the entrance, oblivious to the zombies still feeding in the lounge room. His eyes fell on the internal door to the garage. It was the only place they hadn't checked. He sprung for it, twisting the knob, but in his haste made a mess of it. The brass handle rattled but wouldn't open. Bob's footsteps rushed up to him. Callan tightened his grip and opened it, then stepped into the dim room.

42

"So here's the problem," Steve Palmer said. "You, big man," he tipped the gun barrel at Greg, "humiliated me at the pub last year. Threw me out for no good reason. You're a fucking asshole, and I knew I'd get my revenge at some point."

Dylan turned to Greg and whispered, "Don't say anything." Greg stood taut, but Dylan could see his hands and arms shaking, his hair damp with sweat.

"And you, fuck nuts… well, we all know what your old man did to mine. Although my father is now *dead*, and he died missing a finger. That's your father's fault. And since he's inside probably dead too, you're gonna take his punishment."

Dylan had no expectations that it would end well for any of them. Someone was probably going to die. Steve was either too stupid to realize that or just didn't care. "Great," Dylan said. "You shoot me, I shoot that guy, Greg shoots you, that guy shoots Greg, and one of those muppets lives. Four of us will die. You know that, don't you?"

Dylan glanced to Steve's left and saw a lone zombie wandering up the hill. Steve followed his gaze, then turned and shot the thing in the head from twenty-five yards. It fell into the grass and lay still.

"*You* might miss." He focused on Greg. "You okay, big boy? You look real sick." Greg tottered, sucking in a long breath. "Fuck, man," Steve said, laughing. "We might not even have to shoot you."

There was movement from the back of the Jeep.

"I think three on three is a lot fairer." Johnny stepped out, holding the Sauer S 202 Yukon rifle with the fitted Zeiss scope. "I've got six thousand dollars' worth of gun aimed right at your head, Stevie boy."

Steve's face folded into disbelief. "Johnny, man, what the fuck are you doing? You're one of us."

Johnny chuckled. "I was *never* one of you. You're a bunch of crazy lunatics. For fuck's sake, man, you killed those two people at the hardware store for *nothing*. They were just trying to survive like the rest of us."

Disbelief washed from Steve's face, replaced by a sneer. "You fuckin' rat. You did everything we did."

"I'm no angel, but I ain't at your pathetic level."

One of the men standing up behind the garage said, "We got two more, Steve." A couple of zombies came into view from the back of the house. Dylan switched his aim to the third man.

"Well fuckin' shoot 'em."

The man who had spoken turned away from the boys and fired two shots. The first missed, the second hit one of them in the shoulder. "Fuck."

Steve let out an annoyed breath. "Jesus, Walt, can't you do anything?"

The other man turned and fired, dropping one with a head shot. The second continued its dead shuffle.

"Dylan, cover Steve," Johnny said.

"Got it."

"Let me show you how it's done," Johnny said. He shifted the rifle, paused, then cracked off a shot. The remaining zombie's head erupted, ribbons of blood and chunks of skull flying. It fell with a quarter of its head missing. "There. And I've still got two rounds left for you." He turned his aim back to Steve.

Dylan stifled a laugh. He couldn't believe how it was turning out. The last person in the world he had expected to come through for them was doing just that. Moments ago, Dylan had expected nothing less than death, and now it appeared that Johnny might save the day.

"Nice work," Dylan said, looking toward Steve. "Now we have two choices. You guys climb into your car and drive away and we all live to fight another day, or we start shooting and *none* of us walk away."

Grinding his teeth, Steve glanced around at his mates. It would burn him to give in, Dylan knew, but how important was his life?

One of the men on the hill said, "Let's just go, Steve. There's only three of us left. We'll get 'em another day."

Steve tightened his grip around the rifle and looked out at the lower paddock. "*Fuck.*" Finally, he turned back and said, "All right. Let's go."

Dylan, Greg, and Johnny moved back as the others climbed into two of the vehicles. Steve fixed a menacing glare on the three of them, and Dylan knew that if they didn't leave town, Steve would never rest until he achieved revenge.

The two cars reversed. Steve's car stopped beside the boys and he wound down his window. "Looks like Wayne's been playing with fire again." They all laughed as the car spewed dirt and sped off.

Dylan closed his eyes and rubbed his temples. There had been close call after close call over the last few days, although they had all been facing zombies, not humans. This was more real because they had been *people*. It wasn't supposed to be like that. They should have been banding together and growing stronger in numbers. It was a reminder that not everyone was trustworthy.

Greg dropped the rifle and fell against the hood of the Jeep. He bent forward, hands on his knees.

Kristy opened the car door and slid out. "Greg? You need to sit down." He nodded. "I thought you guys were dead."

Dylan said, "Me too. Those crazy fucks could have gone either way. Nice work, Johnny." He took Greg under the arm. "Let's get him into the front seat. We have to get out of here."

As they loaded Greg through the passenger's side, Dylan saw it on the other side of the house. "Oh, shit." They followed his gaze and saw a plume of dirty smoke towering over the pitched roof. "They've set the bloody house on fire."

43

The garage was silent, almost eerie. From the lounge room, he heard the crack of gunshots as Bob shot the remaining feeders. Callan held his breath, scanning the grey filtered light, looking for his girl. He had heard her scream earlier. It had come from this end of the house. She had to be here somewhere.

He spotted the shattered glass on the floor beside the BMW, and then the two broken side windows from which it had come. At first, he couldn't see Sherry. But then he crept forward and saw a crooked leg curled across the passenger's seat.

"Sherry?" He felt the rise of nausea as he hurried forward. She was hurt. Hurt and—

He felt pain across his chest and then he hit the floor with a thud, the wind stolen from his lungs. The rifle clattered over the concrete and banged into a wooden locker. Scratching for air, he rolled over and crawled toward the car. A foot connected with his jaw and he fell back, his cheek slapping against the hard flooring. Pain invaded his face and head; his chest throbbed. *Sherry. Get to Sherry.* He lay crouched over, breathing heavily. Wetness dripped from the end of his nose. "Bob?" His voice was low, raspy. He put a hand out to defend from the next blow, and turned his head in the direction from which he thought it might come. He saw heavy, worn boots and followed them up to strong legs, then to a thick torso. His eyes had adjusted to the light, although he still blinked back tears from the kick to his face, and he saw the muscles of its chest and shoulders. He couldn't quite define its face in the dimness, but the low growl from its throat confirmed it was a type three crazy.

"I need to check on Sherry," he said, afraid to turn away. He realized what a stupid thing it was to say, but it grunted. He wondered why it wasn't killing him, why it hadn't taken him by the throat and bitten into his living flesh. *It wants me to suffer.* They were that smart, he realized.

The garage light flashed on. Bob stood in the doorway holding the rifle. Callan hadn't realized the gunshots had ceased. The thing turned and looked at Bob. Callan straightened up and saw its greyish skin and the prominent red lines of blood vessels beneath. In its right hand was a length of steel pipe.

Bob lifted the rifle and stepped down into the garage. The monster moved toward him. In the confined space, the noise was deafening.

Blood sprayed over the roller door. The zombie jerked once and fell backward, hitting the concrete floor with a thump. Bob lowered the gun and said, "I'm out of bullets." His voice sounded muted, suppressed by the ringing in Callan's ears.

Callan glanced sideways into the car. Sherry lay at an awkward angle, her face turned toward the windscreen. He didn't need to check on her. Matching the dark shade of her beautiful mane was a massive discoloration on her neck. He watched her chest for the rise and fall of life, but there was none.

Callan began to sob. His eyes filled with tears. He couldn't think about what this meant; all he felt were waves of hurt, filling every cell, his gut, his arms and legs, his chest, smothering his brain and thoughts. He needed to touch her again and started crawling toward her.

"Callan. Wait." He turned, bottom lip quivering. "You don't want to see that." Bob walked between them, glancing into the BMW. "Leave it, mate."

On legs that weren't his own, Callan climbed to his feet. "Leave it? How can I?" He peered into the car, fresh tears spilling. "She's carrying my baby." Somewhere, gunshots sounded, and the vaguest smell of smoke drifted in.

Bob sighed, putting a hand on Callan's shoulder. "You don't want to carry this memory with you forever. Take the others and leave. Remember her the way you loved her."

"Not without Sherry," he said, opening the front door. He dropped to his knees, wiping a flood of tears away.

Her eyes were open, staring at the roof. Her forehead was still warm, and he tried not to look at the wound on her neck. Just to be sure, he took her wrist, pressing two fingers against her skin for a pulse. Nothing. He shifted them, waiting, and tried another position without result. He turned her head and saw her dead eyes follow the roofline. He laid a hand on her heart and waited, pledging to relinquish anything in his life to feel a beat. It was still. Sobbing, he lay his head beside hers, his body shuddering. Was it real? Or was he asleep somewhere, stuck in his worst nightmare? Anything would be better than this. Every one of his dreams had involved Sherry. They had clawed their way back over the last few days. He had been happier, and hopeful. Now it had all been stolen. He would never talk to her again. Never lay with her, or make love the way they had last night, and his child, boy or girl, was gone. Callan felt a hand on his shoulder.

"Leave her. She's gone."

He shrugged it off. "I'm not moving." A bang sounded from the back of the house and the frame shuddered. "I'm staying with her. I don't care if I die."

Bob looked down, nodding. "I get it, I do, but you can't stay with her. She'll turn soon. Into one of them. A bite like that…"

The thought speared cold sense into his brain. Bob was right. She had been bitten by a zombie and therefore would turn into one. Did he want to be around for that? He sat up, an anguished expression on his face. "But I can't leave her like this."

Bob said, "I'll look after her from here."

A flicker of coherence surfaced in his mind. Bob nodded. "I'm not coming with you guys. I never was. I just wanted a chance to say goodbye to my son."

Callan thought of Dylan losing another parent. He would be feeling a similar pain, and he recalled the other night, watching him suffer through his mother's death. He had known pain was imminent, but had not expected to lose Sherry.

He glanced down at her blank eyes, then reached out and closed the lids. He wanted to hug her, cradle her in his arms, and sit with her, remembering the good times. Bob was right, though. She would soon be something else, and that thought was enough to give him some control, though he felt the pain pushing at the edges of his mind.

"Don't think about it," Bob said. "You need to keep moving, get your mind on the next action. You hang around here, dwell on this, you'll die. I knew my wife was dead when I didn't get back that first night. She probably panicked and left the house." He tossed his gun onto the floor. "She was bitten when you found her, wasn't she?" Callan looked away. "Dylan's a good boy. Look after him for me, will you?"

"He's been the one looking after me," Callan said.

"Can you get him for me?" Bob said. 'I'd like to see him before you leave." Bob's stark view of his own impending death drew Callan further back. "You smell that?"

Callan did. It was definitely smoke. "Smoke. Something's on fire."

The door banged and buckled under the weight of fists. *BANG, BANG, BANG.* The two men glanced at each other. The gold knob turned rapidly both ways, then clicked, and the door swung open. Zombies piled in, one after the other, the smell of the dead feeder's blood drawing them like a mouse to cheese.

Above their heads, smoke drifted through the entranceway, then the loudest explosion Callan had ever heard rocked the world.

44

The dark smoke looked like a grassfire to Dylan. He couldn't yet see flames, but the dry grass would quickly catch and the house would be under threat.

A large number of zombies still roamed the property, searching for the prized flesh of humans, or tolerating their own if within easy reach. Many had been shot, but now the last of the resistance had fled and Dylan sensed the force gathering. Initially, the two human parties had been able to fight, but alone, the numbers were overwhelming. They needed to leave immediately, but one major problem still existed.

"I'm going in," Dylan said. "Something is wrong. They've taken too long."

"Hurry," Kristy said. "And be careful."

Dylan ran to the rear of the Jeep and loaded the Remington, then stuffed more magazines into his pockets. Johnny patrolled the area with his rifle at his eye, poised to take down anything that wandered too close. For the moment, they had a fifty-foot radius, but the feeders were edging closer. Dylan overlooked Johnny's treachery toward Callan for now, admitting that some of them might not be alive without him.

Something exploded on the other side of the house. At first Dylan thought it was a bomb, but realized it had to be one of the propane bottles.

"We need that trailer," he said. "Kristy, can you turn the Jeep around so Johnny can hook it on? I won't be long." He ran across the gravel toward the front entrance, an invisible hand tightening around his gut.

The front door swung open, revealing a trail of dead, broken zombies. The plush wool pile carpet and lavish couches were no more. Entrails spoiled the floor like discarded streamers, and bright red stains covered the walls in varying patterns. Beyond the entrance, half a dozen walkers fed, picking through severed arms and legs, one using a discarded head as a bowl. A fat, neckless zombie ambled toward him, hissing. Dylan shot it in the chest and it fell back, hitting the ground with a thud. A lone zombie sitting against the wall dropped the hand on which he was chewing and crawled over to the bulging stomach and began feasting.

Loud voices sounded on his right. He ran across the entranceway and leapt up the carpeted stairs, turning toward the garage. Three zombies stood in the doorway, jostling for entry. Dylan levered the bolt on the Remington and shot the one at the rear in the head, spraying blood over the other two. It fell forward and pushed them into the garage, clearing the doorway.

He stepped up to the entrance, full of terrified energy. The remaining two from the doorway began feeding on their fallen comrade. Dylan shot one through the ear, levered the bolt, and blew the other's face off with a battle cry full of rage.

Callan stood in the right corner pressed against the roller door, defending his position with an intensity Dylan had never seen. Around his feet lay the bloody corpses of several zombies. The tomahawk in his right hand had savaged the two attackers, both bleeding from neck wounds, but still they groped at the sleek Kevlar clothing. He wielded the axe and connected with a bald head in a sickening thump.

Dylan's father was in worse shape.

He lay on the hood of the BMW, fighting off two attackers, a woman with long blonde hair and a pale, scarred face biting into his leg, and a man in tattered overalls scratching at his neck. He knew his father was infected, but Dylan wasn't going to let him die in such a horrible way. He stepped to the car and kicked the male aside. The female released his father's leg and looked at him with disinterest. Callan lifted the gun and pulled the trigger. The top of her blonde head disappeared, splattering his father and the BMW with blood and brains.

It fell aside, and as the short man in green overalls tried to stand, Dylan shot him in the face.

He swiveled, ready to unload again, but Callan had beaten both attackers to the floor. He sat over them, hacking with frenzy at their heads and necks. They were dead, but his arm thrust up and down, the red blade rising and falling with frightening, furious repetition.

Dylan saw Sherry lying across the front seat of the BMW. The glaring wounds on her neck covered him in goose bumps. He had never really liked Sherry, but even her treachery didn't warrant such an outcome.

More smoke billowed into the garage. Callan dropped the tomahawk and climbed to his feet, staring at the carnage. Dylan counted nine.

"I'm so sorry," Dylan said. Callan nodded, his lips pressed together. "I think the house is on fire."

"Go," Bob said, hobbling toward them. "I'll take care of her." Dylan watched him, knowing the farewell was imminent, already feeling the heartache. Was there another way?

Bob shook his head. "Forget it, son." He lifted his leather jacket, revealing a dry wound. "I was bit when you found me, but you knew that."

More gunfire sounded. Callan rubbed at his face tiredly. "What about Sherry?"

Bob put a palm out. "I said I'd do it. Before she wakes back up."

Tears ran from the corner of Callan's eyes. He wiped at them, nodding. "Thank you." He walked toward the door, then turned back as though he'd forgotten something. "I'm sorry I was such an ass earlier. You've done a lot for us."

"Look after them," Bob said. Callan nodded, scooped up the tomahawk, then disappeared back into the house.

"It's gonna burn down," Dylan said.

"Perfect. Fire kills them, too."

Dylan hung his head. He had known his father was infected, and despite trying to push the thought away, it had remained at the edge of his mind. He looked up and saw the ache of failure in the furrow of his brow, the curved down mouth. Bob coughed heavily. Dylan felt the swell of sadness in his chest, surprised his eyes remained dry. What was he to do?

His dad took Dylan by the hand. "You look after the others. You look after Kristy. I know how you love her. You do what I couldn't for your mother."

Dylan ground his jaw until a sharp pain flared in his teeth, and tightened his face to keep away the tears. His father didn't have the same strength. His red eyes became glassy. Bob pulled Dylan to him and they hugged so tight he couldn't breathe.

After a moment, he released him and stepped back. Dylan asked, "And there's no vaccine anywhere?"

"You might try one of the Army bases in Sydney or Melbourne."

"And then?"

"Tasmania. I'd go there. The virus is controllable in a place like that. It's a big island, but…" Dylan nodded, his lip trembling. "You'll be fine," his father said. "Just get out of this place as quickly as you can."

Dylan realized that not even the man he had held on a pedestal, above the trials and tribulations of the world, was immune from death. He hugged his father again and said, "I'm sorry, Dad. I love you."

"I love you too, son. Keep making me proud."

And then Dylan was gone, stumbling across the garage floor and up the stairs, blinded by tears. He let himself sob and hitch, not caring about control.

Flames leapt from the kitchen and family area, sending thick smoke into the lounge room. Even at twenty yards, he felt his skin bake. He coughed twice, covered his mouth, and ran through the entranceway. Smoke drifted out onto the gravel parking area.

The Jeep now faced the road, the trailer attached. Around it were the bodies of a dozen walkers. A handful of zombies still wandered within thirty feet of the car. Johnny shot one in the head, then saw Dylan and jumped into the car. Dylan crunched his way across the gravel and slid into the backseat beside Callan, giving Kristy, who was driving, a quick nod.

As the Jeep rolled off, Dylan lay back with his eyes closed and let the tears flow.

45

Kristy steered the Jeep and trailer down the long driveway, wiping tears from her eyes with the heel of her hand. It had finally happened, the scenario she had been imagining and dreading. One of them was dead, and Dylan's father would end up the same way, too. She glanced around at Dylan, who had his eyes closed, tears on his cheeks. She reached back and squeezed his hand. His eyes flickered open and he gave her a pained smile.

"I'm so sorry," she said, squeezing her lips to stop herself crying. He nodded and whispered his thanks.

As they approached the bottom of the driveway, another wave of zombies turned into the gravel entrance, led by three of the crazies.

"Don't stop," Johnny said from the back seat. "Drive through the fuckers."

Kristy gripped the wheel tighter and squashed the accelerator to the floor. The engine moaned, thrusting the vehicle forward.

"Wait," Callan said, his face close to the window. "Stop the car."

"Are you mad?" But her foot obeyed, feathering the brake pedal, and they skidded to a halt on the loose dirt. Callan opened the door and leapt out. "Callan! What are you—"

In the side mirror, a flash of blue ran through the grass from the left. The rear door clicked opened and floated to the top of its reach. Callan tapped the carpet floor inside the Jeep and the dog leapt in.

"Sit," Callan said. Then he slammed the door and hurried back to his seat. The zombies had progressed past the entrance. "Go. Floor it."

Kristy did, spinning the wheels, then caught the loose rocks and thrust the vehicle forward with a ripping sound. The big zombies stood out in front, clenched fists at their sides, angry, inhuman stares directed at the Jeep. Behind, a long trail of feeders stood, ignorant and empty-gazed. She accelerated harder, and the car rushed down the slope.

"Don't brake," Callan said softly. At five yards, the cognizant walkers stepped aside. "That's him. The one we saw at Mom and Dad's house."

Dylan stirred. "It *is* him."

As they passed, the leader struck the window with a heavy fist. Kristy jumped at the sound. She plowed through the mob, knocking them aside with the edge of the Jeep. Several fell under the front and the car rolled over them with a clunk and bump. The trailer rose and fell with a metallic crash.

"Keep going," Callan said, leaning over into the back with a hand on the dog.

Kristy turned the Jeep onto Silvan Road with a screech of tires as other feeders crashed into the edges of the hood and doors. They thudded off and rolled away.

The path ahead looked clear—for now, at least. She glanced to her left and saw Greg with his head back, eyes closed. He might have been sleeping. They needed antibiotics soon, or he would be in serious trouble. She was amazed at his effort, his ability to push aside the sickness and fight. He was tough, as Callan had always maintained, tougher than any of the others probably realized. Now he would pay for it, though. In the rearview mirror, Dylan's red eyes watched the passing properties. The ache of further loss showed on his face, a stiff, expressionless look, as though the slightest movement would return him to tears. Callan still had an arm over the back, soothing the dog. He returned her gaze and shook his head slowly to indicate he couldn't believe what had happened. Kristy mouthed the word *sorry* and looked back to the road.

The bottom of Silvan Road was less busy, as though the dead zombies and gunfire had drawn all the others away. Walkers were still visible on passing properties, ambling about in overgrown gardens and on broken porches. The zombie population might have dispersed, but where were the five of them going to go? They no longer had a home, or a bed, and only a little food. She supposed they could go back up to the lake, but how long would they last there?

"Where am I going?" Nobody spoke. She supposed this was a defining moment. If they stayed somewhere close, they would have perpetual reminders of what they had seen, and the familiarity of their past lives, haunting them forever. However, leaving meant they had given up on their families and remaining friends. Were they prepared to do that?

"One of the Army bases in Sydney," Dylan said. "My father said they might have been working on a vaccine."

A ground-shuddering explosion sounded, turning all their heads back toward the house. Kristy stopped the car and looked through the passenger side window. A plume of grey smoke reached into the sky, and bright orange flames were visible through cracks in the trees.

"The other propane tank," Dylan said. "Dad…" He turned back toward the front of the car. The others did the same, and Kristy slowly accelerated away.

In three days, their world had spun on its axis, too fast for Kristy to consider much of what had happened. The fear of making a mistake, of losing patients, had diminished, and for the first moment in a long time, Kristy felt capable. She had fought the zombies by hand and with weapon, and had won. As an individual, she had progressed, but as a team, they had suffered. The loss would stick to their bones forever.

"I can't stay here," Dylan said. "Albury's gone. We'll…" He caught the words in his throat and swallowed. "We'll all die if we stay."

"Wagga it is, then," Kristy said.

Could they have been in any greater disarray? She wouldn't have imagined it any worse. Regardless, they had no choice other than to go on, to press forward and fight as they had for every hour of their lives in the new world. Who knew if they would be alive tomorrow? But for the sake of those they had lost already, they would fight on. Kristy tightened her hands around the wheel, lifted her chin, and drove toward town.

THE END

Author's Note

Hi there, and thank you so much for reading my story. This is my first full-length novel, and I hope you enjoyed it, as much as I did writing it. As a new author who is learning his craft, I'd love to hear what you thought about the story, good or bad. You can e-mail me at owen.baillie@bigpond.com.

As the reader, please don't underestimate your importance to new authors like me. The fact that someone has read this book inspires me to keep writing. When I began this, I had no idea how much time and effort it would require, and I found myself steadily increasing my commitment to reach the finish, rising every day at 5am (6am on weekends) to reach my targets. If I had known then, that people would read it, I may have even written faster, and enjoyed the process even more.

Reviews appear to be one of the biggest factors in people giving new authors a chance, so if you could spare a moment, even if it's only a line or two, I would be forever grateful.

I'm currently working on the second book, which I hope to have published in March 2014. If you want to get an automatic e-mail when it's released, or receive the occasional exclusive short story, type the following into your browser: http://eepurl.com/FU2cH. Your e-mail address will never be shared and you can unsubscribe easily at any time.

Also, friend me on Facebook, like the Invasion of the Dead page, or follow me on Twitter. You can also check out my other stories at Amazon.

Thanks again,

Owen
Melbourne, Australia, November 2013.